I0716290

ZAUBERER

A NOVEL

A. DERSTINE

Byzantium Sky Press
Ellendale, DE, 19941

ISBN 978-1-955872-22-5 (paperback)
ISBN 978-1-955872-23-2 (eBook)

Library of Congress Control Number: 2024946052

First Byzantium Sky Press Paperback Edition: October, 2024

Cover & Interior design by Crystal Heidel, Byzantium Sky Press

Manufactured in the United States of America

Cover Design: Crystal Heidel
Raven Cover illustration from Shutterstock.com
DNA and Frame: Freepik.com
Various photographs blended in background: Unsplash.com

For Momma, Crystal, and the Goils for always pushing for me to follow my dreams and playing Imagine with me.

Thank you to my friends and our group from Save Point for giving us a place to stretch our imaginations.

And a big THANK YOU to all my beta readers and my UHC and EH teams. I couldn't have finished this book without you!

ZAUBERER

1

I remembered the night of my accident as if it were a Blu-ray stuck in my head: high definition, all the way. My memories have been sharp since that night. However, this memory has haunted my nightmares and is where my story begins.

"Mom? Momma? I'm here!" I entered my parents' house clutching my degree and white coat from the ceremony. Their dogs, Scarlett and Pippin, bayed and barked until I bent down to give them lovings, which was interesting as they are two very different heights. Scarlett was a sleek Catahoula hound who habitually would put her nose on the table to beg. At the same time, Pippin was an affable dachshund mix about as tall as a corgi.

"Baby-Mine! You made great time." Momma smoothly dodged around the canines. She hugged me against her … ahem … massive tracks of land. All the women in my family are on the curvier side of life, but Momma was on a cortical steroid she had to take every day. It made it harder for her to lose weight, but the benefits far *outweighed* the drawbacks. See what I did there? Don't blame me. The Moms raised us on puns.

"Did you run into any traffic?"

I smiled. "Nothing I couldn't handle. Is there anything you need me to do for the party?"

Mom came around the corner and slipped the dogs treats. "No. Everything is all set up in the back. Annie and Ree took control of the chaos as soon as they got here."

"You just head up to your room and get ready."

Their house was just large enough to house five women, allowing us to rub elbows without stepping on each other's toes. It had been cozy growing up here. I think it was what made us such a close family. Almost all my friends and family fit comfortably for the party between the house and the backyard. The smell of the charcoal grill made my stomach rumble as I went up into my old room. It was just a guest room now, with one of Momma's signature crocheted blankets decorating the top. My outfit for the evening was already laid out. The Moms knew I wasn't the type to go for dresses unless I absolutely had to and had put out a nice set of slacks and a soft cotton tee that read, 'Yeah, I'm the Doctor.' I laughed, taking off my graduation dress that everyone insisted I buy.

Not that I didn't like the spectacular, long column of purple silk with a white wrap. Momma had helped me pick it out for the event and made me promise to keep it on until everyone was done with pictures. It had cut a bit into my clinic fund, but the smiles on the Moms' faces were worth it.

The Moms were always supportive of their girls. Ever since I was born. They had had to get a donor to start our family. Momma carried all of us as she had the self-proclaimed 'birthing hips.' As a result, all three of us looked a lot like Momma. We all had dark hair, hazel eyes, and boobs that could smother people if we hugged them too long. Mom, in comparison, was tall with tightly curled blond hair and green eyes. Ree (short for Marie) was already considering getting a reduction, and she hadn't even hit her third decade. We don't know who the donor is, so we don't know if there are any traits from that side of the gene pool.

The Moms were just as thrilled when Ree joined the family business at Hall Construction as they were when Annie (long for Anne) passed the bar and got a job with the attorney general. But, as much as the Moms wanted to support me through my doctorate, I couldn't let them. I didn't want to put that kind of burden on my parents.

So, I worked at a local bookshop when I got into medical school. Bindings. It was run by a man named Jove Brandt. The store was a fantastic hole-in-the-wall place that did good business with all the surrounding colleges in the city despite the owner's notorious prickly personality.

My parents had never been in the best of health. Mom had chronic anxiety attacks, the kind that left you on the floor quivering. Pippin was her service dog. He would recognize when an attack was about to happen, have her sit on the floor wherever she was, and press his paws against specific pressure points until the episode would pass.

The girls and I had grown up knowing Mom had problems. The one we weren't prepared for was Momma.

She was always the one who took care of things. She'd protect Mom while the service dog did their job. She was always the first to decide what to bring to a bake sale. She was the one who helped us make banners for

Pride. Momma was the one who got the closest to the stage at school plays and cheered the loudest.

And she was the one who couldn't afford her medicine all the time.

Momma had been in the kitchen, making dinner like she usually did while I was in middle school. We were watching some movie about aliens when we heard a crash.

"Babe?" Mom called, "Are you okay?"

The silence was deafening. Mom launched out of her chair and ran into the kitchen, the girls and I on her heels. Momma was on the floor, pasta and sauce spilled all over the linoleum.

"Danni? Danielle?" I could hear the panic in Mom's voice. This was before they'd gotten Pip. So, there was no one there to stave off the attack. It was like watching a person short circuit in real-time. She started shaking and went down on her knees. "No, no, no! What do I do, what do I do, what do I do?"

I looked at my sisters, who were staring. They didn't know what to do either. So, I did what Momma always taught us to do . . . whatever needed to come next.

I breathed a little sigh of relief as I saw Momma's chest rise and fall . . . but it was too shallow. She should have been taking deeper breaths than that. I knelt and made sure to get Mom's attention. I needed her to look at me instead of her wife's still form. I touched her shoulder, and she looked at me with blank green eyes.

"Mom?" I made sure my voice was even. "Do you know what's happening to Momma?"

Her voice sounded hollow, lost, as she answered me. "Momma is asthmatic. She has trouble breathing. She told me she'd be okay if we held off on getting her meds. She–she promised she wouldn't overdo it. She said she could handle it, like she always says."

That was the information I needed. I jumped up and called nine-one-one.

Momma had been diagnosed when she was little, but the medicine she needed to breathe every day was expensive. Her old employers had just changed insurance companies again, and this one had a massive deductible before the insurance would pay for anything. It was a choice between groceries or Momma's meds . . . and she made a choice.

Thankfully, the ambulance arrived before any damage from oxygen deprivation, but the catalyst threw me into medicine. I was going to ensure that no one I worked with would end up in the same situation as my mother. If something as stupid as an insurance company tried to harm my people, I'd make sure I'd treat as many people in need at cost as I could.

"Mira!" cried Momma as I descended the stairs. She hugged me and tucked my long hair behind my ear. "Let me take a look at you! Babe, look! Our baby's all grown up. I've got to go and get the camera."

Mom smiled and held out her hands to me.

"Mira. Oh, Mira." Mom teared up. "You look amazing."

"It's just slacks and a tee." I laughed.

"Still, your Momma and I couldn't be prouder. You're the first real doctor in this family!"

The Moms hung a banner above the expansive back porch that read 'Gratz Grad! Class of 2055!' in rainbow colors. There was a fire pit, yard games, and the grill with my aunts and uncles, each operating a station. It felt like a well-planned family picnic where friends and neighbors could come and have fun, too. I even spotted Pastor Janice in the crowd.

We'd attended Saint John's United Methodist since I was a kid. It was a lovely church. A safe place that accepted our family with open arms. They had this glorious stained-glass window in the sanctuary depicting Christ as a shepherd surrounded by many colored lambs. It was a picture showing how much God loves all of us, no matter how much melanin is in our skin.

There was enough to feed all of South Philly from the look of the tables laden with food and drink. A handbell clanged loudly behind me, and several people laughed when I jumped.

"May I have your attention, please?" Momma shouted in the way only she could. Put a woman in a choir for enough years, and she learned how to project. "Everybody grab whatever you're drinking. I've got something to say."

The people quieted to a murmur as Momma wrapped an arm around my waist. "Mira, you worked so hard for what you've earned today. Endless nights of studying for your exams and working at that bookstore because you knew we couldn't pay for everything for you. This girl right here took the initiative to work while earning a *doctorate*!"

Cheers rang from the spectators as Momma kissed the side of my head. "So, it's the least we can do to throw you the biggest celebration we can. We are so proud of you, baby girl. Everybody, raise your glass for Doctor Mira Hall: General Practitioner!"

I cried and hugged her, and Mom came over and wrapped us both in her arms. I laughed and sniffled as we embraced on the porch. The house and yard were filled with people, music just this side of legal, and a feast to feed the masses.

I spotted my sisters. Annie meticulously organized the food line, and Ree was over by the DJ, giving them grief. I chuckled and wandered over.

"You listen here, you music-slinging shyster. My Momma is the type of person who thinks that if she randomly hears a Queen song, then all is how it's supposed to be. So, I want you to take this die . . . die is the singular of dice you nimrod . . . take this die and roll it after every song. If it rolls a six, play Queen. OG Queen, she can tell the difference. Do this, and we'll give you extra for every Queen song we hear. No cheating. If you only play Queen, or it's like every other song, you get docked instead."

"Ree, don't threaten the DJ. They're just doing their job."

"I'm watching you punk . . . *Mira*! Here's the woman of the hour!"

She wrapped her arms around me in a crushing hug. Ree had the upper body strength of a lifelong construction worker. She had worked her way up from general laborer to her current position of foreman and had the physique to prove it.

"Ree," I croaked. "You're crushing me."

"*Sister sandwich!*" Annie yelled and slammed into us. Pinning me in the middle. She had to have run across the yard to hit us at that speed.

"Have some decorum, counselor!" I laughed.

"Feh, it's a party! A party for *you*! The bestest oldest sister who chose to spend a decade in school *while* also working at a bookshop. What kind of glutton for punishment does *that*?"

"Apparently, this one does." Ree gave me a soft sisterly head bonk before letting go. She nodded at the rest of the party. "So, what do you think?"

"Pretty nifty. You guys thought of everything."

"The Moms did most of it," Annie said. "You know how Momma gets when it comes to party planning. She had the Extendeds sign up for station rotations."

This explained why two of my uncles were working the grill, one of my second cousins was judging the beanbag toss, and Momma's NB sibling, Ankle Kay, was policing the beer. The Hall family was legion, and Momma put them to work like a general assigning troops to war. My sisters were two of those troops.

"She had sign-ups on a special chat so that you wouldn't get wind of it." Ree gave me a noogie before letting me loose.

I blushed. "She didn't have to do that. I would have been fine with us just ordering a metric crap ton of pizza . . ."

"As someone who appreciates high-quality barbecue, I'm glad your Momma did what needed doing." The sassy voice of the only other worker at Bindings, Katie Fynn, rang with laughter. Her green eyes danced as she gestured around the yard. "You know it's kind of fun to get wrapped up in all this. I got recruited to help with the lanterns and string lights."

"That makes you an Extended now, you know." Annie nodded sagely. "Found family is just as valid as blood, and you've been in on enough sleepovers by now."

Katie had been the one to welcome me after Jove hired me to run the downstairs. Katie's demesne was the upper level of the two converted townhomes where the fiction books were. Her parents ran a jewelry store a couple of blocks over in the city, so it was a short commute for her on foot.

"Well, you couldn't pick a better person to do lighting than a photography major." The combination of fairy lights and paper lanterns gave the backyard a mystical feel. It was only a matter of time before Jove lost her to the world of weddings and magazine covers.

She smiled and held up her camera. "Had to make sure everything was perfect. I've got a photo booth set up over by the cake. It only took a second to set up, so I let myself get recruited."

"How'd you get up there, short stuff?" Ree wanted to know.

"Because ladders are a thing that exists, and one of your hot cousins knows how to hold one without staring at my ass."

"Ew! Don't say 'cousin' and 'hot' in the same sentence. They're your family now, too!"

"If I did that, it would take out a quarter of the eligible people 'round here. And unlike *Doctor* Mira Hall, I do not have a thing for professors or librarians."

I flushed and looked away from her dusky, Pixie face and bouncy red curls. "I don't know what you're talking about."

"Mmm-hmm. Right, and I didn't see you checking out his ass as he walked down into that dungeon he calls a basement . . . on *numerous* occasions . . . Like now."

Jove was in the food line in a white button-down with rolled sleeves, tailored gray slacks, and expensive brown suede shoes.

"He's going to regret that shirt when he gets sauce all over it." Annie said, "Those shoes, too, if he finds a poo pile we missed."

He went to get a bottle of water out of a cooler. Katie sneezed at the same time that the bookseller bobbled it, and it dropped to the concrete. Chocolate eyes gave an aggrieved look to the heavens as he ran a hand through dark hair. We all tilted our heads when he bent down to pick it up.

"To be fair," Ree interjected, "the world owes that man's tailor a favor. That plus the German accent? Rowr."

"You don't work with the man! That accent gets real old real quick when he's cussing you out in German. He'd be a scary bastard if I didn't know more curses than he does."

I rolled my eyes. "He doesn't cuss you out in German. He calls out to some old gods and begs them for patience."

She gave me a look that had her red curls bouncing. "Says you. He talks too quick for Google Translate to pick up. Oops, I see some people looking for me at the booth. Congratulations, girl!"

I started going from table to table to greet all the guests. I paused and smiled as I got to the table that held my professors. A few of them I'd given invitations to myself, but everyone was allowed a plus one, and that was when I got my first big surprise of the evening.

Dr. Phineas Alden, the premier surgeon in the state, if not the country, sat like a dignitary holding court. I wasn't sure who brought him, but I was happy they did. Alden had been a guest lecturer for several years. I got to work at one of his hospitals during rotations, but I hadn't worked under him when I did the tour of surgery. Besides, his specialty was neural surgery, and I didn't want to be that specialized. I wanted to be able to help everyone.

The surgeries this man performed were rumored to be borderline miraculous. If there were a hall of my medical heroes, he'd be on a pedestal alongside Joseph Lister and Charles R. Drew. I was a little star-struck that he'd decided to make an appearance at *my* graduation party. Someone sure had some clout to get him to come to some newbie's backyard barbecue.

I smiled. "Welcome, everyone! Thank you so much for coming. I'm happy to see so many illustrious medical community members here. Does everyone have something to drink?"

"Well, it's no Château Margaux." Alden chuckled at my anatomy professor. "But it'll do for now."

"We'll be sure to get it for next time." I smiled tightly. Château Margaux was a stupidly expensive wine, and my parents had already put enough money into the event. This was one of those times when you didn't point out how rude your significant and influential guest was acting.

"Congratulations on your graduation, Mira." My biology professor smiled, glossing over Alden's faux pas. "It's a beautiful venue."

"You'd hardly believe it's someone's little backyard in the suburbs."

"Phineas!"

"I'm only speaking the truth." His cold blue eyes bore into mine. It was like looking into the eyes of a snake. "Don't worry, Hall, with your education, breeding, and brains, venues like this will be few and far between. I want to invite you to work with me at my hospital. There's a position at my office with your name on it."

I took a step back, stunned. I mean, Blathering Blatherskite, the head of the best hospital in the state, just offered me a job. A job in a specialty I didn't want. "I mean . . . wow . . . um . . . I'm flattered, but I have plans to open my *own* practice."

"Well, there's no way you could afford that alone, not with such . . . *humble* beginnings. So, when that fails, look me up. I'll put you on the path to ultimate success."

"I have other guests I need to see to." I smiled politely. "Please enjoy the rest of your evening."

"Oh, I will." He pulled out his phone and started texting on it, obviously dismissing me.

I walked away, a little shell-shocked. Never put a person on a pedestal. The disappointment I felt was crushing. I'd been right at the front of the lectures he'd given at Drexel. I'd bought his books on neural plasticity. I'd had him sign one! My stomach was churning. I hadn't eaten yet, which was good. Otherwise, I'd be in the bushes throwing up.

"Mir? Are you okay? You're making a face."

I looked over to the maple tree I climbed as a kid. It was festooned with fairy lights. The little LEDs made the tree look like it was glimmering with magic. Under the branches stood my oldest and best friend, David Erickson. His bright green eyes and sandy brown hair looked soft in the glow of the decorations.

We'd met in high school. Freshman students who happened to have homeroom together. He had always been 'the shy one' while I'd always been pegged as the 'weird one.' One morning, I noticed an issue of X-Men hanging out of his book bag. I decided that day that he was going to be my friend. David had been wary at first. He thought I was trying to make fun of him, but once he realized I was sincere, we stuck together like glue.

Comics were just one thing we connected on. The more we talked, the more we realized movies, tabletop games, conventions . . . all things nerdy, we seemed to have in common or were open to discovering something new to geek out over.

David's Nordic ancestry didn't stop the nerd pudge gathered around his waist. We would watch anime at each other's homes, munching on whatever we could get our hands on. We'd get popcorn and candy when we went to the theater. We'd munch at diners when we went to cons. We caught some flak from other kids. Most were about our appearance, but others teased us because they thought we were dating. He was a sweet person I could laugh and joke around with, but David had never really shown interest in me in that area, so I was content to stay friends. I wasn't going to push if it wasn't something he wanted.

We both got into one of the best medical universities in Philadelphia. While my goal was human medicine, his was veterinary. He'd always been excellent with animals. When Scarlett had a run-in with a porcupine a few years back, David kept her calm at the vet. The brat graduated before me, so his patient's owners called him 'Doctor' before mine would.

Looking at him under the tree, his hands behind his back, made me realize how far he'd come. He was a big, fluffy guy before getting into the veterinary program. My best friend had now slimmed down while helping patients and their owners. He'd been working more with large animals like cows and horses and had gained some nice-looking muscle in some nice-looking places.

I was still on the curvy side of life. No matter what I did, I never seemed to lose weight, even on the most rigorous rotations. I was a little jealous of him for that.

"Hello? Earth to Mir, are you receiving, Silly Little Space Station?"

I stuck my tongue at him before smiling. "Sorry, Goliath, my mind wandered a bit there. What are you doing over here all by yourself?"

We'd come up with this in high school to take the power back from the bullies. We knew we were big. So, Goliath because he's David and Space Station because I'm Mir. Silly *little* Space Station because while Mir was bigger than Goliath, the I.S.S. beat it out, and David knew I loved alliteration.

"I saw that mountain of a gift table, and I . . . wanted to give this to you separately so it didn't get lost in the shuffle." He blushed and pulled out a vintage doctor's bag. The kind that was made before zippers were a thing. There were bronze clasps and buckles that draped across the leather bag.

"Where did you find *this*? It's gorgeous!" I sat down on the grass to open it. I tugged on David's hand until he sat across from me.

"I found it in an antique store in Quakertown. Then I contacted one of the Ren-faire leather workers to refurb it. The buckles, clasps, and interior are all original. I couldn't do anything about the antique store smell."

"That's okay. It gives it more character. This thing is *huge*! I could fit Momma's crochet project bag in here and still have room for like ten patient files, a stethoscope, and a good first aid kit!"

"There's also an outside pocket for tongue depressors and adhesive bandages." He leaned over and pointed to a pocket. "I also had them add a shoulder strap so you could have it cross-body in case you have to get to someone quick."

"It's *perfect*!" I leaned over and hugged him. "Thank you, David. I love it."

I stood up, hugging the gift to my chest.

"Where are you going?"

"I'm going to put it away so it doesn't get lost in the shuffle." I smiled, "I'll be right back."

The front of the house wasn't nearly as well-lit as the back. The evening shadows were quickly spreading into the night's darkness. I had parked my car along the curb so it would be easier to get out when I wanted to leave. I put the bag in the back with my white coat, degree, and caduceus pin.

"*Guten Abend, Kleine.* Leaving already?"

Jove stood in the shadows, long coat draping over his shoulders, looking mysterious. He did mysterious rather well. Even when we'd first met, he seemed to be able to appear out of nowhere.

I was at the campus eatery between classes, wracking my brain. How was I going to stay independent and get my doctorate? Opening my clinic was my ultimate goal, but I couldn't burden the Moms with my financial needs. They were running things pretty tight, especially with the cost of Momma's meds going up again. I'd gotten lucky by winning some small grants, but my ultimate trouble was housing.

I tried the dorm thing. The biggest problem was that it was about the same as sleeping with an unknown venomous spider unless you knew your roommates like the back of your hand. I'd survived two semesters before I'd gotten saddled with one too many vapid fashion plates whose only goal in life was to charm a man into marriage. The offhanded insults about 'people' needing to 'watch their weight' and how 'insane' it was not to know who said what on Insta. The ever-present derisive giggles inevitably followed this. I'd gotten enough of that in high school. It made me itch.

I was determined to get out of the dorms. I had my eye on a place. It was a small, not quite studio apartment with a kitchen. I'd have to go down the hall to do laundry, but that wasn't a deal-breaker. Oh, and *bonus*! Built-in AC! And it was right in my price range . . . if I could get more income.

At this point, my job was University student. But my classes were in the morning or only some days during the week. I had pockets of time to work and if the employer was willing, I could study on my breaks. I only needed five hours of sleep, max. It was doable.

But I needed somewhere close. I preferred a small business owner. I'd heard horror stories from the Moms who'd met when they both worked at a big box store. Momma liked to joke that she got her spouse from Walmart. I didn't want any part of that nonsense. I was okay with working with the public. You must be able to serve to be a doctor anyway, but to be forced to capitulate no matter what? No, thank you.

Smaller businesses had a higher probability of a boss willing to be on my side occasionally, too.

I heard my name and sighed as I stood to go and get my cappuccino.

"Oh, honey," said the flamboyant barista with dyed hair holding out my drink, "it's only the start of the semester. What's got you so down? You look bluer than my hair."

"I'm staring down the barrel of another semester in the dorms."

He winced. "And you're on the side of campus where that one sorority decided it was better to live on campus than have a house to themselves. You poor thing."

"I'm looking at off-campus places, but I need an income boost, if you know what I mean? Are they hiring here?"

"Sadly, no. But I do know of a place that is."

"You do?"

"It's a little bookstore that does some of the best restoration work I've ever seen. My boyfriend's dog decided my econ book needed to die, and they fixed it like it'd never seen the inside of a chihuahua's mouth. I was just in there the other day and heard the owner say he was looking to hire. Here, I'll get you their address."

The day of my interview, I was shown a hearth made of antique stone. Two wingbacks and a coffee table were there. I sat waiting to talk with who I assumed was the manager. On the table were a couple of books. I smiled at the titles.

Twenty-Thousand Leagues Under the Sea.
Journey to the Center of the Earth.
Around the World in Eighty Days.

I picked up the last one and started reading. I had no idea how long the wait would be, and it had been a while since I'd gotten to read Jules Verne. I usually would have been reading on my phone, but the physical books were begging to be read. I just got lucky that my favorite one was in attendance. I loved how Phileas Fogg and Jean Passepartout acted with one another. One OCD, the other just wanted some stability in his life. I crossed my legs and let myself be pulled into the story.

I blinked when I heard a discrete "Ahem."

I looked up at one of the most handsome men I'd ever freaking seen. His dark brown hair was tousled, not in a styled way but in an 'I run my hands through my hair when I'm stressed' way. Dark chocolate eyes studied me through small, round, antique-looking glasses. He stood very straight, starched shirt tucked into tweed slacks with a vest that almost hid the suspenders he wore underneath. Id, the part of me that liked to run as wild as our ancestors did before wheels were a thing, stood up and took notice with a little bit of internal panting. Ego, the sophisticated part of me that ran most of my human interactions, held her back.

"*Hallo*, are you *Frau* Hall?" His voice was a smooth baritone.

Oh my God, he was German and had a sexy accent! Now, Ego was taking notice, too.

I swallowed before replying, "*Ich bin* Mira Hall. *Wie ghets?*"

His eyes shot up in surprise. "You speak German?"

I smiled. "Taught on my Oma's knee. The old biddy won't acknowledge you if you don't address her in German. She had some trouble with English when she and Opa came over from Dusseldorf."

"I can relate. No matter how long I have lived in this country, there are times when I can only express myself properly in my native tongue. I am Jove Brandt. I take it you like Jules Verne?" He sat in the chair across from mine and looked pointedly at the book in my hand.

I flushed and closed the book, putting it in my lap. "I'm going to buy this, I swear. I couldn't help myself while I was waiting."

"Very few authors can capture the attention as Verne could."

"This is my favorite by him. I've meant to pick up a new copy since mine disintegrated."

He blinked. "Disintegrated?"

"Well, yeah." I shrugged. "That's what I call it when you read a book so many times, the cover falls off, and the glue can't hold the pages anymore. I heard you offer restorations. I might have to use those services for some of the other books I have my eye on. My one aunt is a fan of antique books, and I'd love to get something restored for her."

Jove laughed. It was a kind, gentle thing. "I thought you were here for an interview."

"Oh, I am. But if I completely flub it, then I still want to be able to shop here." I tucked a stray hair behind my ear. "You have a great location. It's not too far from home for me. It's nice and close to University City, too."

"And what are your qualifications? Other than excellent taste in authors?"

"I worked a register at our local farmer's market while still living with my parents. That is, up until I got accepted to Drexel. I worked at several of the stores there each summer. It was the Quakertown Farmer's Market. It's a huge—"

"Ja! I am familiar with it!" His eyes lit up excitedly. "It has been a long time since I was in that area. It got rebuilt after the fire?"

I studied his face, the way I'd been taught to peg someone's age to ensure they weren't buying something too old for them to purchase. I didn't see deep lines in his eyes or on his head. His hands and skin seemed well taken care of but not old. If I had to put a number to him, I wouldn't put him much past my age of twenty-five. I thought, *I haven't heard of a fire in thirty years. You look too young to be talking about the one back in twenty nineteen.*

He flushed and coughed. "I must be thinking of a different market then."

"Hmm, there are a lot of markets in that area . . . that would make sense." I looked around the store. "Is this your place, or does your family run it?"

"Bindings hast been in my family for generations, but I am in charge now. My parents decided to return to Germany for their retirement. Are you familiar with this kind of register?" He motioned over to the heavy antique that adorned the counter.

"That wasn't just for show?" I blushed with embarrassment. "I–I mean, I've worked with one before, but it was only to show a collector that it still worked. Where did you get it? It looks like it's in great shape!"

Jove chuckled. "It is another thing that has been in my family for a long time. We pride ourselves on traditions here at Bindings. I hope to show you how to take care of it once we get the paperwork."

I couldn't stop the enormous smile that felt like it was going past my ears. "So I have the job?"

"What hours were you hoping for?"

We haggled over hours but finally agreed on what would work with my schedule. The pay Jove offered was . . . generous for the position.

"I believe in paying people what they are worth. As you were also referred to me by a trusted customer, I believe this would be a good place for you to start. Now" —he uncrossed his legs and leaned forward with an avid interest in his eyes— "with business out of the way, I would love to hear your opinion on *Journey to the Center of the Earth.*"

We ended up talking for three hours past our appointment. He showed me how to use the register and the turntable, which surprisingly didn't have a radio. Jove claimed to be an audiophile and preferred the sounds of 'pure music.' I would have given him my number if the man hadn't just given me a job. But I needed a place to live over a man to take a bite out of.

I smiled at the memory and the man half-hidden in the darkness out front of my parents' home. "Naw, not yet. I just wanted to put something in the car so I wouldn't forget it. How 'bout you?"

"I am not one for this many people, as you know. However, I wanted to give you your gift myself." He stepped into the streetlamp's glow, and I saw that Momma's barbecue sauce had claimed another victim. Jove held out a small jewelry box. It was too big for a ring, thank Christ, but it still gave my heart a jolt.

He must have seen the relief in my eyes just like I saw the hurt in his. "You know I am no longer your employer, Mira. Please, accept this from me."

Then, something cool fastened around my wrist. I hadn't even seen Jove move. I pulled my hand back and lifted it to find a silver bracelet dangling there. It was beautiful, with four tiny charms hanging from the slim, braided metal. It fit perfectly, as if it had been made just for me by the jeweler.

The first charm looked like a medieval shield with a lion on it. Its flowing mane framed the stoic-looking leonine face. I'd seen this same art style around the shop. There was a carved version above the door to the basement of Bindings, where Jove did his restoration work, and others worked into the newel posts guarding the upstairs.

The second was a green and silver Celtic cross backed with a circle of braided metal . . . that couldn't be wood. It was too small to be bent wood. It had to be metal painted to look like wood or maybe brass. It warmed my heart as I knew Jove wasn't a Christian, but he knew I was. It was nice to have what I considered divine protection.

The third charm was two conjoined Chinese symbols that I learned the meaning of when I looked it up later. They meant 'Protection.' I could use all the protection I could get.

The fourth was an eye. Not an actual eyeball. That would be gross. This was stylized, carved flawlessly from lapis lazuli, and reminded me of things I saw in the Egyptian exhibits when I was little. I wasn't an Egyptian, but I was interested in the stories of their gods and mythologies. The Moms were into all the different legends worldwide, so they shared their interest with their girls.

My stomach sank as I studied it. I couldn't keep this. It was too much like a gift one gave to a significant other and must have cost him a bundle. There were small blue gems in the eyes of the lion and a larger green jewel in the middle of the Egyptian eye.

"Jove, I can't—" but that's as far as I got. I looked up from the bracelet to find myself in an empty yard. He had already left while I was looking at the charms. I smirked—that ninja. I picked up the box that was left behind and opened it.

Congratulations on your graduation, Doktor Hall.

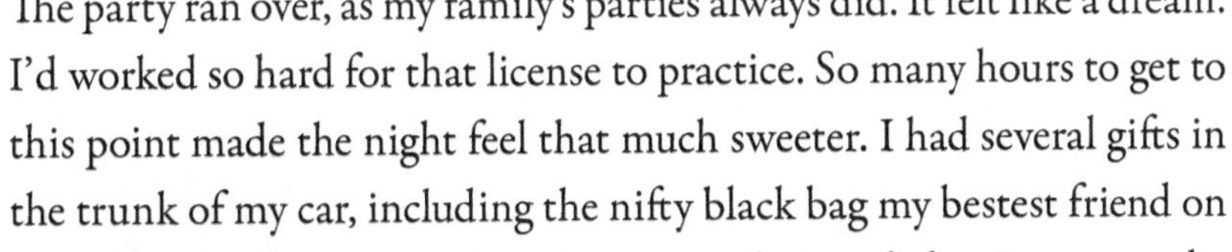

The party ran over, as my family's parties always did. It felt like a dream. I'd worked so hard for that license to practice. So many hours to get to this point made the night feel that much sweeter. I had several gifts in the trunk of my car, including the nifty black bag my bestest friend on the planet had given me. The charm bracelet jangled as I got into the driver's seat.

"Are you sure you don't want to spend the night, Baby-Mine? It will be almost two by the time you get home," Momma said, concerned.

Mom and Ree had just finished stuffing the last of my graduation gifts into the trunk, letting it close with a loud *thunk*.

I lived in a small apartment in Philadelphia, only three miles away from Old City. I could walk to the Franklin Institute on my way to the

Reading Terminal Market and hit the Mutter Museum on the way home. I loved how close it was to my university and Alden's hospital, where I'd done my residency. Yet, it still gave me the pleasure of enjoying the historic buildings, museums, and cobblestone streets of one of the most fascinating cities. Philly is unapologetic, brash, passionate, and creative. There is nowhere else I'd rather be.

It was only an hour away from the Moms. The turnpike was always safer when there was less traffic, especially this late at night. Or so I told myself. I'd done it plenty of times before. I wasn't worried.

"I'll be all right, Momma. I'll call you when I get home, okay?" I kissed her cheek and waved as I pulled away. I wanted to get home to hang my white doctor's coat. The dean had handed it to me folded neatly on top of my degree, and I was anxious to hang them in places of honor at home. I couldn't wait to start opening my clinic now that I had my doctorate. My perfect spot to start helping people. I'd been dreaming about my spot since I took out my first student loan when I started medical school.

The inky night on the drive from my parents' house back to my apartment in the city didn't hinder my happy glow. Despite my delight, I wasn't going any faster than the little white sign on the highway told me to go. Apparently, that wasn't good enough for the truck behind me. When I say 'truck,' I mean one of those *big* trucks that usually pulls huge and heavy loads that you can't see over or around if you happen to be behind them.

The horn blared as the monstrous, massive vehicle pulled up beside me. It started pulling into my lane, forcing me to the rumble strip on the side. Panicking, I laid on my horn and looked out of my window into the truck's cab. From my view in my little sedan, all I could see in the cab was this dark, swirling smoke. My first thought? *Fire!* My second? *'Pole!'* as I crashed headfirst into a light pole that doubled as an emergency call box. The irony was not lost on me. Blackness quickly followed as I slid out of consciousness.

2

According to the authorities, my front end wrapped around the pole, snapping my front axle in two and shoving my dashboard and steering wheel into my middle. The bottom of my car thrust my legs back, causing them to snap at my right ankle and left shin. My airbag kept my neck from cracking, but that didn't stop the glass from the windshield from embedding itself deep in my skull.

It was painful to pull air into my lungs from breath to breath. I ached everywhere. My throat and nose were raw from the removal of the breathing tube. I kept going in and out. It was impossible to stay awake. I blinked at the whiteboard that was posted on the wall. It had my nurse's name, Patrick, the times he was in, and the current date. It was just a day after the party. I closed and opened my eyes, trying to wrap my thoughts around things. I barely had time to meet my nurse and ask for some water before I fell asleep again.

The next thing I saw when I woke up again were the familiar faces of my family and a white cup of water. My sisters were there, along with our parents, who were all trying not to crowd my bed. They were still in their party clothes, which told me they had spent a restless night together. The lights had been dimmed, and the curtains closed, but I could still see my family, which made me so happy.

"Baby-Mine," said Momma, tears clogging her voice. "Can you hear me?"

"Momma, I hurt so bad." I reached out to my Momma with one arm and gently hugged her.

"Oh! Mira, your *hair*!" Mom said in shock as she gently brushed what was left of my hair. "What did they do to you?"

I reached up and felt the gauze. There must have been damage to my skull for the surgical team to go there. Under the gauze, my hair was still long. One of my nurses had tied it back so it wouldn't get in the way.

"I won't have my daughter looking like a broken doll. Once you get out, we are going right to the salon to get it fixed," she promised.

"Well, that was a stupid thing to do, Mira. Now she's going to drag you to Roxy's," said Ree from a nearby chair.

Roxanne LaRouge was the owner of the Moms' favorite salon and spa. I loved going there when I had the money, so going sounded heavenly . . . after I slept a bit more. I was so tired. Ree sniffed, pulling my attention to her. "Years and years at school to get a doctorate, and what do you do? Hit the first pole you see on the way home." Ree always hid her emotions with gallows humor and sarcasm, so this was nothing new. She slid onto the bed beside me and wrapped her arms around me. I tried not to wince. "Don't you *dare* do that again."

How Annie shifted from foot to foot told me exactly how freaked out she was about my situation. "Really, Ree, all the things in the world to say, and you say that?" She rolled her eyes but slid onto the other side of the bed. It was crowded, but I didn't want them gone. I kissed them each on the head and gently hugged them close.

"It was just so shiny. I couldn't help myself," I said slowly, making them laugh a little. I wasn't sure what my prognosis was then, but I wasn't about to let those two get too annoyed at each other, not over me. The door to my room opened, and two people came in. I recognized them both as they'd both been at the graduation party. Dr. Elizabeth Stanton, who'd done my Emergency Room rotation, and the surgeon who had saved my life, Dr. Phineas Alden, entered the room.

"Miss Hall, good to see you awake!" Alden boomed. I winced at the sound and saw Dr. Stanton grimace out of the corner of my eye. Aww, hell, I knew that look. Nurses would give the same cringe when a resident (yours truly) would say something idiotic or just hit people wrong, like asking a curvy woman when the baby is due. The defeated look on Stanton's face also told me that more of the same gaffs were on their way, and they happened all the time with this particular surgeon. Dr. Alden was a legend in his field. I was grateful that he'd been able to work his magic on me. Which was why I didn't correct him.

"A pleasure to make your acquaintance, Mrs. Hall and Miss—" Dr. Alden paused, waiting for Mom to give a different last name.

Momma stepped up, positioning herself between Mom and Alden, "This is my wife, Erica Hall, and Mira's sisters, Marie and Anne. We want to thank you for saving our daughter's life. I wish we would have been allowed to see her sooner than now."

She smiled diplomatically. She knew leading questions like that made Mom uncomfortable. In one short sentence, Momma had introduced my family and made it so routine that no one in their right mind would question it.

"We had to keep the area sterile for your daughter's protection, Mrs. Hall," said Dr. Stanton. She hadn't been around when I was doing my residency, but she had the air of experience. She knew how to handle frantic families and how to unruffle feathers. However, her compatriot seemed oblivious to many of the cues my family was putting out there. He maneuvered around the Moms, barely acknowledging that they were people he had to be concerned about. He moved around my family as a person would move around a table, just objects in his way. Mom had to sit hard in the visitor's chair to avoid getting bumped. Momma's eyes narrowed slightly, but she visibly shrugged it off and gave me an 'I love you, baby' smile.

"Tell me how you are feeling, Miss Hall." Dr. Alden smiled down at me from the end of my bed. I frowned a little at how quickly he had dismissed my parents, and the creepy glint in his eyes. It made me want to curl away. I pulled the covers up more, uncomfortable under his scrutiny. I felt Ree and Annie angle in closer. It felt really good to have them there. I felt less vulnerable with my sisters next to me.

His face was square, with a receding hairline that he tried to hide with a comb-over. His surgeon's hands were delicate but looked solid and steady. The way he carried himself told me that he habitually went to a high society health club to tone. He wasn't overly muscled but seemed to keep up with maintaining his figure.

"That's Doctor Hall," Mom corrected proudly.

"That's right! You were at the top of this year's class, weren't you?" Dr. Alden snapped his fingers as if remembering. The gesture came off as pompous and a little rude. Like he was praising a child for getting an 'A' in macaroni art, it put a little more tarnish on that pedestal I'd had him on.

Momma's eyes narrowed again at the condescension. Mom was typically oblivious to cues such as tone of voice, so Momma usually did most of the socializing with strangers until Mom felt comfortable.

Strike two, Dr. Alden. I wished that he would lower his voice. It was painful when he kept talking at an average volume while everyone else was hushed.

Dr. Alden put his hands in the pockets of his white coat and smiled brightly before continuing, "You should find this fascinating, Doctor Hall. You were in pretty bad shape when you were on my table. Thought we would lose you a couple of times there. But the procedure was perfection itself. Nothing else to be expected from me after all."

"How—" I croaked. Momma handed me my water to sip before I could continue. "How long was the surgery?"

"Ten hours. You had many tiny lacerations and particulates left behind in your frontal lobe. We used a new tool I've been working on to help. A little project of mine, if you will." He expounded on the experimental new surgical laser that helped remove the particulates from the right hemisphere of my brain. His gestures were significant as he went on about how intricate my surgery was. My head throbbed as I struggled to follow along.

I saw Mom's face go pale when his descriptions got too graphic. Pride radiated from the surgeon as he spoke about his machine and the success of the new medication that aided in my healing.

More tarnish went on as he bragged.

"They all expected you to stay comatose for a week at the very least, but not me. I knew the procedure would be a great success, and I was right as usual." He elbowed Dr. Stanton, whose face had gone ashen as he just . . . kept . . . talking. "That'll show them who is at the top, once and for all."

"What did you just say? You just *decided* to use something *experimental* on my daughter?" Momma hissed. That hiss was not a happy Momma sound. Strike three, Doc, prep for Hurricane Dani. When my Momma became angry, her voice returned to the South, where she was raised. That twang would do any Southern Belle proud. She didn't like the word 'experimental' at all.

Stanton got a look of panic on her face. She knew the signs of an irate family member and took a discrete step toward the door just in case she needed to call for reinforcements.

Momma's eyes were slits as she pushed between Dr. Alden and my bed. She poked at his chest, forcing him to take a couple of surprised steps back. Now that he was further away, I felt my muscles relax a bit.

I felt Annie's hand gently stroking my shoulder, comforting me, her eyes fixed on the drama. Her prosecutor's brain was turned on, paying rapt attention to the scene unfolding before us and notating everything that could be useful in court.

Ree, in comparison, went still, but her eyes were steely, hot with rage. I took her hand and felt her tremble as she took a deep breath and let it out. Both my sisters were ready to throw hands with my surgeon. I wondered if he realized it was, at the very least, three against one. I wasn't alone, and right then, nothing could be more comforting.

"At the very least, you should have contacted us for permission to use *anything* experimental on our daughter, you over-entitled, puffed-up, son of a bitch!"

"Madame, there is no call for profanity. Your daughter is an adult, and as an adult, I saw no purpose in contacting you for *permission*." Condescension dripped from his voice as he looked down his nose at her. That man was playing with fire and didn't know it.

"Yes, she is, *however*, as she was near *death* at the time. You should have checked with her next of kin. Especially seeing as I am listed as an *emergency contact*!" She got right in his face, yelling without really yelling. It was a mom power she had cultivated with the three of us. It worked great in movie theaters.

"It wasn't as if he had far to go. We were in the *waiting room, wringing our hands the entire time*." Ree growled.

"What right did you think you had to use our Mira as your *goddamned* guinea pig?" Momma said through her teeth.

"Madam, I can have your family removed from this room at any time," Alden's voice was flat. His eyes had gone tundra cold as he spoke and chilled me to the bone. "I suggest you moderate your tone."

Danielle Hall had a temper when it suited her. My family had every right to be upset. It was unorthodox for Dr. Alden not to consult my family on this. Keeping them out of my room was one thing, but keeping them out of the loop was another matter entirely. That is the kind of thing that causes unnecessary trauma to the family and something we, as doctors, are taught to avoid at all costs.

"Dani," came Mom's soothing voice as she put a hand on her spouse's arm and gently pulled her away from the surgeon. She hated scenes like this, and Momma was winding up for a rant fest. "If Doctor Alden hadn't made that call, hadn't done what he did . . ." She turned and looked at my bed. I had one arm around Ree, and my head was snuggled against Annie. "I don't think she'd be here with us now."

Dr. Stanton agreed heartily. "Absolutely, Madam. Everything done was essential to your daughter's survival and recovery." She wisely took a step or two away from Momma, pulling Dr. Alden with her. "Come, Phineas. We should leave them alone now."

The surgeon glanced threateningly at my mother, who still looked like she was deciding whether to throw the fist her hand was forming. At the other doctor's insistence, Alden allowed himself to be pulled closer to the door.

"I must say I am very impressed with the speed at which Doctor Hall is recovering," said Dr. Stanton, pulling more attention away from Alden as she was pushing him out the door. "She's already awake and coherent so soon after her surgery. Some people don't wake up from this kind of trauma at all. It's borderline miraculous."

"As expected." Alden harrumphed.

"Doctor Alden?" My nurse, Patrick, stuck his head into my room, a neon purple clipboard in his hands, almost running nose-first into the surgeon. "You have a call from a General Howell? It sounded important, sir."

"Yes." Alden nodded and made his way through the door. "I'll be right there. Miss Hall, I will check in with you again at a more convenient time to go over some post-operation procedures you will need to adhere to."

I frowned. He'd dropped my title again. I mean, once was forgivable, but twice, especially after a correction, is inexcusable. We all glared at him, eyes tracking him as he finally left the room.

After he left, Dr. Stanton sighed and shook her head. Her voice was a relief after the constant booming volume of Alden's. "I am so sorry about his behavior, everyone. If he wasn't the best-damned surgeon we've got, not to mention his connections, then I really don't think he'd still be here."

Alden had been more socially inept than I'd been led to believe. I did not appreciate being patronized, infantilized, or disrespected like that. On any other day, I would have been yelling in his face. I don't care if you're God Almighty. You don't treat people like that! I couldn't drum up the energy to fuel my rage much beyond the pleasant daydream of my foot up his elite ass. My head was pounding, and my throat was sore, my muscles ached. I leaned on Annie, yawned, and failed to hide it.

"C'mon, guys. Time to head out," Mom said. "Mira has to rest to get better."

"We'll be back tomorrow, Baby, with some books and your laptop so that you won't be too bored." Momma kissed me on the cheek and stroked the side of my face like she used to when I was sick as a kid.

Ree looked down at me, and her expression wavered. "Jeez, Mir. Where can I touch you where you don't hurt?"

I took her hand and hugged it against my cheek. "I'll be okay. This is just the first part of getting back to 'okay.' I swear. No pie crust promises here."

Pie crust promises were easily made and easily broken, or so Mary Poppins once said. We grew up on Disney, so I knew Ree would get the reference. I'd said it to make her smile, but she broke a little bit then, tears starting down her face. Annie grabbed some tissues out of the box that appeared magically in all hospital rooms and gave them to her. Ree acted so tough sometimes, but she loved us very much. Mom, bless her, quietly shuffled my family out of the room after I kissed each one of them goodbye.

I loved my Moms and the girls. I wish they could have stayed longer, but my eyes wouldn't stay open anymore.

The next time I opened my eyes, the light that filtered through the slatted window shades was considerably darker than it had been when my family visited. It was also just in time for them to deliver my meal. Kathy, my night nurse, came in soon after the dinner hour, knocking gently on my door. "Hey, Doc Hall. Got yourself in a pickle, huh?"

I took a sip of water from the white cup they'd given me with my dinner. "Hey Kath." I croaked. "The pickle was the size of an eighteen-wheeler and made me wrap my car around a pole."

She hissed in a breath of sympathetic pain. Kathy was a pleasant woman whom I'd worked with before during my rotations, so we were on excellent terms. She was a thirty-year pro who loved to help the newbies learn the ropes.

"Heard you got saddled with Asshole Alden."

"I had no idea he lived up to his moniker so well." I tried for a sarcastic smile but only managed a wince.

"Don't push yourself, hun. You'll be back on your feet and being a smart ass soon enough." Kathy took the remnants of my dinner (lime gelatin and water) and noticed I was shivering. "Did you want another blanket?"

"Yes, please." I whimpered. "How come I didn't hear about his assholey-ness when I was here last?"

"*Himself* wasn't around this part of the hospital much while you were doing rotations, but I swear he's been like that since the day they put him on the damned board of directors. He's been impossible to deal with ever since." With practiced ease, Kathy snapped the thin blanket in the air and let it settle over the sheet I already had. "He has this real 'master of the plantation' vibe going, yanno? His patients are more like test subjects or projects. Anyone he considers beneath him he treats like shit. He doesn't really interact with most of his patients after he's had them on his table. Patrick told me A.A. seemed real interested in you, though."

"Me? Why? I'm just your run-of-the-mill vehicular accident victim."

"No idea, hun, but Patrick noticed him taking papers out of your file after the reports had been filed."

What? That wasn't right at all. "Did Patrick try to stop him?"

"Of course, he did, but A.A. just snarled at him to remember that he was easily replaceable and should remember who the fuck he was talking to."

That confirmed that Alden was just as much of an asshole as he projected himself to be, especially to people he saw as 'below' him, which was pretty much everyone.

"Look, is there any way you and the other nurses could make copies of my tests and reports? I don't know what he took out of there, but I'd like to make sure it doesn't happen again."

"It's your right to have access to your records, sweetie." Her grin turned wicked. "It'll be nice to stick it to that asshole. I'll talk to the others, and we'll make up a chart for you with copies of everything. You know what you're looking at, so I know you don't need the jargon-free version."

"Can you also CC Doctor Moore? Just in case?"

"Sure thing." She promised, "I'll take care of that myself. Now you just concentrate on healing, you hear? If you need anything, push that button."

Jove came to see me a few days later. I could sit up all on my own by that point and felt proud of myself for having accomplished the feat. He clutched sad-looking purple tulips in his hand.

He pulled up the chair, positioning it so I wouldn't have to move my head as much. *"Kleine, oh Gött.* Look at you."

"Hey, Jove." I tried to give him a weak smile. And I tried not to feel self-conscious about how I looked, but damn, that was starting to get hard every time someone came to visit.

Jove's bookshop held a special place in my heart. The smell of old books and the location in the historical part of the city made the place feel like a second home to me. It kept me fed and housed in my apartment rather than my parent's house while I went to school. Sometimes literally.

When Jove and I had a shift together, it would often run into the night, past closing, especially if there was a new title shipment coming in. On those nights, we would take turns ordering dinner and eating it on the antique oak counter as we critiqued the latest books. Sometimes Katie would be there too, but mostly it was just me and Jove.

I had to cut my hours to the bone as I did my residency, but Jove never forced me to choose between work and school. I really appreciated that.

"I am so sorry, Kleine." Jove has always called me that. It means 'small one' in his native German. Not that I'm a small person, quite the contrary, but Jove is six-eight, a whole foot taller than I am. The nickname stuck and gave my heart a smiley, gooey feeling every time he said it.

He placed the flowers next to my bed as I studied him. He looked more disheveled today than usual. His clothes were rumpled, there were dark circles under his tired eyes, and, I swear, his shoes had lost their customary shine. His shoulders slumped further as he stared down at the floor. "*Es tut mir Leid.*"

I rolled my eyes and lightly punched him on the arm. Then I winced. Rolling one's eyes after a head injury hurts. "You weren't driving that truck."

He looked miserable after I said that, like a kicked hound. "If I had only known, then I . . ." His arms fell impotently to his sides. "I would have done anything to spare you this pain."

I shifted uncomfortably in my bed to get a better angle to see his face. "Look, Jove, there is no way you could have known something like this would happen. If it didn't happen to me, then that truck would've hit someone else." I touched his hands, clasped together in front of him.

On new release nights after our habitual critique, we would talk about my dreams for my practice and his for the future of the shop. Jove wanted to eventually expand into a franchise with locations all over the world. I dreamt of owning my little general practice, having my own nursing staff, and maybe even an associate or two so I wasn't swamped with patients. I would treat people regardless of their insurance status and improve their lives. However, a medical practice would take time to build unless a retiring doctor would be willing to sell you theirs with a pre-built patient base. I didn't want to piggyback that way.

I wanted to create my own.

I had saved as much as I could so this little bump in the road wouldn't make me starve. It just pushed back my timetable by . . . damn . . . a few years if the insurance didn't pull through. I took one of the flowers, suddenly needing it, and took a shallow, appreciative breath in. "How did you know I liked tulips?"

"Your mother had them in the garden. I asked her about them at the party. She told me she had planted them the month you were born. That makes them a special flower." Jove then suddenly took my right hand and gently squeezed it, bringing it to his lips in one of those European knuckle kisses. His hands were warm and comforting. I jangled the bracelet. It made a gentle tinkling sound that made me smile. I would give it back when I saw him again. Until then, I'd enjoy it. But he didn't visit me after that. The sneaky brat avoided the hospital, so I wouldn't have the opportunity to return the gift.

The first few weeks of recovery were mainly spent sleeping with intermittent tests to monitor my recovery, nothing out of the ordinary. I had visitors every day, either members of my family, friends, or both. David came so often you could set your watch by him. He'd usually come with a board or card game for us to play until my meal would come.

I could tell I was recovering fast, so it didn't surprise me when they moved me out of the ICU and to a different wing. What shocked me was how far away I was from the rest of the hospital. I recognized the area as one of the COVID wings when the disease was still new and terrifying. I didn't like how Alden had me sequestered. All I was told was it was best to be kept in a quiet part of the hospital.

They still kept patients with the virus in this wing when it was some off-the-wall variant, but while I was there, it was eerily quiet, like a haunted sanatorium. It was a sparsely populated section of the hospital, staffed by nurses and techs I wasn't as familiar with. They ran to the stoic and burly. I used to see a lot of those types when I did my rotation in the psychiatric wards. It felt isolating, like I was in a prison wing. The only thing missing was actual guards at the doors.

My time in that wing was filled with inpatient physical therapy, cognitive tests, X-rays, and scans of my brain. Since my nurses had changed, I wasn't getting copied on my results or even what tests were being ordered. I would catch Alden watching me. From the window on my door at first, but once he caught me looking at him, he decided to drop the pretenses. He took charge of my tests himself, ordering the technicians to let him see the results as they appeared on the screen.

We ran into some trouble with the bracelet the first time Alden wanted a PET scan. He was there, looming over the technicians like an impatient, malevolent shadow. I couldn't figure out the trick to the clasp on my bracelet, and neither could the nurses or techs on staff. I could feel his angry eyes bore into me. The fact that the surgeon was there watching the test rather than just getting a report later felt wrong, but who were we to deny one of the board directors if he wanted to take an 'active role' in his patient's recovery?

"Hall, take that damned thing off," Alden demanded sharply, sneering at my bracelet. "I don't want any anomalous data clouding my results."

As if I wasn't the one with the brain in question. My wheelchair had been parked next to the large machine for fifteen minutes by this point. They'd just stood over me and watched as I struggled to take off Jove's gift. I was tired and done with this level of shit. I wanted to lie down, whether that was on the scanner table or back in my room. I didn't care.

"I would if I could, Doctor," I said with a sarcastic, saccharine smile. "The clasp is in a bad position."

"Well, then we'll just have to help you with that. You," Alden snapped at the nearest technician. "Get that thing off her. I don't care if you cut it off. Just get her into that machine. I need to know how well the procedure is progressing."

I pulled my arm in close to my chest. "This was a gift. I don't want you to cut it off!" How the hell could I give it back to Jove in pieces?

"Give me a moment." The Tech's kind eyes pleaded with me for patience. "I'm going to do everything I can to take it off without hurting it first, but you need to understand that if we can't, then we may have to cut it off."

He knelt to try to take it off himself. The clasp moved and slid out from under his hands just as it had my own. When his fingers finally got to the mechanism, it refused to open, no matter how much force the poor man applied.

"Hold her down," Alden said coldly.

I felt a chill race up my spine at his tone. I wasn't really a person to this man. I was a test subject. This was way too many tests for a new medical device. Just what the hell did he do to me in the operating room?

Two burly nurses took two menacing steps toward me. My heart was in my throat, and I held my hand protectively against my chest.

"Hey, what the hell are you doing? There's no need for that," the Tech protested. "This patient isn't hostile. All you're doing is scaring her!"

Alden's eyes narrowed dangerously. "Are you questioning me? I take it you don't like your job then. Technicians like yourself are easily replaceable in this economy. Get this uppity sack of shit out of here."

"I'm sorry," he whispered and stood. A burly-looking guard-type man escorted him out of the room.

The nurses stood on either side of my chair and held my arms against the armrests. Another intrepid tech returned with a pair of metal clippers he had at his station.

He tried to cut it himself, but after several grunting minutes, he gave up and handed the tool over to one of the brawny nurses to try. After several attempts, the clippers clattered to the ground, blades bent. The bracelet dented them, rendering the tool useless. The braided cord looked like pure silver, but there was no way silver would have held up to those clippers.

"That has to be some type of titanium. Unless you want to cut off her hand, sir, then that thing is not coming off."

"For the love of Pete, Alden." I growled, shaking off the remaining burly man. "Just calibrate the machine to account for the anomalous materials or just put my freaking hand in a mitten. It's not like my hand is going to be in the PET anyway, just my head. All you're doing here is flexing your position and attempting to intimidate a patient. Which is illegal, by the way."

I rolled my chair over to him and glared up at his imposing form, "Now, I want to see these scans just as much as you do. I want to see what this medication you've had me take every night is doing. Since this thing" —I held up my hand and jangled my wrist— "isn't coming off, then we just need to work around it."

For a moment, I thought he'd have Hewie and Dewie over there tackle me for being impertinent. Either that, or he wanted to slap me. But then, he looked down at me and smiled. "You surprise me, Hall. You see the worth in what we're doing. You really were top of your class. I didn't expect you to take such an interest in this. All right, Hall. You've presented a solution that I can live with. Go on back over so they can help you into the machine."

Alden went into the computer room, manned by a different, scared-looking tech.

I was laid onto the machine's flat surface. The room was silent, with the edge of fear you feel when something dangerous is nearby. In that silence, they quickly took my blood sugar and clicked the IV with the tracer fluid into the hook-up already connected to my veins. This procedure used to take forty-five minutes, but technology had progressed in the past few years and shortened the time down to ten. Thank God. I didn't think Alden had the patience to wait any longer than that.

The hand that held my bracelet was put in a lead-lined mitten that looked like one of Momma's potholders. I set my hands to my sides and nodded at the Tech that I was ready. Usually, I'd have asked for my headphones so I could listen to some music or an audiobook, but with the tension in the room, I didn't dare. The Tech offered me a set of ear-plugs instead. Her hands were soft but shook from time to time. She'd just watched her colleague get fired, worried she might be next, and had all the earmarks of just wanting to get the day over and done with. But she still took the time to give me a little bit of comfort. I smiled at her as I put in the plugs and started thinking of my favorite Queen songs. I was most of the way through *Bohemian Rhapsody* when the machine stopped and slid me back toward my chair.

"Hall, roll over here and look at this."

I did what I was told, maneuvering my chair into the computer room.

Alden looked like a spoiled kid at Christmas. "Look here, see how these structures are being built along the parietal lobe?"

He was excited, and honestly, I was too. I sat up straighter to make sure what I was reading on the scan was accurate. What we were looking at was incredible. Inside my brain, where there had been damage from the accident, grid-like structures dotted and looked to be spreading like a net protecting the rest of my brain.

"And look here." He brought up a part of the scan with a swipe of his hand in the air and enlarged my right leg. The bone was still broken, but it was now perfectly aligned, and only a hairline fracture remained of the damage.

"That's impossible." I let out a surprised breath. "I had a compound fracture there. It doesn't even ache anymore."

"Precisely. We didn't even need to use any screws on the break when we reset it. Just fit the two pieces back together and let the procedure do its work. Imagine the possibilities for this. People would only have to be in for the procedure once and be healed in a matter of days from incidents even worse than yours."

"Are you saying that this continues *after* a patient has been released? As in self-healing?"

Alden nodded, pleased I'd noticed the application. "As long as you continue on the regimen of medication, you'll be up and walking around in no time at all."

"What do you do when the patient stops the regimen?"

"Eventually, what we are calling NAN-Zero Six will be flushed from the system naturally after six months, leaving all the benefits of the healing process and more behind."

This was the first time I heard the name of the medicine I'd been taking. I hadn't heard of anything like it on the market, which meant that it wasn't only the instruments that were experimental. I swallowed carefully. "What do you mean, 'and more'?"

"Those structures we saw forming around your brain will remain there as further protection for the organ in cases of sudden impact. You'll be more resistant to concussions and damage from an outside source like what happened during your unfortunate accident."

I let my mind ponder that bit. "And you're certain adding something like that won't hinder the brain floating as it's supposed to and not just be damaged at impact as if there was a second layer of the skull there?"

"There were a few experiments where that happened, but with some tweaking, we've gotten it to the point where the structures are flexible and act as a cushion rather than a wall."

I wanted to study my results more in-depth, but the bastard shut the file and ordered me back to my room. Blood work was taken every six hours, like clockwork, and there were plenty of tests that would only require me to give samples but not be in on the results.

I thought it was strange that he was taking such an interest in me. I also thought it was odd that I seemed to be the only one in this trial. With the medication being called NAN-06, that told me there had to have been five other iterations of the drug. Were those failures? Was mine the sixth one in line? Was I only the sixth participant in this trial?

"He just doesn't have your way with people, Doctor Hall," remarked Tammy, my day nurse, when I'd gotten back to my room. She was subbing the shift for my usual nurse in this wing, as they had a family emergency crop up. I'd worked with Tammy for eight months during my maternity rotation—sweet lady but with South Jersey sass.

She handed me a copy of my latest chart with a wink. "When you were a resident here, you were one of our favorites because of how you empathize with the patients and staff. Doc Alden just doesn't have that way about him. He treats us like we're his servants. Just last week, he made Miranda cry, and she's one of our best nurses! Kathy gave us the down low on what was going on. The Moms are supremely pissed, your sisters too! Alden moved you out to wing Timbuktu and restricted who could visit. Family only and even then only from six am to nine am."

That's why I hadn't seen anyone since they moved me. No one could work within those hours reasonably. Typical visiting hours were between nine in the morning and eight at night.

"Ew." My nose scrunched in disgust.

"I know, right? You'd think the man would have *some* empathy for another person, but not A.A. I swear he snaps his fingers at me one more time, and I'm throwing a full bedpan at his head. It's going to be sweet when your family files charges against him."

"Thanks again, Tam. I've been going nuts about this." I waggled the clipboard with my chart on it. "I really like having a copy for my records."

"It's your right, honey. When you're done with it, I'll bring it back up to Kathy for her to put it with the rest of your paperwork for when you get released. You get some rest. I'll check in on you in a bit."

I thanked Tammy again for my chart and opened it to read. I was becoming as fascinated with my scans as Dr. Alden. I understood what they were saying. My brain seemed more active since the surgery. More synapses were firing at faster rates than previously recorded.

Something extraordinary was happening.

Then, late one night, I had to go. You know, *GO*. I didn't want to bother the overworked night nurse. She was already dealing with a screamer who had woken up fully before the nurse could quickly get her blood drawn for testing. Probably the only other damned patient in this wing. But, damn it, I had to go! I swung my casts over the side of the bed. Thank God they didn't go up to my thigh. Otherwise, I'd have to try to wait it out for help. If I kept healing at the rate I was, then I should be upgraded to walking casts soon.

I tried to calculate the distance from the bed to the wheelchair. Too far. Why had the nurse left it there? I just needed it a little bit closer. I stretched out my hand and thought how much closer it needed to be. Then it rocked toward me.

I blinked. It had to have been a breeze or something. I sat up and reached for the chair again, straining. It rocked again, harder this time, almost rolling. I held my breath, listening. If there'd been an earthquake, I would have heard it. Or at least felt the tremor. I looked around the room for anything that could explain what was happening.

"Ghosts don't exist," I said to myself. "I do not have some benevolent poltergeist pushing my chair to me so I can hit the head. The last thing I'd need is to be haunted by a Rona patient screaming 'hoax!'"

I'd heard scary stories like that all through medical school. A doctor sent down to some forgotten hospital wing . . . like the one I was in . . . to a room with only one patient inside. Gulp . . . like I was . . . only to have things fly at them as soon as they entered, the shrill screams of *'Hoax! Liar! I've got the flu, you son of a bitch!'* as sharp implements beat the unsuspecting physician to death.

I shook my head and gave my cheeks a little slap. I was being ridiculous. I was a woman *of SCIENCE*, damn it. There had to be a more logical explanation. My eyes looked around and landed on the discarded little medicine cup. No way, but then again, why not? I've been taking the mysterious Nan-06 for three weeks now. According to the scans, I used more of my brain than anyone else in the world. I had to test this theory.

I looked at the wheelchair in a new light. I focused and stretched out a hand. My amazement scattered my concentration, and the chair stopped moving. I cursed and tried again. This time, the chair rolled to my waiting hand. I did a little hop off my bed and into the chair. The resulting bump reminded me instantly of my need for the chair in the first place, and I rolled myself to the bathroom. I maneuvered over to the porcelain throne and evaluated my options.

Option one: I would tell the doctors and become an instant guinea pig, just like Momma had said in the first place.

Option two: I would keep it to myself and run my own damn experiments.

Guess which one I chose.

It took another month before I was released from the hospital. It was a near thing. I was in walking casts, barely needing the wheelchair. They'd taken my cell phone, and the phone in my room was only connected to the nursing station. My only communication with the outside world was through the nurses Kathy had on my room. They were usually overnight nurses, a brilliant move on Kathy's part. The one shift Alden never interacted with. They were getting messages out to my family. They couldn't sneak any in because they were frisked going in and out.

I could feel the cage tightening around me. When I slept, I had nightmares. Sometimes, it was the accident with flashing headlights, blaring horns, and swirling smoke. Sometimes, it was just a voice singing, 'Guinea Pig, Guinea Pig, Mira Hall's a Guinea Pig!'

The worst nightmare was me strapped to a metal gurney.

I couldn't open my eyes. I could feel the surgical lights hot on my face, but I couldn't see. I couldn't move. I heard the clanking of the surgical equipment on the table. I recognized the sound after so many years of schooling.

Oh God, I'd heard horror stories about this sort of thing. I was awake and, far worse, aware during my surgery. I was already in so much pain. It was about to get so much worse. The beeps on my monitor sped up as the fear hit my heart. My chest felt tight, and I whimpered, but not a sound escaped.

"Doctor, she's up. I hear her." Oh, thank God. I thought I hadn't made a sound, but he'd heard me. Somehow, he heard me. There was a muffled reply that came from somewhere in the vicinity of my head. I felt the panic start to crawl up my throat.

"Shh . . . Shh, it's okay, lovely, let me sing you off to sleep." His voice was . . . calming. It crooned as the man started to sing softly. I heard the snap of a latex glove being removed. Then I felt a light, almost loving touch on my arm and felt the pain ebb away. I was getting pulled back into the darkness of blessed unconsciousness. "Lavender blue, dilly dilly, lavender green, if I were king, dilly dilly, you would be my queen."

I jerked awake, gasping, panting through the terror. I wanted to go home, be in my own bed, hear my neighbors moving around. I wanted to play Dungeon and Dragons at my favorite comic book place, Never Ending Stories. I wanted to play games with David and eat takeout with Jove. I had enough of this.

But every time I brought up leaving, Alden would change the subject. He would wave away my concerns every time I asked, saying we needed more tests. I'd been hospitalized for two months in total. I didn't have any pain anymore, but every day, they still took the blood.

Still every six hours.

It was strange because if I was reading my charts correctly, I was healed enough to start outpatient PT.

According to my night nurses, my parents wanted me home, too. Tammy had managed to get me my phone as that wing of the hospital didn't have the hook-up anymore. I had to hide it under my mattress. That made it a lot easier to keep in touch with my family.

Momma had been particularly insistent. She hadn't liked my surgeon since that first meeting in my room and had no qualms about letting him know about it.

Annie was already compiling evidence for a whopper of a lawsuit for imprisonment, kidnapping, malpractice, and a laundry list of other charges ready for me to give her the go-ahead.

The day the Moms came to pick me up was intense.

Kathy had gotten the paperwork from my primary to prep me to go home. I'd been off the IV for a while now, but I still had the nondescript, white capsules stamped with the letters NAN-06. I handed her the paperwork I signed with a smile.

"All right, Doc. Looks like we've got everything in order here. Your ride said she'd be the one to pick you up." Kathy leaned down. "We made sure to schedule it for when A.A.'s in his board of directors meeting to avoid any unpleasantness."

"I'll be glad to get out of here. It's like a freaking tomb down here." I shivered as I pulled my favorite cream-colored cardigan over my shoulders. My aches and pains were gone, even the ones from the surgery. I had walking casts and a shiny new set of crutches leaning against the side table. Sweatpants, leggings, or skirts were going to be what I got to wear until I could get the casts off.

"I know, right?" Kathy smiled. "I hate working the shift down here. It's so far away from the rest of the hospital, and it's freaking creepy! Like it's haunted or something."

"Ready to go, Baby-Mine?" Momma's voice was a soft coo, and her smile was the most comforting thing I'd seen in months. I was up on my crutches and hobbled over to hug her.

"Oh, I'd say she's ready, Mrs. Hall." My favorite nurse wheeled the instrument of my escape around the bed. "You know the rules, Doc, into the chair with you."

As we left the ward, I felt the tension ease out of my shoulders. The guards on the door glared at us with every step. They couldn't say anything because all of the paperwork was in order.

Every step was a step closer to being out in the sun again. I hadn't even been allowed to do much exploring of the wing. Some of the other nurses, who were more loyal to Alden, had kept me on a short leash.

Tammy and Kathy thought the whole idea of sucking up because of someone's position was asinine and just did what was suitable for the patient. I liked Tammy and Kathy.

The corridors got broader and brighter as we got to the front lobby. I could see the sun shining through the tinted glass of the doors. It looked like paradise and freedom, but my smile disappeared when I heard a roar behind us that made me scrunch deeper into my seat.

"Just what the hell do you think you're doing?" Alden strode up to us from the closing executive elevator. His face was a study in reds and purples as rage exuded from every pore. He glared at Momma, a snake ready to strike. "As I have stated, madam, I will decide when she is ready to go. As her attending physician, I cannot, in good faith, allow her to be taken from the premises. Miss Hall—"

"Doctor Hall." Momma corrected through clenched teeth.

"Doctor Hall requires further treatment." He stood there glaring, waiting for Momma to capitulate as he looked down his nose at her. He was in for a long-ass wait.

"And just what treatment is *that*? She's done with the surgery. She's done with the inpatient physical therapy that you, yourself, insisted on. You've sequestered her in an old COVID ward where there are barely any other people. I wouldn't have been able to find her if that nice desk nurse hadn't given me a map. Why would you have to do that when she hasn't shown any signs of infection from something else? She's taken the medicine you've been shoving into her, a medicine that you *still* have yet to inform our primary doctor as to what it *does*!"

"I do not have to explain my work to the likes of you." Dr. Alden hissed. "Your obvious obesity shows that you have little regard for your own health. What makes you think you are qualified to evaluate the health of your daughter?"

"You absolute self-important, bumptious segment of fresh bovine excrement. You best step all the way back before this 'obese' woman tramples you under my boots."

That wasn't the first time I felt afraid of Dr. Alden. He'd ruled where they'd been keeping me with an iron fist. Whenever there was a protest on how he was treating me, proverbial heads rolled. I saw more people fired during my time at the hospital than I had in my entire life. The staff was afraid of him, and the fear was infectious.

There was avarice in his cold, blue eyes whenever he looked at me. Like I was his property instead of his patient. He wanted me to be his very own research project. The kind of project that would have me locked in a secure government facility where I'd never see my family and friends again. He had been reading the charts and tests as well as I had, though I had gotten mine serendipitously. I worried that I might have to call in the cavalry to keep my freedom. The 'cavalry' was my baby sister, Annie, the prosecutor.

Tammy (she'd won the coin toss on who got to walk me out) held my wheelchair and looked nervous. Even she had to do what the doctor told her when he was right in front of her like this. "Her discharge papers are all in order, Doctor. Have we missed something?"

His head whipped around to face her. "Who signed those papers?" He snarled.

"Our family doctor, Doctor Moore," said Momma primly, placing herself between Alden and my wheelchair. "She came with me yesterday to evaluate Mira for release as she would have done weeks ago if your office had deigned to keep her in the loop like you're *supposed to*."

"We need her to remain here in the hospital to run further tests to make sure the treatment has been successful, Mrs. Hall," Dr. Alden said, trying to sound reasonable but failing spectacularly.

The angrier Momma got, the further south her voice traveled, and she was supremely pissed. I knew the reason for Alden's unusual interest. But the idea of staying here one minute longer made me nauseous.

"Well, it's obvious to anyone with *eyes* in their head that her treatment *has* been a success, Doctor Alden. And our family doctor agrees with us. Mira has completed her recovery here, and you shouldn't have had much of a say in any way once she was moved out of the Intensive Care Unit. You cut her off from us, you bastard. She wasn't even allowed to go outside and see the sky! Believe me, you will be hearing from our lawyer about that," Momma said. She looked like a wolf defending her cub. "Doctor Moore has prescribed her outpatient physical therapy, and frankly, Doctor Alden, I am questioning the *propriety* of your unusual interest in my daughter as she was supposed to be outside of your direct influence by this point. Frankly, I find your behavior . . . concerning."

Alden's face went purple, and he started to sputter. "Madam, *you* are not a doctor and have no authority in this hospital. Your daughter is under my care and isn't going anywhere unless *I* say she can."

"You seem to be under the misconception that you have any further say in my daughter's recovery. We know our rights, and if she wants to go home, then by God, she's going home. Against your orders or not. And believe me, *sir*, that if you make one more move toward my daughter, I will bring you up on charges." Momma's hands were on her hips as she glared at him. "You can't give me a reasonable explanation as to why my daughter has to stay. There are other people here who can benefit *more* from your . . . care. We are taking her home. Your services as her surgeon are complete, Doctor, and *you* are no longer required."

"Nurse, you keep Doctor Hall right where she is. I'm going to call this Doctor Moore to inform her that she should keep to her wheelhouse." Alden stalked to the front desk.

Fortunately, Momma wanted me home, and she was *done* with Alden's shenanigans. My Momma is one of the strongest-willed people I know. She looked at the doctor, her eyes steady. She then took the handles of my wheelchair from Tammy and pushed me out the door to my parents' waiting car, my nurse protesting behind her.

Dr. Alden looked so flummoxed that it was almost comical. His mouth opened and closed over and over, like a trout, as I climbed into their vehicle. As a big deal in any hospital in the tri-state area, he didn't know what to do with a mother like mine. He was used to snapping his fingers and his will being done. Momma left him there, still sputtering as we rolled out of the hospital pick-up zone.

As Momma got settled in the passenger seat, righteous fury in every breath, she said to Mom, "Drive, Honey. Baby-Mine, you tell me if that nasty man makes any contact with you from here on out. If he even says 'Boo' to a goose across the *street* from you, you let me and your sister know, and we *will* take care of the problem."

"Yes, Momma," I said, impressed. My mother had just taken on a god and won.

3

"Good job, Honey." Mom leaned over and gave her wife a peck on the cheek before she turned around and grinned at me. "Before we take you home, we have a stop to make first."

"Roxy's Salon?" I was hopeful. I wore a bandana around my head, embarrassed about how my hair looked. Ree had been teasing before, mostly because she was more the type of person to cut her hair when it got in her eyes. Roxy is a fabulous non-binary person who goes by they/them. They've been the owner of this salon Mom's been going to since her transition.

Pippin thunked his tail against the seat next to me. As Mom's service dog, he goes with them practically everywhere. Pippin is a tan dog with natural eyeliner. The Moms found him as a pup after six months of searching. He was at their local pet store that specializes in re-homing rescue litters. The training was intensive, and because of what Pip was training for, Mom did most of it herself under an instructor. Pip has this natural ability to tell when someone needs him. He crawled into my lap as soon as I buckled in and licked my hand. I snuggled with him and let relief wash through me as we pulled away from the hospital. I had to shake the feeling that I was escaping.

"That's right," Mom agreed. "I called ahead and let them know about your circumstances. Thankfully, the wound from the surgery looks healed up, though they said they'd still be careful around it."

"That was healed up weeks ago, according to Doc Moore," grumbled Momma.

"It's okay now, Babe, we got her out. I know you're mad, but take a breath before you scream." Mom smiled at me again through the rear-view mirror.

Momma took a steady breath in and out. "You're right, love, you're right. Mira, I do believe Roxy's exact words were, 'Get that woman over here for a spa day.' Lord knows you need it after having to deal with that *man*. We should be there in a half hour."

The drive itself was typical. The only remarkable thing was when Mom stopped at a traffic light. I noticed a giant, onyx bird roosting in one of the small trees planted every so often on the sidewalk. It stared right at our car, right at me. Pippin noticed, lunged forward, and gave several sharp barks, the fur on the back of his neck standing on end.

"Pippin!" Mom said, shocked. "No bark!"

"I don't get it." Momma frowned, "He's never barked on a ride. Not even when there was another dog outside barking at him."

The dog anxiously whined in my lap until we pulled away from the intersection. I had been about to point out the giant bird, but by the time I looked again, it was gone. I shrugged it off as just something weird you see from time to time, like rainbows or a pigeon with a cigarette in its mouth.

We pulled up to the store in front of Roxy's. The salon boasted to have worked on everyone from matrons to drag queens and did everything from kid trims to full body massages. I loved it there. Annie had standing bi-weekly appointments with one of the stylists, especially before a big court appearance. She's told me she does it so the opposition will under-estimate her. Ree, in comparison, only went when she absolutely had to, like when Aunt Kate got married. The actual entrance was down a flight of stairs, but they had an entrance in the upper part of the building for people who couldn't manage them, like me.

"Honey, I can't park here on the street." Mom said, sounding strained.

Her hands were flexing tightly on the wheel. Driving in heavy traffic for too long was starting to get to her.

"That's okay, Babe." Momma's voice was soothing, easing her wife's anxiety. It came to her as easily after so many years of practice. "Just put on the blinkers while I get Mira out. We'll meet you inside after you park."

Momma opened my new rental wheelchair and locked it in place so I could sit. I had the crutches, but they were really for short distances. Longer treks were going to require a chair for just a bit longer. I had some practice with this while I was at the hospital using my ability. I was now an expert in moving a wheelchair with my mind.

In front of my concerned Momma, however, I had to be subtle about it. While she helped me to make the transition from car to chair, I *moved* it ever so slightly to make it easier for us to get me in. It was almost like having a third person there to move the chair into just the right spot.

Mom smiled as I got settled. "Huh, that was easier than I thought. Okay, Baby-Mine, let's get you inside."

We waved as Mom drove around to the back of the building. Roxy's was the converted basement of an old office building. The space must have been huge before Roxy and the gang took over. They made it *fabulous* in the best possible way. The front desk was the first thing I saw when the elevator doors opened. The desk itself looked like someone had taken river rocks and made it into a motif with dark cherry wood as the polished countertop. The waiting area was tastefully decorated with comfortable-looking couches and chairs with a white faux fur rug under a glass coffee table. Soothing music piped above our heads with Kalimbas, harps, and hand drums. I could feel myself relaxing already.

"Mira! Baby! *Darling*! *What did those monsters do to you?*" shrieked a low, throaty voice from behind the counter. Roxy rounded the corner from behind the desk. "Your moms told me everything. You poor dear, you must be frazzled."

Roxy was as androgynous as anyone could possibly be. Today, they wore a tunic and stylish pants that managed to look like a suit and a dress at the same time. They were a striking, tall, Korean who used smooth motions to make everything they did simply elegant.

"The rest of today is about *you*, darling. I've got Mimi waiting to do your massage with this healing lotion I got on my last trip to Seoul. Something just *told* me I had to buy it, and here you are in desperate need."

"Roxy, you have no idea how glad I am to be here." I felt myself start to tear up. I hadn't realized how stressed I was until I got here. Alden's face, eyes full of rage and possession, flashed in front of my eyes, and I shivered.

"Oh, *Yeobo*! It's okay, Roxy's got you." They snapped their fingers in the air. "Bibi, bring me that tall cup of raspberry tea with honey I had steeping in the back. Mira needs it *now*."

I smiled. That was my favorite way to take my tea. Roxy really did know everything about their clients. The people here were great and really wanted to make you look and feel your best.

"If only we could have gotten your sisters in here too, we could have made a real family spa day out of it." Their beautiful face pouted, and they handed me the tea with their slim, beautifully manicured hands. Their fingers were tipped with intricate cherry blossom branches that had to have taken forever to get just right.

"Annie has court today, and you know how Ree is. This looks like heaven to Annie and me but a torture chamber to her. Fuzzy rugs not-withstanding." I winked. "She'll be back in when she decides on a new tattoo."

Roxy and Momma hugged and did the air kiss thing while Bibi took the handles of the back of my chair and started to lead me into the back. "We will take care of you, darling."

She helped me into the dimmed room. A screen was mounted flush into the far wall. It was on a continuous video showing simply enchanting underwater worlds with whales and jellyfish swimming and more soothing music. Bibi and Mimi were twins who had been masseuses for years. They helped me into a spa robe and got to work.

I. Got. Pampered.

I was jelly in Mimi's hands as she used the lotion on my battered body. She couldn't massage my legs as they were still in the casts, but I did get them to sign them for me. Bibi signed my right cast, and Mimi signed my left. Bibi decided she wanted to be my primary source of transportation for the day. We rolled to the sauna next.

"To help sweat out all of those nasty stress toxins," Bibi said as she poured water over the hot stones. We'd wrapped my legs with plastic bags Roxy had for just such occasions. They were specialty bags that had elastic at the top to keep my casts dry. The heat felt good, but it also made my head itch. I had the disaster that was my hair under a tight bandana.

"Don't worry, peaches. Hair is next. We just wanted to buff you up and work out those knots first."

"Consider me buffed." I laughed as we wheeled toward the hair salon.

The set-up for Roxy's was purposeful. There was a door in the back that would take regulars right to the salon portion of the spa, but new customers were always shown the long way, "To show them what they're missing, *darling*!"

The overall design looked as if a bunch of hyper-active designers were set loose in an antique store and told, 'If it ain't Baroque, don't buy it.' The aesthetic worked for Roxy's, and it made me smile.

Pippin galloped up to me in his harness, the zip leash extending to Mom, who was already sitting in a salon chair with her hair in a towel. Pip's entire body wiggled in excitement. It's what earned the pooch the nickname 'Wiggle-butt.' Momma's dog, Scarlett, wasn't a service animal, so she usually stayed at home.

"Wheel our girl right over here, Bibi."

There was a chorus of horrified gasps, hisses, and a small scream from the nearby stylists as we took off my bandana.

I started to tear up. I had a *tonsure*! The hair on the top of my head had been shaved down to make the surgery site easier for Alden to access. There had been growth, but not nearly enough to match the length of the rest of my head, which had been down to the middle of my back. I whimpered a little.

"It will be all right again, my darling," Roxy said, squeezing my shoulder. "I've had worse cases than this sitting in my chair. Let's go over your options."

"How obvious is the scarring?" I'd tried to look at it myself in the mirror when I was still in the hospital, but I'd never been able to get the correct angle.

"Gotta give it to them, girl. If I didn't *know* you just got out, I wouldn't have been able to tell. All you have is this little star-shaped scar right about here." I felt a feathery touch at the crown of my head. "This is some of the best post-surgery work I've seen after an accident like yours. You made the *news*, darling. Had us all here wringing our hands for you."

I frowned. That was too far back and too far into the center for a frontal lobe surgery. My chart had shown the proper site for where the incision was supposed to be. The crown of my head was not it. When I got home, I planned on consulting the chart that I'd smuggled out to see what was done and why it differed from what I'd been taught to expect.

Roxy and I discussed my options. I didn't want the hassle of a sew-in or a weave, nor did I want to go with a full wig. With everything that had happened to me so far, I craved simplicity.

"Yanno, Rox," piped up the stylist working on Mom, "she could rock an O'Connor. Especially if she wants to spice it up with some color."

Roxy tilted their head from side to side in thought. "You really would look simply *amazing*, darling, but I think not too outrageous in color. Not yet, anyway."

An "O'Connor," as it turns out, was named after a famous singer from the eighties. It looked perfect for the simplicity I was looking for, but I'd never heard of the singer before. The Moms giggled, overhearing that, and played her music while Roxy got out the clippers to buzz the rest of my head down to size. That resulted in an impromptu sing-along as everyone started to belt out the lyrics they knew. The pandemonium quickly led to the expansion to the rest of the decade, including Momma's favorite band, Queen.

With every note sung and every swipe of the clippers, I felt stronger. Damn it, I *was* a killer queen. I was taking control over what had happened because I was the goddamned *champion* of the *world*, and I was going to take back what was mine . . . somehow. Not that I could fully walk yet, let alone drive.

I hadn't realized how much I'd been regulated and watched while I'd been hospitalized. The tests Alden had been running had already started to go beyond what was required for recovery. I ignored it due to how much I wanted to know for myself, but looking back, I could see how toxic Alden's attention was. God bless Momma for getting me out of there because I have the suspicion that I wouldn't have been there if she'd waited any longer.

We went with a natural-looking red for the color of my new super short hair. I wanted to grow it out later, and I knew the red tips would look cute. We chatted a bit longer. While the Moms were distracted, Roxy gave me the card for a psychologist they knew who specialized in trauma from accidents.

"Your room at the house is still there and perfectly serviceable, Baby-Mine, why not use it?" Momma asked as we turned into my parking space at the small complex. This was where my car would have been if it hadn't been totaled. My apartment was on the ground floor and not more than a half hour from my family. It gave me the privacy I needed to practice my ability and still let them think they were taking care of me. Momma had been against it.

"Momma, I love you and Mom, but I can't sleep right when you blast Queen while she's playing a video game. Besides, don't you guys have D and D with Uncle Eric and Aunt Lynn this weekend? I don't think I'm up to playing, and I really don't want to put you out." I hobbled into my living room and settled myself on my couch. "I'll be fine here.

You have a spare key, so you can come in anytime when you want to check on me."

She smiled softly and got me a pillow and a blanket she'd made for me when I was a kid. Momma and her sisters were crafty. The kind of crafty that requires a limit on yarn purchases. If they were given a problem (and yarn), they would crochet the world a solution. "Okay, but you call us the second you need help."

4

THE NEXT FEW weeks were filled with visits.

The Moms sent over food every so often via my sisters. The girls came by on and off throughout the next few weeks to make sure I was taking it easy but not getting too bored. We ended up having a lot of sleepovers, and I was almost positive they were babysitting me with how often they came over. But it was nice to have help getting to the bathroom when they were there.

I was getting restless. I wanted some video evidence to go along with my experiments with my abilities.

It must have shown because one afternoon, Annie offered to take me on a much-needed shopping run.

"Knock, knock!" Her cheery voice rang from my doorway. "I'm here to kidnap you!"

"Thanks again for this, Annie. I really needed to get out of the house." I hobbled over to hug her. "I know it's hard to get off from work."

"You get out of the house every day between seven and nine." My little sister looks like someone who belongs in the city. She is very fashionable but in an old-fashioned way. Think chic cottage core.

"PT shouldn't count as 'getting out,'" I grumbled.

"Better than nothing. Do you have a list of what you need?" Philadelphia was made for women like Annie Hall. She wore hats, gloves, and pea coats that looked like they were tailor-made for her. It also gave her an unassuming look that she was going for. She liked to keep her opponents off guard. "I want to make sure before we leave."

"The only meds I'm on are sent through the mail." The NAN-06 was sitting in my bathroom next to my sink so I wouldn't forget to take it. "We need Toria food and Me food."

"Okay, David said he has off this weekend, so he'll be around to keep you company."

David had slid easily into the family's check on Mira's rotation. He'd come with a game or movies while muddling around in my kitchen to make popcorn and/or cookies. I liked it when it was 'and.' The man makes amazing snickerdoodles.

"I wish you'd let me file that lawsuit on Alden," Annie said as we got into her car. "He needs to be reminded that doctors are not *gods*. I'd love to have him in the defendant's seat."

I was just happy to get out of there, I thought as I clicked in the seatbelt. "Let's just do the next thing that needs doing first. Shopping!"

I got to ride in one of those motorized carts without having people look at me sideways. By this point, I'd been given the okay to use just the walking casts and crutches. However, I still was encouraged by my physical therapist to stay off my legs as much as possible. I started to try to remember what I looked like without the damned casts on. They were beginning to be a regular part of my daily outfits.

"I want to take a swing by Electronics, too," I said over the electric hum of the cart. "I want to look at video cameras."

She gave me a curious look. "Why? Your phone can do anything that a camera can do."

Yeah, and then it would promptly share it with my service provider. I needed something isolated to record my experiments. Then, I'd have to get it encrypted and stored on a secure cloud somehow. But that was something I couldn't tell my sister. "They have some features you can't get on a phone. Specifically, zoom. You can almost see the park from my place, and I want to watch the kites."

"You mean you want to watch the kickboxers that jog there."

"There's nothing wrong with appreciating the human form in motion," I said sheepishly. "There's also an LARP group that's fun to watch, too. I like making up stories for why they're fighting."

"Nerd."

"And proud." I grinned. I bought a camera, memory cards, and a tripod. I was just about to pay when my cart jostled. I almost dropped my purchase. I felt the person touch my back as he went by with a quick "'Scuse me."

I glared up at the man who'd bumped into me. He was a guy around my age wearing a University of Penn hoodie with the hood up. There was no reason to bump into me. There had been plenty of room behind me at the register.

Annie growled and started to pivot to follow him.

I stopped her before she could go after the guy. "Just leave it, sis. I'm fine. There's no reason to keep an asshole in your life longer than you need to."

"Fucking asshole."

"Precisely." I nodded and made her laugh as I handed the cashier my debit card.

Annie got me back onto my couch and brought the groceries in, asking as she went where I liked things to go.

"Please keep the wet cat food on the counter and the dry in the tupper. I've got them at the perfect height, so I don't have to bend."

"And the bread?"

"Fridge. It lasts longer there."

"So, what are you going to do once you're back on your feet? I know the hospital stay had to have pushed back your plans," she said while putting things away.

I blinked. I hadn't thought about it. I let the fascination with my new ability blind me. What was I going to do next? "Honestly, sis, I've been a bit distracted as of late. Thankfully, the truck's insurance company is helping immensely, so I'm not as far back as I thought I'd be." I was unpacking the camera and tripod. I fiddled with the connector on the tripod, seeing where it should connect to the camera. I couldn't keep the grin off my face. It was like opening up a Christmas gift with all the packaging. "Look at this beautiful thing! Good eye spotting it on sale. Score! It came with a light ring!"

"I still don't get why you don't just use your phone." Annie laughed, her smart bob bouncing. "You get that from Momma's side."

"Momma's side does love gadgets." I conceded.

"Just don't let yourself get too distracted. Though I wouldn't blame you if one of those distractions were David. He is not bad to look at." She opened a drawer and put the notebooks and pens inside as I sputtered. She rolled her eyes at my protestations. "Mira, you should really think about letting him in more. Don't you know there is a whole genre of books and porn dedicated to friends to lovers?"

"I refuse to be some . . . cliché, Annie." I sneered. If Annie was right, then I had to reexamine the entire relationship going back to high school. I didn't have that in me right then, not on top of everything else. "So, what did you mean by, 'What am I going to do?'"

She shrugged, letting the subject of romance go for now. "You worked really hard for that doctorate of yours. What kind of practice do you want to set up?"

It just occurred to me that I forgot to let them in on the surprise because of the accident. And this was the same question loan officers would be asking when I went to get a business loan. I'd double majored between lab work and working with patients, and I loved both. You can do so much in a lab. You can find the cure for cancer given enough time and resources. I felt like a detective when I got to track down the wheres, whys, and hows. I felt so much joy from finding different things under a microscope.

On the other hand, working with patients and their families was amazing. My family practice rotation held a special little place in my heart. I adored kids. My mind went back to the time when I helped a little girl get out of her own cast. She had earned her broken ankle by jumping off her parents' tall couch. Her mother informed me she had been covered in glitter and trying to think happy thoughts. I also enjoyed the immediacy of being able to help a person right away rather than waiting months to get results.

I pulled the camera out of the bag and just held it for a second while I mused out loud. "I want to help people. Out of all the different rotations I did at the offices, the hospital, and the wards, I liked two places the most: Family practice and the labs. I'm thinking of opening up my practice with a lab attached."

"Mira, that's really ambitious." Annie frowned at me. "Not only do you have to find a place, but you have to get approval for it by the DEA and a bunch of other acronyms as well. You have to choose a legal structure, get your credentials, and get malpractice insurance, too. Isn't this going to be awfully expensive, not to mention a little much to put on yourself? You just got out of the hospital."

I loved my sister. She was brilliant and headstrong and I swear she could absorb law books faster than I could bake a cake. "Want to be my first investor, Annie?" I grinned at her. "I'll name something after you."

"Sure." She handed me twenty dollars. "Just . . . don't name the bathroom after me."

"Aww, but my big sister teasing rights!" I gave her a hug around the waist. "Look, don't worry about that stuff. I'm going to be super bored just laying here all day. I'm going to use my time productively, even if that means laying on the couch with my laptop and signing up with all of those acronyms. I'll get things done and still rest. I promise."

I watched her pull out of my parking lot and immediately set up the camera.

I moved a glass of milk around my head and put it back on the table.

It was easy! I felt the weight and shape of the object I was maneuvering, but it felt much lighter than it was. Like I was lifting a glass that was only half full. I sat at the table and smiled at the camera. "My name is Doctor Mira Hall, and this is experiment one."

After I ended the experiment, I allowed myself a little butt wiggle dance of glee. This was only the beginning! I had to push my limits.

I put the camera away and spent hours that day typing up reports and analytics, reveling in the excitement of discovering something new that had never fully been proven by medical science. I didn't know yet how I'd get my blood under a good microscope to find out if the origins of my power could be seen or not, but I'd work my way up to that. A project like this couldn't be rushed and had to have years of research behind it to be taken seriously. What needed to happen now was documentation and a way to keep the information private until I was ready to disseminate it. Then, I ordered some weights online. I needed them for my next experiment.

David called me to let me know that something had come up, and he couldn't come over. "I got bit by a patient . . . it's pretty gnarly. I'm having it looked at now." He sounded like he was in an emergency room. I recognized the codes and dings I could hear in the background. "We'll meet up when I'm patched up, okay?"

"Damn. Are you okay?" It would have had to be serious for him to decide not to come. He loved chilling on my couch watching Doctor Who. "I could get one of the girls to pick me up to come visit you."

"Don't worry about it, Space Station. You're already a mess. We get to be messes together now."

"We've always been messes together." I smiled. "You just described our high school careers."

I heard a knocking sound through the phone. "Doctor Erickson?"

"Gotta go, Mir. I'll call you later. I've got to get stitches now."

"Watch out for those slings, Goliath." I heard him laughing as we hung up.

5

THE WEIGHTS TOOK two weeks to be delivered. Thank god I lived on the ground floor. I think the delivery guy would have boycotted me if they'd had to drag them upstairs. Unboxing them was almost as fun as ordering them. I put them on the floor in a row, going from lightest to heaviest.

I *moved* the camera into position on the array of colorful weights. The heaviest one was black, and the lightest was a pretty pink. I sat behind them on the floor with my legs thrust out to either side like a kid with a new toy. I was using this experiment to double as at-home physical therapy.

The tripod was set up and pointed right at me, the red light telling me that it was recording. I needed to document everything. This could very well be what future doctors looked back on whenever they had a patient who presented abilities like mine.

"I am Doctor Mira Hall, and this is Experiment Two. I'm going to try to lift these weights without touching them until I can no longer lift them in the air. This will show me what my limit is for lifting heavy things. I will hold each weight for two minutes." I showed the camera an egg timer that I placed beside me on the wooden floor. I focused on the first weight, pretending a ghostly 'hand' was wrapped around it and was doing my bidding.

One by one, each weight lifted, held in the air for two minutes, then slowly descended. "I can feel the weight," I murmured as the blue dumbbell marked twenty pounds eased into the air. "But it doesn't feel as heavy as I know it is. Twenty feels like ten. Ten feels like five, and so on. I also find I don't need my full concentration to lift the lighter weights." I stopped talking, feeling the poundage of the equipment as the eighty-pound weight slowly rose into the air. Two minutes later, it gradually descended.

"We have now passed my normal weight threshold. Typically, I'm only able to lift and sustain eighty pounds without shifting my weight to use my hip to hold it longer. I will now attempt the one hundred pounds. I usually can't lift this much on my own."

The purple hundred-pound weight glided into the air, held and slid back down.

"One hundred and fifty pounds." I grunted, feeling sweat start to bead on my forehead. Up, hold, down. My head was beginning to pound with the effort.

"Two hundred pounds." The black weight rattled and moved from side to side before it lurched into the air. I panted as my eyes locked onto the floating weight. It shook in mid-air, threatening to fall. I was going to lose it. It was going to fall on the ground, and my neighbors would call the cops because it would sound like a body hitting the floor.

I threw a hand in the air, focusing my mind on the weight, holding it in place. The shaking stopped. After the allotted two minutes, my breath whooshed out. I didn't realize I'd stopped breathing. The weight plummeted to the floor and landed *hard*. I winced at the dent. I leaned back against the old couch, my head spinning. My fingers trembled as I held a hand to my throbbing head. My phone rang.

"Hello?" I panted.

"Mira? Is that you, honey?" Mrs. Fetterman, the elderly widow who shared a wall with me, sounded concerned. I could hear her overweight Pomeranian barking madly in the background. "Charlie and I heard a big crash. Are you okay?"

She said it like 'Cha-lee.' I smiled. "I'm all right, Mrs. Fetterman. Just doing some at-home PT. The weight got away from me."

"Well, you be careful, dear. I don't want you to overdo it."

"I promise I won't."

"All right then, good night, dear."

"Night, Mrs. Fetterman." I stood and grinned manically at the camera. "Weight. Threshold. Reached. End of Experiment Two."

6

I WAS IN my car, the night inky around me. The glow of the dash my only interior light. Streetlights flashed on as I passed under them. My heart was in my throat. The sign on the highway read fifty-five miles an hour, and the needle of my speedometer matched precisely. My headlights cut through the dark shadows, illuminating the dashes on the road. I glanced over my shoulder. My diploma, white coat, and doctor's bag were all right where they were supposed to be. I hadn't forgotten anything. Why was I so scared? Then I heard it—the hideous blare of a horn.

My head whipped around, and I saw the eighteen-wheeler behind me.

My hands fisted around the wheel as I put my foot down on the pedal, but my foot went through it as if it were as insubstantial as a gust of wind. I tried again, but my right leg just wasn't . . . moving . . . fast enough!

I heard a howl and panting. I looked in my rearview mirror. The truck was closer now, fire spurting out from under its hood. The engine roared, The headlights looked like they were sewn shut with thick twine, and the grill looked like thick needle-sharp teeth grinning with a dreadful, satisfied hunter's smile. The horn roared and howled again and slammed into my car, pushing me over the rumble strip.

I woke up screaming as I hit the pole.

My physical therapist finally cleared me to drive on my own again. I was starting to get tired of how 'amazed' everyone was with how fast I was healing. I smiled and credited it to the medication. After my escape via the Moms, I was sent a prescription bottle by courier with instructions to take once per day. The little capsules were labeled NAN-06, the same medication that they'd given to me in the hospital according to the charts I'd been able to get my hands on.

The bottle itself was different from what I was used to picking up at my local pharmacy. This one had a digital lid with a timer on it to remind me to take it at the same time every day. I thought it was nifty at first, that is, until the thing started whistling like a tea kettle when I was late on a dose. The alarm would get louder and louder until I turned it off by unscrewing the cap. I thought I'd trick it one day and not take a pill out, but apparently, this thing went a step beyond the norm. The alarm triggered louder until I took the NAN-06 out.

I was tempted to flush it out of spite, but the damned stuff was working. I *was* recovering fast. Almost too fast to be believed. What the hell was in this stuff? I held the capsule up to the light. The shell was an opaque white. The chemical composition could have been liquid. It felt heavier than a typical capsule, but I wasn't sure.

The pill reminded me that I needed to look deeper into Alden's work. He would have had to register it with the FDA for trials by law. But when I looked into any trials, I couldn't find anything. Not even a mention of the name Phineas Alden. What the hell was up with that?

I knew some pharmaceutical companies kept their research under wraps until they were ready for human trials. Still, the procedure and medication had to be disclosed. Paperwork had to be signed for trials. Who would have signed my paperwork if the Moms hadn't been let in until I woke up? Alden had money, power, prestige, and pedigree. I knew of several doctors who waded into the political arena from time to time to push their agendas. Could that be what was going on here? I sighed. I wished I had the hacking chops to look deeper than a few intense internet searches. Maybe then I could get some answers and not be so nervous about it. If I couldn't find answers the legal way, then I'd have to find someone to do it the illegal way . . . Not that I had any contacts like that.

Thankfully, finances were one thing I didn't have to worry about. The truck's insurance company was stepping up and taking care of much of the costs from the accident, including the cost of a rental car. This meant my timetable for owning my own practice was only a few months behind instead of the years I'd been worried about.

Ree gave me a big grin when she came to get me from my last physical therapy appointment. "You ready to go, gimpy?"

"Damn straight, but I'm driving!" I grinned hugely and held out my hand for the keys. "I want to pause at the thrift store to donate these crutches."

"Mira, are you even allowed to drive?" Her face grew concerned.

I grinned and showed her the paper with permission from my physical therapist. "Mira Hall is mobile once more!"

She started texting rapidly on her phone, her thumbs flying over the screen.

"What are you doing, Ree?"

"Warning the general populace."

I laughed and shoved her over to the passenger side. When I got behind the wheel, I stared at it for a second as I put on my belt. I worried that I wouldn't be able to drive at all, but I seemed to be okay with the sun up and avoiding the highway. I swallowed, remembering my nightmare, turned on the car, and eased out of the parking space. The sun was high in the sky. It was safe to drive during the day. We were just about to leave the lot when I had to slam the brakes to avoid hitting this enormous black bird.

"Geebus, Mira!" Ree yelped. "You just got out of the goddamned hospital! Are you trying to get back in by giving me a heart attack?"

"Didn't you see that monster bird?" I demanded in defense. "It flew out of nowhere! Are you okay?"

"Just bruised. Jesus, Mir, I was kidding earlier about warning the populace, but I think I may actually want to warn people now." She grumbled before we continued our journey back to my apartment.

I was met with the surprise of my littlest sister, who had pizza and ice cream prepped and ready. "Ree texted me to let me know you were mobile, and we wanted to have a little celebration party for your regained independence."

Pizza, ice cream, and movies. My sisters knew me well. Ree regaled Annie on her narrow brush with sororicide. "And suddenly I'm thrown into the seat belt. I didn't know she was planning on killing me, but obviously, she's been hiding some hidden desire for my death."

"I did *not* try to kill you," I said, rolling my eyes. "It was the kamikaze *crow* that tried to kill you."

"That thing was way bigger than a crow. You should have *seen* this bird, Annie. I think it could have been a raven." She held her hands in the air, exaggerating the size of the bird. "I thought it was done for, but it flew away when lead foot here hit the brakes."

Ravens were not common in the city, to my knowledge. I'd have to look it up when the girls went home. Momma always said it was bad luck to hit a black bird. I was glad I'd missed it. I didn't want to think it was a bad omen, but it made the hair stand up on the back of my neck. The girls stayed a while longer, enjoying pizza and ice cream while we watched another campy movie. I wouldn't have been able to get through therapy and stay sane without them.

I got on the net to research what I needed to do. Annie had been right. Opening a practice, like the one I wanted, took money. I had a fund started, but it was only enough to put a down payment on an office space. A modest space in a modest building that needed a lot of repair work . . . maybe. There were a lot more things I'd need to create a good practice. I had to find investors, talk to banks about loans, and see a real estate agent to start. I didn't even want to think about zoning costs, equipment, or staff yet.

I got my NPI number, applied to the DEA to be able to prescribe, and applied to work with Medicare. I also was scouting for malpractice insurance and a medical lawyer to keep on retainer. It was all very daunting. It must have been written on my face because I felt a poke of Ree's finger in my ribs while she and I were at the rent-a-car place.

"Earth to Mira, would you pick one already?" Ree groaned. Annie was supposed to have been my escort today to finally get me fully back behind the wheel, but Ree lost the bet as to who could drink the most soda without belching. "Your brain is flying off without me again."

"Sorry. A lot on my mind." I felt my cheeks warm with embarrassment.

"Well, get your mind on *this* lot and pick a car to drive."

"Sorry," I apologized again. "After this, could you do me a favor and just head home? I really need to . . . *be* for a bit."

"I mean, if that's what you want. The Moms won't be happy about it, but I get when a person needs space." We picked a blue plug-in sedan that was compatible with the plugs at my complex's parking area. There'd been a big push around the twenty-forties to make EV charging stations available to apartment dwellers like me. I drove by myself for the first time since the accident.

What I wanted was to take my mind off all that worry for just a little while. The best place to do that was the shop I'd spent the years before and during my residency and rotations. I pulled my new car gently into Bindings' sparse parking area behind the old building, promising myself I wouldn't stay past sundown. The idea of driving at night sent cold spikes down my spine. I just really needed a quiet place to think that wasn't my apartment, and the soft wingback chairs by the stone fireplace in the shop were calling me.

I frowned at some new graffiti that had managed to be sprayed on the brickwork, the early afternoon light peeking through the branches of the one lumpy tree that adorned the edge of the back lot. I'll give the tagger this: the art was intricate, like a mural instead of graffiti. Maybe it was something Jove had commissioned. The lion's head was permanently set in a roar, its fangs long and sharp-looking. Surrounding it was a large circle with strange letters written around the exterior. I tilted my head at it as I parked. I wondered if Jove had the artist on commission, as it was in the same art style as my charm.

"Weird." I shrugged and walked toward the white door that had the words 'Employees only' on a plaque in the window. That's when I realized the lights inside were off. It was noon on a Monday. Jove never closed this early on a Monday, not even for lunch. He always made sure either Katie or I were operating the register. Though, since I didn't technically work there anymore, I supposed that was a thing of the past. That thought made me feel a little sad. I really should be entering from the customer entrance at the front, but I'd just automatically parked in the back where I usually did.

"And weirder," I muttered. I dug my key out of my purse and unlocked the door. Somehow, I'd forgotten to return the key when I'd been doing my rotations, and the boss seemed always to forget to ask for it back. One *more* thing I needed to return to the man.

Bindings used to be a three-story home set up as a twin. Jove had purchased both homes, knocked out the separating wall, and turned the backyard into a small parking lot. The two first floors were dedicated to books. The right side of the first floor usually held the harder-to-find antiques and college textbooks. The left was for gifts, stationery, and non-fiction. The left side was also where the register and reading nook were. The second floor on the right side of the building was dedicated to fiction and easier-to-find paperbacks. Katie loved it there. The second floor on the left side and the combined third floor were for Jove's split-level apartment. The combined basement of the place was off-limits and had been for as long as I worked there.

The basement was where Jove went to work on restoring the books. Restoration was one of the services Bindings offered that he charged quite a bit for, but it was worth the price. I swear he could work his magic on a tattered old copy of *Oliver Twist* and hand it back to you, looking as if it had just come off of the printing press. I had him restore a few for my aunt for her birthday. She loved old books. Jove's workshop was *his* space. He didn't let people go down there. When I asked him why, he said there were a lot of chemicals he didn't want Katie or me around.

"Jove? Katie?" I called into the darkness. "Yoo haloo! Anyone here?" The light from the sun played with the dust motes in its shafting light from the thin, old windows. Everything in the store was meticulously cleaned or restored from the original wood the place had been built from. It gave Bindings the air of antiquity that I hadn't seen in other local bookstores. The windows didn't lend enough light to see what was going on in the rest of the shop. I got two steps out of the little hallway into the main room when the lights flashed on.

"*Welcome back, Mira*!" proclaimed a large sign over the main lobby. Jove smiled as he leaned against the ancient counter. He was looking much more like himself today than he had when he'd visited after the accident. Today, he wore a vest with his sleeves rolled up to the elbows, very nicely tailored pants, and shined black oxfords. Gone was the disheveled man from the hospital. Jove now looked like a delicious librarian. He nudged a small, round chocolate cake with one lone candle closer toward me.

"It's not my birthday."

"Well, then just blow it out for luck." The look on his face was hard to peg. It had this soft joy that made me feel like I'd finally come back to somewhere I belonged.

I smiled back and blew out the candle.

"*Mir!*" A voice squealed from behind one of the stacks. A blur of red hair bulleted toward me. I held out my arms and braced myself for Katherine Ferrell Fynn.

I let out a little 'oof' noise as she wrapped her arms around me. I winced. "Katie, dear, I'm still a bit tender there."

She instantly let me go and looked up at me, concerned. "Are you okay? I missed you sooo much! Ooo! Love the hair!"

"Thanks. I wanted something I didn't have to mess with for a while."

I smiled and waved my arm around the shop. "You guys didn't have to do this for me." I looked over at Jove. "How did you even know I was coming over?"

"Marie called. She said you had been worried about something and that you could drive again. When you had such worries with your studies, here is where you came to get lost in the stacks." Jove refused to call Ree by her nickname. He said it wasn't a proper name. She ragged him about it whenever she saw him.

"We missed you, Mira. You were gone so long. The boss here has been driving me absolutely bonkers. How are the Moms and the girls? Did you get to look at new cars yet?" Katie always talked a mile a minute. If I hadn't grown up in a household with four other women just like her, then I wouldn't have been able to follow the conversation.

"I missed you too." I hugged her again. Katie was a grown-ass woman, but there was something about her that had me thinking of her like a third sister. "The Moms and the girls are fine. They've been taking care of me by being over at my apartment more than in their own homes. I'll let them know you asked after them. No, but I got a rental that fits my complex's plugs."

Jove smiled warmly at me and opened his arms for a hug. As he isn't usually a hugger, I took it as the gift it was meant to be. I breathed in his sandalwood and leather scent and smiled. "It is good to have you back, Kleine. I could use your help this afternoon if you are feeling up to it."

"What? Mira's just got out of the hospital! Why are you asking her to help? She's got a lot she's got to get done." Katie's fisted hands were on her hips as she frowned at him.

"Because I saw that you have a shoot tonight that I know you have forgotten about. Your father called to remind me to chase you out before you are late."

I smiled up at him and gave him another squeeze in thanks for understanding why I needed to be here. He gave great hugs, if rare. "It's okay, Katie. I could really use the distraction. I have to be home by six, though.

I'm–ah–expecting a call from a potential realtor." I lied. The thought of driving after sundown made my skin crawl.

Jove released me with an embarrassed cough and went behind the checkout counter to cut the cake. "Have you found the spot yet?" He was talking about *the* spot for my practice. When I had worked here full-time, I would often gush about my dream clinic. The spot had to be perfect.

Not too out of the way so people could quickly get to me and not too close to the city where I would become overrun with patients looking for a quick clinic.

I shook my head and sighed as I separated three plates from the stash we had for occasions like this. I'd had time while I'd been recuperating. Still, I'd also had to set up everything with the government to make sure I'd be allowed to practice legally, looked for malpractice lawyers, and dug as deep as I could into whatever it was Alden was up to. Realtors and office listings fell on the back burner.

"I haven't even found a good realtor yet. It's been hard to find investors, too. There's a lot of equipment and medical supplies I need to get started. I almost wish I *did* have a mentor whose practice I could take over when they retired." I sighed. I'd already made up my mind about starting my own practice. No sense changing it now.

"Mira, if you need the money, I would gladly be your first investor," said Jove, staring down at the cake knife. "The revenue I receive from the shop should help in some small way, should it not?"

"Annie beat you to it." I smiled. "Not that I'm turning anyone away. Maybe I'll name something after you."

"As long as it is not the lavatory." He said it with such a serious face I couldn't help but laugh. "It is good to hear that sound again, Kleine."

"It's good to be able to *make* that sound again. Thanks, Jove. I needed this." I wanted to ignore my far-reaching problems for just a little while. Working retail let me turn off my brain for a bit and deal with the next person in front of me. "I really have to be back at my place by six, okay?"

"*Ja*, Kleine, that is fine. How have you been?" He leaned over the checkout desk, an oaken antique that fit so perfectly with the feel in the rest of Bindings. Intricate carvings in the wood told stories if you knew how to read them. It was a beautiful piece that Annie swooned over the first time she saw it. She goes antiquing with Momma at least once a month.

I rubbed a hand on the back of my neck. "Just a lot on my mind. With the accident, there's so much I have to do yet. It hit me while I was paying for the rental. This accident is going to set my timetable back a bit to build my practice, mostly because of recovery time. Thankfully, the truck's insurance company stepped up to pay most of my bills for me. It was so weird that they wouldn't give me the name of the company. I just continue to wake up and find more money in my account marked 'Insurance.'"

"Whatever you need, Mira, we will take care of you." We smiled at each other a moment, and then both flushed as Katie made an impatient noise or possibly a noise that she thought we were cute.

"Jove, are you seriously just going to stand there and hold the cake knife?" Katie's eyes got huge. "We *are* going to get to eat that cake, right?"

"Can you give us some privacy, Katherine?" He handed her a precisely perfect slice of the confection. "I have much I need to speak with Mira about. Take the cake to your area. Do not get any on the books. It took weeks to get those stains out last time."

"No problem, Boss," she promised and quickly took the stairs, heading to her area of the shop. "Now, if you'll excuse me, this cake and I need some alone time." She disappeared around the corner with an excited little butt wiggle.

I turned to him as he slid another precise piece toward me. The charm bracelet jangled as I moved and reminded me. The time had come for me to return his gift. "Jove about this bracelet. Is there a trick to it?"

"A trick?" he said with a slight frown.

"It's just too pretty for me to have. I've been trying to take it off, but the clasp hasn't let loose." I said as I tried to pull it off, trying to roll it over my hand. "I'm . . . uff . . . afraid I can't accept such an expensive . . . what the hell?" I started searching around the bracelet for the clasp to try again before I broke it.

"*Nein!*" Jove yelped suddenly and practically leaped over the counter, banging his knee on the side of it in his haste. "No," he said softer, taking my hands. My hands felt small in his, and they were so warm. "Do not take this off. Please, Kleine, think of it as a good luck charm. Yes? A gift from a friend. I saw it, and I thought of you."

I looked at him. His eyes looked wild, like he'd stopped me from pulling a pin on a grenade or something. Why was he so panicked? It was just a piece of jewelry. "Are *you* okay, Jove?"

"*Ja*, I am fine." He ran a hand through his hair. He was visibly putting himself back together. The panic was easing out of his face. "I wish you would not exert yourself. Please, do not bother yourself with the price of this. I found it in the jewelry shop across the street. The one Katherine's parents own. They gave me a good price on it."

"Under the Rainbow?" I supplied.

"*Ja*. I saw it, and I thought of you." He was still holding my hand. I was about to say something about it when the entry bell rang, signaling a group of chattering students. Jove dropped my hand and went to the stairs leading to the basement. "I have some books on order. They should be coming in before the sunset. Please let me know when the delivery man gets here."

"You got it, Boss," I said, ready to put his behavior as one of those things I wasn't going to worry about right now.

"Und Kleine?"

"Yes?"

"I like your new hair." I could hear the smile in his voice as the heavy door shut. My heart gave a little kick, and I smiled. I listened to the tinkling sound of the door as it opened to more chattering customers. I hurried to put the rest of the cake under the counter. What was with him lately? Nope, not thinking about it right now. Just help the people with the books.

Lunchtime is not the peak flow for a bookshop that doesn't also offer food. Most of the customers we get during lunch are either super studious or super stupid. The frat boys especially liked to pick on Katie if I wasn't vigilant enough. They needed protection, after all. Katie can and will kick ass if not curbed.

Five English majors came in begging for book ideas for their essays. I had that professor years ago. I know she liked her students to at least attempt to read the classics. One of the more stupid ones decided to hit on me. I handed him a copy of *The Iliad*. Petty, I know, but he was a dork who didn't understand the word 'no.' He deserved a challenging read for class.

It was much later when my little redheaded pal was on her way out for the evening. The sun was on its way down, but I still had some time. "You're staying?" She gave a slight tilt of her head, her purse over one shoulder. "I didn't think you wanted to stay late."

"It's peaceful here. I've only got a few things to finish up." I shrugged. "Besides, Jove is expecting a shipment of some kind, so I figured I'd help him out with unpacking."

"Just don't push it, okay? We just got you back." Katie gave me another hug and headed out the door with a little backward wave. She's such a sweetheart.

I started to sweep the shop. I put books back in their proper places, dusted the shelves, and swept the floor. I was just beginning to dust the counter when a knock came at the back entrance.

"Just a minute!" I called as I put the rag next to the register. I paused to open the basement door. "Delivery's here!" I shouted down the stairs over my shoulder.

I walked to the employee entrance where we typically got our shipments and opened the door. What greeted me on the other side was a vast man silhouetted in the evening light.

He seemed to be about seven feet tall, his form filling up the doorway as if he were a wall instead of a person. He loomed over me, his face shadowed by a hat pulled low. His shoulders were longer across than my arms from fingertip to fingertip. The man's arms at the bicep were more extensive than the span of my hand. He had on a jumpsuit with a logo over his heart. It was the head of a black bird with a gold background. Did I mention big? Whoa, big. His body language wasn't saying, 'Hello, I'm here with the delivery.' It was saying, 'I am the strongest thing in a fifty-mile radius, and I will get whatever I want.'

I took an involuntary step back. Both ID and Ego were screaming at me to get out of his reach.

"Yes," the man rumbled, his voice deep. "Payment greatly accepted. High Raven will be pleased." The mammoth of a man took a menacing step forward. I didn't have time to scream as he grabbed me right around the middle, his hands almost totally encompassing my waist. He lifted me as if I weighed nothing. Tossed me right onto one of those large shoulders and started walking away with me. The breath whooshed out of my lungs as his shoulder met my mid-section.

7

ONCE THE SECOND of shock wore off, I did the most logical thing I could think of. I screamed. Aimed right where I thought the bastard's ear was. I curled myself inward and got as close to his head as I could.

His hat fell off.

I screamed louder. The man had no ears! His head and face were instead covered in oily black feathers. Where his mouth should have been was what looked like a flat beak. Throughout my residency, I'd seen many examples of various deformities, but nothing like this. The man had *literal feathers and a beak*!

I started struggling. The scream must have disoriented him. I felt his grip loosen on my legs. I twisted and braced my elbow at the back of his skull. I then brought my right knee up and smashed it into that inhuman face. The thing let out a squawk and dropped me.

Landing on your hands and knees on cobblestones, especially when you just recently got said limbs out of casts, is painful. They were healed, but the ache still cropped up from time to time, like now. It was a sharp, throbbing pain, like when you jam your elbow.

I wanted to crumple and wait for the pain to pass, but I wanted that *thing* to leave me alone more. It wasn't going to leave me alone for much longer.

I scrambled back to the door on my hands and knees. I screamed for Jove. Fear-induced speed had me going faster than expected. I got to the stoop and sat with my back toward the open door. I wanted to know where that thing was and just how fast it was recovering.

The answer to that question was fast. It was already lumbering toward me, its arms and gloved hands outstretched, reaching for me.

Away. It needed to be further away. I had never used my ability like this before, but I also had minimal options. I *pushed* with my mind, putting all my newly acquired synapses to work. I put my hands in front of me and pushed outward. In my months of recovering, I found that sometimes, putting a physical action with the intent of the thought added to its strength. Such was certainly the case in this scenario. The Bird-boy flew back, violently hitting the inside of the open storage truck that held the boxes of expected books.

I blinked for a second. My breath froze as I listened for movement. I panted and let out a shaky breath. In the silence, I felt a small smile crease my lips. Whoa, had I done that? I must've knocked it out! That's freaking right! I am a Woman; hear me roar.

"Mira! Kleine, are you all right?" Jove appeared in the doorway. His warm hands pulled me back over the threshold of the shop. "Get back in here!"

"Jove!" Relief flooded my voice. I've never been happier to see him. I hurried, hands and aching knees, beside him and sat on the floor. "Call the cops, the National Guard, animal control, *somebody.* There's this *thing* in the back of that truck that wants to get me!"

"Tief Rabe," Jove intoned as he placed a hand on my shoulder. He then babbled in German. My mind quickly translated. *Deep Raven, this was not the payment we discussed.* I looked up at my boss with shock. His tone wasn't saying that this was a monster, but an everyday merchant just like the ones who delivered the new releases.

A sound, much like a groan, came from the back of the truck as the creature climbed his way out. One of the sleeves on the jumpsuit had torn, revealing more black feathers. *"Eine weiße Ziege war Hoch Rabe als Bezahlung auf versprochen, Zauberer."*

A white goat was promised as payment to, full Raven? High Raven? And *Zauberer* meant something close to a Wizard or magician. Jove then stepped out of the doorway and into the light of our small parking lot. Trailing behind him was a rope connected to a very live, genuine white goat. It bleated in my face and started to chew on the sleeve of my shirt before following Jove into the lot.

I'm going to translate here for everyone's sanity.

"*Yes. A white goat.*" Jove sneered. "*Humans are not allowed to be used as payment anymore. Not among polite society, at any rate. We do not want to make the little darlings twitchy.*" He patted my head. I shot him a look. It wasn't a pleasant look.

"*Is she your apprentice?*" The creature quickly tilted its head, just like my old cockatiel used to do when it was curious. "*This woman has power.*"

Jove's eyes narrowed. "*Power?*"

"I . . . may have thrown him into the truck," I said, instantly regretting making any noise and drawing attention to myself. I tried to make myself smaller and pulled closer to Jove.

He pursed his lips. "*Have you my items,* Tief Rabe*?*"

"*I do.*" The Bird-boy's stance was one of reserved violence. Those gigantic arms crossed over the expanse of his chest.

"*You have your payment,*" Jove said, tossing the creature the goat's rope. "*Unload and leave.*"

Three other bird-men melted out of the shadows, dressed all the same as Deep Raven. They had the shipment off the truck and into the basement in fifteen minutes. I stayed on the stoop, too scared to look up at the movers as they went back and forth.

Deep Raven stood where he was, glaring at me and Jove. "*Hoch Rabe will not stand for this deception, Zauberer. He will have what is due to him.*"

My heart thudded in my chest. That really sounded like a threat to me. Soon, the truck roared to life and left. I was much happier with the bird-men gone. My mind was working overtime, replaying what had just happened. There was a brief discussion of power, the apparent fact that the delivery men were not human, and the remarkable fact that Jove knew something about it. I rolled my eyes up to meet his as the truck rolled out of sight. "We have to talk."

We went up to his apartment above the shop. I sat at the table in his kitchen, trying to stop my shaking hands while he made tea. I pondered which question to ask first. What were those things? Why were they talking in German? Why did that thing mistake me for a white goat? Why did it call Jove 'Wizard'?

It was at this point I realized my mind was babbling. Panic will do that. I took a couple of slow and deliberate breaths. In silence, Jove gently set a steaming mug of tea in front of me. It smelled like flowers. I drew in the scent, my mind supplying the names. Marjoram, chamomile, motherwort, poppy, lemon balm, Valerian root . . . Ingredients in a popular sleep-inducing tea? I looked at him and tilted my head. "Why are you trying to put me to sleep, Jove?"

"It is necessary, Kleine. That thing you saw will drive you mad if I do not erase it from your memory. Being asleep will make it easier on you." He sat across from me. He looked exhausted . . . and worried.

I blinked, then again. Wait just a minute—did he mean there was something else in my cup other than tea? I wouldn't have thought him capable of something like that before, but I did see a seven-foot-tall talking bird today, so a roofie wasn't so large a leap. I set the cup gently down and pushed it away a little. "Do what with my memory now?"

"When a non-magical being has such an encounter with something of such obvious magic, it will, invariably, drive the non-magical being insane. We call it Veil-Struck. I can reverse it if we act quickly." He pushed the mug forward. "Now drink your tea."

"Invariably?" I arched an eyebrow. "So, you've done many tests on this subject?"

"Well, no." He frowned. "However, the Spitzhut Männer have ordered us to—"

"The pointy hat men?" I looked at him and burst out laughing. "Really?"

"I did not pick the name! Mira, this is serious. I really do not want to have to do this to you."

"Then *don't do it*," I snapped.

"It is not as simple as that. This is for your own safety, Kleine."

"That's a bullshit excuse." I pushed the tea further away from me with my hand. "How long is it supposed to take for this condition to manifest?"

"It should have happened instantaneously." He ran his hands through his hair. "As soon as you saw his face."

"Well, as I haven't devolved into a chittering mass of flesh, I'll assume things aren't going exactly to plan here. The Bard once wrote, 'There are more things in Heaven and earth, Horatio, than are dreamt of in your philosophy.' And if Lewis Carroll believed in six impossible things before breakfast, why can't I?" I crossed my arms over my chest. There was no way that tea was going anywhere near my mouth.

"Because you are human! I will not—no, I cannot take that risk. Not with your safety." He studied me like he was waiting for me to start giggling manically about pretty birds.

"I'm not struck, Jove, Veil, or otherwise." I tried to put every ounce of sincerity in my voice.

I felt like I was looking at a stranger. He'd said he was going to try to wipe my memory! I'd heard stories in the wards about women who would wake up with hours just, *pfft,* gone! I had to convince him not to. Jove was not a medical doctor. He could have gotten the dosage wrong with whatever he put in the tea. I needed to talk him down from this course of action. Otherwise, it could go exceptionally poorly for yours truly. "Please, don't try to wipe my memory. There's no guarantee that it will work the way you want it to."

"This is a spell I have done many times before, and I cannot take such a chance on this. I came too close to losing you, *Mira Hall*." His eyes locked onto mine as he said my name. There was something very, *very* strange about the way he said my name. Like he was talking to the entirety of me. Every cell of my body suddenly was paying rapt attention to what this man was saying. Have you ever gotten your name said by a parent when you're in trouble? Amplify that feeling you have, just before you turn around to answer, by a hundred.

"Drink your tea."

8

I was humming in the lobby of the shop while wiping down the counter next to the ancient register. The melody was familiar, but I couldn't place it. I think it had to do with birds.

I looked up at an old grandfather clock Jove kept. It was an antique, like much of the other furniture in the shop. Good Lord, it was two hours past the time I had to leave! It was already dark out.

I couldn't drive in the dark again this soon. My breath was coming in fast pants as I clutched the broom I had been using. Concentrate, Mira. Do what the therapist on the internet showed you to work through a panic attack. I started counting the blue things in the room when it dawned on me what I had been humming. I don't often hum *Close to You* by the Carpenters. My grip tightened on the broom handle as it all came rushing back. That son of a *bitch*.

I stomped up the flight of stairs and pounded on Jove's door. I leaned on the broom, bristles in the air, anger roaring in my ears.

Jove opened the door and blinked at me. "Mira? What is wrong? I—"

He crumpled to the floor with a whimper as the broom handle connected with his crotch.

I leaned over him and wagged my finger in his face. "You *ever* do that to me again, you smarmy, arrogant, *Schweinehund*, I swear, I'll shove this so far up your ass you'll think you were Jose Jalapeño." I leaned in closer to his face. "On a steek."

I turned on my heel, my nose in the air as I stormed downstairs and out the door. At that point, I didn't care if I still had a friend or not. I would never set foot in that shop again. He had to have drugged me. That bastard *drugged me*!

I drove home in a fog of colorful German curses my Opa had unwittingly taught me as a kid. That's what happens when you let your grandkids watch you fix things. Hammers slip. When Oma found out, she had some choice words of her own.

Thankfully, rage overrode much of my fear of the dark roads, and I got to my apartment building safely. I barely remember shoving my key into the lock of my apartment and slamming the door closed behind me through the ache of betrayal.

I trusted Jove, damn it! I thought maybe, just maybe, he wasn't like other men who take advantage of women. He was lucky I didn't break his frakking neck, and damn the consequences.

I let the black anger take me. I'd managed to keep it together on the road—barely. I threw my bag on the comfortable tan sofa with a fleece blanket folded across the back. I had an oversized crocheted blanket underneath just in case it was too late for a guest to drive home. (The girls and David came over often, so it just made sense to have a spare blanket and pillow on hand.)

I stomped through the doorway leading out of the living room and branching toward the kitchen on one side and the bedroom on the other. I needed a drink. I turned and dodged around my little table.

The kitchen was small, but it was mine. I stalked into it and started pacing like a panther. Son of a bitch, *son of a bitch*, how dare he have the audacity to drug me?

This kind of big emotion demanded a snackrifice or the world would burn. I wrenched open the freezer door of the refrigerator the girls and I had managed to somehow shove into one corner. This level of pissed required ice cream.

I crashed around, slamming drawers and cabinets as I dug out my weapons of war: an ice cream scoop, a bowl, and a spoon. I set the bowl on the eggshell white counters with the juice stains from the previous tenant. I hated those stains. I lifted the lid and attacked the pint of mint chocolate chip. I built an ungodly tall sundae, complete with cherries, whipped cream, and chocolate syrup. I flopped down onto the couch with an exasperated grunt. I couldn't play a violent video game to get the rage out. I'd never get to my appointment with the bank in the morning.

The couch faced a thirty-two-inch flat-screen television. Between the sofa and the TV stood a hope chest that had made its way down the family line to me. It doubled as my coffee table. A tower stacked with movies and video games stood sentinel on each side of the television, and a well-used gaming console sat on the floor.

Across the hall from my kitchen nook was the door to my bedroom. I couldn't even go to bed. I was too riled up. Damn it all. My bedroom is adorned with replicas of weapons from movies and television—*Star Wars*, *Lord of the Rings*, *Indiana Jones*, and, of course, *Star Trek*. I had swords, shields, whips, and staves all displayed on mounted racks and in one large display case I managed to find on eBay.

I'll tell you, those Klingons sure knew their sharp, pointy things. I have this one bat'leth, so lifelike it would make any Trekkie cry. I keep my weapons prime, too. The more realistic, the better. I fantasized about shoving it into Jove's solar plexus and dropping him out of a window.

I decided to practice with my ability. That would wear me out for sure, maybe without the murderous fantasies. I spooned in the ice cream and used my ability to open my History of Neurological Science textbook and read while I enjoyed the minty goodness as it slid down my throat.

Reading this way was great practice on telekinetic agility and weight training. Weeks of rest at home gave me excellent opportunities to work with my ability when not doing paperwork for the government. Almost everyone had gotten me new books to read while I'd been hospitalized. Since no one could visit after they moved me out of the ICU, I had more than a few new additions to add to my microlibrary (aka the two bookcases in my living room) once I got home. I found if I overworked my ability, it usually left me physically exhausted and sometimes with a slight headache. I had worked my way up, able to keep open three books as I would turn in a circle, but once my concentration was broken, gravity took over.

"'This allows for the direct flow of ions from one cell to another and allows for rapid signal transmission between the cells,'" I murmured, reading aloud from the single textbook floating in front of me.

To test myself, I floated the now empty bowl over to gently set itself on the cedar chest. I winced slightly as I remembered the dent on the floor from one of my previous experiments. I'd have to get that fixed if I ever wanted to move out. I liked my little apartment, but I didn't want to stay here forever. The textbook still hung midair as I mentally turned the page. I then sat down on the couch, crossing my legs, holding the book in the air in front of my face. It made me wonder about the activity in my brain and just how rapid that transmission was.

I jumped as something brushed against my leg. I glanced down at my calico cat, Toria, and promptly, the heavy book fell to the floor with a thud. She streaked away as it landed, heading straight for her hiding spot under my microlibrary, a place she hid often during my hospital stay, or so my sisters had told me.

I sighed and stretched my neck from side to side. Reading and ice cream had been precisely what I needed. I was still pissed, but not to the point of murder anymore. Sighing, I pushed myself up from the couch and went into the kitchen for something to drink. Hot cocoa would do.

Toria meowed at me as soon as my foot touched the linoleum floor. She must have decided it was safe now. You would swear my little girl never ate, the way she carries on. The vet warned me that calicoes were talkative. Boy, was he right. She talked to me when I woke, just before my alarm, of course. She talked to me in the bathroom while I would get ready to go out. She talked to me when I got home, and, by God, she talked to me when it was time to eat.

What's interesting about Toria is her face. Her eyes are green, but one side is a sort of light tan, while the other is a tiger gray with a swoosh of natural eyeliner. Don't let her good looks fool you, however. She's a brat. A fat brat. A fat brat that always begs for treats.

"Just because I'm in the kitchen doesn't mean you're getting fed."

She meowed again and looked over her shoulder at my stove's clock. It clearly said that it was *well* past time for her to be fed, and it was *high* time I did something about it. Sometimes, she can be a spooky little cat. "Okay," I conceded, "*this* time it does." Goosebumps popped up on my arm as I reached into the refrigerator and pulled out the half-can of wet food from Toria's breakfast to dump in her bowl. Toria pounced on it as soon as the food hit the dish.

"Glutton." I chuckled as I stroked along her back. I got down a glass and filled it with water and ice. I frowned over it as I felt myself getting mad again.

"Can you believe that asshole, Toria?" Sometimes, talking to my little cat helped me work through things. This had to be one of those times, or I'd never work through it properly.

"I mean, seriously, who messes with someone's head like that?" I grumbled. My head was a lot sharper now that the 'fog of war' had cleared. It gave me the time to sit at my little table and think rationally. "Come to think of it, *how* did he mess with my memory? Even for that little bit, it was just gone for the most part. Sleep-inducing tea doesn't do *that*. Otherwise, it'd be illegal. Jove wouldn't have slipped me a roofie, would he? Frak, little cat, I don't think he even knows what a roofie is. The tea didn't taste off... He could have used something odorless and tasteless, but those types of things aren't exactly easy to come by."

I chewed on my thumbnail as I thought about what had happened. Jove had wanted me to drink the tea to put me to sleep to make doing something easy. With a roofie, the drug would have made me lose time, *and* would cause a splitting headache. I had been dead set against drinking that tea. But I'd done *exactly* what he'd wanted me to after he said my name. And it was weird how he said my name. If he could do that, then why the hell have me drink instead of just telling me to forget? I stood and went to the restroom to look in the mirror for any signs of being drugged.

I looked at a bright-eyed and bushy-tailed reflection. My eyes weren't abnormally dilated. I had clear recall from the drive back to my place that caused my fast-beating heart, but otherwise, there were no outward signs of being drugged. What if it was something new? Maybe I should go in, just in case.

I'd have to call the cops then. I closed my eyes in despair. I'd have to call the cops on someone I thought was a friend with whom I'd shared my hopes and dreams. But some things just weren't adding up in my brain. *Why* did I drink the tea when he told me to? That circled me back to how Jove had said my name.

I also thought back on the conversation between him and Bird-boy. Zauberer means Wizard in German. He'd spoken of 'Pointy hat men.' There were decorative signs and sigils all over the shop if you knew where to look. I'd thought it was just his aesthetic. Jove was more old-fashioned than Annie was, and she was personally trying to bring back the fashions from the 1940s. I once caught him using a handkerchief to wrap a paper cut rather than a band-aid from the first aid kit.

"Bird-boys are real." I tried to convince myself. "That big, scary Bird-boy had called Jove a Wizard. He did something when he called my name. Pointy hat men . . . Toria, I do believe I've been working for a Wizard."

It was then I heard a light knock on the door.

My brow furrowed. Who could this be knocking at my door? At 11:30 yet.

I looked through my peephole and saw Jove, the aforementioned asshole, on the other side. Pursing my lips in irritation, I turned the deadbolt on the door and opened it. I crossed my arms over my chest. His body language said he was remorseful, but I hadn't decided if I wanted to forgive him yet. "May I help you, Mr. Brandt?" He winced at the razor-sharp edge in my tone. I hadn't called him Mr. Brandt since my first year when I started working at Bindings.

"Mira, we have to talk." The set of his shoulders and how his hands were shoved into the pockets of his long coat came off as adorable and broody. No, Doctor Hall, you're mad at him. He made you lose time, bad Wizard.

"That's what I said hours ago. It would be best if you convinced me why I shouldn't call the police for what you did to me. I'm only going to give you this one chance to state your case." I stepped to one side, silently allowing him in. *Never mind that his eyes are begging you under his hair. Stay strong. Let him say his piece and then toss him out again.*

"May I come in?" He had that kicked-dog look on his face again.

I arched an eyebrow at him. Wasn't that implied? I motioned inside and opened the door wider still. Suspicion tingled in the back of my mind.

"Mira, may I come in?" Jove continued to stand at the threshold, looking sorrowful. Why did he want a verbal invitation? I searched my mind for relevant lore that I had absorbed through movies, tabletop campaigns, and books.

"Well, huh. I thought that only applied to vampires," I said softly.

"And anything that has magic. A threshold can stop some things and greatly slow others. It won't stop me, but it would greatly reduce my power." He looked sheepish.

I regarded him suspiciously. "You've been here before. Why would my threshold work now?"

"You are upset with me," he said matter-of-factly, like that explained everything, which pissed me off all over again! As if I needed to be told how I felt about him at that exact point in time. Something must have shown on my face because he pushed on. "Before you slam the door in my face, please, let me explain. Because you are upset with me—"

"Understatement," I said through clenched teeth.

"Because you are *very* upset with me," he corrected, "your home no longer welcomes me. I must ask permission if I want to keep my power."

That was interesting.

"It varies from lore to lore then. Okay. Go ahead and reduce your power, Zauberer. I don't want you pulling any more stunts like you did after Bird-boy left." I crossed my arms and waited.

"When did you get so stubborn?" He sighed.

"Birth. Cross it if you can." I fought to keep the fascination off my face as Jove forced his way over my threshold. It was interesting to watch. All his features became distorted. His hair went flat against his skull. It was sort of like pressing one's face into a sheet of clear plastic. When he finally made it through, there was a little 'pop' sound, and everything went back to normal.

"Well, you don't see that every day," I said, trying to keep my tone distant and clinical, like an annoyed Vulcan. I kept my shoulders stiff and my head held high as I led him to my little table, sat, and gestured to the chair across from mine. "So, let's talk."

He sat down gingerly with a sigh and looked over at me. It looked like he was still recovering from the crotch shot I had delivered earlier. Good.

Crossing my arms again, I leaned back and looked Jove over. "Why did Bird-boy think I was a goat?"

"A white goat is also a euphemism for a human sacrifice."

"I thought that was a 'long pig.'" I made sure my eyes were flat as I looked at him. More through him than at him, to be honest.

His eyes widened in shock. "*Scheiße!* How do you know *that*?"

"I have a couple of aunts who are into true crime and spooky podcasts. Occult terms come with the territory."

"That is moderately terrifying, Kleine." Jove leaned forward, steepling his hands. "Once Tief Rabe saw a beautiful woman answer the door, he thought you were payment for services rendered." He brought his hands to his face, palms together. "That idiot should have known that the Spitzhut Männer outlawed that option for us centuries ago precisely for the reason I am here now begging for your forgiveness. In all of our records, humans become overcome with madness when presented with something so alien to their knowledge. We call this madness 'Veil-Struck' because it happens the most often if someone's veil is malfunctioning or forgotten."

I felt a bit of heat rise to my cheeks at that 'beautiful' comment. I didn't believe it for a microsecond. If I were so 'beautiful,' I would have more dates on a Friday night—when I wasn't studying my ass off for a doctorate, that is. I wasn't the right shape to be conventionally beautiful, so I shrugged it off and focused on what Jove had just said. I wanted to know more about Zauberers.

"Why were you both speaking in German to begin with?" I watched his face. I was careful to avoid his eyes, just in case other lore was true as well. Stories about being captured in the gaze of a powerful being played through my head. I settled on looking at his nose.

"You know how when the Olympics are aired, they are broadcast in English and French, *ja*?" He waited for me to nod. "Well, it was agreed by the Spitzhut Männer that when dealing with any others in an official capacity, we would address each other in German. It was a prevalent language for some time. They thought it would be a safe bet for business in the new world. When the Americas were founded years ago, English only beat German by one vote."

"Who are the . . ." I had to snicker. The name was just so ridiculous. "*Spitzhut Männer*?"

"They are the leaders of all Zauberers." Jove's face became solemn. "I would not laugh at them if I were you, Kleine. It would be like laughing at a mafia Don. More like laughing at all the mafia Dons at once while they are armed and already annoyed with you." He looked around. "Could I bother you for a drink of water?"

I nodded and got up to get him some. I was feeling very odd about this entire conversation. Essentially, Jove was telling me magic was real. Hell, he'd proved it by walking into my place tonight. I would be laughing in his face right now if it weren't for the very real bruises that were blooming on my knees where I had hit the cobblestones trying to get away from the Bird-boy thing. I winced as my knees reminded me that they were in pain. I grabbed a couple of blue ice packs and a dish towel while I was getting Jove's water and headed back out into the living room. I gently set the water in front of him and pulled up one of the other chairs to prop up my legs to ice them.

"What has happened to your knees?" His brow furrowed in concern. "Did that bastard hurt you?"

"Oh, that was before you came to the rescue, wasn't it?" I hissed in pain as I placed the packs on my knees. "Bird-boy grabbed me, and this knee met his face." I pointed to my right knee. "Then he dropped me, I fell, and knees met ground at force."

Jove winced in sympathy. "Cobblestones are hard."

I smiled ironically. "Built to last. Those roads are a big part of this city's history. They just weren't meant for people to land softly on them. I just have to bring the swelling down. I can take some anti-inflammatory meds later. It's no big deal."

He stood and gestured to my legs. "May I?"

"What are you going to do?" I narrowed my eyes at him in suspicion. "I thought you left your power at the door."

"The majority, yes. I have enough for a little healing."

I was curious if this was going to work as well as his last spell did. Did my enhanced brain negate his magic entirely, or just what was supposed to affect my mind? I frowned at my pants. I was wearing jeans and not the kind that were easily rolled up. "Are you able to do it through the fabric?"

"It is possible, but it will not work as well." He scowled. "If you had only invited me in, then I would not have any trouble at all."

"I stand by my decision. You'd already cast one spell on me tonight. I can't trust you anymore. Stay put while I put on something else." I stood slowly and walked past him, determined not to show just how much it hurt to bend my knees. I concentrated on the pain in my knees rather than the pain I saw on his face.

"Do you need any help, Mira?" Jove whispered before I got to my bedroom door. His voice sounded strangely rough. Like the idea of going into my bedroom meant more than just helping me change or, more likely, the idea of me not trusting him hurt.

Good, he'd hurt me too.

"Nope." I looked over my shoulder and forced a strained smile at him. "I'm good." I got to my room and shut the door behind me. I didn't want Jove to see all the weapons. He'd think I was already crazy and try the memory spell again. By this point, all thoughts of calling the cops had gone out the window. I was going to see some actual *magic*! This was too cool. *Magic was real and existed in my sphere of existence!* The show at the door had been tantalizing. I wanted to see it up close and personal. But no magic on my memory again. That was off-limits.

Now, how to get out of the jeans . . . I ground my teeth together as I shimmied them down to my knees. They had swollen quite a bit since I'd gotten home. Why hadn't I felt the pain until now? Then it dawned on me. Adrenaline. I was scared when I faced Bird-boy. I was angry when I crotch-shot Jove. Both fear and anger produce adrenaline that can block pain for a short amount of time.

That time had run out for me, and both knees throbbed painfully in syncopated rhythms. My breath shuddered out as I pushed the jeans down farther. Breathe through it, Mira, just like in the birthing classes you sat in on when rotation took you through maternity.

I must have taken too long. With my pantied butt in the air, I heard the squeak of the hinges on my bedroom door. I flushed with embarrassment. "Get *out*!" I shouted and *slammed* the door closed before Jove could open it further. Oh God, how much did he see? I didn't even have on sexy, kickass underwear! I was wearing the gag gift set Ree had bought me for surviving the crash. They had the nurse from Pokémon throwing a two-fingered peace sign on them!

I shoved my jeans off the rest of the way and put on some long shorts I usually used for working out. I took a breath. Maybe he didn't see them. I'd been fast with slamming the door in his face. I hoped it didn't hit him too hard. Crap . . . I had been across the room when I did that. How the hell was I going to explain that? Nothing to do but face it.

I went back out to the living room, where Jove was drinking his water in rather large gulps. I felt the blood rush to my face and pulse in my ears. I sat down across from him and sipped from my water. A few minutes of uncomfortable silence ensued before either of us got up the nerve to say something.

Of course, we decided to speak at the same time.

"My humblest apologies. I did not mean to—"

"Are you all right? I didn't hurt you, did—"

That made us both laugh and break whatever silence embarrassment required. After we were done laughing, I said, "The door didn't hit you, did it?"

"No, it did surprise me, however. I did not even feel you gather the power." He smiled. It lit up his whole face. I'd only seen him look like that when we'd get in a rare book. I got a sinking feeling in my stomach. He was about to get the wrong idea.

"Why did you not tell me you could do magic? It explains everything that has happened tonight! I know Tief Rabe said you had power, but I am not one to easily believe one of the ravens."

"Um, because I can't?" I started poking at the rapidly thawing ice pack I'd left on the table when I went to change.

"I beg to differ." He looked me in the eye. I looked away. "You said you threw him into the truck."

"I did." I was going to have to tell him about my ability, and I wasn't happy about it.

"From the back door?"

"No, he'd just dropped me, and I got to the stoop as fast as I could. I threw him from there. I didn't say it was logical." He just looked at me with what was rapidly becoming superior smugness, as if he found me with my hand in the cookie jar.

"Magic is not always logical." He smirked. I felt that annoyed anger well up again. I knew exactly what my abilities were. I didn't need him to explain them to me.

I scowled as I tried to explain. "What I have isn't magic, it's—"

"You have so much to learn, Mira, so much I can teach you." He rushed on as he took my hands, excitement playing in his eyes. That look made my stomach sick. "You must have just come into your powers! I knew there was something special about you."

"It's not what you think." I pulled my hands back, shaking my head.

Jove sat back in his chair and took another drink of his water. "I was not certain until just now when you slammed that door in my face. You were clear across the room from that door."

Damn it. "I could have something set up. Like a button by the foot of my bed, for example, to automatically slam a door." Okay, that sounded ridiculous, even to me. I had to make him understand. My ability could be explained, proven, and repeated. Magic can't. That was why it was called magic.

"You do not have to make excuses to me, Kleine. All struggle with such rationale until it is proven to them." Jove shook his head, smirking again like you do at a kid who doesn't understand why blue plus red equals purple. Wow, that rankled. "Looks like I will have to show you."

I looked away indignantly, propped my legs up on the chair again, and grabbed for the ice packs.

"The whole reason you had to change in the first place was so I could heal that for you, is it not?" Jove came over and knelt next to my legs. "I will show you some real magic, and then we'll see about channeling what you have."

I rolled my eyes. "*You* are doomed to disappointment."

You can't channel what you don't have. Jove just didn't realize that yet. He closed his eyes and slowed his breathing. He then placed his hands just above my kneecaps. So close to the skin, I could feel the warmth from them. He murmured something. I could barely make it out. I had to strain to hear him.

"*Schmerz auflösen.*" 'Pain resolved,' my brain instantly translated. I liked the sound of his voice speaking in his native tongue. I had to avert my eyes for a second as his hands flashed like a camera. My knees got warm. Not hot, not painful, just warm. I sighed as the pain eased out of them. Jove removed his hands, and I watched in amazement as the bruises receded.

"The swelling should go down in about five minutes," Jove said smugly. "Much faster than anti-inflammatories, *ja?*"

"Whoa. It's really *real*, isn't it?" I poked at my right knee to see if there was any residual pain. "Why didn't your spell stick the last time? I know you used more power."

"I was hoping to figure that out by talking to you here. It is not often a mundane human can shake off a spell cast by a hundred-and-fifty-year-old Zauberer." He sat back in his chair and drank his water.

Jesus Christ and all his holy hand grenades. I searched his face for any sign of aging as defined in medicine. He didn't look older than thirty or thirty-five on the outside. I swallowed before stammering, "Y–you look good for your age. Is it some illusion or glamour?"

"Such things exist. However, they are not needed for my kind."

I took a swallow of my drink. The man I'd worked with for over a decade was older than my great-grandfather. I stared into my hot chocolate and debated breaking out the Bailey's. "So, you wanted answers as to why and how I could shrug off your magic."

I took a breath to explain about my abilities. How they manifested, how I got them, how—

"You must have some latent power or someone in your family. You must not be as human as you think. It is something quite common."

What? I gaped at him.

"There are plenty of half this and that running around. As soon as their powers manifest, we scoop them up into the Community. Tell me, do you know of anything that would be odd in your family history?"

I shook my head. "I did a genealogical tree a couple of years back for my grandmothers for Christmas. I was able to trace them back to their respective countries of origin. I piggybacked off my one aunt's work. She's always been a history buff and had a lot of what I was looking into for Momma's side."

Jove stroked a hand over his short beard. "Do you know much about the donor? Your father?"

Jove and I had a quick conversation about my parentage when he first met The Moms.

The family had descended on the shop the same week I'd been hired. There was no way any of us could get a job someplace and the family not visit at least once. Annie loved the antique section and made a beeline there, Ree was browsing True Crime, and Momma grilled my (then) boss while Mom browsed the Science fiction section. My family has never felt any shame about how we came together as a unit. Momma even invites questions. She feels it's the best way to get the correct knowledge directly from the source.

I shook my head. "The donor was anonymous. All we know is the basics along with his family health history."

"I've never heard of someone with power being able to pass on magic that way before, but there is always a first time."

I grabbed the ice packs again to help bring down any remaining swelling and to have something to do with my hands as he stared at me. His brows furrowed, trying to understand.

"What of your Oma? Did she tell you anything that may have seemed like a story at the time? Sometimes magic is consciously passed."

"Nothing beyond the typical '*Schneewittchen und die sieben Zwerge.*' My sisters and I loved it when she told us that one. She had such flair with it." I smiled, remembering many nights at Oma's house, listening to her voice and sitting around her old chair.

"And your Opa?"

"An old-school builder. Our family name used to be Rathaus, but Opa thought it sounded like 'Rat House' when said in English." I shrugged. "He changed it to the closest thing he could say in English that meant the same thing. Hall. He wanted our family to gain respect in America. He and my great-uncle are doing very well doing what our family has always done best," I said proudly. "Building homes and offices."

Jove frowned. "That does not sound like there is any connection with magic there. Buildings are a very human thing. All that steel and glass does not work for most of us."

That's because there wasn't any magic. Not even a crazy Uncle Louie. "What I have going on with me isn't magic," I said with certainty. Then I stood up and made my way to the door.

"Wait, Kleine—"

"You still aren't listening when I'm telling you something. First, it was, 'Don't fuck with my head, I'm not crazy.' Now it's 'Listen, you *Arschloch*, I don't have magic!' I don't know how to say it any plainer. Just . . . Go home."

I opened the door. "I have a meeting in the morning with a bank, and I've already stayed up too late as it is. I've given you a lot of information, but you haven't been giving me any back. I'm tired, and besides, I'm still mad at you. Attempting to adjust someone's memory because it is inconvenient is not cool on any level. Especially when I considered you a friend."

"Please, Kleine, I had no choice," he pleaded. "*Es tut mir leid.*"

"We always have choices, Jove. You just made the wrong one. If you want to continue to be friends, then it's time for you to go."

After I showed him out, I went back into my room and whimpered at the time on my alarm clock next to the bed. Tomorrow was going to be an energy drink day. Damn, I hated those days. Those things always made me jittery and gave me heartburn. I fell into bed and let sleep take me.

9

THE FOLLOWING DAY was pretty much how I thought it would be. An energy drink with my toaster pastry. Eww. My appointment was with one of the loan officers at one of the banks close to the university. I already had my student loans through them. My credit was high enough that I may have been able to get another to start a business. All this talk of banks reminded me I would need to apply for my independent business license later that week. I didn't live far from campus, but it was just easier to take public transportation from my apartment to the school than it was to try to navigate in the city in my rental. There was a bus stop that I could walk to a block or so up. That walk would have been a lot harder if it hadn't been for Jove's healing the night before.

I sighed as I sat down on the bus, plopping my purse down beside me. It was a short ride, but it would give me a chance to think. My entire world had just gotten a whole lot bigger. I put in my headphones and thought about what I'd learned. Magic was real. Bird-human hybrids were real. What else was real? If Bird-boys could exist, and Wizards could exist, what else could exist? How did they keep out of the notice of the general population? Did they have shields or maybe something that deflected attention? Was that why they called those people 'Veil-Struck,' because they saw behind a veil? What else was out there? My mind was full of questions that had nothing to do with how many CCs of insulin a patient with diabetes needed.

I glanced out of the window and saw a large black bird keeping pace with the bus. Weird. Remembering Bird-boy, I shuddered and looked away from it. I frowned. Why was I letting a bird freak me out? I purposely looked out of the window where it had been, but the bird had already disappeared. The bus was going through a busy section of town. The crowded sidewalk was choked with people busily walking to wherever they needed to go, not noticing others around them.

That's when I noticed something interesting while we were at a stop light. There were gaps in the crowd. Rather large gaps where the masses seemed to skirt around the edges. Why weren't these people filling in the gaps to get to where they needed to be sooner?

I looked harder at the gaps, focusing. There had to be something there that I wasn't seeing. I watched, fascinated, as the air in the gap began to move. It was sort of like how the air ripples in the summer when the sun's scorching rays beat down on the city. The rippling moved with the crowd as the light changed. I couldn't help but stare as the movement seemed to consolidate into a shape. It was tall, about eight feet, but walked on two legs, but before I could really identify what I was seeing, the bus started to move and turned away from the crowded street.

What else is out there?

I asked a simple question and got one big, mysterious, complex answer. My eyes were glued to the window for the rest of the trip to the bank, but I didn't see another *air anomaly*. When I stepped off the bus, I had found resolve. I needed to research some things between appointments. Knowledge was a very strong weapon, and it looked like I was going to need as much as I could get.

My appointment didn't go as planned. I stepped off the bus and walked into the bank with its laminated floors and plush-looking seats. I walked toward the luxury area of the bank reserved for loan negotiations and other significant transactions. The bank was as silent as a tomb, with only the soft mutterings from the tellers to the customers behind their acrylic safety shields.

"Excuse me, miss, can I help you?" called one of the tellers. There was a long line of customers, and all eyes were suddenly focused on me.

"Uh, yes, I have an appointment with Trey. I'm here about a business loan?"

The teller looked me up and down. I'd dressed very professionally in a dark pantsuit with flat sandals. They'd seen me walk off the bus because the stop was just outside, and the condescension on her face was thicker than her foundation. "You're *Doctor* Hall."

I firmed my lips but gave her a professional smile. "Yes, and I'm here to see Trey. Are they in?"

"Oh, you're one of *them*. He should be coming back from lunch soon. You can tell he's a *he* because his name is *Trey*."

"Oh, I never assume. It's rude, after all. So is pointing out things like that, at the express volume you chose and at the express tone you chose to use, specifically, to ridicule and embarrass someone you don't even know. Your behavior also tells me this isn't a bank I want to start my practice with anyway since casual cruelty is so prevalent here. You know what they say about assuming. Oh, and if you don't . . . Google's free . . . look it up." And I walked out, almost bumping into a man coming the opposite direction. "Oh, excuse me."

"Mira? Mira Hall?"

I blinked at the man. His dark face and smile clicked. "Trayvon? Geebus. It's been ages! I haven't seen you since high school. What are you up to now?"

He gestured to the building around us. "I work here. I'm the loan manager."

"I had no idea! When I made the appointment, they just said to come in and ask for 'Trey.' Since when did you start going by 'Trey'?"

"Since I went into banking. Racism is still a thing that exists. People are a lot more likely to talk with a 'Trey' than they are a 'Trayvon.'" He glanced at his watch. "I know I'm a couple of minutes late, but I hope you weren't leaving."

"I was . . ." I looked over my shoulder pointedly at the teller. "I didn't feel like my business would be welcome here."

Trayvon shot the teller a fulminating glare before turning back to me. "I'm sorry our inexperienced teller offended you, Doctor Hall. Please, don't think too poorly of our branch because of the actions of one person who *will be immediately* reprimanded and retrained. Please follow me to my office, where we can talk about your loan in private."

We went past the plush seats and into an office with large glass windows at the corner of the building. "Have a seat. I'll be right back. I need to find the head teller for a quick second."

I got shot down almost instantly when he came back. "I'm sorry, Mir, but you need more collateral to show you're solvent enough for us to take a chance on. Listen, if you get more investors, then we'd be glad to work with you, but as things stand now . . . I just can't."

My heart sank. "I . . . understand. I'll see what I can do about investors."

"Please, do," he said earnestly. "I'd love it if I could help you turn your dream into reality."

I blinked, and the meeting was over, leaving me with a lot of nervous energy and nowhere for it to go. I decided to meet up with David for something more substantial than a toasted pastry. I shot him a text to meet me at The Board and Brew if he was up for it. It had been our favorite place to go when things were getting hairy with school.

I was already sitting at our table in the diner, surprised I'd beat him there. The restaurant was an old-timey place from back in the 2020s. They still had counter service for the lone diners but also served anything your stomach could crave. Burgers, wings, and fries were a staple, but so were avocado toast and vegan delights. It was great. And if you were bored (see what I did there) while waiting for your food, you could go to the games and pick something to play. He and I had many of the same classes until I had to do my residency, so we had spent many a night studying at the diner, distracting one another so we didn't burn out.

"Hey, Space Station, rough day?"

I smiled at him and stood to hug him before we sat back down. He was moving slowly. "Yeah, but how about you? How's the wound?"

He pulled his collar to one side, exposing his upper shoulder. My eyes went wide. There was a wide gauze pad taped to where his shoulder met the rest of his neck. It looked like it had been appropriately dressed, but I was tempted to look at it myself. "I'm on recovery leave."

I gave a low whistle. For a wound to need that big of a bandage, it had to have been nasty. "Ouch. Geebus, did you need me to look at it?"

He smiled warmly. "I'd appreciate that. I saw someone right when it happened, but I know it's gonna bug you until you take a look for yourself."

I slid over to his side of the booth. The faux leather squeaked and made fart noises as I got situated.

"They patched me up when it happened, but I'd rather a *real* doctor look at it," he said, wiggling his eyebrows to make me smile.

"That would be me. Now, turn to face me, oh he who gets bitten by patients." He swiveled, our legs brushing against one another. I gasped as I pulled his shirt down to his shoulder. It was bigger than I thought. There were actually two pads taped together at the collarbone, and the wound went all the way down to his left pectoral.

"Be gentle. I'm fragile." He looked at me with playful green eyes.

"I'll be gentle, you big baby. I wish we were in a sterile environment, but beggars can't be choosers." I used the hand sanitizer in my purse before I pulled up the tape. I winced as I got a look at the wound itself. David's flesh had been stitched and stapled where it had been required, proving he'd already seen a human doctor. They'd probably treated him at the veterinary clinic to stop the bleeding then got him to the emergency room.

I didn't smell the tell-tale scent of severe infection. It actually looked like it was healing well, but it was going to leave an impressive scar. The animal had to have chewed and clawed at David to produce something like this. "They did a good job. You're remembering to change the bandages and keep the area clean?"

"Yes, Mom."

I stuck my tongue out at him and replaced the dressings over the wound. My hands sent a signal to my brain, reminding me that my David was starting to get ripped. Down girl, no lusting after wounded friends, Bad Mira. "What happened?"

"It was the last patient for the night, an auto emergency. Old dude moved fast for a super-senior Husky. He had to get shaved down to evaluate his wound properly. The old boy was so docile when they brought him back, but I guess he really didn't want the muzzle. Humph, he got it anyway." He smirked as he pulled the shirt back into place. "I had to wrestle his fuzzy ass to the ground. But he sure as shit got seen to."

"And obviously, he still had all his teeth." I winced and gently slid out from his side of the table. "Be sure to use antibiotics for that. You don't want it to get infected."

"Heh, infected." He snorted.

I frowned at him. "Dude, infection is not something to laugh at." I smacked his good shoulder lightly before moving back to sit across from him. "You've been in some of the same classes I was. Some of those pictures are gnarly."

"Has anyone ever told you your vocabulary is something out of an episode of Scooby-Doo?"

"Like Zoikes, man." It was relaxing sitting here with David. Sure, he was like a worrisome older brother, but he was still the best to hang out with.

He stopped laughing and got this serious look. "Are you okay, Mira?" He looked pointedly at my knee. It was bouncing faster than a two-year-old in their first bouncy castle.

"I'm sorry, I didn't sleep very well last night."

The waitress came up and took our drink order.

I got ice water to help level out the taurine from this morning.

"And so, you had an energy drink this morning." David crossed his arms and stared wryly at me.

"And a toaster pastry," I added.

"Mira, you hate those drinks. You once told me they all taste like melted gummy bears. Are you having nightmares again? Is that why you're not sleeping?" he whispered after the server left. David was the only one who knew about them. I didn't want the family to worry about me.

"No, I just couldn't sleep." I smiled and patted his hand. I couldn't exactly tell him about my sudden discovery of the world of the weird, even though we bonded over the nerdier things in our lives. I really wanted to tell him, if only so I'd have someone to geek out with.

"You know I'm just a phone call away if you need me." His face was concerned as he watched me. "A pastry and an energy drink don't do the body good."

"Hey, that was our go-to breakfast when we pulled all-nighters!"

"Until we saw what diabetes can do to a body. I got a reminder of that at the clinic. You should have seen this one man who brought his Pomeranian in. Poor guy was in so much pain from neuropathy, it was hard to watch."

"The man or the dog?"

He nudged my water closer to me. "Both. That crap you've had this morning isn't good for you, Mir."

Thankfully, the server came about that time with our food—a steak and mashed potatoes for David; fried shrimp, a salad, and fries for me. "I'm running on about three hours, if that. I got home late from the shop." I rested my head on my hand.

"I don't see why you still hang out there. It's not like you work there anymore. The guy treats people like dirt, he's rude, and he wouldn't smile if the Joker pumped him full of laughing gas."

"He'd have to know who the Joker is first." I chuckled, pointing with a French fry in my hand. "And you just don't like him because he called you cute."

His eyes narrowed, an embarrassed flush spreading across his cheeks. "He called me 'Snooki.'"

"No, he called you '*Schnucki.*'" I corrected him, lifting my water glass.

"The difference being?"

"One means 'Sweetie pie.' The other is that one chick from that reality show your grandma used to watch." I tried for the laugh, but he only scowled at his steak. That steak didn't do anything to deserve a look like that. "He's a good person, David, if you'd give him a chance. And Bindings . . . it's a place for me to feel . . . safe, and I kinda really need that right now."

"How does a grown man in this day and age *not* know who the Joker is?" He grumbled, stabbing at his steak. "Hasn't he gone to the movies in the last twenty years? The man has no taste."

"Not all of us are so well-versed in the life and times of Batman." We both laughed. I smirked and took a swig of my water. He laid a finger on my bouncing knee to stop the movement again, something he'd always done when we were studying together.

"How are your legs?" He spoke around his steak. Then he swallowed and took a swig of his water before continuing, "I know you were worried about having residual arthritic pain later."

I had been worried, especially since my recovery period had been so unusual. I thought of the healing Jove had done on them at my apartment. That also reminded me of what happened before he came to my apartment. Maybe David was right. Maybe I should take some deliberate steps back from Jove Brandt.

"Mir?"

"Hmm?"

"How. Are. Your. Legs?" David repeated slowly, a slight annoyance sneaking into his voice.

I flushed with embarrassment. "Sorry, my head's in the clouds today. They're better. Much better. I'm making sure to exercise them twice a week just like they told me to in therapy."

He nodded once. "Good. The way you sprinted through PT, I was worried you didn't take anything to heart. I didn't want to have to remind you about your Momma and her 'weather foot.'"

"One little horrific auto accident won't keep me down," I said, popping a shrimp into my mouth. I could practically feel my system leveling out. That's right, food. Soaking up all those sugars and chemicals.

He took a shrimp out of my basket and ate it. His eyes went severe, his mouth set in a firm line. "I should have been with you. I should have taken you home myself that night."

"David, there is nothing anyone could have done. If you'd been with me, the only thing that would have changed was how many people were in the hospital. And I barely survived. There would have been a very high chance you wouldn't have."

He shrugged. "It's this nagging feeling I've got. Like if I'd just been there—"

"I don't want to think about it anymore." I shivered. "You're already hurt enough, and . . . I just don't want to dwell. It could have been a lot worse."

"Worse than emergency brain surgery? You're going to have to think about this sometime, Mir. I'd rather you do it with a professional." He took my hand. "Listen, everyone over at the game store is anxious to see you again. We should—whoa!" We both jerked back when a fast, black blur slammed into the window next to us.

"What the hell was that?" I yelped, my heart in my throat.

"A bird, I think. Too big to be a crow. It might be a raven. We must be near a nest or something. They're rare around here, though. Let's go out to see if it needs help. With a blow like that, it could be stunned." David stood up from his clean plate. I still had some of my salad left, but I suddenly didn't have the desire to eat more.

I had a terrible feeling. My eyes scanned the trees as I leaned down to pick up my bag. "Look, I've got to get going anyway. I'll see you later." I put my share of the bill and the tip on the table.

"Are you sure you don't want to help the bird?" He tilted his head to one side, confused. "That's not like you, Mira."

"You're better equipped than I am to take care of an injured bird, David. I've got another appointment in a half hour across town anyway . . . with a professional. I'll text you later, okay?"

"Okay, be careful," he said incredulously as I left. His voice was almost too quiet for me to hear. I nodded and waved goodbye. I couldn't blame him for his disbelief. I *wasn't* acting like myself. I'd have to blame the lack of sleep later.

The bus dropped me off about a block away from my next destination. I looked down at the card in my hand that Roxy had slipped to me. The nightmares were becoming more frequent since the surgery . . . I felt like I was dangling off a ledge and falling into a chasm of constant panic. I had to do something about this to nip it in the bud.

That meant therapy.

I called and made the appointment with Rosalinda Jimenez. Thankfully, she had appointments available during the day so that I could get myself here. Her office was a converted Victorian, complete with turrets. The wraparound front porch creaked as I stepped onto it. It didn't look neglected. Instead, it felt . . . homey, like being welcomed to my Nanny Smith's house.

The entrance was welcoming. A smiling receptionist greeted me as I walked in. "Hello, I'm Andrea. May I help you?"

"Yes, I have an appointment with Rosalinda Jimenez at one," I replied nervously.

"First time?"

I nodded.

"You must be Doctor Hall, then. I saw your name on the books and thought you were coming in for a consult. Have a seat right over there. I'll come and get you when Rosalinda's free."

The waiting area looked like it would have originally been the drawing room or lounge of the house—the place where Madam or Sir would entertain company. There was even a tea service on a small table against the wall. The only thing that smacked of the modern age was the single-serving, automatic coffee maker. The dispenser next to it had a variety of teas or coffee, packets of sugar, sticks of honey, and a small, laminated sheet of paper that gave instructions on its use.

My hands were cold. They shouldn't be. It was that time of year in PA where one day it could be freezing, and the next it could be blazing hot. Today was a hot day, but my hands were still cold. I followed the instructions and got myself a raspberry tea. I'd just started stirring in the honey stick when I heard my name called.

"Doctor Hall, it's good to meet you face-to-face." Rosalinda was a comfortable-looking Latina in her fifties. Her melodic voice rang with the slight accent of either Mexico or somewhere further south. Her black hair was layered and framed her face fetchingly. She smiled at me and opened the door further. "Please come in; feel free to bring your tea."

This room was smaller, more like a bedroom than an office. There were couches covered in floral prints with soft-looking throw pillows. Built into the far wall was a bookcase that looked like it was an original part of the house. The windows looked over a nearby highway. It must've been a fantastic view before the ever-growing city swallowed it up.

"Please have a seat. That tea smells so good I think I'll join you in enjoying it." She walked over to another table with its own tea service, complete with honey sticks. She nodded at my cup. "I get the sticks from a honey stand I pass on my way into work. It's run by this family who are just starting to get into beekeeping."

"It's always good to support local businesses," I said carefully. I could feel the knot in my stomach start to ease. This was better. We were just talking.

Rosalinda's tea smelled like orange blossoms as she settled herself on a couch across from the one I was sitting on. "So, Roxy gave you my card?"

I nodded. "Our family's been going to them for years, so when I went after escaping from the hospital—"

"Escaping?"

"Yeah." I blushed. "It kinda felt like we were escaping." I told her about being separated from my family and Alden's behavior while leaving out the crucial bits, like how I could lift my couch with my brain.

Rosalinda sat patiently, waiting for me to finish before exclaiming, *"Ai Dios mio!* No wonder you called it 'escaping!' Are you bringing charges against him?"

"No. I just wanted to get out and be left alone, yanno?"

"How awful it must have been. I'm sorry, Mira, it had to be hard."

I shrugged. "I'm alive, and I'm free. It could have been a lot worse."

"Mira." Her dark eyes were serious and full of concern. But I didn't see pity. I would have hated to see pity. "You don't have to dismiss how you felt. Just because it could have been worse does not diminish how bad it was to begin with. You don't have to be grateful that things weren't as bad as they could have been."

I felt my throat close up. Sometimes, hearing obvious truth spoken aloud can remind a person that others care about them. I'd seen a lot while doing my rotations—accidents, trauma, fractures . . . death. So, I'd pushed down on my concerns. I shouldn't complain because it could have been worse . . . I felt a tear run down my cheek when I looked into the therapist's concerned amber eyes.

Rosalinda handed me a tissue box. "It's okay, *chica*. You are in a safe place. It's okay to feel what you're feeling."

I honked into the tissue.

"What Doctor Alden did was illegal, unethical, and wrong. It was also, in no way, shape, or form, your fault. You said this was right after the accident with the big truck?"

I nodded.

"So, it's not even your fault for how you ended up in that man's clutches. Would you like me to help you work through your emotions on this?"

I swallowed some more tea. "Yeah, I think I do."

I went to set the cup back on the table when I heard it. The distinctive, blaring howl of the horn of an eighteen-wheeler sounded. It felt unreasonably close, right on top of me close. Close enough to force me over the rumble strip and into a pole. I could smell the exhaust and electric ozone of arcing wires. I froze, and my tea hit the floor with a dull thud, spilling its contents on Rosalinda's carpeted floor. My breath started coming out in pants. I lost focus on the world. Quickly, Rosalinda knelt by me and took my hands.

They were shaking so hard.

"Doctor Hall, can you hear me? I need you to breathe, *chica*. Slow breaths in and out. You are here, safe, in my office. Nothing can harm you here. Good, in through the nose . . . hold it for two, three, four, five . . . and release. There we are, Mira." She slipped fresh, hot tea into my cold hands and rubbed my shoulders while I breathed. I didn't remember her getting up to get more, but I was grateful she did. "Has this ever happened before?"

I shook my head and looked morosely into the dark liquid in my mug. "Never this bad before. I've been avoiding the highways and driving at night. It hasn't been hard to avoid with my family driving me around everywhere lately. I'm fine with anyone else driving with me in the car at night . . . just not me. Smoke too—though my sister can burn incense that doesn't bother me—but big bonfires . . . any dark black smoke does it." I looked back up at her, hesitating for a moment. "I'm having recurring nightmares—one with the truck and one from the surgery. I wake up in sweats, thinking I'm about to throw up. And I keep hearing that. Damned. Song."

Her eyes searched mine. "What song, Mira?"

"'Lavender's Blue.' Every nightmare I have ends with that song on the line, 'You will be my queen.' Like some twisted promise." I swallowed back a sob. "I hate it."

"I would like it if we could meet often to talk about this. A lot is going on, and I want to help get you back to living how you want to live. You've heard of journaling, yes?"

"Of course. We had a class on it when I was still deciding on what kind of doctor I wanted to be."

Rosalinda walked over to a desk behind the couches. It looked more like a craft table than a desk. There were stacks of bound notebooks, pens, crayons, and even paints propped up in a way that would let a person see them. "What color would you like?"

Of course, I picked the one in Who Blue. It went along with the sonic screwdriver pen I had at home.

On the bus ride home after my appointment, I kept a wary eye out for the air anomalies that I could only suppose were things that didn't want to be seen. The phenomenon still left me with so many questions. How did they work? What did they hide? It helped me keep my mind off my failed loan interviews and the bird incident. Just how many were there? Then I realized I had my very own answer guy. Jove wanted to know more about my family and I wanted to know more about his world. He'd just have to cough up the knowledge after I'd been so generous with my personal information. I'd see him tomorrow morning before the shop opened.

It was only fair.

10

"No." Jove crossed his arms and leaned against the ancient wood counter.

I had to keep an eye on the time so I wouldn't miss the bus to get back to the apartment. Sure, I had a new car, but depending on public transport gave me more time to be out and about during the day. I wasn't the one driving, and the buses are about the same size as a truck, so I felt safer.

"No, I am not going to just tell you these things."

"And why not?" I crossed my arms and glared at the Wizard. "I think I've been more than forthcoming with my personal, *private*, family history. The least you could do is tell me more about all of this."

"That will not work on me, Kleine. I have heard you tell strangers stories about your mother's uncle who rammed into a museum guard while he was pretending to be a superhero. You share your family history with anyone who will listen. This is something you should curb from now on. You never know who may be doing the asking."

That was a chilling thought. I didn't want to expose my family to danger. I mean, look what happened to Spider-Man.

Jove turned away from me and walked toward the display that always needed straightening. "You do not know what you are asking of me with these questions. What you want is not mine to give you, and besides which, they could get you killed." Then he mumbled in German, "*It is fascinating that you can see the veils in the first place. It's unheard of among the Community."*

"The Community?" I pressed. I followed him as he paced around the store, going from stack to stack, making minor adjustments to the books. "What Community?"

"*Scheiße*!" he cursed.

"Forgot you can't pull that particular language trick on me, huh? Do you need another broom reminder?"

He crossed his legs and winced. "No, Kleine, I do not."

"Humph," I said to myself. "Didn't know there *was* a community. Why didn't I know there was a community?"

Jove smiled, showing a bit of smugness again. "That is how it is supposed to be. Our people work hard to keep it that way. The Community of Philadelphia, to be precise. That is all I am allowed to say. With the advent of your abilities, it has proven impossible for me to cast memory magic on you that would last. The choices we have in this situation are limited. At my mentor's advice, we will be bringing you into the Community as a member."

A mentor? Jove had never mentioned anyone he'd learned from before—not family, not school friends, no one. And the way he said it not only conveyed a deep respect for this mentor but perhaps more. I opened my mouth to ask about it when he put his hands on my shoulders. His hands were warm and soothing.

"I know you have questions, Mira. You have every right to them, but not yet."

"I don't have to like it." I shrugged him off and took a step back. His hands were starting to feel too good, and I was still annoyed at the attempted mind wipe. "I could find out on my own, you know."

He shifted and was suddenly *way* too far into my comfort zone. I thrust out my chin and didn't back down. Go me. I felt like I was looking up at a small giant. We were toe-to-toe when he spoke again; his voice was rough, his eyes desperate. "Can you not tell how much danger you are in? You have *no* idea what is waiting out there to eat you, Kleine. The Unkindness knows who you are now. Do you think they are going to stop taking notice now that you *threw one into a truck?*"

Unkindness? This was a new phrase I was going to research the crap out of once I got home. My eyes narrowed, and I tilted my head. "You're upset about more than the Bird-boy. What is it, Jove?"

"You have always been very observant, very . . . clever." He took a step closer, crowding me against the stone fireplace built into the wall. "It is one of your most attractive traits."

I felt my heart start to pound in my ears as an embarrassing blush heated my cheeks, but I didn't drop my eyes. "Don't be an ass. You know I have, and you know why. Back off." I took a little step back. There is a point where you just are not comfortable with how close someone is.

He reached out and braced against the brick hearth, leaning in and trapping me with an arrogant smirk. "Make me, Kleine," he said, stroking the side of my cheek.

"You got it." Jove's eyes widened in shock as I *pushed* him back a good five steps with my ability. Added to that, I was annoyed enough to *trip* him. His ass hit the floor, and he let out a satisfying 'whoomph.' I pointed at him and snarled. "You ask before you touch me, got it?"

Jove started laughing. This was not the reaction I'd been expecting. I arched an eyebrow incredulously.

He sat up, his face glowing with excitement. "That was amazing! I felt no gathering of magic at all!"

I nudged him with my shoe. "You are an assbutt, Jove."

"Assbutt?"

I ignored the question. I didn't expect him to get the reference to Supernatural. "You ticked me off so you could test if I were really using magic or not," I accused. I leaned down and stuck out a hand to help him up. He took it with a look of glee on his face.

"See? Clever. I had to test it. You are such an enigma, and I could not help myself. I pored over your family tree last night. Your book was a great help, but I could not find anything in your family tree, even using my magic. I mean *nothing*." He grunted as he got back to his feet. "Even a normal person has at least a lesser Fae or a bit of brownie. Your family is exceptional in its mediocrity."

"I don't know if I feel insulted or not." I mean, I knew we were just human, but to be called mediocre is a different kettle altogether. Then I paused and narrowed my eyes at him. "And just how did you go over my family tree? I know I didn't give you my copy of that book."

He flushed. "Magic? I put it back after I was done with it."

I *threw* a copy of *Oliver Twist* at his head. Original version. Embossed hardback. When he ducked, I focused harder and used my ability.

"Please, Kleine!" The book chased the Wizard around the stacks. It hit him three times before settling back in its place on the bookshelf with an irritated ruffle of pages.

"Permission, Brandt. It's a thing you need to remember."

"I had to find out if you were telling me the truth as you knew it before telling you more about the Community! Your bloodline is full of average humans: carpenters, window makers, ironworkers, and smiths in general. Even one of your mothers works with computers. Even though some of us would call that a kind of magic, her powers are purely scientific and learned. You do not even have a priest or druid in your background." He laughed again and ran a hand through his hair. "I had to resort to other means to look into your donor, and even he had no magic in his line."

"You found our donor? You have his name?" My world slowed a little at that revelation. The man had literally been our sperm donor. Suddenly, I had access to his name.

Jove looked soberly into my eyes. "*Ja*, Kleine, would you like to know it?"

I thought about it seriously before I shook my head. I was grateful for the man who had donated a tiny part of himself to give my sisters and me life, but he had nothing else to do with us. I walked behind the counter to give myself some space. My heart was still beating a bit too fast for my taste.

I reached into a box of specialty books that had been ordered. I slid one of the books into a special bookcase behind the register. Even though I wasn't on the payroll anymore, it didn't feel wrong to help with the stocking like I always had. The shelves were labeled alphabetically behind locked glass. Each employee had a small key that fit into the case. Some of the ordered books were rare and valuable. Precious things, indeed. Even though I wasn't technically an employee, Jove had never asked for the key back.

"I told you that you wouldn't find any magic," I said. I knew my abilities came from either the surgery or the medication I've been on since. I still had a half-full bottle of NAN-06 looming in my medicine cabinet. It still felt vital to take it, but I still didn't know exactly what it did. I could feel Jove watching me. I couldn't figure out if I were unnerved or not.

"Just what are you, Mira Hall?" came his softened voice from behind me.

"To my knowledge, I'm human—nothing more, nothing less. My brain has just been in a type of controlled overdrive. Who knows, in a couple of generations, these abilities may start occurring naturally." I turned back to him and gave him an indulgent smile. "It's not magic; it's science."

"Then how did you break my spell on your memory?" His hands were in the pockets of his slacks as he regarded me like a puzzle he hadn't figured out yet. "What I cast on you was most definitely magic."

"A part of my mind retained the knowledge. It closed it off from the wipe and reminded the rest of me." I smirked. "In the form of The Carpenters, of all things."

"'Close to You'?"

"Right on the button," I said, tapping my nose. "I'm surprised you know that one."

"I listen to music," he said indignantly. "I just have to hear it in person, or I have to be far enough away for my *abschwören* not to interfere. Though it has been a while since I have heard that song."

I smiled, imagining Jove at a Carpenters concert. "Me too. I hadn't heard that song in years, and suddenly, it was playing over and over in my head. Just the one line involving birds." I leaned over the counter. "What's an *abschwören*?"

"Something we will speak of . . . when you are inducted into the Community. So what happened after the bird reminder? If the spell had worked, you would have just gone home as if nothing had happened instead of marching upstairs, calling me names, and assaulting me."

"Consent is paramount. I never consented to have my memory fucked with. You deserved every moment of what you got." I sniffed in indignation. "What was that thing you did with my name?"

"I used your *titel*, the name you gave me yourself when I hired you." He came around to my side of the counter and started putting away the other books from the shipment. "Every creature of knowing has one. With you, I only had a partial *titel* as I do not know your whole name. A *titel* can also change with how a person sees themselves. It is no longer as powerful if the subject no longer recognizes the *titel* as part of their name."

"Like how someone knows their maiden name, but connects more with their married name, if they change it, because they've been using their married name longer."

He nodded. "It is also something you should hold precious. Never give a magical being your full name from your own lips."

Creature of knowing—that was an interesting way to put sentient. This magic could be a dangerous thing in the wrong hands. "It gives you power over them?"

"*Ja*, it calls someone on a primal level. Once you have their attention, different things happen. Humans pay attention and usually do the next thing they are told. The Fae will answer when they hear the call. It is dangerous to call the Fae." His face paled, and he shuddered. "Incredibly dangerous to call the Fae."

"Got it." I grabbed the cleaning cloth from under the register. "And the air anomalies?"

"No, Mira, just no." Jove got serious, then. "If they know you can see through that, then you are nothing more than meat. Especially if you truly are just human as you claim."

A customer came in then, interrupting our conversation. Jove shelved the books in his hands, and I operated the register. It was as natural as breathing to jump in again. Just after the customer left, a loud crash came from what I affectionately called Jove's dungeon.

I jumped from behind the counter. "What the hell was that?"

Jove growled, grabbed an old book off the shelf, and made a beeline for the basement.

11

"Verdammt, I lost track of time! Stay here," he snapped, shutting the door behind him. I locked the entrance to the store and put up the closed sign temporarily. There was no way I was getting left behind, not when I was finally getting some answers. I then grabbed the handle to the dungeon and pulled. The heavy door opened with a groan. Jove was already down the short stairway and chanting in German. It sounded lyrical, like music, but with only one note.

I'd never been down here before. It didn't really register when I'd been working here. I just thought it was an area with toxic fumes, and Jove didn't have enough personal protective equipment for us. I blinked to help my eyes adjust faster. Surprisingly, there were candles everywhere. Everything from small votives to twelve-inch pillar candles were placed strategically throughout the basement, giving the place an eerie glow. It reminded me of the Phantom of the Opera's lair but with less river water. "Uh . . . don't you restore books down here, Jove? One would think you wouldn't want fire."

"That is not the real problem here," he intoned, keeping in time with his chant. "I must bind it before it burns down the store." Something chittered angrily at Jove from one of the many dark corners.

"Well, don't you sound like a bundle of cheer?" I murmured, scanning the dim room. There were bookshelves lining the one wall in various stages of repair. Opposite them was a table with glue and thread to rebind some of the older books. Next to that was a tub with unidentifiable chemicals in it. Stacks of books stood as tall as most men in various places around the room. Candles were everywhere, providing the only source of light. I should have brought a flashlight.

I only caught a glimpse of the creature, but it was a small, lithe creature with big eyes and ears that were perfect for the gloomy basement. It had two thin legs and two scrawny arms, but it used them as if they were all legs. It stuck to the wall, just like a bug, the candlelight shining off its dark, leathery skin. It looked like how my Opa had always described an imp or gremlin in stories. The damned thing was fast, the talons on its feet tapping against the worked bricks of the basement floor.

The creature popped up on the top of a stack of refinished books that stood almost as tall as the pillar candle next to them. The candle stood between the books and a sink full of chemicals. The thing looked at me with an evil little grin.

Imagine one of those tiny carnivorous dinosaurs from Jurassic Park. Now, make it smile at you. Creepy, isn't it?

Sharp, pointed teeth glinted in the candlelight as it reached out with one hand-like claw and pushed over the candle. Before gravity could pull it any further, I grabbed the candle and dropped the broom.

"Why, you little hell monkey." I then *grabbed* said hell monkey with my ability and held him squirming midair. "Where do you need it, Jove?"

"Fair lady!" the thing screeched in a tiny voice. "Pretty lady, let me go!"

I almost did out of sheer shock. I bobbled it in the air but quickly righted it again to look it in the face. "You can talk?"

"Oh yes, Pretty lady. I can do anything you want if you get me out of this evil Zauberer's laboratory. Please, please! Let me go!"

"Mira, put it into the circle I have set on the floor," Jove said. "Once it is bound again, all will be well."

"Sorry, little dude, he's the boss." I gently walked with the creature floating beside me to the chalk circle on the floor. "No hard feelings?"

"No, I understand. Is it so bad that I want to stretch my legs occasionally?" The thing sighed, drooping. It looked like a sulking cat when it wasn't grinning maniacally. Its large leathery ears drooped as he mourned. "The Zauberer works me all the time, and I don't even get a day off!"

"That little liar must be goaded to work all the time," Jove said. I gently placed the imp in the chalk. Its clawed feet touched the concrete in the center of the circle. It lit up as if it had an electric current running through the chalk lines. Jove stopped chanting, sighed, and approached the circle. "Was this really necessary, Gr'heghg?"

I blinked. The creature's name was Greg? It sat and scowled at Jove, crossing his thin little arms over a bird-like chest.

"You knew our contract was up today, buddy. It was your own fault you were late for our meeting." From nowhere discernible, Greg pulled out a pair of reading glasses and a stack of papers. It started flipping through until it got to the part it wanted to read. "The party of the first part will relinquish control over the party of the second part unless the contract is renegotiated and approved by the party of the second part. The penalty for being late for the aforementioned renegotiation is the destruction of whatever the party of the second part deems fun."

"I was only ten minutes late!" Jove protested.

"Twenty." Greg threw the glasses and paper into the air, where they disappeared in a puff of yellowish, acrid smoke. "And on top of it, you brought another Zauberer into the mix. Since when did you get such a powerful partner?"

"I hate to interrupt, Greg," I said. "However, I am not—"

"Not one of concern to you, gremlin." Jove put himself between me and Greg. I guess he didn't want the imp to know about me.

"It's Gr'heghg. If you're going to use my *titel*, use it correctly." It smiled around Jove to look at me. The smile made my skin crawl. "Call me, and I will come."

"For a price," said Jove, crossing his arms. "Now, if you are finished destroying my lab, let us get down to business." Jove sat cross-legged in front of the imp. "To extend your contract by another twenty years, what are your terms?"

"The promise of your firstborn?"

"*Nein.*"

"Your full *titel*, from your own lips."

"*Nein.*"

"Oh, come on, you've got to give a little here."

"A coin from my pocket," returned Jove.

"*Nein,*" said the imp. "What do you take me for, Zauberer? A human?"

"The first letter of my *titel.*"

"You know *titels* don't work like that!" Greg stamped a little clawed foot in anger. "I'd need the whole name to make any use of it whatsoever! I already have two parts, Zauberer. It's only a matter of time before I weasel the others from your lips."

They went at it for over an hour. I sat on the stairs, watching them. This was a rare insight into this new world. I wanted to absorb as much as I could. I wished I could have taken notes.

Jove offered little things, and Greg demanded big things. There was a massive argument about a strand of hair. Apparently, such a thing would give Greg a lot of power against Jove. I watched, fascinated. Opa had told me stories about gremlins and how they would work their way into factories and airfields, loosening bolts and stealing small but vital parts of things. Opa claimed that a building he was working on once collapsed because an imp damaged the cornerstone. And here I was looking at one.

I smiled. I had an idea. I went upstairs to the small drawer beneath the register. We had a clear tub I had marked 'lost and found.' It only took me a minute of digging to find my prize. It had been there for years, so I doubted the owner would be back to retrieve it any time soon. I grabbed the object in my hand and returned to the basement.

"Hey, Jove, I—"

Jove held up a hand for quiet. I shrugged and sat down next to him.

Okay, fine, I have an answer to your problem, but you don't want to listen to me? Casually, I started pushing the buttons on my prize, activating the digital pet inside. It chirped and cooed at me as I played with it.

"What is that?" Greg's voice filled with wonder. It craned its neck around Jove again to see what was making the noise.

"A gadget," I said simply, feeding the pixelated dog.

"Can I see it?" Its face was pressed up against the magical field and flattened as if it were pressed against glass. He looked like something out of a cartoon if the cartoon was of a creepy anthropomorphic micro dinosaur with long arms, that is.

I shrugged casually. "I'd be glad to let you see it . . . but . . . it's not mine. I borrowed it from Jove here." I let the toy lie flat in my hand, and then I *slowly* raised it up with my mind and let it turn between my hands. "Neat, huh? Imagine all those little bits and pieces that make these things work."

Greg whimpered and snapped its gaze back to Jove. "I will do your bidding for another twenty years if you keep me supplied with those."

"I don't know . . ." Jove scratched his chin. "Those don't come cheap. You want me to keep you supplied with them? It would cost you fifty years."

"*Fifty?* That is outrageous!" Greg's slitted eyes flashed an otherworldly green. "Twenty, and I'll toss in an extra year for free." I made the toy float just out of his reach.

Jove must have been tired of me teasing the imp. He snatched it out of the air and held it in his open hand. "Thirty years, and I will give you a microwave to play with at Christmas."

Greg's eyes danced. "Done!" He snatched the toy out of Jove's hand, smiling with triumph. "A pleasure doing business with you, Erik Brandt."

Huh, I didn't know one of his names was Erik. Jove stiffened, his body at attention. Aw, hell, that little bastard just used Jove's *titel*. I wondered if it worked the same on Zauberers as it did on regular humans.

"Kiss the girl, Erik. She just saved your lab," Greg said. Jove turned to me. His eyes didn't look right. Jove was like a zombie as he stood. Not seeing, not hearing, he *had* to do what that little monster had told him to. Apparently, it worked the same on Zauberers. Eep.

"Why, you smarmy little mutant!" I snarled at the imp. "And what if I don't want a kiss?"

"Then you'll have learned not to interfere with a contract that isn't your own." Greg cackled as Jove leaned over and tried to grab me. I *pushed* myself to a standing position and took a couple of steps back. Then, for an instant, his eyes changed. Jove looked hurt. It stopped me in my tracks. I didn't want to hurt him. He grabbed my hand and bowed over it. I felt his lips warm against the back of my hand. I blinked in surprise as my heart gave one big thud. Whoa. Where the hell had *that* come from?

"You never have to fear me, Mira," he said, his eyes dark as he looked up at me over his glasses. His eyes were the color of warm milk chocolate. Why hadn't I noticed that before? He turned my hand over and kissed the inside of my palm. It felt incredibly intimate, very different from when he'd kissed my hand at the hospital. Goosebumps went up my arm as his breath tickled over the pulse point. Blink, thud, whoa.

I was still getting my bearings when Jove turned back to the gremlin. "That was uncalled for. You are not to use what part of my *titel* you do have as stipulated in the original contract to force my behavior during negotiations." I couldn't see his face, but I could tell he was smiling. "As punishment, you restore fourteen magical tomes free of charge."

Greg chuckled. "Worth it."

I hate gremlins.

12

I surprised myself by getting back to my apartment at a half-decent hour, giving me plenty of time to work on my research. After the disappointing meetings, the 'lunchus interuptus,' and the imp, concentration was proving challenging. I tried to distract myself with another experiment.

I turned on the video in the kitchen, framing my shot. I had on a baking apron at the table with a bowl in front of me. I'd moved my little table so I could show how my ability was able to control multiple things at once. If I did everything right, I'd have a cake to go with my ice cream.

I smiled at the blinking red light. "I'm Doctor Mira Hall, and this is Experiment Three. Having found my weight threshold, I am now working to find out how many things I can do at one time. So, today, I'm baking a cake."

I held out a hand, and a box of cake mix flew into it. I'd left the cupboard open to have one less thing to concentrate on. The camera *panned* and focused on the refrigerator. The door opened without a hand to guide it. I began to read off the ingredients I needed from the back of the box.

"Three eggs and a cup of milk." The eggs and milk carton pulled themselves out and floated in mid-air.

My smile widened. It was working! The camera panned, following the flight of the food.

"I also need oil, a spoon, and a cake pan while I crack the eggs into the bowl to mix."

The camera moved to the cabinets as they, too, opened to accommodate my demands. While the camera followed the flight, there was the sound of a smashing egg. The rest of the flying implements fell to the floor with various clatters and bangs.

"Well, hell. I'm going to have to work on that. Note: do not hold too many things mid-air at once. Not until I can keep my concentration in check."

Which was nigh impossible. My brain was running in too many directions. I had too many questions and not enough answers.

So, I did what I always did when I was like this: I hit the net to do some research.

After seeing Bird-boy, all my hindbrain told me was, 'Scary monster! Run!' Which wasn't helpful. My parents had always taught us to combat fear with knowledge. So here I was, go-go-gadget Googling. Ravens are known as highly intelligent, greedy, and determined birds. Jove had called them 'The Unkindness.' Unkindness is an archaic name for a group of ravens. It figured a bunch of half-birds took it as their name. Folklore had them as creators and destroyers, angels, and demons. I'd describe them as chaotic neutral. Out for themselves—at least, that's what the research told me. I'd finally gotten back into a good rhythm with my typing and writing up the first few pages of a thesis, and I was really starting to get sucked in.

I wasn't expecting the single hard knock on my door. I had been in the middle of an extensive train of thought, completely lost in my work. The sound was so loud and jarring that I jolted, bobbling my laptop. I managed to *catch* it with my ability before it hit the floor. The knock came twice more before I realized there had to be a person on the other side.

"J—just a minute!" I grabbed the laptop out of the air and set it gently down on the couch.

I looked through the peephole. A chill raced up my spine. I couldn't see anything but black swirling smoke. *Oh, my God, FIRE!* I thought. Just then, the fire alarm screamed through the air. Had I not heard it before now? Was I that far into my work? I shook my head. No way. There was no way I'd have missed a fire alarm.

I twisted away from the door and grabbed Toria's carrier. I was not evacuating without her. She must have seen me get the carrier. That cat managed to squeeze herself between one of my bookshelves and the wall where I usually couldn't reach her. Normally. I opened the door to the carrier and set it on the floor in front of the cat. One telekinetic push later, I had a very confused cat securely in her carrier. I snagged my purse and my laptop from the couch and raced to the door.

I tapped the doorknob to estimate if there was a fire on the other side. Not only wasn't it hot, it was *cold*. Very cold. That made me pause. Something didn't feel right here. There was *frost* on my doorknob. I opened the door slowly and stepped back. The door was blocked with black swirling smoke, but instead of rolling into my apartment, it stayed on the other side of my threshold as if glass blocked its path. I felt my heart stutter in fear as I peered into its depths.

As I watched, the swirling darkness changed into countless wings and feathers. Birds—no, Ravens—flew in front of my now-open front door. Instead of caws emitting from their throats, it was the unmistakable sound of a fire alarm. The screaming siren became croaking calls and fluttering wings. A cold wind blew into my living room, making my arms break out in goosebumps. I felt my body start to shake as I stood my ground.

It was like something out of a horror movie. Sharp beaks and talons looked like they wanted to tear me apart. I was frozen to the spot, my face pale, as I stared at the spectacle before me.

Toria hissed and spat from inside her carrier. I felt my right hand move on its own. The bracelet jangled musically as my fingers squeezed the locking mechanism on the wire door. As soon as the bars moved out of her way, Toria launched out of the carrier. Claws extended, ears pinned to the sides of her head, my little cat pounced into the mass of fowl. I screamed, lost my balance, and landed on my ass. The birds recoiled from the cat, roiling away as they flew down the hall and out of sight as if they'd never been there. I heard a thump, and then deathly silence reigned. I was moving almost before I got my feet under me. Please let her be okay. Please, be okay, kitten.

In the middle of the carpeted hallway stood my cat, blood on her mouth and a feathered neck in her teeth. I goggled at the body of a large black bird. Its neck twisted at an impossible angle. Toria dragged the fresh carcass over to me, her legs waddling around the body of the bird as she dropped it at my feet. Then she meowed at me and gave me a look that said, *THIS* is how you hunt.

"You are getting treats for dessert for the rest of your fuzzy life," I informed her, picking her up. She protested. My little girl hates being manhandled. "Now, what to do with it." We both looked down at the body. I shuddered. I couldn't leave it out in the hallway for anyone to find. God only knew what might happen. I went back inside and tossed Toria in my bedroom, closing her in. I then went to the kitchen and got a plastic bag from the stash I usually used to get rid of cat litter. I inverted the bag on my hand so I could pick it up without technically touching it. I put the body on the table and stared at it.

My mind kicked into overdrive, replaying everything that had just happened in slow motion. The smoke, the fire alarm . . . it'd been an Unkindness trick. Going through it again in my head, none of my neighbors had opened their doors to escape the 'fire.' The smoke had been familiar as well, the dense color and swirls just like the smoke that had filled the cab of the truck the night of the accident. They had used my fears against me. They'd used that night against me. I felt myself getting pissed off again but took a deep, calming breath instead. I had to think logically.

Why would the Unkindness use their powers on me? For what purpose? To get me out into the hall. And I *had* gone out into the hall, but instead of taking me when I went to get Toria, they'd let me be. Birds and cats had a tendency to be natural enemies. Maybe they'd been afraid of my little cat getting another one of them. So, then, why get me out of my apartment? Just to be mean? No, that didn't play. This had to be because of the deal with Jove that went sour. My blood ran cold. They had wanted to take me. Bird-boy had said that High Raven would want proper payment. I owed my tiny Toria high-quality, expensive treats. My next move was to call Jove. He would know what to do with the body of a mythical creature.

He made the half-hour drive in ten minutes.

"You shouldn't have been speeding," I chided him when I answered the door.

"If you have what you say you have, then I was not going fast enough."

"Please, come in," I invited him verbally. We were dealing with magic. I wanted the only Wizard I knew at full power. I crossed my arms over my chest and led him to my little table.

He froze, staring at the plastic bag. "Is that it?"

"Yup." A loud meow came from the direction of my bedroom. "And that would be our little heroine." I opened the door, and Toria sauntered in, deliberately ignoring me to look up at the Wizard. She meowed again.

Jove bent down and scratched between her ears and under her chin. "*Ja*, you are a mighty huntress, pretty one. Not every cat can bring down such a beast."

"Oh hush, she'll put on airs for the rest of the year." I smirked and went into the kitchen to get the treats. "Not that she doesn't deserve it." I poured the little morsels into Toria's food and told Jove everything I'd seen. My hands were shaking as I started a pot of water for tea. I needed something to do with my hands, or those needles of panic were going to pull me down onto my knees.

"Smoke is one of the favored illusions of the Unkindness. They are masters of trickery. They use the panic of being suddenly presented with the threat of fire to make the victim waltz into their waiting wings." He leaned against the door frame, watching me. "Many people do not think of such illusions being dangerous, but they are very wrong."

"Tell me about it. I really thought there was a fire." I shook again. "Just like with the truck."

"From your accident?" His tone sharpened.

I nodded, my face grim. "Yeah. The smoke swirled just like that. I still can't believe the police couldn't find it afterward. With smoke like that in the cab of a truck, he would have had to pull over. I even got payments from their insurance company."

"What was the name of the company?"

"No idea; money just started appearing in my account that read 'Insurance payment.' The bank couldn't give me any information on how to contact them, and the driver didn't show up at the hospital to swap info. I thought it was something Momma set up. She's worked with insurance companies for years. She would have known what needed doing."

"So, you do not know the truck itself or its origins. Or even if it was an 'accident' at all." His voice sounded grave.

Why would creatures I had no idea even existed try to kill me? Jove was silent, his features drawn. The water heated to the point just before boiling. I turned off the heat and added the tea bag to let it steep while I thought about when I'd last seen that look on his face. It looked the same when he brought me those sad tulips in the hospital.

"What do we do with the body?" I held teacups, handing him one.

He took it gently from me while he considered. "We wait. The Unkindness will send someone to collect it. However, we need to put it in something a tad more dignified than a plastic grocery bag. We do not need them to be angry at us."

"You're worried about *them* being angry? Don't I have the right to be angry?" I felt the quickening in my blood as my face flushed. "What if I had just rushed out into the hall, screaming? I have several nosy neighbors. It would have drawn attention."

"They would have had a plan for that. They were using their magic to dampen or alter the sound. They would have taken you, Mira. However, they would not keep you for long. I would not permit that."

"Bullshit. If they are the ones who caused my accident, then, for all I know, they came to finish the job. In all the research I've done about the Raven stories, they don't mention kidnapping. He steals things and tricks people."

"The thing they would have stolen was you, Kleine. To them, you do not count as 'people.'"

"Well, I am *not* a thing to be stolen. They'll have to see what it means to tangle with someone who knows where all the nerves are."

"You amaze me." Jove chuckled. "Instead of running for the next county, you do research."

"I'm not going to just sit around after meeting a supernatural being without researching to learn as much as I can about the lore. Think about it, Jove. I've been seeing ravens flying around me for a week now." I crossed my arms over my chest for warmth, thinking of the incident at the diner. "We're assuming they want to take me. This attempt was bold. Thankfully, less potentially lethal than a car accident, but bold all the same."

Jove paled and blinked. "You said you did not go out into the hall. Why? Most humans would have at least had some part of their body cross the threshold. That would have been what they were expecting you to do."

I shook my head. "Something wasn't right. The doorknob wasn't hot. It was cold. It was like sticking my hand on an ice cube. It had *frost* on it, for God's sake. It wasn't right. If there was an actual fire, it should have been hot."

I watched as Jove slid the body of the bird out from one bag and into another, more dignified, silken sack with a red drawstring. The bag had an angular rune embroidered in gold. Jove saw me looking at it. "It is a rune of protection. We want nothing else to happen to this poor fellow to hinder his journey to Raven."

"I have something else we can put that in, so we aren't just giving them a bag, if we are talking about respect for the dead, that is."

He paused, considering. "What do you have?"

"Just a minute, I'll go grab it." I put my teacup on the table, headed into my room, and closed the door behind me. I felt myself getting more and more enraged with every step as the thoughts of what these people wanted to do to me swirled in my mind. Whether they wanted to take me or finish the job from my accident and kill me was inconsequential. They had no right, *no right* to make me feel unsafe in my home. Fuck that. *Fuck that!* This rage, however, did not mean I was going to treat the body of a sentient being poorly. I took a few deep, cleansing breaths before kneeling and reaching under my bed.

I pulled out a wooden box with an ornate fatherly face carved into the top, surrounded by ivy vines, from under my bed. I picked it up at a yard sale, so I wasn't terribly attached to it. It reminded me of one of the legends Momma told me as a kid. The Green Knight was one of my favorite ones. It was gory, but it was a story of true honor. I heard a low whistle behind me and flushed with embarrassment. "Expecting a war, Mira? You are positively armed to the teeth."

I flushed. Of course, Jove followed me. Damn it. I'd been so furious about my attempted kidnapping that I hadn't heard him behind me. I didn't even hear the door open. "I don't suppose you'd believe none of this is mine?"

"Not on your life. Is that a bullwhip?" The sound of wonder in his voice made me laugh.

"Along with a replica of Doctor Jones' hat, yes." Still kneeling by the bed, I opened the box and upended it onto my bed.

Out poured some of the miniature replicas I had, as well as my practice pair of nunchucks, cleaning oils, polyhedral dice, and whetstones. I'd find another place for them or try to get another box online. The inside of the box was lined with black felt and smelled a little like cherries. "Respectful enough?"

"Oh yes." He gently took the box and helped me to my feet. "Who is Doctor Jones? Is that one of your professor doctors from school?"

I arched an eyebrow at him. "Seriously? It was only one of the most awesome roles Harrison Ford ever played! Second only to his role as Han Solo in Star Wars."

I must have looked shocked. Jove started to look uncomfortable and turned back to the living room. "Come, we have a body to deal with."

"True," I said soberly, following him through the door. I tried to wrap my head around never seeing a movie in theaters. *Ever.* It made me sad for my Wizard friend.

Jove was solemn as he laid the body to rest in the box. *"By the stars in the sky and the stone beneath our feet, rest easy on this leg of your journey home,"* he said in German. It sounded beautiful . . . like a heartfelt prayer. I closed my eyes and offered up a small prayer of my own. No matter what this raven had done to me, I believed in asking for peace for the dead. I'm not a great Christian, but I believe in Him, and I like to think He believes in me, too.

As soon as I unclasped my hands, a knock sounded at the door again. Much softer this time. I shot a look at Jove, who gently closed the lid and latched it before turning toward the door with the box in his hands. I had to speed up to match his pace to open the door for him.

On the other side of the door stood a beautiful woman with short blonde hair done in a reverse bob and dressed in a black business suit. She looked . . . competent, like she always had everything under control. On her neck was a broad silver choker with a charm dangling from the middle. The charm was a flying bird. "I am here for the member of the Unkindness whom you murdered."

"Murdered?" I protested.

Jove nudged me to be silent. "We have him," he said solemnly. "In return for his body, all we wish is to be left in peace."

"The woman will answer for her crime," she said through her teeth as her eyes narrowed at me over Jove's shoulder.

"Wait one single solitary minute. I think I deserve to know who is accusing me of murder." I crossed my arms, annoyed.

"I am Ms. Corvis. That is all you need," she said crossly.

"*Ladies, perhaps we can make a deal?*" Jove appeased. His voice was smooth as it spoke in his native tongue.

"Zauberer." Ms. Corvis hissed. "I should have known. You are the other reason my husband now lies dead."

"You can't have it both ways. Either this is my fault or his, according to you." I moved to stand beside Jove.

"If the Zauberer had been honest, High Raven wouldn't want *you*." She jabbed a well-manicured finger at me. She started to pace on the other side of my threshold. Her high heels tapped a rapid staccato on the hall floor. Her face was stoic, but her eyes flashed with a gleam that told me she'd rather be pecking out my eyes. "High Raven would never have had this bastard's precious tomes delivered if he knew he was getting a mere *farm* animal."

"In my defense," said Jove, "pure white goats are hard to find."

Ms. Corvis crossed her arms and aimed a steely glare at me over Jove's shoulder. "High Raven *raged* when the low raven brought it back. The low raven told the flock how the Zauberer had tricked us. He told us about *you, human*. Your beauty, your fighting prowess, and how you have *power*. You, Mira Hall, are the payment we expected for procuring those books for your Zauberer."

I was really starting to wonder why everyone kept saying I was beautiful. I have brown hair, hazel eyes, and big boobs. I'd received enough teasing throughout my school years to know that I was more than a few inches away from the standard of beauty. Nothing I did ever took the weight away from my arms, legs, or belly. I'd pushed aside the hurt from the constant teasing at school when Momma had her incident. It hardly matters what some idiot calls you if you're never going to see them again after you leave school, especially when someone actually important needs you. So, I pushed it aside and left it there.

"So good to have confirmation on something you suspect . . . like abduction. Welp, better than murder, I suppose."

"We *never* wanted to murder you. Idiot." Her voice was so sharp it made me want to flinch. She must have been hell in a boardroom. "It hardly seems fair that my husband is the one to pay that price. You were *supposed* to come racing out of your apartment, like a *normal* human, run out where the Unkindness was to gather you up and bring you to High Raven, where you belong. As *originally* agreed." She sent a pointed look at Jove. "You owe us proper payment, Zauberer."

"So, you were going to abduct me. I'd suspected as much once I had a moment to think," I said finally. "I saw through your illusion, Ms. Corvis. I would have never stepped over my threshold. I defended myself, and you failed. Ergo, not a murderer."

She quietly raged. "How dare you? You low-born bitch. You released that vicious beast who slew him as sure as if you'd shot him. You had no idea you needed to protect yourself."

"There were clues," I disagreed. I put on my cool doctor's persona. The one that you show to abusers who bring in their victims. The ones who scream in your face when you get in their way. The bullies who grew up and didn't know what to do once their victim pool shrank. I may not have a slew of nurses at my back, but I did have a legit Wizard and a cat. I let my cold stare meet her hot one. "No fire causes a doorknob to be cold. No smoke would be stopped by a threshold like it was stuck in a fish tank. I was able to penetrate your illusion by my means. I am not at fault for seeing through your tricks."

I softly laid a hand on the box Jove still held. "I am, however, deeply saddened that there was death over this. You had no way of knowing about my pet. I offer you my deepest condolences. I pray this, in some small way, shows my regret for your loss."

Gently, I took the box from Jove.

I then knelt on the floor and slid the box over the threshold. I didn't want her getting any fancy ideas about grabbing me and taking me to

High Raven herself. "Take your man. Lay him to rest in your fashion. Please tell your leader that I am now aware of his tricks and am not so easily fooled. My deepest condolences to you and your family." I bowed my head respectfully as she knelt and opened the box.

Her hands shook as she reached down into the box. Tears fell as she touched the dead through the dark cloth. Her breath came out in a ragged sob, the façade of concrete confidence cracking under the pressure of her pain. "You have given my husband such respect. I would not have given the same to you. Thank you for this. I will deliver your message to High Raven." With a soft click, she shut the lid on the makeshift coffin and lifted it. She rubbed her wet cheek against the wood. Holding it in her hands, she turned and walked down the hall.

"This is not the last you will see of the Unkindness, Mira," Jove warned softly as we watched the elevator doors close behind Ms. Corvis.

"I know," I heard myself say, but it sounded hollow. I was too drained to deal with anything more by this point.

"I did not know High Raven would fixate on you when he discovered my deception." Jove's voice was starting to sound desperate.

I couldn't tell what he wanted me to believe here. Maybe he wanted a show of my sympathy, maybe my forgiveness. I don't know. I was reeling from what I'd seen in Ms. Corvis's eyes. I'd been so angry, so self-righteous in defending myself from these magical beings. But they really were beings with love, terror, despair, and pain . . . just like me. Despite their monstrous appearance and their terrifying power, they were beings, if not *human* beings, and my cat had killed her husband.

I didn't know what to say to Jove other than another, "I know."

"That was a good thing we did for Ms. Corvis and her husband," he said hopefully, trying to have me engage more.

My voice softened as I gently pushed him over the threshold and out of my apartment. "Yeah, we did. Good night, Jove."

13

THE NEXT DAY, I could almost feel myself becoming hyper-aware of my surroundings. I was cringing at every slight sound, just in case it was the Unkindness back to take me. It was only paranoia if someone wasn't really after you. Nothing was as creepy as knowing someone wanted to abduct you.

I'd seen some instances of women being drugged by a napkin or flyer on their windshield. The assholes would drench the paper in chemicals that can cross cellular membranes and poison their victims to make them more pliable. That's why I was planning on using public transport today. I'd pick up a box of gloves somewhere on my way home. I hoped the Unkindness didn't know about those chemicals. I expected the pepper spray and the panic alarm in my purse would work should the need arise. I'd almost left the apartment when I got this niggling feeling on the back of my neck. So, I also added a whistle to my keychain and tossed in a pink camo stun gun that Ankle Kay had given me the day I moved to the city. I took a breath and headed out the door to my next bank appointment.

My shoulders slumped as I walked with the crowd to get to the bus stop afterward. Another short meeting, another quick rejection. "We're sorry, Doctor Hall, but the market isn't good right now. We can't take the risk on someone who hasn't been in a practice before."

I wasn't doing well in getting my business loan started. It was almost as bad as trying to get a job right out of school with no experience. These loan officers kept looking at me like I was just some kid. I was frustrated and annoyed.

The stop I was at was next to Penn Park. Maybe I needed to take a walk through the park to level out. I angled away from the bus stop and went to the entrance that connected to the street.

Almost immediately, I felt like I was stepping out of the city and into a quiet place full of green-growing things. The morning was bright and sunny. Light peeked shyly through the branches and leaves of the surrounding trees. It was peaceful, happy, and super contrary to my mood. It should be gloomy and raining, maybe with some slow, sad blues playing in the background.

I practically leaped out of my skin when a hand landed on my shoulder. I spun around, my fists up.

"Whoa there, Rocky." David stood there holding up his hands. "I didn't mean to scare you."

I let my arms relax. "Sorry, I've just . . . got stuff going on. What are you doing here?"

"We have a demonstration here today for agility rookies. It looks like there is some heavy stuff on that mind of yours. Come on, I'll buy you something to eat. You look like you could use it." He fell into step beside me. "We were just cleaning up anyway."

"You saying I'm too skinny?" I smirked. He and I both knew I'd been complaining about being too heavy for years.

"I'm not falling into that trap, Mira. You've got circles under your eyes, and you're pale." I heard concern creep into his voice. "I can tell by looking at you that you haven't slept well."

"Yeah, well, rough night." At his look, I shrugged. I couldn't tell him the nitty-gritty about what happened last night. So, I tried a lie. "It was no big deal, just some kids playing a stupid prank on me."

Fibber, fibber.

"Be careful then. People be crazy." David walked closer to me. It was starting to bother me. I took another step to the side to put some distance between us. I didn't want him to trip over me. "What kind of prank?"

"Smoke bomb. It really freaked out some of my neighbors. It was really only a dinky thing. We didn't even need to call the fire department." I didn't look at him. I'm not the best liar, and David usually pegged me when I lied to him.

He would tell me it was the Force that ratted me out or his mutant telepathy that he learned from Professor X. But not today. Instead, he wrapped an arm around my shoulders, pulling me close to him. It felt awkward and borderline creepy. But this was David. I never got the creep vibe from him. Knowing that didn't stop my skin from crawling at the contact. "Must have been horrible, frightening."

"Yeah." I was glad he let it go so quickly. I wouldn't say I liked lying to him. He would have me put up in the mental health ward if I told him birds were trying to abduct me. I didn't know why he was being so clingy. It was starting to freak me out. Speaking of birds . . . I looked around. How did we get in a more secluded part of the park? Why wasn't I hearing any? I didn't like being this far away from other people. "We should head back," I said, trying to take another step back from him. "My next meeting with another bank is soon. I have to get a move on to make the bus."

"Aw, pretty Mira, what's the rush?" His arm tightened around my shoulders. I looked up into David's face. It warped before my eyes, sprouting black feathers around his rapidly changing features: broader nose, darker eyes, and a wicked grin.

Crap on a crepe at Christmas, this wasn't *my* David. My hand dove into my purse and pulled my spray. The man was lightning-quick and grabbed my wrist before I could bring the spray to his face. He shook my arm, forcing me to drop the canister. Instead of falling to the ground, as gravity really wanted it to, it floated, nozzle pointed at faux David. The Bird-boy gawked at it. "It is *true*. You have power." I sprayed it in his face. He let out a squawk-like scream and released me.

Coughing, I ran toward the fountain in the center of the park, my lungs burning from the residual capsaicin in the air. Some of the spray had gotten into my lungs and stung my eyes. I struggled a little as I ran toward what I hoped would be a more populated area. Maybe someone in there could help me. This time of year, mothers let their kids splash in the water.

I heard a *whoosh* sound behind me and was quickly blocked by the Bird-boy. "That wasn't very nice, Mira."

"Neither is abduction. In fact, I'm positive it's a felony." I dodged to the side to try and get around him. Damn, he was fast. "Your boss is trying for the direct approach, huh?"

"You were promised to us—"

"Was not!"

"High Raven will get what he wants," Faux David said, ignoring me. He took a step closer. "And what he wants is you."

"I'm warning you now, you son of a hen, I will defend myself. I belong to no one." I used my ability and grabbed the camo stun gun, slammed it against his chest, and pulled the trigger. I ran in the opposite direction while his body jerked and twitched. I wasn't sure how fast he would recover. I didn't make the typical mistakes movie heroines make. I didn't stop to look over my shoulder. I just ran. My heart pounded in my ears as fast as my feet did over the grass. I had to move fast before he recovered. I stayed away from the tree line that marked the thicker part of the park's trees. I didn't want to be anywhere near those trees. A girl could get ambushed like that.

"Whoa, Mir! What's the matter? Why do I smell pepper spray?" David suddenly appeared in the direction I was running.

How could I be sure this was *my* David? My mind raced, and I came up with a pop quiz. No one knew Marvel movies like David Erickson. "Quick." I panted, stopping a few feet away from him. "According to the X-Men movie in two thousand, why was Magneto so sure there would be a mutant genocide?"

"Because, when he was coming into his powers, he was in a concentration camp. Duh, Mira, we saw that movie together, remember? We were at my parents' place."

I went over to him and hugged him tight. I was shivering from running … yeah, running, that's my story, and I'm sticking to it.

"Mira, are you okay? You're pale and clammy. Holy Hell, you're shaking!" He ran his hand over my hair and looked around. "Why did you use your pepper spray? I can smell it on you."

I looked over my shoulder and saw the Bird-boy melt into the shadows of the tree line. I shuddered. "There was a mugger. I used the pink stunner on him, too. He tried to grab my purse. I'm okay now."

Concern overtook his features. That and something closer to rage. He pulled me in close. This felt much safer than it had with his doppelgänger. He growled. "Where are they?"

"I don't know. I sprayed them, stunned them, and booked it. Look, could you walk me to the bus stop? I'm not feeling so hot." I shivered again as we walked toward the park exit. I was going to ditch that appointment. I didn't need another rejection on top of what I'd just gone through.

"I'm going to do you one better. I'm taking you home—my car's right over there. We're gonna get you home and maybe get in an episode or two of *Doctor Who*. That'll level you out."

I nodded as he led me to his little blue Volkswagen. It took longer than I want to admit for my hands to stop shaking. David set up a little marathon of my favorite episodes and bought pizza from my favorite place.

I snuggled under the heavy blanket I kept under the couch with my best friend, selfishly using him for warmth. I shouldn't have felt so cold, but his face warping into the cruel, beaked face of the bird man was enough to make my skin crawl. I found myself constantly studying David's face to make sure it wasn't moving or rippling. He camped out on my couch. I knew he would. The man had the uncanny ability to tell when I wasn't feeling safe and needed to have him there.

I stared up at the stucco ceiling in bed and contemplated the last twenty-four hours. I'd been so full of it last night when I had a Wizard at my back. What had I been thinking—challenging them like that? I thought I had this under control. I knew they were after me. I knew they had the power of illusion. I just thought forewarned was fore-armed. Clearly, I was wrong. I was now down one can of pepper spray and one stun gun. I was less armed than ever. I had to be a lot more vigilant than I had been. I was as susceptible to illusions as ever. That would have to change. I wasn't going to let anyone within six feet of me without checking somehow.

But what was a good way to check?

I remembered the bloody corpse of the raven that Toria had killed. Their blood was red, just like any other bird—nothing to go on there. The air didn't shimmer around them like it did on the air anomalies, so I couldn't tell that way. The Unkindness seemed to have their own power to hide themselves rather than relying on whatever created the veils. But their illusions weren't perfect. I needed to know more about the Unkindness and their abilities if I was going to go against them.

⁂

"They're getting bolder, Jove," I said softly when I went to Bindings the next day. "I was barely able to tell this fake David from the real one. Is there some law against abduction in the Community?"

"There is, yes. However, said laws get mired in murk when a group as powerful as The Unkindness is involved. Especially seeing as *you* are not a member of the Community yet. One more reason to get your name in the Charter sooner rather than later. I am working with my contacts to get someone here to get it done. Sadly, we are being mired down by Zauberer politics."

On Wednesdays, I would bring dinner for the three workers of Bindings, and Jove would make tea so we could get the displays ready for the new releases. I was going to miss things like this when I got my practice up and running. I separated the white boxes of Chinese food for Jove and Katie to grab. I opened mine to mix the rice and the walnut sauce with my chopsticks. I wanted to keep some of our usual rituals even though I didn't technically work there anymore. Jove and Katie were friends. I wouldn't stop seeing my friends because of some birds. Katie hadn't come down yet for her portion.

"What happened when you realized the person was not *Schnucki*?"

"You know, he hates when you call him that."

"Ah, but his face is so adorable when I do." He grinned. Jove had been dusting the rare books in the locked case behind the counter when I came in to tell him about the flock's latest movements and to bring dinner. He had his shirt sleeves rolled up to the elbows with his glasses perched on the end of his nose. Part of me wanted to take a bite out of him instead of my walnut shrimp.

I paced in front of the register, still working through what happened. "His face started to shift around and sprout feathers. It was bizarre." I gestured with my chopsticks. A thought struck me. "Was that me penetrating his illusion?"

"Yes. Your ability is proving dangerous to Community secrets, and that is dangerous for you." Jove sipped tea from a steaming mug on the counter. "However, your ability was only part of the reason you were able to see the truth."

"What's the other part?" I started to dig into my little white box.

"I have to tell you something about your bracelet." He leaned over the counter, took my hand with the bangle, and smiled. "Mr. Fynn crafted the bracelet itself. However, the magic woven into it is my own."

The *for you* was left unsaid but hung in the air and wrapped around me like a warm scarf. I blushed and pulled back my hand.

"Should we be talking about this with Katie in the building? The food is going to bring her down eventually," I pointed out.

Jove gave me a sly smile. "You do not need to worry. I gave her the night off."

"Really? Usually, you need the extra help on Wednesdays. We're going to have a lot of leftover food here." I'd gotten used to the routine of the three of us eating Chinese and chatting about books and customers. I then noticed that Jove had only brought out two teacups. I took a sip and was surprised to find he'd already doctored it to my liking. I used the cup to gesture at the rest of the food boxes. "What are we going to do with it all?"

"I will give it to the gremlin. He likes the sound of the names of some of the food. Kung pao and pu pu platters make him laugh." Jove chuckled. "I cannot believe you called him 'Greg.'"

"That's what I thought I heard you say." I shrugged. What had happened in the basement flitted around my mind—especially the heart-thudding kiss on my wrist. I was finding it more challenging to relax when it was just Jove and me. Alone. Like now. I drank a little deeper from my teacup and tried to change the subject. I held up my wrist and let the light play over the charms. "You gave me this right before the accident."

"Correct." He nodded, swallowing a teriyaki noodle. We'd gotten lucky, and the new Chinese food place down the block did fusion food, blending Chinese with Japanese. The sushi was worth it.

"Why did you give me a charmed charm bracelet, Jove?" I watched him as he set his tea back onto the counter and picked up another one of the small white cartons, presumably to make up a box for Greg.

"It is a protection circle with charms against different types of magic. The Eye of Horus helps you see through illusions." He forked some pork fried rice into his mouth. Jove always refused to eat with chopsticks. I waited for him to say more, to explain why he'd given it to me before the accident, but he kept eating.

"Is that why I can see the veils?" I spoke around my food. I grabbed my water bottle to wash it down.

"No." He shook his head. "Veils are much more powerful. I do not yet know why you can see those. Your other charms are subtle." Jove put down his food and came around the counter. He took my tea and placed it on the nearby coffee table. Holding my hand in his, he pointed to each little charm on the bracelet. I couldn't stop the little thrill the contact shot up my spine. "These are the Chinese symbols for 'protection.' They help direct you to do things to protect yourself."

"Like how I opened Toria's cage? The charm made me do it?" I wasn't sure I liked the idea of being controlled by anything. I'd already resolved never to tell Jove my middle name. God knew what he could make me do with my complete *titel*. Not that I didn't trust him, but I didn't want anyone to have that kind of power over me.

"Yes, it did, but it only does that in extreme cases when you are not sure of what action to take. It can guide your actions, but it cannot force you to do something you would not normally do." He pointed to the next charm. "This is a Celtic cross."

"I recognized that one." I smiled. "My aunt has one tattooed on her ankle."

"I thought you might. This one will help protect you from Demons like the imp. Stronger Fallen may overpower it, but as long as you are resolved to be against them, they will not possess you. I also thought you would like the look of it."

He wasn't wrong. I loved the delicate look of the charms and the tinkling sound they made when I moved. I frowned over what he said. So, Demons were real too; I'd wondered after the episode with Greg. The thrill turned into a chill. I'd heard, read, and watched horrible stories about possession. It was something that put fear right into my soul. I was glad it was a cross that was protecting me from that. I pointed to the last charm. "What about this one?"

"That is my personal shield. If you are ever lost or taken, I will be able to find you." He pulled my hand up and kissed the inside of my wrist. "You mean much to me, Kleine."

Thud. Whoa. I felt heat rush into my cheeks. There hadn't been a magical compulsion on him this time. Nothing forced him to kiss me like when Greg had used the *titel* before. I swallowed audibly. I had been about to pull away when Jove looked into my eyes. "You know I'm not your employer any longer, Mira."

"Yet, here I am, still working."

"Only if you wish to."

I gently tugged my wrist back. It was still tingling from where his lips had brushed. I looked away from his dark eyes. I was not prepared to go down that particular path yet, so I went back to the subject at hand. I walked over and sat in one of the wingbacks and shoved some rice and shrimp into my mouth. I felt the tips of my ears burning. I swallowed before I could talk again. "You said you were sorry when you came to visit me in the hospital. That wasn't sympathy, was it? It was an apology."

He bowed his head. Jove looked ashamed. Usually, he was a very confident man. He sat hard in the chair on the other side of the coffee table. "Ms. Corvis was right when she said it was my fault High Raven has an interest in you. What she was incorrect on was the timing," he said morosely. "The Unkindness does extensive research on their clients before they take them on. This was the first, and I swear to you the last, time I've used them for deliveries. High Raven knew about my employees before I met with him to discuss payment for their services."

Jove dropped his head into his hands. His voice was ragged with emotion. "They had pictures of your accident. Low Raven showed them to me when we discussed what happened to people who could not pay for services rendered."

I felt the world drop out from under me. I'm glad I was already sitting. I should have made the connection when I saw the smoke in my hall. I knew it looked familiar. Maybe some of my brain cells hadn't fully regenerated yet by that point. "They're worse than the mob."

"Very much so, but without using them, I would have never gotten those books."

I shot him a steely glare. Books? He was more concerned with the *books*? That wreck had put my family and I through hell for months. If it hadn't been for Doctor Alden's miraculous surgery and the NAN-06, I would have been in heaven with my ancestors.

"Was it worth it, Jove?" I seethed. "I could have died in that wreck!" I shot out of the chair and started pacing, gesturing with my chopsticks in one hand. "It took me weeks of recovery in the hospital and months of physical therapy just to get to *this* point! There are times when my body aches, Jove. So much that it's all I can do to breathe. I have nightmares where I relive the accident over and over again. I can't drive at night anymore without a panic attack! So, I am going to ask you again, Mr. *Brandt. Was it worth it?*"

Instead of answering, he stood and motioned for me to follow him. "Come with me." I pulled back, but he waited patiently. "Please, Kleine."

Reluctantly, I nodded.

Jove led me up into his apartment. He pulled out a seat for me at his kitchen table. As I got settled, he went into one of the back rooms and soon returned with an honest-to-God crystal ball.

Jove set it up in the middle of the table, waved a hand over it, and spoke. "*Verbindung zu* Cristos."

The orb glowed, and shadows appeared on its 'face.' The shadows coalesced into the visage of a woman in her forties with wavy brown hair tied back into a loose bun. Her eyes were on Jove as if she couldn't see me at all. Then, a bright smile lit her face. "Zauberer Jove!" the woman said in a surprised voice. "It's so good to hear from you again."

"Alesha, I am calling to check on your daughter's condition. How is she?" He smiled into the globe with the same sort of smile I'd used myself during rotations or seen from a trusted pharmacist.

"Since you got us that potion last week?" Her voice trembled. "She's getting better, Jove. It's slow. It is always harder when it's slow, but she's getting better. She called me 'Mama' again just last night. I don't know how we can thank you." The woman sniffled and wiped her face.

"Just keep her away from strange-looking fungi, *ja?*"

The woman nodded. "Thank you again, Zauberer Jove. I'll send my husband along with some cornbread for you tomorrow. I made it just this morning."

"It will be good to see him again. I can never get enough of your cornbread. Have him stop by the shop tomorrow, and I'll have a book for you all to read together. It will help with the healing. Let me know if there is anything else your herd may need."

They said their goodbyes and the crystal went dark. Jove looked at me over it. "The Cristos are a family of Centaurs who live well outside of the city. Their little filly, Pix, ran afoul of Lethe Mushrooms. They are magic fungi that steal your memory. It made her forget how to use her veil as well as who her family was. Without that veil, she would have been taken and put onto a dissection table."

He stood, taking the crystal ball gingerly in his hands. "Without those books, she would not have recovered at all. The potion to counteract the mushroom is extensive and complex. It is also ancient. I had to restore four tomes to get the ingredients and the recipe right. They had to be hand-delivered from Greece. Do I need to tell you what would have happened if I had gotten the formula incorrect?"

"I imagine the same thing if you get something wrong in any medication. Varying results from a mild itch to death." I looked up at him. "Can you do more with those books than just the one potion?"

"Oh, yes." He smiled. "I can do so much more to help the Community."

"Then it was worth it." I believe in helping people. If those books could help people, then it was good . . . But it was also something I'd want to go over in therapy.

14

I COULD HEAR the rhythmic beep of the heart monitor measuring my pulse, the machine breathing for me, hissing next to my ear. But my memories were jumbled. I got flashes of my childhood. There were storms where we grew up—the kind that could knock out power for a few hours. It would scare the girls when we were kids. The Moms both had to work, so there were a lot of times when I was the one watching them.

The lightning flashed, and the girls screamed. I pulled them down into our basement and lit a hurricane lamp. Was there someone at the top of the stairs? No, it was just the three of us. The shadow was gone when the lightning flashed again.

"Okay, guys, since the lights are out for now, how about we imagine?" It was really just the three of us improvising what we would do in our favorite cartoons if we were there, but it took their minds off the loud booms from outside.

"This is the perfect setting for Batman," Ree said with false bravado.

"Nuh-uh Daredefil!" Annie had just lost her two front teeth and couldn't say her 'v's right.

"Well, what would Batman do if he met Daredevil? I mean, they're both ninjas, and if they're in the same city at the same time, then some freaky stuff has to be going down." I grinned at them. "And since they're in different universes, I'm betting the Kingpin is up to his dimensional shenanigans again. Now, who would he hook up with Gotham-side?"

"Mr. Freeze! No cap!" Ree chattered. "He's obsessed with his wife too, and if Freeze went looking for Nora in a different dimension at the same time Kingpin was looking for Vanessa . . ."

The lightning flashed again, and the four of us . . . no, the three of us. There were only three of us in the house . . . *If I were king . . . dilly dilly . . . you would be my queen.*

I gasped as I tore myself out of the dream. This time, it was the surgery. It started the same. I groaned as I got out of bed. My head was pounding. I stumbled to the bathroom just as the alarm started on my meds.

The sound spiked the pain in my head. "Ah, damn it." I rushed to get the lid off and stop the sharp sound. My ears rang at the sudden silence as I took out the pill, put it on my tongue, and swallowed with a bit of water from the sink. I chased it with a couple of pain pills before stripping and getting into the shower.

I just had to do what came next.

I got out of the shower, dried off, and got dressed. I fed Toria, put in more digital paperwork to become a practicing doctor, and got out the camera to continue my experiments.

"My name is Doctor Mira Hall, and this is Experiment Four. I've realized there is a lot my ability will be able to do once I have the proper dexterous control. I might be able to clamp off hard-to-reach veins or arteries during surgery. I could stop a muscle from spasming. I may even be able to stop the hiccups mid-hic. I want to be able to use this to help people, which is the entire point of medicine. However, I must work on my mental dexterity to be able to apply my ability to the utmost."

The camera panned the lens on me with one of my medical books on the floor in front of the couch. (I still had to fix the dent in the floor.) I had the book open to an anatomy page showing how the diaphragm works. Beside me, I had a water bottle with a taut rubber balloon stretched over the opening and what looked like little lungs inside. Today's experiment was an important one. It was to start showing how I could use my abilities to be helpful in my work.

I placed the bottle in front of me. "This is a rudimentary look at how the diaphragm works with the lungs. What I'm hoping is that I can use my ability to stop it from moving involuntarily."

I pulled the end of the balloon, making the little lungs inside fill up with air. But when I let go, instead of the balloon snapping back into place and forcing the air out of the lungs like it's supposed to, it stayed where it had been pulled, and the lungs remained filled.

"I am using my ability to keep the balloon inflated to interrupt the diaphragm from its involuntary movement. This can be applied when someone has hiccups or is hyperventilating, for example. I'm light years away from daring to try this with a person, only because it is so dangerous to mess with the muscle that makes a person breathe. However, if I am in an extreme situation, I don't see why I shouldn't try if it will help the patient. End of Experiment Four."

Sighing, I saved my work in the secure thumb drive that I used for my experiments and notes. I knew I was using the experiments to stave off the looming depression that had been hovering over my head.

For weeks, I had been going from bank to bank and loan officer to loan officer. No one was willing to take the risk on a newly minted doctor without a pre-established practice. I didn't want to bite the bullet and integrate myself into an existing clinic until I had enough capital to get some actual funding. I might not have a choice if things didn't change. That thought had my shoulders slumping. I really didn't want to go that route. I remembered how the patients always seemed a little disappointed not to get the doctor whose name was on the door. I wanted my name to be on the door, dang it! I wasn't ready to give up yet. I rolled my eyes heavenward. "Please, God, don't make me have to go to GoFundMe for this…"

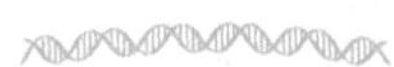

The guy at the dealership was thrilled with my choice of an electric blue sedan. "Electric really is the way to go when talking reliability nowadays. You never have to worry about the price of gas again with this baby. Technology has come to a point where you can charge your car in the same amount of time it would have taken to get gas twenty years ago. Many apartment buildings are putting in charging stations."

I knew that. Hall Construction had won some bids where the charging stations were mandatory. So, my old forest green sedan became my pretty blue EV. I named her Nimby. The old car had been officially dubbed totaled, and my insurance company agreed the accident hadn't been my fault. The payments from the mysterious insurance company were more than enough to purchase a new vehicle.

"Okay, Nimby, let's get going to Bindings. Jove's got to have some reference books on how to get backers to start a business." I murmured. Talking to one's car is something I picked up from Momma. She spoke to her old Ford for years and cried like a baby when Bertha finally died.

I heard them before I saw them. Ravens croaking in the trees around me. It sounded like hideous, mocking laughter. I ducked into Nimby and locked the doors.

"Where do you think you're going?" whispered a voice right next to my ear. My eyes darted around the vehicle. There wasn't anyone there. Black night swirled in front of my car, turning into the road I'd had the accident on. The blaring of the truck's horn sounded, and lights flashed into my eyes from the rearview mirror. Why did I come alone? I wanted to feel in control again. I thought the best way to do that was by picking out my new car by myself. I felt the panic clawing at my throat.

"Just come along," crooned the voice. "We'll take good care of you."

My wrist jerked. It felt like a gentle tug. I rubbed at the charms until I noticed one that was warmer than the others. I glanced down, and the eye was glowing gold, the color of the ever-shifting sands of the desert. I held up the charm and looked through it.

The world snapped back into sanity. My way was free and clear, but some men in dark jumpsuits were quickly making their way across the lot. Fear clogged my lungs as I smashed the start button on the car and peeled out of the lot. A few other drivers honked at me, but my main priority was to get somewhere safe. Home was safe. They couldn't get over my threshold without an invitation.

When I got back to my apartment, I went online to look up raven anatomy. I wasn't going down without throwing hands, metaphorically speaking, of course. I didn't want to kill anyone, but a broken scapula or two was just what I was looking for.

The next attempt came a few days later. It was dangerous outside. I had almost everything I needed right at the apartment except food. But that was okay, too. I could just order my groceries to be delivered. Then I wouldn't have to go outside where it was dangerous. Stupid, I know. In my defense, I wasn't exactly thinking clearly. My apartment was old enough to have Judas holes instead of cameras. It looked like my regular delivery guy. It sounded like him, but when I looked through the eye, black feathers started to emerge.

I put my medical knowledge to use.

It was surprisingly easy, like snapping a twig instead of a bone. I focused on where his shoulders were and put my hand against the door like I was performing the five-finger death punch. My physical fist hit my door. My mental one broke the bone I was aiming for.

His buddy, who'd been hiding behind a veil, had to knock the bastard out and carry him away.

They didn't come to the apartment after that.

Days later, while I was at Bindings, I got a call from the Moms. Momma had another attack . . . a bad one. She was in the hospital. Mom was freaking out because they wouldn't let Pippin in with her.

"What do I do? *What do I do?*" Her sobs made me flashback to the first big attack.

Momma on the floor, barely breathing. Her lips turning blue. Mom's face paling, her eyes darting around for answers.

I forced my voice to be steady . . . even. "Mom, I need you to breathe. I'll meet you at the hospital, and we can go visit her together." As long as she wasn't by herself, Mom could manage. "Just hold on. I'll be there soon." I grabbed what I could and ran out into the parking lot.

I didn't feel a thing. I didn't hear that 'thwip' sound they make for darts in the movies. I just looked over my shoulder and saw a tranquilizer dart connected to a black feather protruding from my shoulder. Disorientation struck almost instantaneously.

"Well . . . shit," I said as I went down. I blinked hard, trying to stay awake. It didn't work.

I woke up nauseous in darkness, and I felt the terror like a hand around my throat. Were the Moms okay? I began panting as my situation became painfully apparent. It had to have been an illusion. They had to have spoofed Mom's number, then used her voice to give it just that right tone of panic to lure my ass outside.

I prayed that was what happened. The alternative would have made me lose my mind.

I knew my eyes were open, but I still couldn't see anything. They'd used a tranquilizer dart to drug me and had taken me from the parking lot at Bindings. I'd been abducted . . . taken away . . . I disappeared.

What had they done to me while I was out? My hands flew over my body to make sure I still had clothes on.

Like that means anything! My brain screamed, *They could have raped me and just put back on my clothes.* Was this headache just an aftereffect of whatever the hell they used on me, or do I have something else wrong with me now? Tranquilizer darts don't work that fast on humans. What other poison was in what they shot into me? Was the back pain a sign of my cells starting to break down from poison? *I'm going to die. I know I'm going to die here in this dark place all alone.*

I heard someone sobbing softly somewhere nearby, but it could have been me. I had to get myself under control before anything else. The clawing feelings of panic, despair, and doom were *not* helping at all.

I forced myself to sit on the cold, stone floor and closed my eyes against the darkness. I silently repeated the Litany against Fear from the Dune series by Frank Herbert. It was surprisingly effective in helping me focus on my next step: notice five things outside of myself in the room. The air smelled musty and damp, like that of an old, defunct wine cellar. The cold stones under me were large and cobbled. The structure I could feel beneath my fingers made me think of some of the structures I'd seen in Old City that had been preserved by the Philadelphia Historical Society. I could hear the sobbing somewhere behind me and the echoes of dripping water. The sound was deep, as if it were falling into a bucket or trough. I opened my eyes again and still only saw darkness, but now the black didn't seem as terrifying. I'd broken myself out of the attack, and now I could do what needed to come next. Rosalinda would have been so proud of me.

"Hello?" I said into the darkness toward the sobbing sound. "Is someone there?"

"Shut *up*!" hissed a man's voice farther away but in front of me. "D'you want their attention, huh?"

I lowered my voice instantly. "Where are we?"

"Huh." Chuckled a woman with a thick Jersey Shore sound to it. "She must be new. They always keep it so dark here. It's hard to tell when they open the door to feed us or to bring anotha mouth to feed."

"Are these singular cells, or are we in a communal one?" I sat up in the darkness and crawled toward the sound of her voice. It had sounded closer and friendlier than the man's command had been.

"If communal you mean if they put us all togetha, then no. They tend to put two of us in a cell. Same-sex. Apparently, they don't want us to mate. Doesn't mean we don't have fun from time to time. Gotta take the edge off, yanno?" The woman laughed.

I wondered what they did with trans people like Mom and shuddered, deciding I didn't want to know. I heard a closer sound and tried in vain to look around. "Who's there?" I whispered. My question was answered with a snuffling sound to my right.

"My name is Deirdre. My name means 'sad one.' It's cause I'm always crying," said a very young-sounding voice to my immediate right. It had a melodic sound, like it was from across the pond. Ireland or Wales. Katie's dad sounded like that. My eyes were slowly adjusting to the darkness. I could just make out a shape. A small form was crouched in the middle of the room. Knees pulled up tight in protection. Holy God, it was a kid!

I went over and knelt next to the child. "Hi there, Deirdre. My name is Doctor Hall." My training was kicking in. Comfort the crying child and find out what hurt. "Why are you crying?"

"You're gonna go away just like all the others, and I'll be all alone again. You could die before they take you away. It's always so dark and cold. I don't get to see the sun as much anymore." Deirdre reached out a hand to me.

Good God, she was tiny. The small hand gripped mine. It was bony and thin, with none of the signs of having healthy flesh. I had no doubt she was suffering from the first stages of malnutrition. Her hands were cold to the touch. Gently, I rubbed the hand between mine to warm it up. "You poor kid."

She sniffled. "It's always so dark. You hear noises in the dark. You can't get out, even though there's no door."

"No door?" I looked around uselessly. I hadn't felt any bars when I'd made my way to where Deirdre sat wrapped around herself, but I'd assumed there'd have to be bars in a prison.

"Yeah, do you see the marking on the floor?" She pointed. I could barely see her pale skin and long black hair in the darkness. I followed where she was pointing and moved to go toward it.

"Stay away from that, Newbie!" The woman's voice snapped from my right, then it gentled. "You don't wanna turn into a crispy critter."

Deirdre took my hand, slowly moving toward where she had been pointing, guiding me with her. We didn't have far to go. Suddenly, she stopped and said quietly, "I need a strand of your hair."

I rubbed my hands over my buzzed hair and came up with a few stubby bits to give to the girl. She gently tugged on my hand until we were crouched low to the ground. In the inky darkness, I could barely make out a white chalk circle on the ground. "It's gonna be bright," she warned. "But you gotta see it. You gotta know where it is so you don't touch it."

Her hand opened, and I assumed she dropped the hair. The flash was blinding as it turned the bits into tiny puffs of smoke. The burning follicles gave the air an acrid smell. "They turn it off and on when they bring us food or a new person. People always try to walk out of here. They never make it." Deirdre stood and walked over to the back wall. I heard her sigh turn into a sob as she slid down to sit on the hard floor.

"Psst. Hey, newbie, come here." The woman beckoned from the side of the cell. I went over. There was nothing on the floor to hinder my path. "Hell of a show, huh? Did a piece of hair fall on it? Some light show, huh? I usta do that when I was bored. The name's Issa. You got one?" Her voice was high. It sounded like she should be chewing gum between every other word.

"Mira. Where are we?" I reached out and found that there were bars to this prison after all. They were just between the cages. Apparently, Deirdre and I had a corner cell that was stone on three sides and bars between us and Issa that started at shoulder height. I assumed it was for privacy.

"Hell if I know. There ain't no windows, so I think we're underground." She leaned her back against the bars. "It feels like my uncle's basement down here before he got it finished."

"How long have you been here?"

"Best I can tell, I've been here for about a couple a months. Been marking the days by when I sleep. But I deserve to be here afta what I did."

Her voice changed. Issa wasn't really paying attention to me anymore. My heart went out to her. Unfortunately, healing the mind isn't my kind of medicine. But I could let her talk it out if she needed to.

"You think you deserve to be here?" I couldn't think of what someone could do to believe they deserved to be put into a lightless pit like this. I was almost positive it was against many laws of unlawful holding.

"Why sure. I hit a Raven with my Escalade. Turned out to be one of their kids learning to fly. They took me only two days later and threw me in here."

"No trial?"

"They ain't like you and me, honey. Their justice is quick and accurate." Issa paused as if remembering. "I was stupid then. I didn't care about nothing or nobody except me . . . and maybe my little brotha. But once they told me I killed a kid . . . that was the game changer." Issa's voice filled suddenly, choked suddenly with tears. "I thought I just hit some stupid bird, yanno? They had me brought up in the middle of the funeral. Chained me up good. The mother was with the kid's body. Just sitting in a chair looking lost, you know what I mean? He was in between, yanno, so he still had some of those feathers around his little face. I ain't neva felt shame like that, *neva*. It was like looking at my brotha after our dad got drunk. Laid him out flat."

She blew out a breath to steady herself. "I knelt right there and started bawling like a baby. I lost my mother in a car accident like that. My uncle is a surgeon, and he couldn't save her. I knew how that little boy's mother felt. I musta been crying like that for twenty minutes before I felt a shadow over me. I remember looking up into his mother's face. Gawd, that was the worst feeling eva." Issa's silhouette leaned against the bars, crossing her arms over her chest, the heel of her hand rubbing her eyes.

"The mother screamed and started kicking me. Over and over and over. What right did I have to cry for her son? I think I heard my ribs crack. Then she broke my arm, my leg, and my collarbone. Crack, crack, crack, just like that. Then she reached down and grabbed my head, leaned over me, you know? And she told me how she'd given me every injury I'd given her son except the one that killed him and how I was to tell her why she should let me live. You know what I told her, Miri?"

"Mira."

"Whateva." Issa turned to face me. She was grabbing the bars now, her face resting between them. She was sobbing, too, but not the same way Deirdre had been. These were tears of madness. "I told her to kill me. I didn't deserve to live for what I did to her kid. I didn't deserve life for what I did to her family. Then she threw me down and told the guards to bring me back here until she could figure out what to do with me. They patched me up, and I have been here ever since. So yeah. Some of us . . . we belong right here. Whadda bout you? What did you do to deserve being here?"

I was stunned for a minute after she finished her story. Her experience was completely different from mine. Issa really believed that just because she hit a bird with her car, she deserved imprisonment. In no way could she have possibly known that the bird was a child. Things like that don't enter into the mind of modern man. We are taught that there is no magic, no wonder, and, in some cases, no god. Why should she have taken it to heart when she hit the bird?

If it had been me, I would have felt bad for hitting it. Sure, that's normal. Momma also had some family stories about hitting birds being bad luck, but this was a whole new level of guilt trip. There was something seriously twisted with this poor woman. Or maybe this was what it looked like to be Veil-Struck.

I swallowed a few times. It took a bit for me to find my voice. "I didn't do anything to them. They think I am *payment*." I bit out, rage filling my voice. "They delivered some special books to my former boss, and they thought he was trading me for them. Even though his people haven't dealt with debt in humans for two hundred years."

"Two hundred years? Who are these people you're talking about? The mafia?"

"Come on, Issa. You know these Ravens aren't human. Do you think they're alone? There are so many more things out there." I sobered, angry at my confinement. "Their justice isn't always so accurate. So, I am going to get out of here."

"Didn't you see what happened to your hair?" She protested. "Your whole body does that if you try to get out. I seen it happen when people get tired of being here."

Her voice was urgent. It didn't seem as tainted with instability now. "Jumping over it doesn't work. Praying before you walk over, it doesn't work. It's just zap, done."

"There's a way, I just have to think." I turned away from Issa. My eyes had adjusted to the point where I could make out the contours of my cell. There was a toilet in the corner, as well as a sink. Two blankets and two sorry excuses for pillows were on the floor. Deirdre was curled under one of the blankets. She'd gone back to where she had been while Issa and I were talking.

I doubted the poor kid was asleep. She had all the earmarks of someone who was traumatized. I worried about malnutrition but had no idea without a proper examination. I tried not to think about how her hand had trembled when she took me to the ward? Spell? Lock? What the hell was that thing anyway?

I sat on the empty blanket next to where the girl lay and stared straight ahead at the open cell door. That was maddening. Freedom was all but screaming at me, and that damned thing on the floor was stopping me. Suppose I thought of it like a force field from Star Trek; then I found myself not as tempted to go through. I clasped my wrist with my hand and made a startling discovery. I still had on Jove's bracelet. It felt warm against my skin.

"They tried to take that off you," said Deirdre, still facing the wall. She must have heard the charms clink together.

"Really?" I smiled, fingering the charms. Just like at the hospital, then. My charmed charms weren't going to be taken from me easily.

"Yeah." Issa giggled manically. "Fried one of 'em really good. Where'd ya get it?"

This was a good thing. This meant Jove could find me. Not that I was going to sit around and wait for a rescue. "I just know the right people, I guess."

"It's Zauberer-made, isn't it?" whispered my little cellmate. "I can smell the magic on it. It's potent."

That got my attention. "Now, how can you do that?"

"I'm special, too. That's why they keep me, why they put you with me. I can do things with plants." Deirdre sat up again and stared at the open door. "They always put the special ones together. They make the ward stronger for us, too. I haven't seen the sun in so long." She sounded lost. My heart ached for her.

"How long has it been since you've eaten, Deirdre?"

"Couple of weeks now. I don't want to eat the stuff they give us." She inched closer to me. "It's not good to eat."

The tone of her voice changed abruptly. So quick of a change from sniffling to curious. It was so abrupt it made me blink in surprise. "So, what can you do? You must scare them to have them put you with me."

"I move things with my mind," I whispered back, adopting a conspiratorial tone. "Deirdre, I'm going to try to get us out of here."

"I heard you tell Issa. I don't want you to die, Mira. It's too soon after the last one." Her voice trembled.

I didn't want to die either, but there had to be a way out. "Do they always keep us down here? Do they ever take people out for exercise?"

She shook her head. "We never get to see the sun. Not unless they have a task for us."

"Have they always put special people together?" Maybe I could use my ability to get us out of here.

"I know what you're thinking. The ward will taste your magic and eat it like sugar candy," her whisper dropped. It was breathy and near silent. "They always put our kind together. Part humans."

"Darling," I whispered, "I'm all human."

"Then how can you be special?" She scoffed. "Zauberer Magic? Fae magic?"

"Science." I *lifted* my pillow and made it do a little dance in front of us.

"Wow, that's amazing! I don't smell magic at all when you do that! My magic can't work while I'm in here. You just might be able to do it." I heard the smile in her voice. It made me happy. I decided right then that if there was any way to do it without getting us killed, I'd try to take her with me when I escaped. Deirdre and I settled down on the threadbare blankets. I'd given her my pillow. Let the kid have some extra comfort.

I couldn't sleep anyway. The noises Deirdre had told me about were real. The tiny scratching and chittering that sounded almost next to my ear made any sleep impossible. I also found myself becoming more protective of Deirdre. The poor girl had obviously been traumatized by these monsters. She was whimpering in her sleep—tiny, helpless, animal-like sounds. I crawled over to her and gently put her head on my lap, stroking her hair.

"Don't worry," I said when she twitched in the darkness, "I won't let them hurt you." Deirdre sighed and settled back onto my lap, falling asleep almost instantaneously. She slept soundly as I sat watch. I've always been protective of people younger than me: my sisters, my friends, everyone. If there was anyone who needed protecting, it was this little girl.

When they came to feed us, it was a shock. I was staring into the gloom. My eyes had adjusted as much as they were going to at that point. The cell was empty for one second, and then suddenly, a large, bulky Bird-boy was standing between us and the ward. My quick intake of breath was enough to wake Deirdre. I pushed her behind me, keeping me between her and it.

"It's okay, honey." Issa giggled. I was really starting to think she was entirely insane. "It's only breakfast. They don't usually come around wantin' stuff until later."

The large dark form bent and placed two covered trays on the floor. It reminded me of the covered dishes we gave patients at the hospital. After delivering our food, the Bird-boy melted back into the darkness.

"Creepy," I murmured. They seemed to use their illusions for almost everything.

"You ain't kiddin', honey," Issa said around her food. "Freaked me out my first day. Food ain't too bad, though."

I edged out, away from the wall, wary of the Bird-boy coming back. I grabbed the tray and brought it back to the wall. I could smell food. When I opened the lid, fresh fruit, cheese, and bread with butter greeted me. It looked like food. It smelled like food, and I was getting hungry. When I reached for the spork, Deirdre stopped me.

"Don't eat it. It's not food." She hissed. "Not this time. Sometimes it's food, but not this time."

"What do you mean?" I heard Issa snarfing hers, and my stomach growled. "I'm hungry, Deirdre."

"Just *look* at it!" She sounded desperate.

Something in her voice made me heed her words. I lifted my wrist and looked at the food through the eye of Horus charm. It was like looking through a tiny magnifying glass or one of those crosses with the Lord's Prayer in the little gem. The objects on the plate warped as the charm stripped away the illusion. The girl had been right. The food on the plate was moldy and rotten. What had been the sweet smell of fruit turned foul and made me gag. I cringed away from it.

"When people get sick from the stuff, they take you away to make you better. Then you feel grateful to 'em for healing you." Deirdre sighed quietly. "I haven't eaten anything in a while."

I stared at the rotting food. Once I'd seen through the illusion, there was no going back. I studied the dishes. "There may be some of this that's edible. We just have to cut around it carefully." I picked up an aging apple and the cheese, pointing out the good parts.

"But how do we get to it? It's not like they let us have knives."

"Then we'll use what we've got. If I use this spork the right way, it won't snap." Carefully, I worked to separate the flesh of the fruit. I found once I had a small gash, I could separate it the rest of the way with my ability. It was slow, tedious work, but when I was finished, there was enough to take the edge off for Deirdre. I ended up not eating myself, but I could stand to lose a few pounds anyway.

"Eat it slow," I instructed the girl. "You've been starving yourself, so I want to introduce foods back into your system slowly. I wish we had oatmeal or applesauce here. I don't want you cramping by eating anything too complex too soon."

"You sound like a doctor," she said around a bit of apple.

I smiled. "I am one, remember? I just got my white coat. One day soon, I'm going to open my clinic." I smiled as I pictured the sign on my clinic door. *Doctor Mira Hall: Family Laboratories*. Yeah, I liked the sound of that.

"I want to be a florist or a farmer when I get out. I have always worked best with plants. I want all my pretty plants around me all the time. They're a lot better than people." She sighed a very grown-up sigh. "If they let me go, that is. High Raven keeps making me all these promises, but they never happen."

That got my attention. "You've spoken with High Raven?"

"Yeah, he's kinda mean. He doesn't like it when things don't happen the way he wants 'em to." Deirdre was starting to perk up now that she was finally eating something. "Do you have any friends back home, Mira?"

I smiled down at her. "Yeah. There's my friend Katie. She's a little fireball and bounces all over the place. She's got red hair and freckles that dance over her nose. I think she'll like you. My friend David will, too. He's a veterinarian, an animal doctor."

"But you're not gonna see 'em anymore." Issa giggled. "Once the birds take you, they neva let you go."

I watched in horror as Issa put a slice of apple on top of one of the rotten hunks of bread. A maggot crawled over the flesh of the fruit. "You probably shouldn't eat that."

"Who are you, my mother? I'm hungry, so I'm gonna eat it. Carbs aren't good for my figure, but who the hell is going to see me in here?" She purposely slipped the bit of apple and the bread into her mouth, past her thin lips. The bread was green, and the apple had squished far too easily between her straight teeth. I flinched away, swallowing to keep my breakfast down. Now that I'd seen through the illusion, I couldn't unsee it.

I stood, went over to the ward, and crouched by it, forcing myself to look away from Issa's cell. I had to get to work. There had to be a way around that ward. Otherwise, how could the Unkindness come in and out without harm? I held up my bracelet and looked through the charmed eye. It showed nothing. That only told me the darkness wasn't an illusion, and neither was the ward. I had to pay more attention to the pattern it made.

I hunched over the marks on the floor. "Watch your eyes, Deirdre. I need to see the ward in action again. Are your eyes covered?"

"Yes, Doctor Hall," said, her music-like voice from the gloom.

"Good." I ran my hand over my scalp and frowned. I had no way to tell if I'd been successful this time. It'd been a miracle I'd gotten a viable sample last time. I chewed off a sliver of my thumbnail and used that. The ward flashed. It hurt my eyes since I had already been in darkness for an untold number of hours. Damn, it had been like a flashbulb on a camera. I replayed the memory in my head frame by frame. The ward was circular, like one of those old plastic maze puzzles—the one where you get the little silver ball into the hole. It looked complex from my perspective. I didn't know anything about magic except what I had read in stories and my players' handbooks from various tabletop games.

"It's okay now," I said, opening my eyes. "I'll have this figured out soon."

Moans of distress started in Issa's cell. That wasn't a good sign. I'd heard those sounds before during rotations, just before a kid threw up on my shoes. I stood, heading toward the bars between our cages. "Issa, are you okay?" Her body was prone over the toilet.

"I don't feel so good, Miri." She moaned. "I'm gonna throw up now, just to let cha know."

I winced as she proceeded to do exactly that. The sounds of Issa getting sick weren't pleasant to hear. A choir of other people voiding their stomachs sang out like a malicious toddler slamming on a toy organ. I had to focus on Issa. She was the only one I could see in the gloom.

After a long while, I wasn't sure what she was throwing up anymore. The meal she had was obviously down the drain by now. She was dry heaving, at this point, hard. If she didn't stop, she was going to tear something vital inside. I could hear similar sounds from up and down the hall of cells.

"Issa, you need to stop now," I said, an edge to my voice. "There's nothing left in your system. You've got to stop before you hurt yourself."

"Ugh . . . I . . . can't." She managed to gasp between heaves. She had to stop.

I could make her stop. She was the only one I could see, so she was the only one I could help. I'd only tried this once before, but that was on a plastic bottle in my living room. I hadn't planned to try this on a human until I'd managed to do clinical trials! I took a couple of steadying breaths. Issa could really hurt herself if I didn't do something. I *concentrated* on my ability. I knew the human body. I aced every single one of my anatomy lessons. I knew I could stop her by making specific muscles stop contracting against Issa's abused stomach. The diaphragm and core muscles all had to relax to give the woman a chance to breathe. If only for just a moment.

I had to be extra careful controlling the diaphragm because it was so integral to breathing. The heaving stopped. I released my hold on her diaphragm almost immediately. I had just wanted to interrupt it, not stop it entirely. I nearly smiled as I heard Issa gasp in the air. I wished I had her in an examination room. I couldn't tell if she really had torn something without touching her. I relaxed my hold on her muscles. At least now she wasn't dry heaving anymore.

"She needs medical attention," I heard myself say. I wished for a second that I could teleport to the other side of the bars instead of my telekinesis. I knew I could help her. I needed to get my hands on her to help her. I raised my voice to shout over the loud sounds of people getting sick in their cells. *"Get your feathered asses in here! This woman needs medical attention!"*

Two large Bird-boys came in, melting out of the darkness almost instantly as if they'd been only waiting on me to call out. They primarily presented as male, and calling them Bird-boys made them seem less frightening than they were. One gently took the unconscious Issa in his feathered arms while the other stared stonily at me. I glared at him. "She needs medical attention," I repeated. "And not to be fed rotten food. Corvus Corax may be able to digest things like that, but not humans."

He grunted and turned to walk out of the cell. He shot me a final look over his shoulder as if daring me to speak again. I narrowed my eyes back. I observed as they took Issa. There was no flash of light. They must have done something to open the cell to get in, but they did nothing after they left. It made sense. What would be the purpose of locking the door on an empty cell?

I felt Deirdre's thin hand clutch mine. "I don't want that happening to me, Mira. Are you sure it was okay to eat?"

"I cut off all the bad bits, remember? You'll be okay." She snuggled closer to me. Poor kid. I wrapped an arm around her in a hug. It was so hard to judge her age in the darkness. I was trying to judge only by feel. That was never a good way to do things if you're not used to it. "You said your magic doesn't work here. Do you know anything about their magic?"

"Only a little. I've been here a long time. So, very long. I've had time to watch them when they have me up in the main hall. When they want me to grow something." Deirdre's voice was soft, like she wasn't used to talking to another person. It made my heart ache to hear.

"So, you sort of have a green thumb, huh?" I made sure the smile came through my voice to encourage her.

"Oh, it's much better than that." I could hear the responding smile in her voice. It was good that she had pride in her ability. "I ask seeds to grow, and they do, quick as you like. They like me."

"That sounds cool! I'm not so good with plants. I always forget to water them." I gave her a light squeeze. "I'm going to have to get back to work on the ward. How long do we have until they usually come around again?"

"They'll come for some of the others soon. They usually wait until the retching slows down more. Then they bring up the ones they need to do stuff for them. What's the use of having free labor if you're not going to use it?"

The kid had a point.

"They're not going to come and get me today. They had me grow so many plants just yesterday. I'm out of juice. I couldn't ask a plant to grow right now, even if I really needed to." She sighed. "I'm going to take a nap, Mira. I'm tired." She settled, pillowing her head on her thin arms. I pulled up the blanket and covered her, tucking her in a little.

"Okay, I'll wake you in a bit," I said as I stood. I walked away from her and back to the entrance to our cell. I sat cross-legged in front of the ward, where it was situated on the floor. Closing my eyes, I brought the image of the ward in action up again. It must have seemed like I was in a meditation trance the way I was sitting, or I may have looked constipated. Who knows? I knew there had to be some way to turn the damned thing off. If only I could watch as the Bird-boys did it.

"Hey, you!" A voice above me snarled. "Back away from there!"

I looked up and saw my wish was about to be granted. One of the burly guards stood there glowering at me. I held up the eye charm to my eye and blinked when I saw there was actually a second Bird-boy there, crouching on the opposite side of the ward. He was closer than I thought. If I'd reached out a hand, I would have been able to push him on his tail feathers. He had a flashlight in one hand and, with the other, was finishing the circle. It was just a quick, small swipe of a movement. I almost missed it. Almost. I had to force myself not to grin. Who says God doesn't answer prayers? The secret to the ward wasn't an addition. It was a subtraction. Something was erased to make the ward inactive.

The burly guard entered menacingly, all swagger and intimidation. "High Raven wants to see his newest acquisition."

"Leave that one alone! You gave her to me! She's *mine!*" I heard Deirdre scream as the Bird-boy reached down to grab me. I didn't want to let them know I still had my power as well as my bracelet. That would have been bad. I slapped his hands hard enough to knock it away and stood on my own. I don't think he expected that as he recoiled and blinked.

I bared my teeth at him. "Was that really necessary? You're scaring the child." I didn't take my eyes off him. I just stared into his avian eyes as I addressed my cellmate. "I'll be okay, Deirdre. Don't worry, this one's just a big bully. We'll see what High Raven wants, and then I'll be back."

I heard her sniffle a quiet 'Okay' that didn't really sound convinced, and I strode past the guard and out of the door where the second Bird-boy waited. He held a rope to bind my hands. Thankfully, he tied them in the front rather than from behind, keeping one end firmly in his feathered hand.

We walked along a long corridor lined with the other cells. The smells from the other cells worsened the further we got away from the cell I shared with Deirdre. I heard sounds of retching from a few of them as we passed. I couldn't stop to help them. That tore at me. Now that I knew I could help ease their pain just by *concentrating* on it, it was torture not being able to stop and help the other prisoners. I kept stopping from time to time, trying to get a glimpse inside the surrounding cells. When I did, they would roughly jerk me to keep me walking like a dog on a leash that had stopped for a sniff. From the other cells, I could hear manic laughing, crying, and, in one case, very creepy singing. I almost felt safer between the two burly guards.

When a non-magical being has such an encounter with something of such evident magic, it will invariably drive the non-magical being insane.

I could almost hear Jove's voice in my ear as I remembered what he said that first night when my world went Wonderland on me. I wished it had gone to Oz instead. Oz is a lot less frightening than what Lewis Carroll had cooked up. I stared at the other cells as we passed. Was this the evidence of The Veil-Struck condition? Could this happen to me if I let it? The thought terrified me. Soon, we came to a wooden spiral staircase. There was finally light here, emanating from twin torches marking either side of the stairs. As we ascended, I noticed that every few feet, there were oil bowls topped with fire— very medieval-looking.

"I guess you people haven't discovered electricity yet." That earned me a shove from behind to move faster.

The wooden stairs echoed as we marched up them, quickly becoming the only sound to reach my ears. We marched on for approximately twenty minutes before coming to a pair of ornate wooden doors. I was panting by that point. This fluffy woman was not built for a quick march up more than a hundred stairs. My head was already spinning with fatigue when we finally got to our destination.

The doors opened, as if they were automatic, to a grand hall. I was dragged behind, forced to take awkwardly large steps to keep up. My feet sunk into the carpet. Honest-to-God wrought iron chandeliers were hanging from the thick wooden rafters, the kind with candles in place of light bulbs for which I was thankful. The flickering light of the candles was easier on my eyes than any other form of light would have been. I still blinked my eyes, needing to adjust from the prolonged exposure to the dark. Everything had an ethereal glow to it. Tapestries were hanging along the walls. They were a deep red with the Raven's symbol carefully stitched into each one in gold thread. The tables were arranged in a semi-circle, leaving ample space in the middle of them. A stage for the entertainment to be viewed from all sides. At the head of the room were two thrones, one black and the other gold, set apart from the different tables. The deep green carpet led the way as I was dragged to the thrones.

The Bird-boy jerked his hand upward and threw me toward the thrones. I landed on my elbows and knees. I cried out in pain. If I kept injuring my legs, I really *would* be able to predict the weather. I heard laughter all around me from invisible sources. Veils—I could see them shimmering in the air around each of the chairs. I managed to get to a sitting position, my butt on my heels. I raised my bracelet to my eye and looked at the black throne.

"I can see you," I sang. See, I can do creepy, too.

The air shimmered one final time as the illusion dropped. "Damned Zauberer magic." The man who was suddenly on the throne growled. He didn't look like one of the Bird-boys at all. His face was angular with a strong jawline. His dark eyes were sharp and looked as if they were looking straight through you. The man had his hair long but professionally styled. I saw a long black braid travel over one shoulder. It seemed downright majestic. I couldn't even say his features were avian. Damn, that cut off any line for Penguin jokes. I went with sarcasm instead. "Annoying of them, isn't it?"

"*Silence*," rumbled one of the guards behind me. "You are in the presence of His Eminence, High Raven. The highest of all Ravens of our flock, you will give him the proper respect."

I stayed silent. Not agreeing, not disagreeing. The best thing for me to do was to watch and wait. I still held onto the hope that Jove was on his way to get me. I just had to hold out and not get killed. I looked away from the throne. High Raven made a gesture, and one of the Bird-boys grabbed my head and forced my face to the man.

"The low Raven was right," High Raven mused, leaning forward on his throne. "You are definitely better payment. Your employer was . . . foolish to think I would accept a lowly animal in place of such a fine specimen of your species."

I bared my teeth at him. "You are foolish to think you can keep me here."

He threw his head back and laughed. "*And* spunk! It will be fun to break you."

A chill raced up my spine. Breaking didn't sound so fun to me. The feathered hand on my head gave me a quick, hard shake for insolence. My eyesight gave a painful little spin.

"A shame that it will not be my fun to have." His fingers drummed on the arm of the throne. "You have a buyer."

"A buyer? You *sold me*?" Anger burned in my belly. I was *not* property. I would not be property in any sense of the word. Anger quickly gave way to rage as I spat at him. "There is nothing so low as a *slaver*."

"I am a businessman who provides my clients with the goods they desire. They desired you. They were precise. Mira Hall, the voluptuous woman who worked in Bindings with mahogany hair and witchy eyes."

My hazel eyes were angry slits as I glared at the Unkindness leader.

"You will find her on the road leading to the city the night of the new moon. Maim her well, but do not allow her to die. We delivered you to the client. However, you seem to be a slippery one. The client paid more, and we had unfinished business with the Zauberer. He was supposed to use you as payment so we could acquire you faster."

Who the hell had that kind of pull with the Ravens? Was it just a matter of money? Who had that kind of money that knew who the hell I was? "Humans haven't been allowed as payment in over two hundred years, so I'm told." I sneered.

"Silence, your better is speaking!" I got another dizzying shake. Much more of that, and *I would* have to throw up.

"Payment has finally been rendered for that transaction, even if we had to work for it." The fact that someone had paid them to 'maim me' was sickening. It didn't do anything to curb my rage.

"Slaver." I spat. They seemed to equate status to height, so I went for that. "You are a slaver and the lowest thing I have ever seen! Worms are higher than a slaver! *Amoebas* look down on those who sell other beings!" The burning was spreading now from my gut up to my chest.

I felt the Bird-boy's grip tighten on my head as he slammed my face against the floor hard enough for me to worry about whiplash. "Silence Human! You will not speak to the one who flies the highest above us."

"Sentient people are not property! *I* am not property!" I snarled against the stone. I *grabbed* the guard's fingers with my mind and twisted them back upon themselves. Several loud, sickening cracks rang in the hall just before the creature started screaming. Then, the world distorted around me.

The faces of the flock seated at the tables elongated, their eyes becoming black voids. Color became too bright, shadows too dark. Frightening doesn't begin to describe what I saw. It was like looking into madness and hell at the same time. My mind couldn't grasp it. It came on too fast. My concentration was scattered. I screamed.

The misshapen blob that was sitting on the throne flickered as it sped toward me. My heart pounded in my chest as fear overrode anger. My body froze in terror as the thing came so very close to me. My nose smelled rotting flesh. My eyes saw the distorted body that my brain could only connect to a 'Demon.' This was the thing that had caused me so much pain and so many months of agony as I recovered. I let out a small squeak as it loomed over me.

I cringed as it came close to my ear. Hot, fetid breath brushed my ear, causing my flesh to crawl. "I will do with you what I please. You are *property* and, for the moment, *my* property."

"Back *off*!" I screamed, pouring all of my scattered concentration into the word. The specter flew back and slammed into the wall behind the too-bright throne. The world snapped back into recognizable shapes and colors. I panted and glared at High Raven, who was being helped to his feet by two Bird-boys.

"Why wasn't I told this one had this much power?" He snarled as his courtiers helped him to his feet. He looked like an average human now. Tanned-skinned with long black hair, he looked very regal from a human standpoint and, more importantly, not like a monster anymore. "We should have left her in the drainage cell for longer. The wards should have drained more of her magic than this."

"She was left inside with the drainer for a meal," stammered my guard. Drainer? What was a drainer? I doubted they were talking about the plumbing.

The guard was bowing low but twisted his head to look up at his leader. An avian movement if there ever was one. "As you ordered, High Raven. She showed no sign of sickness, no sign that the cell worked on her at all."

He snarled as he got to his feet. "You have caused us much trouble, Human. You escaped from captivity after we so graciously left you alive on the street. You dared to see through our illusions, get one of my third-highest Ravens killed, and have maimed no more than three of my most trusted . . ."

"Sir, we don't have much time available to us," murmured a Raven in the seat to his right. This one seemed more feminine in her bird form and strangely reminded me of Ms. Corvis. "The fledglings are in need of a cure."

"You think I don't know that?" I heard desperation in High Raven's voice, and for the first time, he sounded almost human. "We have no choice. The flock needs . . ."

A cure? That implied there was some sort of disease. That meant they needed a doctor, and the buyer had obviously promised them one. Someone who could take care of their problem but keep their secret. Someone like me.

I thought about all those people in the basement. I could help them *if* I could get High Raven to listen to me. I knew Jove was coming. I might be able to make it easier for him, too. I needed to get out of here with the least amount of fuss. Why fight an army if you don't have to? Treyvon had told me I needed investors.

I swallowed. It felt like forcing glass down my esophagus. I spoke quietly, "...*Vielleicht können wir ein Geschäft machen?*"

High Raven's eyes sharpened. "Are you a Zauberer that you use their tongue? Were we lied to when they told us you were only Human?"

I shook my head. "While I resent the 'only human' bit, I just used their language to get your attention. While I am no Zauberer, I am, however, a doctor."

With some effort, I managed to get to my feet. "The night you ran me off the road was the night I got my doctorate in medicine. I am *Doctor Mira Hall*. I am the top student in my class. I have survived your flock's ministrations. I saw through your lies, defended myself and my home, and I have a wager for you, High Raven. If you're willing to take it."

He loomed over me again, suddenly standing where he hadn't been a second before. "Why would I do that? I have you here. Your buyer was very specific in wanting *you*, and we have already gone to great lengths to procure you. What your buyer neglected to tell us was that you had power. That makes you very attractive and worth much more than the buyer was willing to pay, and a lot of trouble for us to keep until he gets here. Why would I take this bet?"

Who the hell *was* this buyer?

I swallowed and tried not to tremble as I balled my right hand and shook the bracelet. The charms tingled musically against the Unkindness' ropes. "You know this is Zauberer-made. The one who made it for me is bound to come looking for me, and rather soon, I'd wager. In fact, I'll bet he'll be here before this 'buyer' of yours. It's a fair bet with even odds."

"Just how much would you bet, my dear?" He tilted his head to one side, his piercing yellow eyes watching me. It was the first avian thing I'd seen him do. "What would I gain if you lose this wager?"

"You keep me here, and I treat your flock of my own free will at any time, day or night, at no charge. I live where you tell me to live and do what you tell me to do. I assure you I have earned my doctorate and would be able to treat you better and faster than anyone the 'buyer' would have gotten for you."

"And if you win?"

"I leave here with my and Deirdre's freedom. You treat the people in the basement better. Rotten food, lightless dungeons, and constant vomiting are just unnecessary torture. I will no longer be considered property and will no longer be hunted or 'procured' by the Ravens. You loan me enough capital to start my practice with your logo on the door. I will still treat whoever needs treating, and I will treat your specific flock free of charge when you need me. In other words, High Raven, I would work for you, uplifting your flock in the eyes of the Community. Healing your sick and injured in your names."

High Raven crossed his arms, considering. He, too, was looking at me just like all those loan officers who had been shooting me down for the capital to start my practice. Then he smiled, and his entire demeanor changed. "It seems we have much to talk about while we wait. Would you like something to eat? I assure you this food is not what we serve to those below."

Soon, we were sitting at one of the large tables, or rather, High Raven was seated, and I was standing, my hands finally free. Plates of food sat in front of us. I checked the food with the charm anyway as we spoke. It was bread, cheese, and fruit, but this time nothing was spoiled or rotten.

High Raven threw his head back as he lounged on the comfortable-looking seat, his laugh sounding more like a croak. "...'on a steek!' You really told that to a Zauberer?"

"He should have trusted that I kept my sanity." I tilted my chin up. I was standing at my most professional. I made my voice prim, making him laugh harder.

Momma always told me one of the best ways to sway someone to your side was to make them laugh. Don't get me wrong, I knew High Raven was one scary son of a hell monkey—er—bird. I wanted to get on his good side. He still turned my stomach to think about all those people down below in the dark. But if I could win this bet, it would get them some much-needed quality-of-life upgrades.

High Raven was one canny negotiator. We were hammering out a verbal contract of what would be expected of me if Jove got there first. High Raven agreed to most of my terms, with the exception of Deirdre's freedom. We had finished negotiating and were just about to get to the meat of the Ravens' problem when the ornate double doors exploded inward with a brilliant flash of light and smoke.

"Release my woman of Power, High Raven!" boomed a voice in German through the falling debris. It would have been impressive, really, if I were still in danger. As the dust settled, I beheld the sight of my former boss decked out in what looked like a purple bathrobe with moons and stars sewn on, a far cry from his usual tailored appearance. He had a thick, long, wooden staff raised into the air, and I think I saw sparks starting at his fingertips.

I snorted—*his* woman of power? Since when was I *his*? We were going to need to have a long discussion about throwing around owner-ship. "Can't you see we're trying to conduct business here? Looks like I've won the bet, High Raven. My Zauberer beat your buyer. I'm sorry about the door. Some people don't know a business meeting when they see one. Now, where were we?"

Jove dropped his arms with a flummoxed look on his handsome face. Here, he was all prepared to be the hero and save the damsel in distress, but the scene in front of him clearly didn't match up with his expec-tations. The cognitive dissonance was still playing over his face when High Raven spoke again.

"I believe you were pointing out the advantages of becoming an investor in this clinic of yours, Doctor Hall. After all, you have just won our wager. You say other races in our Community will see us in a more favorable light?"

"Ah yes, indeed they would." I smiled professionally. "Think of it: if your people help fund this venture, then the Community will be singing your praises to the high heavens. 'Did you hear what the Ravens have done for us? A place where we can bring our sick and injured without the threat of exposure!' It would also bring jobs to the Community, as I'll need trained nurses and techs, ones who won't have to hide what they are all the time. And then, of course, everyone would instantly think of your company for their other needs as well."

I smiled again, keeping my focus on the more dangerous creature in the room. I made sure to keep my eyes on High Raven rather than looking at Jove. I heard the Wizard's tentative steps stop behind me. I felt his hand on my shoulder and gave it a comforting squeeze. With the Zauberer at my back, I continued my pitch. "'Who can I call to get that charm I need for Grandma? Of course! The Unkindness! Ruthless enough to get the job done but kind enough to think of the rest of us!' Though I may suggest going a bit lighter on the . . . penalties of nonpayment occurring *before* the transaction occurs."

"We don't usually do that," High Raven admitted, showing absolutely no shame. "You were a special case. What was done was a part of your buyer's orders. 'Maim her well, but do not kill her.' Those were the orders."

I felt Jove's hand stiffen. High Raven snorted, seeing Jove's reaction and not caring.

"And would you be able to tell me who that buyer might be?" I spoke sweetly.

"Unfortunately, no, I cannot. It's a standard clause in all of our written contracts. Information like that would cost you far more than medical services and a bit of advertising." High Raven continued, folding his hands over his knee. High Raven was still a frightening presence in the room, but in the same way the CEO of a large company is frightening. "What assurance can you give to prove you can provide services without exposure?"

I paused. How *did* they know I was trustworthy? I'd as good as killed one of their flock and maimed at least two, if not three others.

Jove's voice rumbled from over my shoulder. "*She will be watched closely by my people. We will be her Aufsehers. Is this satisfactory?"* I found his German comforting. How fast Jove had gone from avenging angel to businessman. He'd just offered to watch me to make sure everyone's secrets stayed safe.

High Raven nodded. "That is satisfactory. Be aware, Doctor, that this is not a donation. This is a loan you are to pay off over the next thirty years with a twenty-seven percent interest rate. I am willing to put out capital for you with the option of refinancing and extending our business arrangement. The Zauberers will watch you to be sure you keep our Community's secrets. There will be a penalty if you default on the loan and a punishment if you divulge information about us to anyone, a dire one."

I gulped audibly and nodded that I understood.

"Do you accept these terms as well, Doctor Hall?"

"I do." And we shook on it. When our hands clasped, I felt a burning sensation on the inside of my left forearm. I tried to pull away, but High Raven's grip was firm. The burning only lasted a moment. When he released me, I pulled up on my sleeve to see a dark tattoo had appeared. It was the shape of a black flying bird. I had no doubt was a raven.

"The deal is made and witnessed," High Raven rumbled. "You will hear from my people to explain our medical needs and to confirm the account has been activated. Prove yourself, and we will let you treat our people."

"May I also inquire again about the girl I was imprisoned with? She needs things, things I may provide her. She said she was hungry. She . . . needs . . . me." My voice was strangely dreamy when I spoke of her. I wanted to get Deirdre out of the darkness. I had to get her out, though the urgency of getting her out had seemed to have strangely waned.

"I cannot agree to the release of the one you know as Deirdre. Her power over you is already fading the longer you are out of her influence. Something you must know is there was no girl child in the cell with you. She's a wonderful mimic of a girl, but she is far older than you are and far more dangerous. Her actual name is Willow Weep. She is a wood wife and feeds off the emotions of the other prisoners. We use her to drain humans who have power but don't know it. It makes them easier to control." He leaned forward. "She especially thrives when she makes people want to take care of her. Do not feel sorry for one such as her. She is where she is because she deserves to be. What I find more interesting is that her power didn't work on you."

I had a hard time believing what I was hearing. Deirdre was just a little girl who could do plant magic. She wouldn't hurt a fly . . . would she? I had to protect her, get her out of the clutches of the Unkindness . . . didn't I? My head was starting to ache. I thought back and realized when she'd taken me over to the ward . . . Hannah's holy hand grenade . . . she was as tall as I am. Too damn tall for the six-year-old I thought she'd been. The more I thought about it, the more my temples throbbed. I was about to press the issue, but Jove squeezed my shoulder before I could inquire further. I felt the pain ease with the weight of his hand. With a stuttering breath, I realized just how completely Deirdre's magic had taken in me. "She doesn't just do plants for you, does she?"

High Raven sat in stony silence by way of confirmation. I'd been ready to break back into the cells to get the 'kid' out, and High Raven knew it. His pause stretched until he saw realization dawn on my face. His features softened slightly. One might attribute it to pity or compassion. However, he certainly hadn't shown it to any of the other people in his basement.

I thought I almost heard concern in his voice when he said gently, "Had I realized that you had such power at your command, Doctor, I would have never put you in the same hall as her, let alone the same cell. I'd assumed she would drain your magic, make you docile, and you would be helpless and compliant when you were brought to me."

Jove cleared his throat. "Are we to sign a paper of some sort? Maybe documentation to be sure of who owes what to whom?"

"We do not need that."

"I am afraid I must insist that a formal document be drawn up. For the safety of Doktor Hall and the Unkindness under the laws of the Community."

"You are both well aware of what happens if a deal is broken with the Unkindness." High Raven's smile was cold, and I shivered as I remembered my accident. He then leaned back in his chair. "Zauberer, make sure she signs the Community Charter as soon as possible, and then we will ratify the doctor's deal in writing."

"My word is not good enough?" Jove asked in German.

The leader of the Unkindness narrowed his eyes dangerously. "Your word by itself is less than stellar. A fucking goat."

"I will set up the signing as soon as we get back to the city," Jove promised.

"You'd better. Doctor, you will find the money deposited into an account we will set up for business when you get home. Welcome to the Community of Philadelphia." I felt a chill down my spine as High Raven stared at me intensely. It made me feel small.

As I left the grand hall with Jove, I couldn't shake the feeling it had been more of a threat than a welcome.

15

WE WERE ESCORTED up more stairs by a couple more Bird-boys until we reached a door. Unlike the one downstairs, this door was much more modern, with a metal push bar like you would find in many public buildings. One of the Bird-boys pushed the bar, and I blinked at the sudden harsh light. We were suddenly in a small convenience store. The floor was old wood that had been painted a dull brown. Small and claustrophobic, it was one of those stores that just made you feel like you had to get out of it as soon as you found what you were after, complete with a surly-looking older man scowling at us from the counter by the door. One would *never* think that something like The Unkindness was dwelling just below their feet.

We were just about to pass the dingy counter when the old man cleared his throat. "Fed that monster you call a vehicle, Zauberer."

Jove gave a wry smile and dug out his wallet. "How much do I owe you this time, Joe?"

"One hundred and seventy-five. Forty for the feed and the rest for my gravel you tore up. Not to mention the scare you threw into everyone."

"I was in a rush." Jove looked sheepish but relaxed, as if he'd been expecting the high cost.

"Yeah, well, you pay the price for charging into somebody's home, spells blazing." The old man snorted and spat into a trash can beside him. "You owe us a boon as well. High Raven will be in touch."

Jove's smile fell, clearly more upset about the boon than the money. "I was only—"

"'I was only' *nothing*!" The man slammed his weathered fist on the counter. "The spells you were gearing up weren't no joke! Barreling your way through our home scared the heebies out of our fledglings. Your woman was fine. Such things tweren't needed."

"Excuse me, I'd just like to point out that I'm not *his* woman," I interjected.

I've never been so promptly ignored in my life.

"Come, Joe. You and I both know there are no fledglings here," Jove said.

The old man harrumphed. "Well, them spells would have scared them if they *were* here. The price stays put."

Jove placed the money quietly on the counter and left so quickly that I had to hurry to catch up.

The car he brought looked like a prop from *Road Warrior*. The black chassis was lifted on imposing shock absorbers. Its oversized tires had large treads with spikes sticking out of the hubcaps. Dangerous-looking battle chains and an angled, snowplow-looking grill that looked like it could ram down a wall at the Pentagon made this machine ready to leap into battle. If I squinted at it, I could almost see the muscle car under all that danger metal.

Jove reached up and ran a hand along the hood of the car like he was calming a fierce guard dog. I watched in amazement as the vehicle shifted and rippled. The shocks shrank, the spikes shortened, the chains became a paint job, and the grill flattened into something a lot more docile and almost friendly. It was like an attack dog that had been called off and was now giving a panting smile. Jove opened the passenger door for me and motioned me inside.

He and I drove away from what I could only assume was a mix of a prison and an asylum camouflaged as a tiny backwoods gas station. Whatever they had doped me up with must have been strong. It was almost an hour of driving in the dark before we saw the golden glow of the main highway. Jove hadn't said anything yet, his face set in grim lines. Finally, Jove sighed. "I need you to come to the shop tomorrow at dusk."

"Why dusk?"

"Now that the Unkindness knows you, it has become imperative to make you a part of the Community, officially. Hopefully, I can convince my people that you are to remain under my care during your introductions to our community. Tomorrow at dusk is the fastest I can think of for this. I have to make some calls."

I nodded casually in the dark. It made sense. "I need to get my name out there, anyway, if I'm to build a client base. I want the Community to come to my practice. Is there some magical Google or something I can put an ad in?"

"Do you have *any* idea how much trouble you're in?" Jove snapped suddenly. The headlights of the car flashed, and the horn sounded off. I assumed it was his power making itself known. "Making a deal with the Unkindness is akin to making a deal with the Fae. And did you forget that it was the Ravens that were responsible for your accident?"

"It wasn't like I had much choice there, Jove! I had to do something to stall for time." I crossed my arms over my belly as it started to quiver now that I was out of that place. "They were going to sell me, Jove. According to High Raven, I was *specially ordered*." I rubbed the new tattoo on my arm. "So no, I'm not likely to forget how dangerous they are."

The car increased in speed as Jove cursed loudly and long in a string of German. I couldn't help but smile as my brain translated. "I'm not sure that is anatomically possible."

His accent was thicker when he spoke again. "They knew I would agree to any payment when I saw the pictures of your wreck. I was out of my mind mit anger und fear for you. They demanded for the white goat as payment to keep them from causing more harm."

Jove's knuckles whitened as he gripped the wheel and spoke through his teeth. "But now, you are telling me you were 'specially ordered?' This means there is much more to their games. They never meant to take what was offered as payment. I would have never given them you. I must find out more about this special order. If they are trafficking in humans, it will have to be reported and dealt with."

"How? Aren't they stupid powerful? The only thing you've really told me is how scary they are!"

"Yes, but they are not the only game in town." His eyes were stony as they focused hard on the road ahead. "Kleine, what deal did you make mit the Ravens? I need you to share all with me on this." His accent was going back to normal, the temper storm ebbing away.

I told him what had happened from the point when I had been taken in the parking lot until he had come into the grand hall. "High Raven practically jumped at the chance to use me instead of"—I shuddered—"delivering me."

"Your price must have been too high. You maimed at least three of his flock, calmed one of their prisoners, and because of you, a member of his flock was killed. Too high of a price to hand you over to a buyer."

"It did sound like the Ravens are desperate. I got the impression that I was a special case. You are missing something else," I said as the chill that had started in my shoulders raced down my spine.

"What?" He concentrated on the road.

"Someone else is after me, and they don't mind putting me in mortal danger to achieve their goals. You have no idea just how much that scares me."

For the rest of the ride, we were silent. Jove walked me to my apartment door. He always was a gentleman, but this time, he insisted on inspecting it first. I didn't stop him. My car was magically in my parking spot, my purse and phone still in the driver's seat. It seemed I'd only been gone a few hours, but my new, wonderful world just got a lot scarier.

16

The following day felt like a new beginning. The sun was shining, the birds were singing, and I didn't have a single financial worry. The amount High Raven had put into the business account in my name was *generous*, to say the least. I'd gotten an email with the account information. What was frightening was that the account was already in my name. I checked on my phone before I even got out of bed. I would be getting the paperwork in the mail within the week.

I was a little giddy as I went into the bathroom for my morning routine. I got as far as looking at myself in the mirror before last night's nightmare engulfed me.

"How much longer?" A man's voice rose in rabid anticipation.

A second voice was older, more mature, muffled, and unintelligible. "I wonder if the others will like her. She's going to be perfect for the ACS."

I felt a gloved hand on the side of my cheek. ACS? What the hell was that? I doubted it had anything to do with Atlantic City or air conditioners.

"What do you think her protocol will be?"

The other voice sounded like a male version of the teacher from the Peanuts cartoons. Wah wah wah waah. It was surreal.

"It's okay, lovely. Let me sing you off to sleep." His voice was . . . calming. It crooned as the man started to sing softly. I heard the snap of a latex glove being removed. Then I felt a light, almost loving touch on my arm and felt the pain ebb away. I was getting pulled back into the darkness of blessed unconsciousness. "Lavender blue, dilly dilly, lavender green, if I were king, dilly dilly, you would be my queen."

The last thing I felt was a warm hand caressing my face.

I gasped and found myself sitting on the tiled floor in my bathroom, shivering as my heart thundered. My hands shook as I pushed myself up. I filed it away to analyze later. I had too much to do today. I had to hit the net. With my new capital provided by the Ravens, I needed to find my spot. I also needed to talk to Jove about how to modify it to suit the needs of the Community. I needed to put this away.

I squeezed my eyes shut as the nightmare swam back into my vision again. I stumbled, barely making it to the toilet. I threw up what I'd eaten the day before. That song started repeating in my head. But it felt . . . alien. Not like when my brain starts swirling and painting doom scenarios. This felt outside myself.

Lavender blue, dilly dilly,

Lavender green . . .

"Stop it . . ." I said through gritted teeth as I *pushed* the alien feeling out of my head. The sound that wasn't a sound stopped. My hands were up to my ears as if that would halt imaginary noise. I had to calm down. All of this fear was scattering my mind. I took a deep breath, forcing myself down from panic-ville.

What the hell was that alien feeling?

I had no idea who to talk about this to. Jove? No, he'd think I was going insane after all. Hell, maybe I was. I took my shower, making the water extra hot to chase away the chill both from the nightmare and the night I spent in the cell. Maybe I could talk to my therapist about it if I were abstract enough. I'd best not, on second thought. This had to do with the mysterious Community.

"You're okay now." I reminded myself as I let the heated spray wash over me. "You're safe now. You are neither weak nor powerless. It's okay now. Fear, by itself, cannot kill you unless you allow it to."

While I was toweling off, a beeping sound started in the bathroom. It was almost ominous-sounding after remembering the nightmare. I opened the medicine cabinet and stared at the offending bottle of NAN-06 as it reminded me it was time for my next dose. I stared blankly at it, the beeping getting louder and shriller with each passing moment. I wanted to cover my ears again—anything to block out that noise. I grabbed the bottle and tore at the cap. Blessed silence fell when the cap left the rest of the bottle.

I put my hands on either side of the sink and stared down at the open bottle of white capsules.

I was healed now. Nothing really hurt anymore from the accident. The aches and pains were mostly psychosomatic. There was no actual injury to feel the pain from anymore. Why should I still be taking these pills? My legs were fine. It was even hard to tell on X-rays where my injuries had been. Same with my skull. Was continuing to take this doing more harm than good?

The bottle cap started to beep again. Hastily, I snatched out a pill and twisted the cap back on top of the bottle.

I snorted at myself. I was being ridiculous. I knew from experience that when you are given medication, you should take it. I'd take the meds as *prescribed* until I ran out. Simple. I put it on my tongue and swallowed it down with some water before I could second-guess myself. Then, I left the bathroom to find my therapy journal.

This was something Rosalinda and I came up with after the trauma from the accident.

The nightmares had been bad, and I told myself I could handle them, but the panic attacks were debilitating. I wanted to take things slow.

We worked out the mantra that helped me keep panic attacks at bay. I really didn't want to have such an attack while on the road, where I would be dangerous to the people around me. It was something I *had* to tell her at the next meeting, though I would have to edit it to keep the Community safe and hidden.

I then started searching for commercial realtors.

I can't let these attacks stop me. I have to do what comes next. Sometimes, that next thing is just putting a foot down to walk.

I'd write about the dream in my journal and talk to Rosalinda about it at our next session.

That dream may have shaken me, but I wasn't going to let it stop me for the rest of my life. I had things to do this morning. I sat at the computer and paid some bills that had been a little behind. It wouldn't do to lose my place because I'd been laid up for a couple of months. I made backups of the video experiments I'd been making to my personal secure server and my external hard drive. I locked the hard copies in my hope chest. Paranoid? Me? Nahhh.

I sent some emails out to get with a reputable realtor and find my spot.

Life now had some fascinating possibilities.

I wanted Jove to tell me more about the Community and what sort of problems I would most likely see as their doctor. Especially the Unkindness. Odds are they would be my most prominent patients. I looked at the phone to check the time and decided I had enough time to get out of my apartment for a bit and get back before dark. Now that I had a car, I should be able to make it there and back again before dark. I grabbed my purse from the old-style coat rack and slung it over my shoulder.

"I'll be back later, my tiny Toria." I opened the door to the stairs. I liked the stairwell in my building. A couple of theater students reside two floors up. They love to use the acoustics on the stairs to practice. I just liked the music. With me on the ground floor, I got to listen. It was always fun around the holidays. Sometimes, I'd join in.

It was silent today, only the echo of my shoes on the concrete as I crossed the short distance to the outside parking lot. I thought more about how interesting my life had recently become. No one could have predicted how much everything changed because of my accident. The same accident my current benefactors caused at the will of some unknown person or persons who wanted me maimed. That thought still sent shivers down my spine. My phone rang in my pocket, the sound making me jump as it echoed around me. It was The Carpenters. I hadn't put that ringtone on my phone before. I looked at it like it was possessed before I hit the green answer button.

"H–hello?" I answered tentatively.

"Doctor Hall, this is Ms. Corvis." I recognized the clipped, professional tones of the woman who had been on my doorstep to collect the body of the Raven Toria had killed.

"Yes, Mrs.—"

"Ms." she snapped. "You should address me properly since you're the reason I'm no longer married."

Granted, it was Toria who did the deed, it didn't stop me from feeling shame. "I apologize, Ms. Corvis. How may I help you?"

"We require your assistance at one of our corporate buildings." Her voice sounded like a high-powered CEO whose underlings didn't dare to cross her. "There is a car waiting outside for you. Please hurry."

"I'll be right there." The fact that she'd said 'Please' concerned me. I zipped back into my apartment and grabbed the black antique Gladstone bag David had given to me for graduation (one of the few things to come out unscathed from the accident). I threw in some essentials for when you didn't know exactly what was needed; I raided my first aid kit from my bathroom. Gloves, sterile thread, gauze, bandages, masks, and some disposable sleeves for thermometers were all pushed into the antique bag. I made it outside faster than I ever had before. I went through the door of my building to see that Ms. Corvis had been honest. There was a shiny black limousine waiting on the curb for me, the door wide open.

I looked from side to side, making sure this really was to be my ride. I slid into the leather seat, and the door closed smartly behind me. I hadn't touched it. It had closed all on its own. The interior of the car was dark. It took a moment for my eyes to adjust. When they finally did, I swallowed a surprised gasp.

"Hello, Kleine. How are you?" Smiled the owner of Bindings. Today, he was dressed in his leather overcoat with the always well-tailored suit underneath. I once asked him why he didn't wear ties. He said he'd rather not have a ready-made garrote around his throat. I'd laughed and told him about the breakaway sort.

"Jove? What are you doing here? I was on my way to see you when I got the call."

"The Unkindness saw fit to pick me up at the shop first. However, they did not see fit to tell me why or where we are headed."

"There is some problem at one of their corporate buildings. Ms. Corvis said they needed my expertise." I pulled my purse into my lap and placed the Gladstone down by my legs as I settled into my seat. "I'm just hoping it's something that doesn't require an ambulance instead of a doctor's visit. I'm not equipped here to deal with things that are gushing."

"We will find out soon enough. I think I feel us stopping."

The car door opened by itself once more to what looked to be a run-down building. Common enough in the city, but this one . . . felt . . . different. The entire building had the shimmer of the air anomalies around it. I would have to ask Jove later why the Unkindness didn't use their own illusions to hide buildings.

"We should hurry." Jove helped me out of the car. "Something does not feel right here." Jove picked up the pace until we were practically running toward the dilapidated doors across the empty parking lot.

I shot a look at him as we ate up the asphalt of the old, asphalt-broken lot. "I don't know what we're walking into. I don't know if I brought the right tools for the job."

"Tell me what you need, and I will provide it." He huffed.

"I'll grill you on the how of that statement later." We pushed through the doors at the same time, and the world changed. Instead of being a dilapidated building on the inside, it was a gorgeous lobby. There were trees inside, the tops of them near the ceiling, which was a good ten stories above our heads. Glass-walled offices circled the lobby and had greenery hanging from the walkways on each floor. The outside may have looked like a dull old factory in dire need of repair, but oh, WOW, what it hid!

"Art thou the physician?" said a voice to my right. I looked and blinked, shook my head a bit, and looked again. It was a Centaur dressed in the uniform of the Unkindness—the human half of him, anyway. The Centaur's horse half looked like a wonderfully groomed piebald with feathered fur over his hooves. The little girl in me silently squeed in delight. He had a worried look on his face.

"Quit it with the old talk, Horace," said a small, smoky voice clearly from New Jersey. I looked around and focused on where the voice was coming from. It was a small ball of light that was flying around and landed on the Centaur's shoulder. It flew up to my face and put tiny hands on its hips. I could see very well that it was presenting as male now. Dressed in a natty suit that matched Horace's, his name badge read Larson. "Well, are you the doc, or ain't you?"

I could only blink at him, stunned, until I felt Jove take my arm. "She is; I am her attaché, Zauberer Jove. We were called by—"

"MS. CORVIS!" my voice exploded out. I hadn't even realized I'd been holding my breath. There was a flying tiny person and a literal Centaur standing in front of me. Life was becoming so cool. I cleared my throat, getting back to being professional. "Ms. Corvis called us."

Larson buzzed over to look at the clipboard his partner was carrying. "You are here at Ms. Corvis's request?" asked Horace. "We had thought, mayhap, you two be lost travelers. We get them from time to time."

Jove nodded sagely. I leaned closer to him by shifting my weight to the other foot. "Is that a fairy?" I whispered.

The ball of light was suddenly in my face again. "Listen, Lady, I know you're here to help the boss, but I will *not* put up with insults. I am a *Pixie*. Fairies are bastards."

"I'm so—"

Jove's hand clamped over my mouth. "She has learned, *elfin*."

The Pixie pouted. "You ruin all my fun, Zauberer."

I peeled his hand off my mouth. "Was I about to do something that would have been detrimental?"

"Never apologize. Or thank. Or say you owe them one."

I arched an eyebrow at him. "Is there some kind of book about this sort of Community faux pas, or did you come by this knowledge the hard way?"

"There is a book. You will get one soon."

The Pixie laughed, a high, bell-like sound. "I like this doc, Zauberer. I hope we get to keep her around. Follow us, ya mopes."

We didn't have too far to go. The Centaur and Pixie took us through a set of double doors and led us down a long hallway that looked like it led to a kitchen. Stainless steel pots and pans were hanging on the walls. Someone had cleared one of the stainless-steel preparation tables to lay the body on it. I observed and relaxed as I saw his chest go up and down. At least my patient was breathing. Ms. Corvis stood over him, looking grave in her black business suit.

A gold Unkindness insignia was embossed where a breast pocket usually would be. The businesswoman's arms crossed as she coolly gazed down at the unconscious form on the preparation table as if he were simply a problem that needed to be dealt with. "Doctor Hall. You're prompt. Good."

"Tell me what happened." I set my purse and bag down on a marble counter and immediately started washing my hands up to the elbows at a nearby double sink. I *opened* the Gladstone with my ability and pulled out the box of gloves I'd shoved in there. I was able to open the package and pull out two, landing them directly in my hands. No contamination here.

"This man is Mr. Aiden Alfenheim. He is one of our . . . associates. We were at a conference when Mr. Alfenheim lost his composure and collapsed." Ms. Corvis' face was totally businesslike, but there was something in her body language that betrayed her stress. She kept shifting from foot to foot in those elegant stilettos. The way she'd said *associates* felt like it was a substitution. Like saying someone was your driver instead of saying they were a getaway driver for when you'd just robbed a bank. I really didn't care if he was a coworker or a lover. I just needed the details.

"Why hasn't an ambulance been called? This man should be in an emergency room, not laid out on a stainless-steel table in a kitchen." I tilted his head back to check his nose and mouth. His airway seemed clear, but his breathing was raspy. The lighting where they had him was terrible. His face, overall, was handsome, if unnaturally pale. There were red, angry blisters around his mouth.

Ms. Corvis rolled her eyes at me and said, in a tone as cold as the Antarctic, "You mean *other* than *you* being at our beck and call as per your agreement with the Unkindness? Mr. Alfenheim is half-Fae and would die if they used man-made metal on him."

It was then I noticed the thick plastic, towels, and parchment paper that separated the man from the table. Effective. "So traditional needles are out. Thank you for letting me know," I mused. I looked over my shoulder at Jove, who was talking to one of the guards. "Jove, could you come here a sec? I have questions."

"At your service, Kleine." He gave me a little bow that came off as a little patronizing.

I rolled my eyes. "I need to know if all of the parts in Mr. Alfenheim are in the same spots as if he was all human."

Jove's eyes got a faraway look in them as he gazed at the man on the table. "Yes, they are." Hmm, he said that like he had firsthand knowledge. "Is that all you needed to know, Frau Doctor?"

"No, I wish I knew much more. You have no idea how vital a patient's medical history is." I started to rummage in my bag for the tools I needed. "The first thing that comes to mind is an allergy, so I'm going to need some things. Tools mostly."

"I just told you he would die from man-made metals," Ms. Corvis snapped. "How, exactly, Doctor Hall, do you plan on healing him with conventional tools?"

"Seriously? When is the last time a doctor has seen you?" Ever since I started school, my family would always have me check their temperature and look down their throats, so I got in the habit of bringing a thermometer and a tongue depressor everywhere I went. The thermometer was plastic, and the depressor was wood. I wiped them both down with an alcohol wipe. I slipped the plastic thermometer sleeve over the instrument and gently pressed the thermometer against his temple. "How long has he been comatose?"

"Twenty minutes," supplied the Pixie. He was floating over the man's supine form.

"Did he eat or drink anything recently?" I started to press and probe Mr. Alfenheim's torso, searching for irregularities. No lumps other than the normal. He was in excellent shape, like a swimmer with a lot of upper body muscle. His pulse was strong, which was a very good sign, but I needed more.

"We had just finished lunch," Ms. Corvis said as if she were stating the expected weather but didn't really care about what it did. "He'd had the same thing we all did. Management ordered sandwiches."

Her eyes watched as I looked over Mr. Alfenheim. It was starting to bother me. I would have much rather had him in a private examination room rather than out in the open with all of these people.

"Ordered?" asked Jove. "Not made in this kitchen?"

I glanced around before going back to my exam. Everything here was totally spotless. The floors, sinks, and fixtures lacked any scars or nicks like you'd see on something that'd been there a while. The knives hanging on the wall over the double basin still had the maker's marks on the handle and had never seen a sharpener. I doubt they'd ever been used.

"This is a new addition to this building," Ms. Corvis said. "Nothing has ever been cooked here. We are still waiting for the glass utensils, pots, and pans so we may provide for our allies with sensitive systems."

"They can't even cook in metal?" I felt my eyebrows go up in surprise.

"It would be like cooking in a pot made of plutonium, Kleine," Jove said gently.

The thermometer beeped. I scowled down at it. 102. That was high by human standards. I wasn't sure if it was high for half-Fae. I *grabbed* the penlight out of my purse with my ability—no reason to get my nice clean gloves dirty digging in my purse. One has only to empty an old purse and run a hand along the liner to see just what a nasty place it is.

I opened his mouth and let out a hiss of sympathetic pain. The inside of his mouth was covered in tiny, painful-looking blisters. It looked like he had gargled tiny hot coals and then decided to swallow.

I motioned Jove over to have a look. "I take it this is what happens if a Fae comes in contact with metal?"

"All metal except silver. Yes." Jove's eyes had sharpened. He looked this way when he'd found something disturbing in a book he was restoring for a customer. Sometimes, he would see things tucked into books when people brought them in to fix. They weren't always pressed flowers.

"Ms. Corvis, you said this man 'lost his composure' before he collapsed. I take that to mean he purged?" I *turned on* my penlight and shone it down my patient's throat to get a better look at the damage we were dealing with. Inwardly, I winced. This was going to be extremely painful for him once I got him conscious, probably for weeks.

She cleared her throat uncomfortably. "Yes."

"I saw it happen." Larson let out a low whistle as he looked down where my light shone. "The mope upchucked all over."

"Thank you, Mr. Larson. That will do. We would need a lab to study the remains of his lunch. I take it he wouldn't knowingly consume metal if he knew about his allergy." I closed my patient's mouth and turned to Ms. Corvis. "No Fae or derivative thereof would knowingly consume that which would kill them. Not unless the person in question is suicidal. Barring that, I worry about poison. Is the place your managers ordered from aware of the allergies of the patient?"

"Our people have properly vetted this particular establishment, and it is Community-owned." Ms. Corvis looked offended. I didn't care. I needed to know. "We have a temporary facility here you may use until your own laboratory is up and running. It is more private." Ms. Corvis abruptly turned, leading the way. Maybe she was more disturbed by this than she was used to showing. "Guards, bring Mr. Alfenheim."

We exited the kitchen through the opposite end that we entered. Those doors led to a long, empty hallway. The farther we walked, the more I felt like I was back on rotation at County. Soon, we came to another set of double doors, which opened to a fully equipped triage center. Just looking at some of the machines made my mouth water; it looked like they'd opened up the medical science catalog and ordered everything. I darted over to a medical refrigerator and started pulling out what I needed. Saline, oral anesthetic, ice. They really had everything I needed.

I felt Jove's hand on my arm, holding me back from the others. "Be careful, Kleine. I recognize that look in your eyes. Everything is here, is it not? Everything you need for your clinic."

"And more. Why the *hell* didn't they bring him here instead of the kitchen?" I demanded as they moved the man on the rolling kitchen table closer to a proper hospital bed. The bars on the side of the bed were made of clear plastic or glass rather than metal.

"The Unkindness is always out for itself first. I suppose they wished to see your reaction to working in not ideal conditions. Be careful, Kleine," he said as he leaned close to my ear. I could feel the soft brush of his breath against my skin. Jove's voice was low, probably to make sure I was the only one able to hear him. "They will offer you your heart's dearest desire to bind you closer to them. More so than you already are. I had been hoping to get you properly inducted this evening, so things like this would be harder for them to do. When all is said and done, they will offer all of this to you. In exchange? More than you will wish to part with."

"You paint us unfairly, Zauberer," Ms. Corvis called over her shoulder. She was more than halfway across the room. Average hearing wouldn't have been able to pick up what the Wizard had said. She pointed to an examination bed with one well-manicured finger. "Put him over there, and remember to pull that paper over the bed before laying him on it." Ms. Corvis looked over her shoulder at me. "Pillow under or over?"

"Uh . . . under the paper and his head." Despite Jove's warning, I was experiencing a little location envy. Some of the equipment I saw was expensive and not something you'd even find in well-funded urgent care.

"You heard her, boys." She nodded, and the guards got to work. Larson flew to the bed and pulled the paper over while Horace gently placed the unconscious half-Fae on the bed.

A man allergic to metal, almost all metal. The scientist in me itched to get his blood under a microscope. An entire race was afflicted with the same disorder. I could help them. But I had to help Mr. A first. I rolled up my sleeves and got to work.

Jove was an excellent assistant. I only had to describe what I needed and he reached into my Gladstone and pulled out what I'd described like it belonged to Mary Poppins. At one point, I asked for a silver hypodermic needle to test him. He pulled out new, plastic-sealed, silver hypodermic needles in various gauges and put them gently in my hand with a smirk. Smartass.

Everything in the treatment room was stainless steel, which would've only hurt my patient more. I donned new gloves and got Mr. Alfenheim hooked up to the saline bag to keep him hydrated while I pumped his stomach. I coated everything I could in the oral anesthetic to at least attempt to make things less painful for my patient as I shoved the plastic tube down his throat.

Apparently, a pump was all his system needed. The allergen had scored his esophagus all the way down to the entrance of his stomach, but once all other traces were removed, he started waking up. I had to remove the tube quickly before he regained full consciousness.

Mr. Alfenheim seemed surprised to be alive after he woke up. "Well, then. I seem to be alive." His voice grated. He had a charming Irish brogue to his scratchy voice. I felt my patient take my gloved hand. Gently, Mr. Alfenheim kissed it. "Do I have you to thank, then, pretty miss?" He flirted with me as I got him started on his way to recovery.

"Welcome back, Mr. Alfenheim. I am Doctor Hall. You are in the offices of the Unkindness. You gave us a bit of a scare there, sir." I pressed him back down gently when he tried to sit up. "Just relax, sir, breathe slowly. I know it's painful, but that should ease up with the medication we've put into your IV. We've pumped your stomach to get out the allergen you ingested. The best thing for you right now is fluids. Primarily, I want you to drink milk. I also suggest ice chips to suck on. I'm going to give you a prescription for some mild pain medication for your throat. It will most likely be very raw and sore for a while until it heals."

I gave him instructions on what to eat and not eat until his throat healed and a prescription for the pain medication. No sharp foods like chips or raw vegetables, and it had to be bland—no salt unless he wanted it to be irritated.

Ms. Corvis pulled me aside by my arm and said, "The contents of Mr. Alfenheim's stomach will remain here in a lab we are setting up for you. You will be called again once it is set up. Your driver will be prompt, and we expect you to be as well."

"Hold on one minute here." I pulled back my arm. "Ms. Corvis, my agreement with High Raven had to do with treating your people specifically. It stated nothing about lab work whatsoever."

She scowled at me. "Such things are your *job*, Doctor Hall. It's why you're *here* instead of in one of our cells with the rest of the chattel where you belong."

"I may have the training for laboratory work, but as it was not in my original contract, then I would expect to be paid for my services." I glanced over my shoulder, checking on my patient. "Our agreement makes it so I will treat your people, the Unkindness, free of charge. I suspect Mr. Alfenheim is not technically one of the Unkindness. Still, I will let this slide as I didn't stipulate if it were only the Unkindness or also the people the Unkindness employed or worked with. My bad there. In other words, this one is a freebie, but I won't let it slide again." I kept my gaze steady on her cold eyes until she snorted and looked away.

"I *will* speak to High Raven about this," she promised direly.

I had to bite the inside of my cheek to keep from agreeing to do the lab work myself. With Jove's warning flitting in my ear, I didn't want it to seem like they could order me to do everything, no matter how tempting it was. Forensic work had been entertaining when I was doing my rotations, and I was considering making it part of my practice, but healing people is what I love best.

I felt Jove take my arm as he handed me my purse. He had my Gladstone in his other hand. "Please inform Hoch Rabe that if he wishes to modify the terms of the contract, then please contact me as Doctor Hall's *Aufseher.*"

Aufseher meant overseer, controller . . . keeper. I wasn't sure I liked the sound of it. It made me seem like a creature at a zoo.

"You should not have let him do that," Jove said as he led me to the doors leading outside. Oh God, he wanted to talk, and his voice had that lecture-y tone to it. I first heard that tone when I accidentally put Tolkien next to Dumas. I almost whimpered. I just wanted to go back to my apartment and take a nap before whatever was going to happen at Bindings tonight.

"Do what?"

"Kiss you like that." The Zauberer scowled. "That man was an emissary for the Fae, Kleine. That means, while he may be a half-breed, he's got connections to the Courts."

Not many patients kiss your hand after a stomach pump. I thought it was sweet. Jove, apparently, did not, but I was so tired by this point I really didn't care. "So, Seelie and Unseelie or Summer and Winter?"

"They are interchangeable." He opened the limo door, then he stopped in shock. "Wait . . . how do you know about—"

"Jove, you've seen the inside of my bedroom, however briefly. You know I'm a nerd, the daughter of two nerds, in fact. I'm pretty sure it's a generational thing in my family. Now, since everything that has ever been turned into a bad Hollywood remake seems to be real, I'm assuming that most of the stuff I've read over the years has at least a basis, in fact."

"So, while your family does not have any sort of magical influence . . ."

"We're always fascinated by it." I grinned tiredly. "Hell, at my great-aunt's wedding, she had the inscription from 'the one ring' inscribed on the bottom of the wedding cake. And don't tell me you haven't read that book. It's on your classics shelf at the store."

"I am shocked nothing strange happened at this wedding. Tolkien was an elf." He smiled back at me.

"So, the runes from the book?" I asked with a yawn.

"Real."

We both started laughing. It took the edge off. We started chatting about all things nerd, which I was fine with. Usually, I only got to talk about things like this with David, my family, or at conventions. Our conversation turned to the nerdiest thing my family liked to do: tabletop role-playing games. Mom and Momma had a monthly running game.

"I will have to learn more about these nerds." He smiled and nodded. "I had no idea so much of the Community's information was out there already. And you say that people pretend to be Zauberers and imps in this game?"

"Not those exact words. I know Aunt Kate has played a druid, Aunt Kris as a vampire, and Momma as a Shukenja. Are those real, too?"

"Depends on what a Shukenja is." He frowned again, his voice grave. "Some of what you have told me is spot on. However, there is important information that has been left out. You have a brilliant mind, Mira, but you are also so very new to our world. There are so many dangers that could harm you."

"Like the Unkindness?" I leaned my head against the window again and watched the city pass us by.

"Yes, very much like the Unkindness. However, even the Ravens fear the wrath of the Fae."

That frightened me.

The Unkindness was the most powerful thing I'd run into so far. If they were scared of the Fae, so was I. I already knew the Fae were dangerous. Momma didn't just read us fairy tales. She also read us the legends with the darker sides to them. Her mantra with them was, 'You don't fuck with the Fae.'

"You are tired, Mira," Jove said after I yawned for the third time.

"No shit," I said with a sneer.

"And moody. You have not slept?"

"Not very well," I admitted. I told him about my nightmare from that morning. I watched as his frown deepened as I told him. I prayed he didn't think I was Veil-Struck after all.

"That sort of thing should not be happening. Your bracelet should prevent it."

I ran my fingers over the bracelet, letting the charms jangle. "I don't understand what could be blocking my memory. I remember everything else from the accident so clearly. There was one other thing. After I woke up, I heard a song, but no one was singing. It didn't feel like a memory. It was like someone was singing directly into my brain."

"That does not sound like anything I know of. If it were a ghost, you would have felt more of a presence. But they are unable to do anything to you without your cooperation. If it were some sort of Demon, it would only need your permission. Be careful with Demons. They are as dangerous as the Fae."

"I figured." They even scare me in movies and books. I could barely watch Coraline when my sisters insisted on watching it. Anything with Demons in them would haunt me for days.

"Here is your apartment building, Kleine. Did you need me to help you with anything else? I am able to place another ward on your home if you wish."

"Would it stop the nightmares?" I asked quietly. It felt so embarrassing to have to ask for help like this. I felt like a kid asking for a blankie.

"No. If they are not of magical origin, then, sadly, I cannot stop them other than the traditional way," he said with a small, private smile.

"What is the traditional way?" I quirked an eyebrow at him.

"To hold you until you feel safe again, Kleine." His chocolate eyes were intense as he took my hand. I flushed but didn't pull back right away. That really didn't sound all too bad. Maybe it was time to look into these feelings I had for this man. He wasn't my boss anymore. I'd been using that as an excuse to keep him at arm's length. We stayed in the back of the limo, holding hands until the ride came to an all-too-soon end. I reluctantly pulled my hands away.

"Have you any plans for the rest of today?"

I shook my head and climbed out of the vehicle. I still wanted that nap. "I had planned to look at a few properties today, but that got tossed out the window when Ms. Corvis called." I glanced down at my watch. "I'm going to have to call the realtor to reschedule. Then I'm going to take a nap. I'll see you tonight. How does five-thirty sound?"

"That will be fine, as long as you get to the shop before dusk. Summer is just beginning, so five-thirty should give us plenty of time."

"And I'm assuming you'll give me a lift home?"

"Of course, Kleine, I am at your disposal."

17

I CLOSED THE door and gave Jove a wave as the black limo pulled away. I rolled my eyes as I read the license plate: RVN1. I turned back to my apartment and almost ran smack into David. He grabbed my arms to steady me so I didn't fall on my ass. "Whoa. When did you get there?"

"Hey you." He smiled. "I was just about to knock on your door. Instead, you got delivered to me . . . out of the back of some weird black limousine." He was wearing a gray hoodie with a pair of well-worn jeans. The hoodie had the school's blue dragon across the chest. It had been tighter on him before he lost the weight around the middle. I was beginning to miss the comfortable squish he used to have.

"I had a consult with a patient. Seeing as I don't technically have an office yet, I went to their home. They're rich, so they offered to send a car for me. What are you doing in these parts?" David lived across town, a fair trek in Philly.

"Just thought I'd come by and see if you wanted to eat. You have a bad habit of forgetting to when you've got something big going. I figure you getting out of that limo was something big. We can grab a bite and talk about what you've got going."

The mention of food made my stomach rumble loudly.

David laughed. "There, your stomach agrees with me. What do you say? My treat."

"Did you have somewhere in particular in mind? Is it close?" I could go for a pizza if it wasn't too far away. I didn't want to be late to Bindings for the mysterious ritual.

"Yeah, actually, one of the puppy parents suggested a place just outside of the city. It's a little out of the way, but apparently, the food is worth it. It's called Lunar Seas."

I grinned. "Oh, how gloriously punny! Lunacies!"

He stopped short and snorted out a laugh. "How did I miss that? It even has that cartoon wolf from Looney Tunes on the door!"

I liked David's laugh. It helped put the picture of Mr. Alfenheim lying on a table out of my head.

"You didn't grow up with prolific punsters for relatives." I sobered. "That sounds like a dinner sort of place." I didn't know if I had time for a dinner kind of place, especially if it was too far away.

"It's a diner. They serve food all the time." David pushed his hands into the pockets of his hoodie. His shoulders were hunched. He seemed way more tense than the situation called for.

I glanced at my watch. "How far outside of the city are we talking?"

"Hour and forty-five minutes."

It was already after three; I'd never make it back by dusk. "Damn, if only you'd asked me earlier. I've got a thing." Please don't catch it. Please don't catch it.

"A thing," he deadpanned. "At the shop you supposedly don't work at anymore, I bet."

Damn, he caught it. "Yeah, Jove needs me at the shop tonight." I hated to beat around the bush with this, but I couldn't exactly tell my all-too-human best friend about the world of the weird.

"So not just a thing, it's a thing with Jove. Mira, you're a doctor now. Why do you still have to jump to his majesty's every whim?" He growled.

It wasn't really a question, but . . . I heard the venom in his voice and decided to take it as one. "I've *chosen* to help at the shop. There's a big shipment coming in. Jove needs help with the setup because Katie has a final tomorrow. Jove asked me, and I promised I'd help."

"So, make it a piecrust promise, then choose to come with me instead," David begged as we walked into my little hallway. "Brandt can handle the setup on his own. His place is *not* that big of a shop, and I really want to show you this diner."

He took my hand as if he were going to tug me along with him. He did the same thing when we went to conventions and he wanted to go to a specific panel. No blaming the Unkindness this time. This was definitely my David. He was still acting strange but not totally alien like the Bird-boy.

"So, you're asking me, though your tone makes it sound more like an order—and believe me, we *will* talk about that too. You're telling me to break a promise to a friend just to go to dinner. You know me better than that." I mean, I *do* love food, but I wasn't willing to back out of this. Really, I couldn't back out of the ritual. I needed to be there to stay involved in this magical world that'd just opened up to me.

I pulled my hand from his and blinked at the pain I saw in his eyes just before they went cold and angry. "I can always tell when you lie to me, Mira. Jove may have asked you to come in, but it wasn't for you to help him with some *stock*. You know, if you just don't want to hang out with me, you can just say so. You don't have to make up excuses. If you've decided that you want to start dating him, then all you have to do is tell me."

"David, where the hell is this coming from? Dating? Me and Jove? Even if that were the case, it wouldn't be your business unless I decide to tell you about it." I felt like I had to defend myself. I wrapped my arms around my belly, which had started to ache. I really wasn't enjoying this conversation. "It's not like that anyway. I have something important at Bindings that needs doing. If it wasn't important, I'd go to a restaurant with you in a micron."

"That's a unit of distance, Mira, not time."

"That isn't the *point*!" David was acting like a jealous boyfriend. I didn't like it. I sighed. "Look, I'm going to go inside, order a pizza, watch an episode of *Doctor Who*, and *hopefully* take a nap. But the way I'm feeling, I'm not sure I want you to join me. You may as well just go the hell home."

His shoulders sagged, and he looked down at his feet. When he looked up again, his eyes were sad again instead of angry. Pathetic and a little ashamed. "I'm sorry, I'm out of line here. I know you don't break a promise when you mean it, not unless someone's health is on the line. I'm acting stupid. I've been having some trouble at the clinic, and it's spilling over. I just really want to spend time with you. Pizza's on me for being an ass, but I'm hoping you'd still be willing to check out this diner soon if tonight's no good."

"Okay, I can work with that. Apology accepted, but I get to pick the episode."

"But you've watched that one a million times! You can practically recite the script!"

"Asses don't get options. *Allons-y*!" The Doctor makes everything better, or at least as better as he can make it with the tools he has. It was an episode that I loved, but I'd also seen it maybe twenty times before (certainly not the estimated million), and I was also so exhausted. I fell asleep on my best friend's thigh after the pizza, but before the Doctor figured out how there was water on Mars.

No dreams this time, thank God. By the time I woke up, David was gone. He'd made sure I was snug under the blanket with a pillow under my head before he left. Something was going on with him; I just couldn't peg what it was. Was it really just problems at the clinic? It was super random for him to bring up dating. We'd talked to each other about dating other people when we were still in high school. Who was hot, and who was not. We'd both tried dating other people, just never each other.

I caught a glance at my watch and cursed. I'd have to hurry if I wanted to get to the shop in time. The sun was setting by the time I pulled into the parking lot. The tall grandfather clock in the corner by the fireplace read 6:30 by the time I walked in the door of Bindings. How strange this felt. I'd walked down that entryway millions of times when I worked here, but now . . . it felt different, more important that things go just right.

Most of the lights were off, giving the fireplace a chance to cast its dancing shadows on the furniture. The firelight danced over the silhouettes of three wingback chairs. Tsk, Jove had forgotten to put up the screen again. It was strange to have a fire going at all with it being so close to summer. The heat it threw off made me glad I'd worn something light. I'd warned him before about the hazard of a fireplace in a bookshop. His answer was to put a fire extinguisher next to the pokers.

"Ah, here is the lady of the hour." Jove's voice came from one of the wingback chairs. Okay, so tonight we were talking in German. I could work with that. Both men stood as I stepped into the firelight.

The man standing with Jove was slightly shorter and slimmer, whereas Jove was rangy. He had short salt-and-pepper hair, a long hawkish nose, and striking blue eyes. A long cane with a gold lion's head for a top was an excellent accessory for the sharply dressed man in an Italian suit, shoes, and a bowtie. On the small table in front of them was a dark bowler hat and a massive leather-bound tome. The book had thick, handmade pages that looked like they'd been sewn into the spine with some thick twine. The leather was a dark cherry color and was titled 'Charter of the Community' in gold. The gold looked like it had been overlaid on the words that had been burned into the cover like a brand. Either that or pure molten gold had been used to handwrite the title, which I wouldn't put past a magical tome.

"Kleine, this is my colleague, Zauberer Xavier Zimmer. Zauberer, this is my woman of power, Frau Doktor Hall."

Phew, try saying that one five times fast. I frowned at the possession I heard in Jove's voice. It made me feel squitchy—not good, not bad, just . . . maybe not ready to analyze it yet. I held out a hand to shake.

"Fräulein." Zimmer took my hand and kissed it. It felt a little cold and slimy. I kept on my patient/customer smile despite his condescending

tone. What was with the Community and hand-kissing? I was going to have to invest in hand sanitizer. *"Zauberer Brandt has told me much of your power but little of your beauty."*

I brushed that off and pulled back my hand but kept the smile in place. *"He neglected to tell me anything about you, Herr Zauberer."* I took the chair across from the two men as we all sat down. *"I hope I haven't kept you waiting too long."*

"No, no," Zimmer assured me. *"I had suspected you to be late; most humans have trouble being prompt."*

Eww, racist much? I had to swallow my snide comment, but I felt my spine stiffen. This man held my practice and, very possibly, my life in the palm of his hand. I had to be polite and professional. Even if he was giving off evil, malevolent vibes.

Jove frowned. *"Frau Doktor Hall is one of the most accomplished and prompt humans I've ever had the pleasure of working with. She has earned respect."* Apparently, Jove didn't have to be polite.

"She may have your respect, Zauberer Brandt, but she has yet to earn mine," Zimmer said with a slim-arched eyebrow. I didn't like the look in his eyes as his cold gaze landed on me and studied me. I gave back my professional doctor stare, looking like I wouldn't blink if a psych patient screamed in my face.

Jove growled and stood. I shot him a look. I didn't need him to make things worse with Zimmer for me. The younger-looking Wizard nodded and took a seat back in his chair, steepled his fingers, and glared at his colleague. He looked cute when he pouted like that. I had to bite back a grin before speaking to Zimmer again. *"I understand I have to earn my place. I am not offended."*

He sneered down at Jove and spoke to him like a tenured professor to a misbehaving college freshman. *"I am here as a favor to your mentor, Brandt. I, personally, don't see why we need one such as her. We are the premier healers in the Community and shouldn't be so welcoming of . . . competition."* Zimmer turned his attention back to me. *"You call yourself 'Doktor.' Do you truly believe you have the skills to effectively treat members of the Community in ways that rival our magic?"*

"I do." I nodded, looking him in the eye. He had deep-set, steely eyes set in a long, pale, gaunt face that didn't seem to have much capacity for compassion. I felt my skin crawl.

"And what gives you such certainty?"

"Herr Alfenheim lives," Jove answered from behind his hands. I glared at the younger Wizard. He had no right to talk to Zimmer about what happened this morning. Mr. Alfenheim had a right to his privacy, and this man had no right to any information about one of my patients.

Zimmer's hawklike gaze snapped to Jove. *"What does the speaker for the Bright Court have to do with this? I was under the impression that this mess you've gotten us into had only to do with the Unkindness."*

"This morning," I began reluctantly—I was careful with my words to stay within my oath and HIPAA guidelines. *"I received a call from the Unkindness. As I made a deal, I intend to honor it. In exchange for my freedom, I will treat their members and employees. They called me for Herr Alfenheim."*

"What did you treat him for?"

"I am not at liberty to tell you more than that. Really, Zauberer Brandt shouldn't have brought it up." I gave Jove's chair a tiny kick.

"Why? Have something to hide?"

I felt my jaw clench as I lifted my chin defiantly. *"Doktor-Patient confidentiality. My patients have a right to their privacy."* I crossed my arms. *"I will not tell anyone anything more than that without the patient's express consent."*

"So, you are just." Zimmer smirked patronizingly. *"This, however, does not protect you from divulging secrets if you are placed under a spell. If I wished it, Frau Doktor, I could make you tell me."*

And then you'd meet the business end of a broom handle, you son of a . . . I took a breath. Professional, Mira. Be professional. *"So far, I have found that I do not remain under Zauberer spells for long, Zauberer*

Zimmer. Jove once tried a memory spell on my person, and I was able to break it within an hour." It gave me so much pleasure to see his face as it went slack with shock. The delicious cognitive dissonance was painted all over it. I couldn't help but smile.

"This is the true reason I suggested putting her in the Charter, Zauberer Zimmer," Jove said. *"She has true power to protect her patients. The Community needs her. Our healing spells and potions take precious time and are sometimes very costly to create and use. Why go through so much trouble when we have a human-passing doctor that our Community can make use of?"*

"I would also be working closely with Zauberer Brandt for those potions and spells when they are needed. This way, I wouldn't be competition, per se, but an asset."

Zimmer leaned forward and placed a bony hand on the weathered tome. *"Zauberer Brandt has taken it upon himself to push us to be your wardens. Do you understand what this means?"*

"To be honest, Zauberer, no, I don't know what it entails." I shrugged but wanted to squirm in my chair. *"Zauberer Brandt and I have not spoken about it in depth before now."*

Zimmer snorted. *"That idiot . . ."*

"I am sitting right here, you know," Jove grumbled.

"Fine," snapped Zimmer, his hawk nose pinning Jove like a mouse. *"YOU idiot! It was your responsibility to explain at least the rudimentary basics of being a part of this Community! I swear, if I didn't owe Rhoades a favor, I'd have sent a better spellslinger over here to do the job of modifying her memory properly and putting this whole business to bed. If spells aren't sticking to a mere human, then obviously, the fault lies with the caster. You are young yet, Brandt. I would have suggested more seasoning before giving you a post of your own—especially this far away from your family."*

Jove snorted this time, but Zimmer ignored him. Between the two of them snorting, they reminded me of two bulls trying to share the same pasture. It was starting to get a little ridiculous. My stomach churned at the thought of anything being 'modified' without my consent. If Jove was young at a hundred and fifty, just how old was this snakelike asshole?

Zimmer's tone became simplified, as if he were speaking to a young child. *"Being your wardens means we are responsible for any mistakes you make in the Community and are required by the Community Charter to see to any disciplinary actions up to and including death."*

My heart rate kicked up a notch in fear. Death was a pretty significant deterrent. Did I really want to join this Community? I didn't think I had the option to back out at this point. I had to have more information. I blanked my face before asking, *"Whose death?"*

"Yours if you break our laws. Theirs if you are put in harm's way. That is what this is." The old Zauberer motioned to the book sitting on the table between us. It opened by itself as his hand waved over it. The pages flipped by themselves until finally opening on a blank page. "We will speak your language for this part, Doctor Hall. By signing this, you are swearing an oath to our Community. Our laws will be your laws when dealing with others."

"Does the Community follow the laws of the land as well?" I asked carefully. "I don't want to have to call the police if a punch to the gut is something's way of saying 'Hello.'"

"A smart question . . . for a human." He sniffed.

Asshole. He reminded me of that one adult from youth group who told me I danced well . . . for someone my size.

"Yes, we do follow the laws set forth by the countries we live in. However, for obvious reasons, you do not call the police should such a thing occur. You should contact Zauberer Brandt should the occasion arise."

I nodded. "Are Zauberers the police for the Community?"

"That would make the most sense as we have the experience and prestige, but no." He grumbled. "More's the pity."

"It would be disastrous to only have one group of people in charge of all the rest when there are so many different types of people who are members of the Community. The Unkindness would no more take direction from us than we would from them. It would cause wars among ourselves when we need to be helping one another survive. So, it was decided to create an organization made up of all people from the Community called The Watch. They are set up much like modern police stations are," answered Jove. "They go through training and ranks, just like the police department in the city."

"We, as your *Aufsehers*, would be the step before calling upon the Watch. Zauberer Brandt will help you with the acclimation after you sign the Charter, of course. Should you decide not to sign . . ." His voice took on an ominous tone, his thin lips twisting into an unsettling grin. "We leave you to the Unkindness."

"Do you always enjoy trying to frighten people into doing things?" I used the same tone back at him. I wasn't as afraid of the Unkindness as I probably should be by this point. They were firmly in my mind as patients, and you shouldn't be frightened of patients because acting out could just be their way of expressing that they are in pain. "I'll read this first, before I sign."

Zimmer laughed snidely. "It's in *elvish*, human. It would take years for you to decipher." He handed the tome to me with a chuckle. "However, you are free to try."

I didn't tell him about my aunt, who was obsessed with Tolkien's books. Or the fact that she gave me an Elvish-English dictionary for my twelfth birthday. At the time, we thought it was a gag gift to go along with the Klingon dictionary on my bookshelf. I'd taken it to heart and became obsessed with learning fictional languages. I had Elvish and Klingon on my shelves at home and had my eye on one in Dothraki that I planned on buying when I had spare money again.

The Charter was heavy and smelled the way old books are supposed to smell. Its pages were handmade and sewn into the binding. I tried to turn the page to the previous entry, but they wouldn't budge. Were they playing a prank on me? I'd seen the pages flip when Zimmer waved his hand over it.

"Magic prevents anyone who has not signed from seeing who has," Jove said gently.

I nodded. That made sense. A secret society—no Community—of people who wouldn't want their identities known to just anyone who got a hold of this book.

I started at the top of the page. It took a bit of time to decipher the first lines. It became easier as I went. This was way more than just a town charter. This was a binding legal document that would hold in any court. "According to this, my signature must be in blood from my dominant hand when the moon is rising." I glanced at my watch. "Which is in about twenty minutes this time of year."

"*You mean to tell me she can actually read that?*" Zimmer snapped at Jove. German had a particular way of sounding very harsh when people snapped at one another. Still, I could also hear the shock and malice in the older man's voice.

"*Yes. My woman of power is full of surprises.*"

I made a face at him. "I'm not your 'woman of power,' Jove. Does it also have my designation here as a Gewalt? Why doesn't it say I'm human?"

"Mira, we cannot go around saying you are human." Jove frowned. "Please understand, Kleine, doing so would send a huge ripple of panic throughout the Community. You would never see any business and never pay off the Unkindness. At that point, they may think it is more profitable to sell you to your original buyer."

Damn, he had a point. The thought of that made my skin crawl. "So instead, we make me out as a new species?"

Both men nodded.

"It was the best the Spitzhut Manner could come up with on such short notice." Zimmer scowled at Jove. "Had we been notified sooner, much of this mess could have been avoided."

I tilted my head at him. "Avoided how?"

"We would have used a stronger memory spell cast by a more capable Zauberer to make you think your encounter with the Unkindness had merely been a bad dream and then slowly brought you into the fold as a new Zauberer." He glared at Jove again. "You should have notified us sooner, Brandt."

"Notified about what, precisely?" I interrupted. I was done being polite and done being patronized. I narrowed my eyes dangerously at Zimmer. "My kidnapping or my accident?"

"The magical happenings connected to your . . . ahem . . . incident." He cleared his throat. "I am speaking of the origin of your magic."

I rolled my eyes. "As I've told Zauberer Brandt on *many* occasions, I don't *have* any magic. My abilities are attributed purely to science. Quantifiable, repeatable, science."

The mage waved a hand dismissively. "That is hardly consequential, Doctor Hall. To suit our purposes here and now, you are the first Gewalt. This is now your race's designation."

"I'm only going to agree to this on one condition." I pointed at my chest. "I define what a Gewalt is. Not you. We keep my actual species in the definition." I crossed my arms over my chest. Zimmer was about to protest when I held up a hand. "I realize I don't have much leverage here. The only reason you're here is because you owed Jove's mentor a favor. None of us want an incident between my people and yours. However, I also refuse to be defined as something inhuman. It would not only be lying to my patients. It would sit wrong with me."

Jove and Zimmer stared at me for what felt like forever. In actuality, it was two minutes and forty-five seconds. Zimmer finally broke the silence after rolling his eyes, clearly thinking I was being ridiculous. "If we agree to this, will you sign the Charter and refer to yourself as a Gewalt?"

"I will." I nodded.

"Very well, what is your definition?" asked Jove gently.

"Gewalt: A Homo sapien who has been augmented by scientific means to have abilities beyond that of the cultural norm for Homo sapiens,"

I said primly, adding, "This may be accomplished through medical or biological means only."

The old mage nodded. "We will keep your 'definition' in our most secure tome in our most secure stronghold. It will be very hard for anyone to find. You will not give it to anyone."

"After all of this negotiation, that would be foolish of me to go shouting it."

"I've found humans to be foolish from time to time." He smiled.

I really didn't like this man. "What assurance do I have that I will not be blamed if someone figures it out, Zauberer Zimmer?"

"It would be better if no one 'figured it out.'" The old man's voice was ominous. "We are of an accord?"

I nodded.

"The only people to know what you truly are will be the Spitzhut Manner, Zauberer Brandt and myself. Now, we have little time before the zenith. Please, fill out the empty page in the Charter and we'll have you sign."

Name: Doctor Mira Jane Hall
Occupation: General Practitioner of Medicine
Race: female Gewalt
Date of oath: 09/01/2055
Preferred language when dealing with your race: English

I hereby swear to obey by the laws of the Community and do my best to help my neighbors in times of trouble. I will use my abilities in their defense if I am so called. Their secrets are my secrets and will be kept as such when pertaining to the Community.

Signed:

———————————————————————

My hair stood up on the back of my neck. I suddenly felt like something was too close to me and I felt trapped. I looked up. Zimmer was looming above me. He had a wicked-looking knife in his hands. Its handle was some sort of bone and etched with runes; the blade itself looked silver and sharp. I only had the chance to make a small panicked sound as he snatched my right hand up and twisted the tip of the blade into my forearm.

I yipped in pain and scowled at him. "Did you have to use something so . . . large to poke me?"

"It is tradition. The Community relies heavily on tradition." He handed me an old-style quill pen, the kind you dip into an inkwell. Only this time the ink was going to be the welling blood on my arm.

"You enjoyed scaring me like that," I accused. He smiled—that bastard.

"Oh yes." He grinned. "You are arrogant, Doktor. The price of arrogance in our world is high."

"It's high in mine as well. If a physician gets too arrogant, they have a tendency to miss things. Things that can save a person's life. Zauberer Zimmer, how long have you had that pain in your right foot? You may want to consider coming in for a checkup. It could be plantar warts. We might have to operate. Burn them out."

Jove snorted; both Zimmer and I glared at him. Using my ability, I *pulled* an alcohol swab, some medical tape, and a gauze pad from my purse to clean the wound after I set the bloody pen to thick paper and signed my name as the clock struck the hour. Zimmer watched as the supplies floated out of my purse and zipped down the hall to my waiting hand.

"Remarkable," he said, sounding impressed for the first time. "There was truly no magic in use when you did that."

"As I said, Zauberer." I nodded as I saw to my wound. I'd suspected there would be some sort of blood ritual with this signing tonight. There always is when something like this was coming into play in just about every book and story. When everything says the same thing, there are good odds of it being true. Thankfully it wasn't more than being poked with the tip of a knife longer than my forearm, but the bastard had pushed deeper than was necessary, so I had to use the gauze pad instead of the adhesive bandage I'd hoped for.

As the old clock chimed, the tome throbbed under my hands. My bloody signature seemed to be absorbed into the paper and then suddenly reappeared in blinding gold. I gave a little gasp and stared at the page I'd written on. I felt myself being compelled to lean in closer. How had it done that?

I didn't get a chance to investigate as Zauberer Zimmer snatched the throbbing book from under my hands and placed it in a canvas satchel at his side.

"The price of curiosity is high as well, young woman," he chided snidely. "It is done. Welcome, Doktor Hall, to the Community. You will receive your copy in due course."

Zimmer wrapped his spindly fingers around the ornate cane, placed the bowler on his head, and suddenly vanished.

"Pompous bastard," Jove cursed.

"I couldn't agree more," I said as I stood and walked back to my purse to replace the tape. Jove stopped me as I went to toss the bloody alcohol wipe away in the waste bin.

"Not there, Kleine. Now that you are part of the Community, you will show up in all of the copies of the Charter that exist. There is always a . . . rush of interest, shall we say, when something new is written that hasn't been seen before. You must be careful with your bodily leavings like hair or nail clippings." He pulled out a silver bucket that had been under the register. I'd seen him use that bin before from time to time, but I'd thought it was just another waste bin. He held it up for me to toss in the wipe.

I arched an eyebrow and tossed it in. The thing made a slight *fwoosh* sound as it passed the lip of the small metal can and incinerated, leaving behind only ash at the bottom of the bin. "Oh cool! A mini-incinerator! I take it that it works on magic, as there's no electric power going to it and the speed of the incineration that just happened there. You can't even smell it burning! Wow! Can I get one or two of those for my practice?"

Jove smiled broadly. "Yes, I will get you in contact with a seller after you open. I have one for you to take home with you. Think of it as a welcome gift. Use it for things such as that. Blood, hair, and other bodily fluids can all be used against you by some very nasty things, so be careful."

He handed me a similar silver bucket wrapped in gauzy gift wrapping that had a silly bow on it. I cradled it on my hip and grinned at him. Then the ticking of the grandfather clock reminded me about how late it was.

"I should get going. Toria'll kill me if I'm too late with her dinner again."

"And we cannot have that. The little hero deserves her due." He handed me my purse. "Here. I will take you home."

18

I WAS DOING all right with him walking beside me. I was fine as he opened the passenger side door for me. I was hunky-dory as I sat down, but when the door closed, my breath caught in my throat. Why was it happening now? I thought I'd be fine as a passenger, but the sound of the door closing pulled me under.

Air rushing by my ears and smoke clogging my nose. Pain everywhere. Darkness all around me as my horn blared because the internal workings of my car were wrapped around the pole and pinning me to my seat. I couldn't breathe . . . couldn't . . . breathe . . . COULDN'T BREATHE!

When I came to myself again, the cheerful green gift bag sat sideways on the ground, and I was cradled in Jove's arms and sitting on the gravel of the parking lot at Bindings. He was stroking my head, which was leaning against his chest, and singing something soft and low. The rhythmic music with the beating of his heart under my ear made me breathe out a shuddering breath. I was okay. I was safe. Nothing could hurt me right then. Not when I was protected by Jove's strong arms.

"There," he crooned to me, "there you are, Kleine. You went away for a little while there."

"I'm sorry, Jove. I—I don't know what happened," I lied.

"Yes, you do. You were having a panic attack." David wasn't the only one who could see through my lies, apparently. "Why did you not tell me that this was happening to you?"

I pushed away a little. My legs felt too weak to hold me up just then, but I didn't want to be comforted. I pushed away and leaned against the side of my car. I rubbed my hand over my face and eyes to wipe away any tears. "It's not something I'm proud of. I'm working on it with my therapist. Damn it, I'm going to have to put this in my journal. I'd really hoped I was far enough along for this"—I gestured up and down at myself—"to not be something that affected me so much anymore."

"Mira, it has been only a few months since the accident. No one is expecting you to be exactly as you were so quickly. Things like that change lives! Look at how much it has changed yours." He stood and held a hand down to help me stand. "You are an amazing woman. Your abilities were strong and remarkable even before the Unkindness harmed you. You can choose to view this as a setback, or you can take it as your next challenge and overcome it as you have everything else this life has thrown at you so far. Will you let me drive you home now?"

"How will you get back if you drive my car to my place?"

He smiled wryly. "I am a Zauberer. I will use magic, of course."

I chuckled. "Oh, of course, how could I forget?" I let myself lean against him as he picked up the wrapped waste bin and handed it to me again. I put it in the back seat, then opened the door to the passenger side. Jove had to adjust the seat to fit his longer frame. I'd put it back to its original position in the morning when the sun kept these attacks at bay.

We chatted amicably on the way back to my apartment. Jove said it would take a few days to get my copy of the Charter, but now that my name was included, I'd be able to see the names and designations of the other signers of the Community. Apparently, it was something that was usually done when a child became an adult, and it usually got accompanied by a big party with the signer's entire family. Since I was the only Gewalt so far, no big party for me, but it was still customary to get a gift. Hence, the rubbish bin of concentrated flame.

True to his word, once he saw me safely to my door, Jove winked out of sight similarly to how Zimmer had earlier, though I think Jove had more panache with it.

I got back to my apartment later than usual, and Toria let me know it. I was constantly surprised that none of my neighbors ever came over to ask about the noise when she complained at me.

"Meowing at me is not going to make me move any faster, little cat. You've got too much pudge around your middle to be *that* hungry." She yowled again as I picked up her dish. "So, I had an interesting day. I saved someone's life, pissed off my best friend, and, after all of that, I joined a secret society, and had a grand mal panic attack." I scratched her behind her ears as she dove into the food. "Not that you care anything about any of that as long as you get your food on."

After feeding the cat, I fed myself and took stock of the day. All in all, it wasn't a horrible day, just tiring. I shoved a small dish of leftover spaghetti into the microwave and hit reheat. Lunch with David had been nice, with us having the Doctor to distract us from what had happened outside. That had been too weird. He had never acted like that before. Then he'd shaken it off like a dog shakes off water. I'd have to keep an eye on him. What if the dog that bit him had rabies?

Munching on the hot pasta, I mused about the ceremony. Zimmer just rubbed me the wrong way. I didn't like his bigotry against humans, or his feeling of superiority for Zauberers. I didn't like how he enjoyed scaring me, and I really didn't like how his eyes had a look of glee with that knife. The experience hit on my creep-o-meter. Momma taught her girls to pay attention to the creep-o-meter. Zimmer hit an eight; I never wanted to be alone in a room with him.

That left me pondering Mr. Alfenheim. What the hell could he have eaten to cause that severe of a reaction? Why wouldn't he have noticed it in his food? Oh sure, I told the Unkindness it wasn't my job to deduce what had happened, but I was damned curious. I really wanted to be the one to have a look at that bile under a microscope, but I wasn't about to let myself be pushed around. I could *not* look weak to them. They'd already seen me at my most vulnerable, and I was not about to let them see that in me again.

The Fae have a species-wide allergy to metal. Though, now that I had time to think about the procedure, I realized Mr. Alfenheim had a wicked-looking knife on him. It had been in a sheath attached to his right calf. I'd checked him all over to make sure the pathogen hadn't been injected somewhere other than his throat. I'd only seen the pommel, but I was assuming the blade had been made out of silver or some other sharp non-metallic component.

Why would Mr. A have eaten metal without tasting it? Decorum? The motive didn't matter, not unless he was trying to kill himself. I could still feel where his lips had been on the back of my (then) gloved hands. The man had been grateful for his life. So, then the offending metal must have been small enough for it not to have been able to be tasted. It could have even been masked in the condiments, especially strong-tasting ones like mustard, vinegar, or horseradish. Why would anyone do that? Did they want Mr. Alfenheim dead? Was it only in Mr. Alfenheim's food? It was too late to call Ms. Corvis and ask. I rinsed out my dish and left it in the sink to deal with in the morning. I needed sleep. I got ready for bed and turned on the camera aimed at where I slept.

"Sleep diary. Day two. I've had a trying day. I'm not looking forward to the dreams tonight. I don't have the correct equipment to monitor myself properly, yet. Note to self: look on eBay for proper equipment." I let out a snort. "Not that I can afford it on my own yet. I may be able to stretch it under my private grant." I got into bed and yawned. "Goodnight."

19

I was dreaming of pastel ponies who were taking me on their adventures and treating me like a close friend. We were having a great time having parties and saving the pony world from rats with wings that breathed fake fire. I was helping one of them load a cannon with confetti when I heard it.

"Lavender blue, dilly, dilly! Lavender green. If I were king, dilly, dilly, you would be my queen."

"I'm no one's queen," I muttered. "And that song is getting old."

"You would be if you came with me," said a familiar voice in my ear. I could feel warmth against the side of my face. "You would be treated like a queen by our people, and by me."

I looked to see where the sound was coming from. Cresting the cartoonish green hill confidently strode a man. He was taller than me and dressed like a knight with a peculiar crest on his tabard. It was black, green, and red, depicting a black knight on a red horse, his black spear stabbing mercilessly into a green dragon. His chest piece shone in the sunlight of my dream; he had a long broadsword at his side and a large shield on his back. His hair was cut short and blond with frosted tips, matching perfectly with his perfectly shaped eyebrows and clean-shaven face. He had the perfect face, perfect hair, perfect armor, and perfect muscles. *Too* perfect for my tastes.

He didn't fit in the pony world.

We were suddenly sitting in a medieval tavern at a small round table alone, a candle in between us and plates of pasta set in front of us. The perfect date.

"Is this more to your liking?" He was now dressed in a white suit with the undershirt's top two buttons undone. This was closer to my usual fantasy, but something still felt wrong.

"You can read my thoughts. I don't know if I like that." I jabbed at the food on my plate; more spaghetti, like I'd had for my actual dinner. "Granted, I don't know if you are a figment of my imagination, or"—I jabbed extra hard at a meatball—"an invader."

The man held up his hands. "Mira. I'm no figment, but I have invaded your sleep. I'm sorry." He didn't sound sorry at all. It was a very casual apology. "I just have so much to tell you. I'll admit I got impatient. The Doctor always says it's one of my few flaws."

"There was no way the surgery that's in my medical records, the one after the accident, had only a doctor and one assistant. Not with the amount of damage I had going on."

"You're so smart, Mira. I love that about you. You're right. The procedure where I got to meet you for the first time isn't something you'll find in your official records. You looked so soft and innocent then. We'd planned on bringing you to the compound as soon as you were recovered enough, but your family . . . got in the way."

I felt a shiver go down my spine. It had to be Alden. The surgeon had been far too desperate when the Moms busted me out. I wasn't sure if he was the head honcho or the middleman, but my not-so-dear colleague was in this up to his pompous neck. If only to deliver me to this 'compound' the man was talking about. "That would make you . . ."

"Matthew. At your service, my lady." He grabbed my hand and kissed it. "Please, don't be afraid. I'm not a bad guy. I should have waited and introduced myself slowly, like he told me to. I was just too excited. There are only a few of us right now, but that will change soon, with your help."

"I'm confused. How and why am I going to help you?" I pulled my hand back. "So far you've invaded my mind and my privacy. Tell me, why should I help you?"

Matthew blinked and looked genuinely surprised I'd asked. "Because you're one of us, one of the new race of humans. A superior race. We are the selected few. The remedy to the evils around us."

"Us being?" I felt my stomach twist with every word he said, but I had to know more.

"We are the ACS. The Anomaly Catholicon Shepherds. The Doctor chose us, plucked us out of the masses and created us to protect the people from *them*."

"Them being . . ."

"The monsters," he said quietly. "They're all around us and no one even knows! Well, some people know, but they don't come out right after they find out."

I sat quietly and thought of my favorite Queen song. It started playing in the background; mustn't let the crazy man find out you know he's crazy. "You mean the Community. The one I just joined today." No reason to lie to him, he'd read my mind anyway.

"You're right about that. Not that you can lie here anyhow." He shrugged, took a bite of his food, then he got this look of horror and revulsion on his face as what I'd said finally took root. "Why in God's name would you go and *join* them? All they want to do is make meals out of humanity! They literally eat human souls! Okay. It's okay. I'm sure the Doctor can work with this. So, when you wake up, you need to call the phone number I'm going to leave on your bedside."

That sent a shock of fear through me. The music came to a screeching halt. He was in my apartment?

"Yes, it gives me a better connection when I'm touching the person I want to communicate with. I don't like what you've done to your hair. It looks like a boy's cut. It'll grow out thankfully; it was so much prettier when you had it long."

"You are reading my thoughts pretty well, but you seem to be missing out on some things." My voice was low and dangerous. How dare this arrogant, pop-star wannabe invade not only my dreams, but my home? Touch me without *consent*? I felt an animalistic growl claw at my throat.

"Oh? What's that? Wait, 'pop-star wannabe?'" Matthew's face twisted in confusion.

"Emotions aren't really your thing, are they? You are a telepath, so you miss things. Like right now?" I *shoved* him away from the table. This was *my* dream, *my* head. Invaders had no power here. "Right now, I am very angry." He flew into a human-sized hanging cage and I locked the door behind him. There was a sound of glass breaking as he slumped to the bottom of the cage.

I smiled with satisfaction as he sat and cursed. If he was feeling pain, that meant he most likely got shoved into my display case in my bedroom. Damn, that also meant I had to replace the glass in my display case after I woke up.

Waking up sounded like just the right thing to do just then.

I jumped out of bed to find Matthew passed out in my main display case, Doctor Jones' hat covering his face. He looked a lot like he had in my dream, minus the white knight complex. I checked his pulse and cursed. Blood was starting to pool underneath his body. I had to find the wound, plug the hole. The camera was still going but was now facing the carnage. "Fuck. Don't die on me, fuckwit. I'm so getting the police in on this jazz."

I cursed again when I noticed one of my sharp, pointy replicas had sliced his arm. That was the only wound I found on his body, but the blood was flowing fairly fast. The slice was dangerously close to a major vein. I ran into my bathroom to get the first aid kit from under the sink. I had some black emergency thread in there along with some gauze. I *closed* the wound with my ability as I stitched him up. While he was still passed out, I took the opportunity to tie him up.

Time to call the police. Not that they would believe me, but all I had to tell them was that I got the drop on an intruder. I had to turn to get my phone from the nightstand. There was the phone number Matthew had left, as promised. When I turned back, there was a woman kneeling beside the telepath.

She had long blond hair tied back in a tail and wore tactical black from the neck down. She glared at me and put a hand on Matthew's chest. I blinked and they were gone, leaving me with glass and blood to clean up. I sat on my bed dumbfounded. I *turned* the camera back to face me.

"End of Sleep Tape Two," I said, and with that, I shut it off. I had to do some cleaning before I could sit down and think of what to do next. The bleach took the blood up from the hardwood no problem, but it still took some time to make it safe to walk again.

My phone told me it was three in the morning. I kept shivering when I tried to get back to sleep, but I didn't feel safe anymore. It wasn't until I took the replica of the Axe of Whiterun from *Skyrim* from its place in the case and set it in the bed next to me that I could finally get back to sleep. The axe had been a gift from David on my birthday the year I started playing the game. He said it was just in case I had to fight a dragon at home.

I woke, annoyed, the next morning to a pounding at the door. I'd only gotten to sleep three hours ago if my clock was to be believed. I couldn't call the police when the intruder had literally disappeared. The pounding became harsher as I pulled on a light robe. Someone was very insistent.

"Hold on, I'm coming." I growled. I didn't expect a growl in return. Was that someone with a dog? I didn't get much farther than my bedroom doorway before my front door broke, sending shattered bits of wood flying through the air like shrapnel. I dove behind my couch with a scream. It felt like a bomb had gone off on my door.

Weapon. I needed a weapon. I could see the shattered case from the open door of my bedroom. I saw the handle of the axe replica on the floor. It must have fallen as I slept. I *grabbed* it and *pulled*. It wobbled on its slower-than-usual journey from my bedroom floor to my hands. I shook my head hard. The fear was scattering my concentration which, in turn, was scattering my ability. I focused and sighed with relief as it found its way into my hand. I clutched the wooden handle tightly; the silver design on the axe head seemed to glow in the hazy light of the dawn peeking in through the bottom of my windows. I pressed myself against the side of the couch, moving into a crouch. My ears strained in the sudden silence as I tried to be as quiet as humanly possible. Where was it? *What* was it?

That's when I heard the growl again. It was low and deep. It shook me to my bones and woke a kind of fear that humans have had in our blood to warn us of predators. I started to shake. I forced my breathing to be slower, to try to calm myself. I couldn't let this scare me more. The last thing I needed right now was another panic attack. Jove had to be coming, right? The wards he put on my apartment should have gone off when this thing broke the door.

Momma would have chided me for sounding like a damsel in distress. She used to yell at Disney princesses to help the hero fight instead of standing there wringing their hands. Mom thinks it's cute and laughs at her while she's ranting at the screen. I gripped my axe tighter and slowly looked around the side of the couch.

Wolf.

Big wolf.

Very big wolf.

Its tawny fur seemed gold in the miserly shaft of dawning sunlight that trickled in from my only window that faced our complex's inner courtyard. Why was it lying down? Unless crashing through my door took more out of it than it had planned. The wolf snarled and tried to stand up again, only to fall back onto its belly. I didn't think it could move from where it had landed. Slowly, I stood, axe in hand.

Its eyes were closed as it struggled under some unseen weight. It wasn't me doing this, so it had to be one of the effects of the ward Jove had set. I breathed in and out slowly. "Okay, okay. There's a wolf, somehow pinned to my living room floor, by magic."

Saying things out loud can be calming. I didn't expect it to calm the beast on my throw rug. The wolf stopped struggling and let out a breath and a long whine, not unlike my parents' dogs. It sighed deeply, and I could have sworn it was a sound of relief.

"I'm betting you're going to be staying there until I can get a hold of Jove." My phone rang. It was playing "Magic Dance" by David Bowie. Jove's ringtone. "Speak of the devil and all that jazz."

"*Mira!* Kleine!" Jove shouted after I answered. "I felt the ward go from the shop. I am right outside." He breathed hard, and, as if reading my mind, added, "I used my magic to get here as fast as I could." I heard the slam of the apartment complex doors that led to the parking lot as the man himself barreled through. He was in the middle of shoving something into his pocket, but it looked too large to be a cell phone. It looked like the handset from an old landline unit.

"Did anyone see you?" Some of my neighbors were nosy so-and-sos who'd record anything on their phones to show the world.

"Never mind that." His panicked eyes looked me over. "Are you all right? Are you injured?"

"I think I'm okay here. My door is now toothpicks, but there's no physical damage. Your spell did its job well." I motioned to the still-pinned form of the wolf with my axe. "He's real, right?"

Jove nodded. "The Unkindness have never been invited into your home. They would be incapable of this Werewolf on your rug."

I froze. "*Were*wolf?"

"You thought it was a large dog, perhaps?" I made a face. He chuckled, waving a hand over the shattered bits of corrugated wood. "Here."

The door reformed in the frame. All of the bits of shrapnel collected and flowed together, mimicking water more than wood. I arched an eyebrow at the Wizard.

"A simple mending spell," Jove explained, closing the reformed door behind him. "We do not want nosy neighbors."

It was impressive to watch something like that happen for no apparent reason.

My life was weird.

I blew out a breath I didn't know I was holding. That was one of the few times I'd seen Jove do such obvious magic. Warmth on my aching knees was one thing, but this was so cool to watch happen. I walked forward and put my hand on the now-intact door. It didn't look like anything had happened to it at all. "Whoa."

"Perhaps we should see to your guest's needs. It will be easier for him to explain himself if he is in human form. I am going to alleviate some of my weight spell so you are able to change, *Blutwulf*. No funny business. I will not hesitate if you mean harm."

The wolf rose into a sitting position and hung its head. "It is not her fault you were caught." Jove preened. "I am just that good. Mira, if you have a blanket, he will be naked when he shifts back."

Before I could move, the wolf stood and pulled out a throw blanket I always stored under the couch.

"He is someone you know?" Jove looked to me.

I shrugged. "If he is, then he didn't let me know he wolfed out once a month." The wolf lightly snagged the corner of the handmade blanket and deftly tossed it into the air, quickly diving under it.

I got a sick feeling in my stomach. I'd only seen one person able to do that. He did it on winter nights when we were marathoning shows. One of those silly things he did because he wanted to prove he could.

"Oh, David, why didn't you tell me?" I covered my mouth with my hand. "You could have told me."

20

His voice was garbled under the blanket. He sounded like he was in pain. The blanket moved in ways the human body was never meant to move. "This is a new development for me, *MirRrrah. RRrrrrr*, I didn't have the chance to *grrrr* tell you." He groaned as bones popped back into place. There is no mistaking that sound once you've had to set a dislocation. "I . . . uhhh . . . came over to see if you wanted to go see if the mall had any new"—a whimper—"Who stuff. Then I smelled the blood." He growled. "I thought you were hurt."

David was panting hard, in obvious pain. It served him right for breaking my door. I scowled, then my expression softened. This obviously wasn't what he'd originally planned.

I walked carefully around to secure the blanket around my friend. "It's okay, Goliath. I'm all right. It's not my blood."

He shook his head. "No, I smelled *your* blood, too." David looked pointedly at my still-healing arm, the cut from Zauberer Zimmer. "You *are* hurt."

"It's okay, that one I did on purpose, and I've treated it. I used antiseptic and everything." I showed him the patch I'd put over the wound from the ritual.

His head then cocked to the side as he saw my other arm. "Is that a tattoo? When did you get a tattoo?"

"Good to see you again, *Schnucki*. You are looking as muscular as ever," Jove said with an appreciative smirk. David pulled the blanket a little tighter around his shoulders and leaned away from the Zauberer, an angry pink coloring the tips of his ears.

"You thought David was not smelling your blood. A good question then, Kleine, is whose blood did you think he smelled?" Jove's voice was chilled. I rolled my eyes. What was I supposed to do, tell him about my nighttime visitor when my best friend just shape-shifted in my living room?

"Mir, do you have a spare pair of pants I can borrow?" David's voice sounded raw, but at least the sickening noises of rearranging bones and sinew had stopped.

"I'm going to get you some tea, too, for that throat." I turned away. "But for breaking in my door, I'm choosing what you wear."

"What is she talking about, *Schnucki*?"

"She's mad that I broke in her door, so she's going to make me wear something embarrassing." I heard a growl as I walked toward my room. "And don't call me 'Schnucki.'"

"Play nice!" I shouted over my shoulder. I closed the door behind me and sat hard on my bed.

I took a deep breath in and blew it out slowly. My heart was still racing. My hands were having trouble holding my axe. So, I *held* it in the air while I took a few more deep breaths before pulling the bottom drawer and getting some sweatpants for David. I grabbed the pair of oversized plain gray sweats. Let him think I'd give him the pair that said 'Juicy' on the ass. I frowned at the empty frame of my broken case and *set* the axe back in its slot.

I had to tell them, after getting dressed, of course. I put the sweats on the bed and grabbed out a Smithsonian tee and a pair of jeans for myself. In short order, I was dressed and slipped the chip from the video camera into my pocket.

David was sitting on my couch looking miserable, wrapped in my blanket. He looked at the sweats in my arms. "No 'Juicy' ass?"

"I figured you'd suffered enough with the shift." I looked at his face. "You're still in pain, aren't you?"

He grunted. "I can't take anything you've got here," he said, practically reading my thoughts. He always could do that. "My metabolism is through the roof, and nothing you'd give me would work for long anyway. I'll be okay, Mir."

"I'm still getting you that tea. High metabolism or not, it'll make you feel better." I stopped short. "Is your body affected by your wolf DNA when it comes to food and drink?"

"From what my sponsor told me, when I'm in human form, I can eat and drink what I like. In wolf form, I have to be more careful. Sure, I'm a strong son of a bitch now, but caffeine and cocoa would do bad things to me when I'm the wolf."

"Where *is* your sponsor, Schnucki?" Jove asked.

"It's 'David' to you," David said with a curled lip at the Zauberer. He took the pants from me and made his way into my bathroom. "We're not friends, and I sure as hell am *not* your sweetie-pie."

"Oh, but you make the cutest faces when you are angry," Jove teased. "However, it is highly irresponsible of them to let a new wolf out in the world alone."

"I don't have to answer to you." David growled through the door. "Mira didn't have that big-ass knife wound on her arm when I left her place yesterday. That means she got it while she was with *you*. She should have been with *me* where she would've been *safe*." He appeared in the sweats, shaking his head like he was clearing it. "Mira, can I talk to you? Privately?" He stalked into my bedroom.

I looked to Jove, and he reluctantly made himself scarce, disappearing as he had last night after the ritual when he brought me home.

The tone of David's voice told me this was going to be one of those serious conversations.

I quietly closed the door behind me. David was sitting on my bed, looking miserable. I sat next to him and stared at the ruins of my cabinet.

Long shards of glass jutted up out of my little trash can like the teeth of an ice giant.

"So . . ." I said.

"So, yeah," he said.

"I take it there's a reason you came over this morning? You don't usually just show up without warning. You usually at least shoot me a text."

"Mira, I wanted to take you out, really out. A nice dinner, a movie, maybe some dancing." He let out a morose sigh. "I had a bouquet."

"A what?"

"Flowers, Space Station! I bought you flowers. Purple and blue tulips. I dropped them when I smelled your blood. They're probably smashed into the hallway carpet outside."

"Dinner, movies, dancing, *and* flowers? That . . . sounds a lot like a date."

He nodded. "I've been wanting to tell you for so long how I've felt about you."

He grabbed one of my pillows and started slowly twisting it. "I just . . . couldn't find the right way, the right time, to tell you like I wanted to. To tell you I've been in love with you for a long time. I just never thought I could be the type of guy you deserved. Someone strong. Someone you could depend on if something bad were to happen."

He stood and started pacing. "There are some good things that come along with the shift. Look, I'm built like Cap now." He held out his arms, my pillow still in his hand, to show me the admittedly impressive muscles he'd grown.

I sucked in a breath and let it out as I sat at the end of the bed. I waited until he sat back beside me. I didn't look at him. "I never cared if you looked like Cap. You've always been there for me. You already are someone I depend on. You get my jokes! Though I'll admit, this is one hell of a way to find out your best friend wants to be more than friends."

"But how do you *feel* about it, Mir?" His voice sounded a little desperate.

"To be honest, David, I don't know. I really don't. I've only been awake for, Jesus God, three hours after one of the worst nights I've ever lived through. I take it they had you sign the Charter as well?"

"Yeah, the night after my first shift. Amos had a big to-do after I signed and assigned Jerimiah to me as my mentor. You'd like him. The guy's built like Everest, but is sweet on the inside."

"Similar for me, but no mentor and no big party. After that whole thing, these two people broke in. The guy you smelled? He was in my head, David. In my *dreams*, he told me that I had to join up with him and his people against the monsters." I made a claw-like mocking gesture with my hands. "He was right here in this room touching my head while he was talking to me in my dreams. Oh, and joy among joys, he told me there was another procedure. One that's not on my official charts where he had a front-row seat. But I've scoured my records. They don't show a second operation. This group . . . the ACS . . . they're turning people into . . . into something else."

I didn't realize I was shaking until I blinked and looked at my hands. "I think they turned *me* into something else."

I *lifted* the pillow gently out of his hands with my ability. His eyes went wide as they followed the pillow into my arms. I hugged it close. "You aren't the only one who's had some new developments, David. This is why I was allowed to join the Community. They're calling me a Gewalt. And, dear God, I'm scared."

I felt tears sting in my eyes. I told him about the Unkindness and the deal I had to make with them to secure my freedom, my tears making my voice stutter.

David gathered me in his arms. They felt warm, strong, and made me feel safe. It felt so comforting, just to be held for a minute. For just a moment, I wasn't in the arms of someone wanting to be my boyfriend, but instead, I was in David's arms, my best friend. He held me like this once before when Grandma Smith died. I could find solace in those arms. I broke and started sobbing in earnest. I clutched at one of his arms as he started to rock me. He waited until my sobbing calmed before he kissed the top of my head. "Well, that explains the random X-Men trivia in the park. I knew something was wrong that day. You were pale and smelled scared. It was like burning plastic and rubber. Acrid. I had to ask Jerimiah what the smell meant."

"What do I normally smell like?"

"It depends on what you did that day. Like now, you smell like bleach and blood."

"You came too early for me to hop in the shower and re-dress the wound on my arm."

He made a sound deep in his chest. It wasn't an entirely human sound.

I shoulder-checked him. "It needed doing. I had thrown one of the Unkindness into a truck with my brain."

"So, while I became Cap, you became Jean Grey." David laughed before getting serious again. "Mira, I know you're scared right now and overwhelmed, but . . . that doesn't change how I feel about you. How I want us to be a thing together." He looked directly into my eyes and my breath caught. Since when did being this close to David do *that*?

He leaned down and touched the side of my face with his hand. "Oh God, you're gorgeous."

He brought his face down the rest of the way and angled it so his lips covered mine.

Fizzle-pop! Unexpected shutdown in progress, prepare to reboot cranial function. His lips were soft, questing, but not demanding. And I was responding. My heart was kicking as I let him continue on his quest. We pulled apart and panted like divers coming up for air.

Then he breathed in deeply through his nose. He moved to smell against the side of my head.

"Really?" I snorted. "Are you really sniffing my hair right now like a creep?" I poked a finger in his ribs.

"I—I think I have his scent. It doesn't smell like you. I have to ask Jerimiah what to do next." He stood up and held out a hand for me. "If you're ready, that is."

I took his hand. "Yeah, I think I'm done bawling for the moment. It never solves anything for me anyway."

"But it's barfing for the *soul*," he said with mock passion. It made me laugh.

"Yeah, well, I don't much like barfing either. I've got footage of the bastard while I was doing my sleep study. It'd be easier just to hook the damned thing up to the TV."

David grabbed the camera from the tripod. "You're the only person I know who'd set up their own sleep study rather than going in to get one done."

"I've been doing other experiments too. I could use an objective eye on them if you're interested."

"Maybe later. I want to find out if there's a way to track this guy." David pulled out his phone and started texting. "Jay can get here in two shakes and, much as I hate to admit it, you should probably call Magic Man back and have him come over too. He's the closest thing you have to a mentor who is familiar with the Community."

"I'm not sure." I shifted from foot to foot. Mentor didn't feel right. Especially how Jove made me feel when he'd kissed my hand. "The Zauberers are more like my wardens. Or that's how it was explained to me. It feels like I'm on probation. I'm glad it's Jove rather than Zimmer, though."

"The guy with the knife." David's lip curled. "He sounds like a bigger asshole. At least Jove has a nice ass. Even if he does have questionable taste in entertainment. Seriously, I was talking about Two-Face with Katie the other day and he thought we were talking about Dr. Jekyll and Mr. Hyde."

"Admittedly, very similar characters," I pointed out.

"Text sent." He grinned. "I wonder who would win in a fight?"

"Two-Face. He has goons *and* guns," I said. "Hyde was a bruiser; beat his victims to a pulp with his cane. Bullets beat cane unless you're bulletproof."

"Yeah, but if you take away the weapons? Then it's just two assholes beating each other. Hyde reportedly had the muscle to be a contender."

"But Two-Face would *still* win by virtue of better healthcare. We had better medicine in the twentieth century when he made his debut." I smiled and settled in for a good debate while we waited for the Wizard and the Werewolf.

21

Jove got there first. "I was not far. I knew you wished for privacy, but Schnucki is a *new* Werewolf, Kleine. Such interactions should be monitored. As your *Aufseher*—"

"Do you realize the more you lecture me, the more you sound like my parents, right?" I narrowed my eyes at him.

His face went through several indignant contortions. "I do not see you as a child!" Jove stammered.

"Then quit treating me like one," I said coolly. "I know I'm new to the Community, but I'm not an idiot. Not only did I grow up with large dogs who have very similar body language to wolves, I trust David with my life. Human shape, wolf shape, doesn't matter. I have plans if things go sideways."

I used my ability to zip the silver axe to my hands. I saw David wince. "Sorry, Goliath, just trying to make a point. I was able to *grab* this when David broke down my door. I am *not* helpless." I took a deep breath. "Jove, you were *there* when I tossed Bird-boy into the back of the truck. I can defend myself."

"You could haf been *killed*, Mira!" he shouted, then his shoulders curled forward and he looked away before whispering, "You could haf been killed by der Unkindness twice over. I was frantic when they took you. Most who disappear into their Aviary are never seen again. They haf no problem getting rid of bodies. Ravens eat carrion."

Jove sat on the couch. "But when I got there, imagine my shock to see you sitting and laughing with High Raven. Making your own *deal* with them."

"Mir's always been like that, though." David smiled. "A self-rescuing princess. More likely to be halfway done solving the problem herself."

"Waiting around can get people killed. I had to do *something*." I blushed.

David gave a 'well, there you have it' gesture. There was a knock on the newly reassembled door. "That's Jay." David's shoulders hunched like he had just gotten in trouble. Slowly, he went to answer it.

I moved to stop him, but Jove took my hand to keep me back.

David opened the door to a rather large, intimidating man.

The man's upper torso reminded me of several bodybuilders my class once studied to learn about the different muscle groups. These muscles were barely restrained by the white tank top stuffed into black pants. His skin was as dark as the evening just after sunset, and he sneered at David through a pair of mirror-reflective shades. I caught the gleam of a gold insignia on the temple of the shades. Ray-Bans, of course. The light from the hallway bounced off his smooth scalp. This guy practically oozed badassitude.

"I felt your shift, pup. I expected more bodies." He turned his attention to my friend. "You told me you were going to get your girl and then we'd hit the mall before it gets too crowded. You need to relearn how to interact with strangers, and having someone to protect, especially someone normal with nice tits, helps keep you in check."

I crossed my arms over said tits and glared at the man. I also wasn't David's 'girl.' I was his friend. Sure, he wanted more, but hearing things put just that way put my teeth on edge.

He gave a cursory, dismissive look around my apartment. "So, did you eat her? Is that why I smell blood? No, it's a male's blood and bleach I smell. Did you find her cheating on you, pup?"

I was shaking with rage. This *stranger* comes to *my* door and starts saying such vile things to my Goliath. Nope, I don't think so. I was so tempted to get my axe again.

"*Peace*, Kleine," Jove murmured. "The last time you had that look in your eye, you had a broom in your hand."

I stepped around the couch, scowled at the man at my door, and put my hands on my hips. I felt rage leap up, chilling my voice. "You aren't allowed in my home until you learn some better manners." And with that, I *slammed* the door in his face with a flick of my hand from the middle of my living room.

There was a tense silence for about two minutes before we heard the roar of laughter on the other side of the door, followed by a gentle knock. This time I strode forward before David could grab me and opened the door. The giant had a huge smile on his face this time.

"My dear lady, would you please allow me entry into your home?" His voice sounded like he was trying to put on a production. It sounded different than the West Philly cadence his voice had earlier.

"Depends, are you going to continue to be an asshat to my best friend and insult me more?"

"I gotta say lady, I admire your grit." He actually bowed and tilted his head to one side. He then looked up and briefly met my eyes over the glasses. It reminded me of some of the wolf documentaries Momma watched. Yellow irises looked at me over the rim of his Ray-Bans. They flashed and melted back into the human brown I'd originally expected. "But only so far. I apologize profusely and ask what boon you would have of me."

"Give me your name and I may grant you entry."

"My entire name? Lady, I could tear this ward to shreds if I wanted to." I heard Jove's voice scoff behind me.

"Just your first name will do," I conceded.

"I am Jerimiah."

"Welcome to my home, Jerimiah. I am Mira." I held out a hand and shook his as he entered my apartment, which had been kind of funny to watch. The bulk of his torso stopped him from entering straight on—he had to sort of sidestep to get in through my door. He was broad-shouldered; his biceps looked like he could lift a bus without a spotter. He reminded me of a seasoned bouncer at clubs I couldn't afford to go to. The kind where celebrities stroll in with a smile and nod.

"The pup didn't say you were a Zauberer," he rumbled, towering over me. What was with the Community and freaking huge people?

"That would be because she isn't one, *Blutwulf.* We registered her in the Charter just yesterday evening as a Gewalt."

"A who do what now?" The big man cocked his head to one side.

"I am a Gewalt," I said with a quick glance at David. "That's what I was doing last night. It's why I couldn't go with you to the diner. I guess you can consider me a new species." I gestured to the couch. "Please, have a seat. I take it you are David's sponsor."

He folded himself onto my couch. Usually, it was large enough to seat four, but Jerimiah made it look like a loveseat. His knees were almost touching his chest. "I am. So, why'd you text me to get my tail over here if it wasn't for cleanup?"

"I had some intruders last night. We thought either of you might be able to help track them."

David held up the camera. There was a funny look on Jove's face, but it passed before I could get a good look at it.

"We can't track him right from here. You used bleach, and a lot of it. It's covering up the whiff I caught when I first came in. I barely smell anything out here now but us and the cat." Jerimiah rumbled. "Unless you let me have a sniff at you."

"Oh, you are so not sniffing my hair." I snorted as I made my way into the living room. I knelt to the hope chest and opened it to grab the cables I needed to hook up the camera to the television.

"My magic will not help much in this situation either. I am unable to lay a curse on something I cannot see. I may call a storm if your door is molested, I can charm your windows so only you may open them . . ."

"That won't work on a teleporter," I said, wrapping the cables around my hand.

"*Excuse me?* What ist a teleporter?" Jove sounded incredulous; apparently, he'd never heard the term before.

"A person who can appear in a room, as if by magic, by way of brain power alone," David supplied superiorly. Then he blinked. "Wait, like Nightcrawler?"

"Yeah, but no sulfur or smoke smell left behind." I went to move the television to get to the ports when David came up to me and gently took the cables from my hands.

His hands were warm and the light brush of them against my skin made my heart pound. "I'm assuming you want to hook this up so we can get a good look at the bastard?"

I nodded as I felt how close he was to me. Damn it all to hell, this hadn't mattered to me when I didn't know how he felt. Now I was noticing the way he smelled like cinnamon and how my heart was starting to flip-flop.

"I'll need those cables to get you hooked up right. You'll have to let them go, Space Station." Did he say that sensually? Did he mean it to be sensual? My brain scrabbled.

"Huh?" Images rushed to my mind of what exactly we could do that involved cables. Heat rushed to my cheeks.

He laughed quietly and shook his head. "I've waited for years for you to look at me like that. You need to give me the cables, Mir. I'll hook up the camera." David smiled at me. Smoothly, he stood from where we'd been crouched behind the television. Were his moves more graceful now because of the wolf? There was a low growl from Jerimiah and David hunched a little before taking his seat next to his sponsor.

I grabbed the remote and pushed play. I suspected that Matthew had gotten into my apartment the same way he'd gotten out, but that wasn't confirmed until I saw them appear next to my bed. The woman had gotten a chair from my dining area and set it next to my head so Matthew had better access. He looked almost identical to how he had in my dream, though he'd given himself more muscles. I shivered as Matthew ran his fingers through my hair. I felt like I needed a shower. A hot one. Maybe with lye. I felt a comforting arm come around me. It was Jove.

"It is okay now, Kleine. You are safe." He pulled me away from the television. The screen flickered a second and I worried that there was something off with the recording, but it corrected itself as we moved away.

Was I safe, though? I stared straight ahead and watched the video.

"Leave me alone with her, Sable." Oh, God, he looked like a preppy putz. His voice sounded like that one guy in college who was only there to play ball and party while Daddy paid for everything. His voice also sounded possessive and made me want to throw up.

The woman shook her head. "The Doctor told me to stay in case there's trouble. We don't know if she's presenting a Protocol yet, Matthew, so just keep to the plan and get her to come in."

"I can't concentrate with you hovering. Make yourself scarce." He made a shooing motion with his free hand.

"Fine." The woman snorted, a slight curl to her lip. "But, I'll be listening in case you need me."

"Yes, fine, whatever." He waved again impatiently at her. "Go away already."

Matthew ran a possessive hand over my cheek as Sable disappeared from next to him. We watched the video the rest of the way through. I didn't realize just how much it bothered me until I found my hands shaking again.

"I wish to see the place the woman vanished from. She should not have been able to do so through my ward . . ." Jove's voice said gently from behind me. Hearing him gave me something to focus on other than the feelings of violation.

"The rules we know don't apply here." Jerimiah's eyes were locked on the screen. "You know, just like I know, there are always new rules when new people are put in the Charter as they make themselves known."

Jove hummed as if in agreement, then said, "I did not expect them to be so apparent so soon. Nor the fact that Mira seems not to be the only one of her kind."

There were cheers all around when Matthew flew away from my bedside. "You do that, Ms. Hall?" asked the big Werewolf.

"*Doctor* Hall, and yes, I did. I am a telekinetic. I threw him in my dream and that translated to throwing him into my display case. It's why there was blood that I had to clean. He impaled himself on my bat'leth. You see me there stitching him up."

"Why'd you save him?" Jerimiah asked. "If you'd left him as is, then he would have been one less thing for you to worry about."

I shook my head. "I can't do that. I am first and foremost a doctor. I had a job to do. That and I wanted him to face breaking and entering charges. I didn't know about the woman, Sable, until she popped in to take him." She and Matthew disappeared on the screen. "Like that."

"We have to get back to Amos; he'll want to know about this. We'll have to do the mall thing another day." Jerimiah pulled off his glasses and winked at me. It was only slightly disturbing. He stood as the video ended with my intruders disappearing from the wreckage that had been my display case. Jerimiah put on his sunglasses and snapped his fingers. "Come, David."

David looked sheepishly over his shoulder as he and Jerimiah left, like he wanted to stay but he couldn't. Where the hell did Jerimiah get off ordering a person around like that? I began to call them back when Jove put his hand on my arm to stop me.

"He does not have the same choices anymore, Kleine."

"What the hell are you talking about?" I snapped, glaring at him.

"He is Pack now," Jove explained. "Until he proves himself, he will be at the bottom of that pack, incapable of going against a direct order or else it will seem like a challenge. Challenges have a tendency to get bloody and involve collateral damage. I do not want you to be collateral damage."

"I think your English is getting messed up, Jove." He only did that when he was pissed off. "Why are you mad at me? I'm the one who all of this crap keeps happening to."

"I am not mad at you, Kleine." He scrubbed his hands through his hair and sighed. "I just watched some strange man touch you as if he owned you in that video. My magic meant nothing to him and that woman."

"There's something else you need to know, Jove. Something the video didn't show. They're building an army. One specifically to go against the Community." I handed him the paper Matthew had left on my side table. "Matthew called us monsters and told me to call this number when I woke up."

"He touched this? You are certain?"

"You saw him put it there himself."

Jove growled in frustration, took me by my shoulders, and leaned down to look me in the eye. "I feel I must provide some clarification as to why my English is messy." Jove pulled me close, wrapping his arms around me before bending down and delivering a soul-searing kiss.

My brain rebooted as I lost feeling in my feet and my knees wobbled. He murmured something softly in my ear, *"Unsere frau der macht. Wir lieben dich."*

Our woman of power. We love you.

I stepped back and gaped at him.

"I must speak to the Spitzhut Männer about this. You did well to wait to show me until after the wolves left. We don't want to cause a panic." Jove brushed a hand across my cheek, his thumb brushing my lips. He stepped back and turned toward the door. "I will reinforce the wards. I have an idea that may help with this 'teleporter.'"

22

"I AM DOCTOR Hall, and this is Experiment Five. My abilities continue to grow." The video pulls back to show me sitting on the floor in front of the couch. The couch behind me levitates above my head and gently sets back down. "I've started lifting weights with my physical arms rather than with my mind to expand my weight limit." A marble on the floor then lifted and did a complicated dance in the air, followed by a small pool tube. The glass sphere flew through the center and orbited around the outside. "My dexterity is improving, as well as holding more than two things at a time. However, my ability still scatters if I am surprised or interrupted."

I frowned, annoyed. "In all of the science fiction, it never says anything about concentration being so crucial to the use of abilities like mine. They focus on emotion. I suppose that is what separates science fiction from science fact. No real studies have been done in this sort of depth before. Or rather, nothing that was publicly published, recordable, or repeatable. Today's experiment is on telekinesis and emotion. I need to find out: if I am under emotional distress, would my abilities be compromised or not? With things that are happening in my personal life, I cannot afford to lose such a useful tool."

I took a deep, cleansing breath in. "I'm going to remember something frightening while having the marble orbit through the hoop."

I wasn't sure if this was going to work. Essentially, I was trying to induce a panic attack. I let myself remember the accident; my breathing became faster and faster. The video showed the marble speeding up in its journey through the hoop, faster and faster until it became a blur. I opened my eyes with a gasp. Reliving my car hitting the pole again in such vivid detail made the marble and tube fall to the floor. I curled my legs up and clutched them, a short tremor running through my body. "End of fear experiment. I, unfortunately, may have to revisit this experiment depending on the analysis of this segment."

I turned off the camera and picked up the marble. It had been two weeks since the break-in at my apartment. Matthew and Sable hadn't repeated their performance, yet I still had this feeling of being watched. I didn't know what new wards Jove had put in, but they seemed to be working so far. I put the marble in my pocket and picked up the pool toy just as my phone decided to ring. I took a deep, cleansing breath before answering it. "Hello?"

The cool, dispassionate voice on the other end of the line was almost soothing after having to remember the moment I hit the pole, but the fact that it was the Unkindness calling didn't do much to lower my blood pressure. "Doctor Hall, this is Ms. Corvis. We need you to do the analysis of the . . . ahem . . . sample we took from Mr. Alfenheim."

I arched an eyebrow. I secretly really wanted to get my hands on that sample to see what the heck was going on with that man's biochemistry to have such a violent reaction to metal. Jove's warning about the Ravens giving me everything I wanted was ringing in my ears. I had to keep the excitement out of my voice. "Why?"

"The Court, that Mr. Alfenheim is a representative of, obviously refuses to let us send his sample to a human laboratory. They want to keep off human radar at all costs, and rightly so. Any such contact would surely spell doom for us all." Her voice was condescending, like an adult speaking to a child who didn't know better.

"If you knew this already, then why didn't you tell me?"

"I *did* attempt to get you to do this analysis in the first place, if you remember correctly, Doctor." She sounded annoyed. "We even provided you with the necessary equipment to do so."

"That equipment of yours comes with more strings attached than what was agreed in the original contract." I snorted. "Forensic lab work has an entirely different goal than, say, working on a cure for whatever illness is hitting your fledglings."

Ms. Corvis made a sound somewhere between a hiss and a choke. "How did you know about that?"

I figured if I let a little of what I knew slip, then I'd be able to barter a better deal for the lab work they wanted rather than a carte blanche monopoly of my time and skills. "I've ears, Ms. Corvis. I heard what one of the other Ravens told High Raven when he brought me up from the dungeon."

I took the phone over to my couch and sat down. "Why haven't you called on me to look at them yet? When there is a disease that comes into play, the longer we wait, the worse the pathogen can become. Has it already started affecting the elders?"

"High Raven has his reasons," she demurred.

Translation: I wasn't trusted yet. I understood the reasoning. I was essentially an unknown faction. Sure, I had a deal with High Raven but to them, I was a human with some weird powers. "So, this is what, a test of my skills?"

"Call it what you will." Her voice returned to that prim yet always disdaining sound she'd somehow managed to perfect. I heard her perfect manicure drum against a wooden tabletop. I bet she was sitting at one of those desks for the high-powered corporate overlords. "You will use the facilities we have provided to work on what nearly killed Mr. Alfenheim."

I was learning not to like Ms. Corvis. She had this way of making it feel like I was a janitor that cleaned the bathrooms and did a shitty job of it. "I have to think about it. I'll be in touch."

"Very well, I will expect to hear from you soon." She hung up with a click. I shrugged and looked at my watch. I had about an hour to meet with the realtor downtown. I grabbed my purse and told Toria to have a good day.

Later at Bindings, after my first futile search for a clinic space, I was feeling melancholy. When I feel low, one of my favorite spots to sit and think is the wingback chairs by the fireplace. There had always been these types of chairs scattered around the different levels of the shop. Though they were leather, they still managed to be comfortable and welcoming. Jove must have used magic to keep them silent as people moved around on them. Otherwise, we would have had the constant squeaking of leather whenever someone sat down. This place was so quiet and peaceful, you'd never suspect we did a blood ritual here two weeks ago.

I went upstairs to Katie's domain first. I didn't want to deal with Jove Brandt yet. I'd been avoiding him. *Wir lieben dich.* The words echoed in my mind as I climbed the stairs. 'We' not 'I'. Did he realize the implications of saying it like that? I couldn't deal with that, not right away. I needed an infusion of Katie Fynn first.

"Nothing yet?" she asked, organizing the endcap she was working on.

"Nada. This woman has had me all over the city, and we still haven't found the right one. I'm starting to hate her, Katie." My hands balled into fists. "She's got this overly perky 'I know the perfect place for you!' look on her face, but *then* she shows me residential places rather than commercial ones!"

"No way of getting a different realtor?"

"She's got this area cornered as her territory." I moaned. "I tried getting a different realtor with the same office, and they just referred me back to her! She's got me booked this whole weekend. Maybe if I write 'I need a commercial space for my medical practice' on a piece of paper and tape it to my forehead, she'll get the hint!"

"Why does she keep showing you residential places?"

"She says it's because there are 'so many' doctors' offices that have converted homes into businesses that it's practically in vogue. That doesn't change zoning laws. Momma would have called her a Karen."

Katie looked over the shelves and arched a dark eyebrow at me. "Is her name really *Karen*?"

"No, but she gives off some heavy 'Karen' vibes. Sweet to your face, but psycho to anyone she views as beneath her." I clasped my hands together. "Katie, please come with me this weekend? I need a buffer between her and me so I don't go insane."

"Okay, I can be your Karen-tamer, but you are treating me to food both days."

"You are legit the best, and I may owe you my firstborn."

"Just name them after me and I'll be appeased," she said smugly. "Now go away and flirt with Jove. I've got work to do and you're keeping me from it."

I sighed as I went downstairs to settle into one of the chairs. Specifically, *not* the one Zimmer had stabbed me in. I felt tension ease out of my body as I snuggled in. Jove handed me a cup of hot tea on a saucer from behind the chair. I pushed complicated emotions aside and took a grateful sip.

"You have much on your mind, Kleine. More than just finding a new space for your business."

I sighed and gave a quick look around to make sure there weren't any people who could hear us. "The Unkindness wants me to run the tests on the half-Fae guy."

"I suspected they would. Have you decided if you will?" He took the chair across from mine. Today he was in a dark blue waistcoat with a gold chain hanging from the pocket. Knowing how old he was made his aesthetic make much more sense. He was a man out of time in the way he dressed and acted. Jove's tailored pants were brown today and perfectly complemented the color of his shoes. He gave off an air of someone who had been taught manners when they still meant something.

"To be really honest? I want to. I really want to. What is it biologically that makes them react this badly to metals? Is it all metal, ferrous metal, man-made metal? I know what I was told about the exception being silver, but I'd be stupid to just take that at face value without any sort of proof.

There are so many questions, and it's almost choking me to know the answers," I paused, looking at Jove. He was listening intently, his dark eyes on mine. "The Unkindness are using this as a test of sorts."

"A test?" He nodded contemplatively. "The Unkindness are slow to trust others, but why would you have to be tested?"

"I think it's a test of my medical skills. I must have made good headway with helping Mr. Alfenheim, but they want to see how broad my talents can go. Can you think of any other reason why they would test me this way?" I couldn't divulge what I'd heard in the bowels of the Aviary. Especially if the Unkindness were to become patients. I knew the fledglings were sick, but I didn't know anything beyond that.

He shook his head. "They are a secretive bunch. They have no desire to let one such as myself know too much about their home and hearth."

"If something were wrong, who would they go to for help?"

He looked at me curiously. "How do you mean? I've never heard of them asking for help from anyone else in the Community."

"Would they ask for help from another flock?"

"I suppose they would if it were serious. The Unkindness does not like to show weakness. None in the Community do, as there are so many that are predators. Weakness is viewed as a sign that a person is prey. Ready to be culled. I have not heard of one flock helping another, but it is not information they would readily offer to an outsider."

I took a drink of my tea, trying to form my next question in the right way. "Remember when you told me about why you had to deal with the Unkindness when this whole mess started?"

He frowned and looked away. "Yes, Mira, of course I do. I have told you why it was needed. What happened to you tears at me daily."

Oh. I hadn't meant it like *that.* "Jove." I reached out to try to make him understand, but he just pulled away.

"What was done was done. I regret that I did not see what they would do to you just for being one of mine." The sadness in his voice made me want to hold him like he'd held me the night of the ritual.

I felt heat in my cheeks and my ears. We already knew it hadn't been his deal with them that had the Unkindness target me. I'd been ordered by some other third party. I was almost positive it was Alden. But if it was, then how had he avoided becoming Veil-Struck? I frowned. I didn't like how inconsistent the condition was. I would have to study the victims more closely if I was to make a hypothesis. "I meant about the ailment the girl had. The Lethe mushrooms. Do people of the Community come to you often for stuff like that?"

"Well, yes. Quite often." He blinked as I dragged him away from his inward attack on himself. Guilt where guilt didn't need to be was damaging. I wasn't going to let Jove hurt himself like that. Not over someone like me. The only reason I recognized the signs was from my sessions with Rosalinda.

"Why wouldn't the Unkindness come to you?" I set the tea down and bit the tip of my thumb to focus my thoughts. "There'd have to be a reason why they wouldn't come to someone in the Community if the flock needed help?"

"They have their own magical practitioners to take care of such illnesses and ailments as what befell the Cristos family. Other than messengers and deliveries, the Unkindness are very private and keep to themselves. I am glad I put that locator on your charm bracelet. Otherwise, I would not have been able to find you."

There was something wrong with the flock. Obviously, it was not a weakness they wanted to spread around the Community. They were sick. Sick enough for a grunt to stick their neck out and remind High Raven about it when they pulled me up out of their dungeon. Something magic wasn't affecting and dire enough to make them seek outside help. And there was this person who 'ordered' me, someone with access to a top-tier lab and doctors. Someone the Unkindness decided was too 'expensive' to deal with any further. So, they took my offer even knowing I had only just received my white coat.

"High Raven apparently wants me to pass this test of theirs before he'll even consider allowing me to really know about what is going on with them. Ms. Corvis was really off guard when I mentioned what I already knew." I leaned against the back of the chair. "If I want to be able to help them, I'm going to have to first figure out who poisoned Mr. Alfenheim and with what."

"It is interesting, Kleine," Jove said with a smile in his voice. He had his leg crossed at the ankle and was watching me with his head in one hand propped on his knee.

Wir lieben dich . . .

I looked over at him and picked up my tea. I should play it cool. He was hitting all my yummy buttons posing like that, but one did not let one's tongue loll out like a hound in heat. "What is?"

"To hear you speak so like a Zauberer."

I didn't know how to feel about that. I chatted a bit longer with Jove when he wasn't busy with customers. I wonder if he knew I was watching him while I was reading. I was glad I'd stayed away for those two weeks to even out. Now I enjoyed the game of it, watching him and pretending I hadn't been. Bindings wasn't busy to the point of me feeling like I should take up the spot behind the register, so I let myself have some fun before deciding to be an adult again instead of a flirting teenager. I still wasn't positive about how far I wanted to take this, but it was fun walking on the edge for a little.

I hadn't committed myself to either Jove or David by this point. Hell, neither of them had asked me on an honest-to-God date, even though both of them had made my wires cross and short-circuit. I sighed and pushed out of the comfortable chair. I waved goodbye to Jove and went out to my car.

If I was going to put myself out there to the Community, I'd need some form of advertisement that would get to my target groups. I'd have to get some cards made up to pass out. It was off to the office supply store to buy some card stock and ink. On my way back to my car from the parking lot, I puzzled more about the strange case of Mr. Alfenheim. I could hardly wait to get his samples under a microscope. I bit my lower lip as I opened the driver's door. I was going to have to use the Ravens' facilities again if I wanted to do a proper analysis on the samples I'd gotten. I didn't want to get too comfortable there. The lab was mouth-wateringly fantastic. It had everything I could possibly need in order to do my work. I opened my cell phone and hit redial.

"I expected you to call sooner, Doctor." Ms. Corvis sounded smug. She knew I couldn't resist getting the answers to my questions about the Fae. I didn't care.

"I'll do it," I said into my phone. "But I want to be paid."

"Of course you will." She sounded like it had never really been a question. "You'll start Monday, of course."

"Of course," I agreed. I tried not to let her tone get under my skin. I leaned against the driver's seat and tapped a finger against the steering wheel in annoyance. "I assume it will be in the same location?"

"Naturally. Your laboratory is waiting for you. We will have a car sent for you at eight o'clock Monday morning."

"Send it at seven. I want to get started right away." I kept my voice as cool and professional as I could. I was already planning on which tests I wanted to run first.

The weekend proved fruitless in my search for a clinic location, even with Katie helping. She would send me locations that she'd find online, and I'd forward them to my realtor. I felt like I'd walked all over the city and still couldn't find anything that felt right. Katie was a lifesaver—going with me to brave the endless empty spaces that didn't fit what I kept telling the perky woman I was looking for. After the last office space we looked at, we hit Moriarty's on Walnut Street. We loved going to that pub, especially on Saturday nights. It almost took my mind off the rat droppings at the last place the realtor took us. I was starting to lose hope that I'd find my spot close enough to the city to be worth it.

"Don't worry, lady," consoled Katie over a pint. She loved getting those. She said it was a homage to the Irish side of her heritage. "The spot is out there waiting for you. We just have to find it."

"It's starting to feel like I'm holding out for perfection. Maybe I should just settle for that place we saw today." I stabbed at my admittedly excellent steak and potatoes without as much joy as it usually brought me.

Katie's nose crinkled. "Not the rat-shit place . . ."

"No, no. The one with the itty-bitty bathroom and the moldy smell in the hallway." I put a piece of the steak in my mouth. "I mean, it was definitely in my budget, especially when I add the costs I can find for equipment."

"You'd end up sinking way more into it than it's worth, Mira. Calling that place a 'fixer-upper' was being far too generous. It's not as if Ms. Perky-pants was only showing us crap places, but you made faces at all the high-rise offices and some of those shined like a new penny!"

"I just *need* something that's going to be accessible without making my patients feel like they have to apply for security clearance to make an appointment!" All the places we'd seen had so much exposed metal. Elevators of manufactured, cold, brushed stainless steel or painted metal staircases—sometimes being the only way to get to some of the locations—put my teeth on edge when I thought about what part of Philadelphia I wanted to tap into. I wanted to be accessible for *everyone* in the Community, then I needed something older that wouldn't kill some of my future patients with allergies to metal.

"Don't look so blue, Mira. I'm still here with you for this. We'll find your spot." She rubbed my arm across the table. "Even if you're getting pickier with it."

"I love you, Katie—"

"Like a third sister." She laughed. "I got you, lady. Now let's enjoy our food and you tell me what the hell is going on with you and the boss."

I coughed and sputtered around my drink. I think my ears burned off, they felt so hot. Katie let me suffer for a minute until I collected myself, cleared my throat, and said primly, "I don't know what you're talking about."

"That is the biggest load of bullshit you've ever told me! I saw you on Friday flirting with him in front of the fireplace." She pointed a finger at me as I opened my mouth to protest. "You are not about to open that mouth of yours and lie to *me*, Mira Jane Hall. I told you to go flirt with him, and you went above and beyond. You had that man *posing* and preening like a peacock. I was damn near surprised as shit that he didn't sprout feathers out his tailored ass and dance for you!"

"You saw all that, huh?"

"Girl, I was giggling at the top of the stairs!" She leaned in on her elbows. "So, now that you have him acting like a fool, what are you gonna do with him?"

"Hell, Katie, I don't know!" I raked my fingers through my buzzed hair. "I only just found out that he's got feelings for me. I wanted to see how it felt to flirt a little back. Baby steps, you know?" I thunked my head on the table with a little moan. "What's worse is, apparently, David has feelings for me too!"

"Our David? Nerdy guy with the nice butt who gave you the doctor's bag at your graduation party? Hell, I could have told you he had feelings for you! Mira, you are *blind* sometimes when it comes to men wanting you." She took a bite of her burger and washed it down with a bit of her pint. "So, you've got the boss bookworm *and* the nerd pining after your sweet ass."

"It's a fat ass. I have no idea why all of a sudden they're acting like this." I tunneled both hands on either side of my scalp. It seemed to relieve some of the stress pounding behind my eyes.

A look of realization dawned on my friend's bronzed countenance. "*You* don't know what to do now that you are finally realizing that people are being serious with their interest in you. Usually, you brush compliments off as people being kind instead of them flirting with you. You used to have your studies as your primary goal, and you let it blind you to anything else for the past decade. Honey, Jove's been interested in you since you started at Bindings. I don't know David so well, but I'm betting his feelings have been brewing a while, too."

She sat back against her seat and crossed her arms. "You know, there are some men out there who *like* more curves on their partners. Looks like David and Jove are two of them." She frowned at me over her cup. "You also know damn well your weight has nothing to do with how pretty you are. You are a beautiful woman and should *own* that shit right now. I mean, damn, I wish I had tits like yours, and your hips are a thing of song and story."

That made one side of my mouth quirk up. "You always have lusted after my hips."

"I would've made a pass at you myself if you swung my way."

"I would have taken you up on that if men weren't so pretty," I said, eating another bite of steak and potatoes. "I feel so dumb. Jove was always pretty to look at, but I had him in this box labeled *thou shalt not touch* because I didn't want any special treatment while we were working."

"Didn't you notice he always made sure to work the same shift as you? Hell, even when you cut your hours and made your shift weird to fit with your residency, Jove made damn sure he was there when you were."

"And David's been my friend for years! Was he just messing with my mind this whole time? I mean, I thought he saw me as a sister or just as another nerd. A buddy to go to cons with! He's helped me corset up for cosplay!" I felt my cheeks flush with embarrassment.

"He was safe, and now he's not so safe. You're rethinking every inter-action you've had with him, and now you have to reexamine them," Katie said. "Was he flirting then? Was I leading him on? Did I do anything to make him think I wanted something more? Do I *want* something more?"

I moaned as she patted the back of my hand.

"And then Jove."

"And then Jove," I agreed. "I'm in so much trouble, Katie."

"Mmm-hmm," she agreed.

23

I ALMOST FELT like a professional as I walked out my door with my bag and a cup of hot chocolate, dressed to get shit done on Monday morning. I didn't have the white coat on. The school had replaced it, my diploma, and my pin for me when they heard about the accident, but it had yet to be delivered. It didn't feel right when I didn't have it on when I was working at what I went to school for. I earned that long coat, and I wanted to freaking wear it.

Instead, I had on one of my more professional polyester tops, dress pants, and sensible flats. I was going to get to work in a lab again! Running tests and going from machine to machine always left me a little drained, but the *results*...oooh, I couldn't wait to get some answers to these mysterious people.

I was feeling confident, until I looked up.

Jove was standing there, in his long dark overcoat and a fedora hat that somehow managed not to look old-fashioned. Under his coat was his typically tailored shirt, waistcoat, and slacks combo that always suited him so well. His hand wrapped around a long, twisted wooden staff, and a satchel hung down over one shoulder. He looked good—a little too good. I had to play this off with some levity.

"You look like a noir cosplayer from Comic-Con. This looks a bunch better than that bathrobe when you barged in to 'save' me from the Unkindness."

He gave me a long look, up and down. "And you look like a mahogany-haired Professional Barbie, but with better curves."

Did he just make a reference to a kids toy?

Naw, it must have been an accident. "Barbie is way thinner than I am."

"More the pity. She always looked like she needed to be fed. Who would want a woman like that?"

Maybe Katie was right.

"How do you know what Professional Barbie looked like?"

He snorted and gave me a look that I was starting to recognize as an annoyed Wizard who's trying not to find me funny.

I blew out a breath. "What was up with that bathrobe anyway?"

"That had not been what I put on that morning, I assure you." He smiled.

"That guy said you'd just barged your way in." I looked at him skeptically. "'Spells Blazing,' if I remember correctly. The rest of your wardrobe is tailored. Or at least everything you wear to the store. Ratty bathrobe isn't your usual aesthetic."

"I was not as prepared as I should have been for their traps. You can take away the fear you have of something, like a Zauberer on the warpath, when you can make them look ridiculous. That bathrobe was an illusion the Unkindness stuck to my coat to make me look silly. It was such a benign thing; I did not recognize it as a trap."

I noticed a blush creeping up the back of his neck and decided to change the subject. "Are you going to come along every time I have to deal with the Unkindness?"

"Yes."

"You are going to be bored to tears," I warned. "Lab work is incredibly long, tedious, and boring."

"You made it sound so exciting while you were in school."

I ignored his comment. "Is now a good time to ask about your *abschwören*? We've got time to kill while we're going to our destination." I sat back and watched him.

Jove shrugged. "Now is as good a time as any. This is all common knowledge and can be found in the Charter."

"And when will I be getting my copy?"

"Soon." He chuckled. "Zauberers are born with an innate talent for magic. From when we are very young, we can see the twinkling of objects and people that have power. Meine Mutti used to weave beautiful clouds of magic to lull me to sleep while she sang. When we come of age, around fourteen or so, there is a ceremony to increase our power. We decide on something to give up. We call it our *abschwören*—something to abjure forever. Whatever is abjured directly correlates to how much magical power we receive."

I nodded, understanding. "So, there's no cheating. No giving up ketchup in exchange for cosmic powers."

"Precisely. But we all have tried to 'cheat,' as you say. We give up something that is not that important to them. We all try to think of something that is important but that we will not miss. Unless someone wants power above all else." Jove's chocolate eyes became sad. "For some, there is no limit on what they would give up. The most powerful of us become Spitzhut Männer. They give up the most to be able to do the most for the rest of us."

"Did you try to cheat? What did you pick?"

He cleared his throat and looked out the window before answering. "I chose the radio."

My eyes just about popped out of my sockets. "The RADIO? The thing that started just about every form of entertainment and a whole slew of technology that all of our current society needs in order to function? *That* radio?"

No wonder the man didn't get any of the pop culture jokes! He'd literally never been able to go to a movie or enjoy a television show. I mean, if the movie was old enough, then he might be okay, but the two technologies merged at some point where one started to influence the other until they became intertwined. I let out a low whistle.

Jove blushed and looked away. "I thought it would be a fad. My favorite music was always available on the phonograph and later on vinyl. And I have always enjoyed the theater, so being rid of something so small seemed like a good bet."

"What do you do if someone's listening to a radio when you walk by? Or if there's one of those outdoor movie events?"

"Most times, I would just not notice whatever was going on, or it would just sound like unintelligible noise to me. Grating . . . constant . . . noise. Sometimes, the item in question malfunctions in some way. Either way, it is almost a relief when the sound stops."

That didn't sound very pleasant. I'd be grumpy, too, if everything I heard out of a radio just sounded like that. I vowed to get him some new music on vinyl for future gifts—or maybe earplugs—poor man.

A soft smile graced his lips. "Then, as time went on, my power grew."

"Because the thing you picked became more important as time went on."

"More than I would ever know. Televisions and radios are practically different things in this modern age. If a new Zauberer were to choose it, they would not have the gains I have seen. Because of my *abschwören*, I am unable to use a computer or cell phone or be in close proximity to televisions or radios. However, I would not trade it back if given the chance. The ability to use magic . . . it is indescribable." Jove made a motion with his hand, and the outline of a purple tulip manifested in the air between us before solidifying into the real thing. He plucked it from the air and handed it to me.

The part about the computer didn't sound right. I didn't think computers were related to radios. I'd have to think about it when I had more time. "What counts as important?"

"It depends on what is significant to the Zauberer. One of my schoolmates chose to give up ever eating fish because she hated the taste. She is able to do small magic but nothing of significance. The strongest I've ever heard of gave up turning left. He is rumored to have an enclave on the dark side of the moon. I hope to meet them someday." He sounded wistful, like how David sounded when we got in line to meet Chris Hemsworth at the San Diego Comic-Con. I guess everyone can have a nerdy hero. This Zauberer who couldn't turn left was Jove's.

The black limo again pulled up to the curb. One of the doors opened, and a tall man in a chauffeur's hat opened the closest door to usher us inside—this was probably due to the fact that a few of my neighbors were at the mailboxes.

I nodded my thanks and sat inside. I waited until Jove was settled to continue. "The results of lab work are exciting; getting to those results is time-consuming. It could be a long while before I figure out what happened to Mr. Alfenheim. Most lab equipment is also computer-based, and you, sir, are no good around computers." It was uncanny how they tended to glitch out around the man.

"I will stay on the outside of the room." He patted a leather satchel. "I have brought a few books Gr'heghg could restore for me. I have to translate them."

"Why not have the little mutant translate them as well as restore them?"

"It is not in the contract. He would want much more for that as well as the restorations. It is better that I do it myself." He smiled. "One of the advantages of a longer lifespan is having ample time to study different languages."

"I'm still not magical, Jove." I sighed. "There's no promise that I'm going to have a longer-than-normal lifespan."

"That, Kleine, is a matter of opinion. Your entry into the Charter is but a few weeks old. We do not know much about your ascension into a Gewalt."

I had to give him that. My abilities were steadily growing with practice, and seeing the abilities of two other people was an eye-opener. I needed more information: did they both have the same procedure I did?

Walking into the building was less amazing than the first time. Maybe because I was starting to get used to all of this fantastic stuff. We even chatted with the same Centaur and Pixie guards. It turns out Horace and Larson were now our personal guides in this facility. A fact that Larson wouldn't shut up about.

"Yessirree, Ms. Corvis was so happy with our work the last time you were here that she gave Horace and me a raise. Ain't that right, Horace?" The tiny humanoid elbowed the Centaur with a smug smile that brightened his entire little body for a second. I wondered if it was a type of bioluminescence and what evolutionary purpose it could have had. Was it a leftover from their ancestors? I remembered Aunt Kate telling us stories about the will-o'-the-wisps and to not follow any steady floating lights at night.

The Centaur grunted and led us down a different hall. I'd fully expected us to go to the triage room again. I was positive I could scrounge together the materials I'd need to set up a rudimentary lab. But we turned away from where that room was almost immediately. I had been about to ask when Jove put a hand on my arm and signaled me to keep quiet. We followed the duo down a narrow hallway, Larson still expounding on how lucky we were to have our own guards in the building. I was starting to suspect Ms. Corvis did it to punish us when we abruptly stopped in front of a silver door.

"We hath arrived at thine laboratory," intoned Horace, earning him a tiny slap from Larson on the shoulder.

"Quit it with that talk, Horace! You live in the United States of America in da twenty-first century! You're gonna make me look bad."

Horace sniffed. "Some of us like to show a little decorum whilst a lady is present." His lip curled into a small sneer. "Where did you learn to speak, Pixie? A mummer, mayhap? You sound like one of the cartoons my foal watches."

"Hey, whyiotta . . ." Larson balled his little fists and held them up in a classic boxer's pose.

"This'll be fine, guys." I'd never get to work at this rate; I still had to make sure they had the right equipment for what I needed to look at.

Horace bowed. "Of course, my lady." He grasped the handle and opened the door. "It is my pleasure to present . . . your lab."

I think I gasped. Oh, for the love of Stan Lee, this was an awesome workspace. Everything was shiny and chrome-edged with white plastic. I may have purred in pleasure as I ran my hand over an ICP mass spectrometer. "Oh, aren't you pretty? They didn't even have this model at school, Jove. This looks like it's never been used!"

"None of it has been," said the prim and proper Ms. Corvis. I jumped a little; she came out from behind one of the taller machines in the back of the room. I frowned at her.

She'd obviously wanted to catch me off guard. "All of this has been recently procured by the order of High Raven. He wants this mess settled as quickly as"—she sneered—"humanly possible. When will the results be ready?"

"Hey now, give me some time to get properly introduced to these babies. If they're straight out of the box, then I'll have to run some diagnostics to make sure you weren't sold any lemons." I looked around the lab and took note of several machines that I wouldn't be needing in order to run the tests on Mr. Alfenheim's bile. The space was on the large side and kind of looked like High Raven bought a forensics buyer's guide and just bought one of everything. Top of the line on everything—that admittedly made my hands itch to use them—but still superfluous to the task at hand.

"I'll have them up and running properly in a couple of hours. I'm glad I got here early." I shifted my weight to look over her shoulder to Jove, keeping his distance outside of the room. He was leaning against the wall opposite the door. The light played in his dark hair, bringing out oil-slick highlights that were usually lost in the lighting at Bindings. He was already holding a large, leather-bound book and reading intently. My eyes did not mind the journey.

I took a step toward him. "You know, Jove, this is going to take a while, and I know you have to open the shop soon. I should be fine here if you want to go." I didn't really want him to go, but I also didn't want his business to suffer because of me.

Jove didn't move. He didn't even breathe. It was like looking at a snapshot. GQ Zauberer. I straightened, looking more intensely at my former employer turned warden. "Jove?"

Ms. Corvis stepped up beside me. "It's no use. We appear as a blur to him. Time moves differently in this room."

"What?" My heart just about stopped.

"It was the only way the Fae would allow us to work on Mr. Alfenheim's . . . samples. This room is now a miniature Faerie mound. Time will move faster or slower as is needed."

The temporal anomaly alone made me grin. I took another look around the room. "How can this room exist? There were other doors right next to this one, but I don't see any others that would open into this one."

"The dimensional space is also a part of the Faerie magic."

I had to stifle an epically major nerdgasm. I felt tears in my eyes. "Do you realize what you've just given me access to? Ms. Corvis, I could kiss you."

She gave me a startled look and then narrowed her eyes. "Was that a threat?"

Time distortion, plus it was bigger on the inside. The Unkindness had just given me a stationary TARDIS, and I was having trouble managing my imminent geek-out. "This is absolutely the best thing anyone has ever given me."

"This was not meant to be a gift for you, Doctor Hall," she said severely. "Time is something we cannot afford to waste. Do what you're being paid for, Doctor."

"Paid?" I perked up at that. Even though she had agreed to that yesterday, I'd assumed they would force this to be under the aegis of the deal I'd made with High Raven.

She smirked at that. "I brought your concerns to High Raven, and he agreed with you. This work is *technically* outside of your original contract with us. As such, you will be recompensed for your time and energy, with a bonus if we are satisfied with the work."

"You'll find I am good at what I set my mind to," I said coolly as I turned back toward the plethora of machines.

She gave me a small nod. "I will return later to check on your progress." She walked to the door, her business heels clicking until she crossed the threshold. Then, she froze, her foot at an impossible angle to keep in the air without following through with the step. Jove was looking up at her now as she exited, but both were as frozen as a scene in a painting.

"Oh, this is too cool." I rubbed my hands together and turned to the computer. I lost myself in the work for a little while there. Only two of the machines gave me any issue on startup, so I was able to get to testing faster than I thought I would. Horace and Larson stayed in the room with me, which was handy. I had Horace move the two lemons to one side where they would be out of the way and got to work.

The bile was already answering so many of my questions regarding the Fae. I don't think they realized how much can be told about a species with so little. As nothing but lore about them was readily available, I had to work from the ground up. Carbon-based, but that is to be expected of anything that originates on this planet. Platelet count low in comparison to humans. DNA of some cells not able to be exactly matched with anything on file, but very closely related to humans to the point where the two species could crossbreed—which was obvious due to Mr. Alfenheim being only half-Fae. The other cells in attendance were totally human. My patient was literally half-Fae. Genetically, that should be impossible, but evidence can't lie. There were only subtle differences between the cells. If I had only been casually looking in a normal environment, I probably would have made an appointment with my optometrist the next day.

Usually with forensics, I went from big to small with testing, stopping once I found the culprit. However, I wanted to wring as much information as I could from the sample before I had to turn my findings in. So, I decided to do my testing the opposite way: small to big.

I glanced over my shoulder to see that Ms. Corvis was now standing with Jove, having what I could only assume was an intense conversation about me. Jove's face had gone slowly from a brood to a scowl, which was almost as attractive now that I was paying attention.

I paused. Crap on a crepe, what was I going to do about *that* situation? Both Jove *and* David had now expressed interest in yours truly. Neither of whom had said anything of the sort before my accident. An accident that turned out to be not so accidental after all. It still made me mad to think that I'd been 'specially ordered' and then messed with by some asshole with a doctorate who did something to my body without my permission. Mad and scared.

How long had he been watching me to choose me as a candidate for his group? Did the Unkindness have any inkling that this man was building a small army specifically to go against the Community? No, they couldn't have. There was no way High Raven would put his flock in danger. He sounded pretty desperate to get a cure for the fledglings. To the point where he was willing to make a deal with a human doctor. The illness had to be affecting many of their young and possibly their elderly. How would the not-so-good doctor have treated them?

My musings were interrupted when I clicked up the magnification on the microscope.

"Holy hellcats," I murmured as I peered through the scope at the bile and was shocked to see a microscopic war unfolding in my petri dish. Tiny, metallic, spider-like things were attacking whatever living Faerie cells were in the vicinity with extreme prejudice. I was suddenly immensely glad I'd been called in as soon as I had. My patient could have had some extreme complications if he hadn't vomited *and* had his stomach pumped. I took a closer look at one of the spider things.

These were nanites destroying the cells, attacking them as they would cancer. I observed that the nanites were leaving the human cells alone.

I pulled the dish out and replaced it with the sample of the offending sandwich. The sandwich was practically crawling with the beasties. Watching them made my skin crawl.

I had my answer as to what had made Mr. Alfenheim sick, but had it been a targeted attack on him, or had the others in the meeting been affected and not known it? The one thing to call us to quick action had been his reaction to the microscopic metal, not the damage being done by the nanites. I rushed for the door. I had to let them know immediately before someone else got sick.

I learned something as I crossed that threshold. If one is going at an increased rate of speed through a time distortion, the rate of that speed wants to normalize as soon as possible. Thus, forcing the body to launch out of said distortion and into the nearest Zauberer who acts like a cushion so one doesn't smash into the wall. It kind of felt like being unable to stop on roller skates when I was a kid.

"Umph! Kleine? What is it? What is the matter?"

No time to enjoy being in his arms; people were in danger. I looked sharply at Ms. Corvis. "Have the others from the meeting gotten sick yet?"

"Yet?" The expression on her face reminded me of a surprised bird.

"Yeah. Yet. You said you'd eaten from the same place, right?" I grabbed her arm and dragged her back into the lab. "I need a sample from you to make sure you're clean. What I've found is really nasty and hopefully we've caught it before anything permanent has been damaged."

"Just what do you think you are doing, you—ow!" she screeched as I pricked her finger.

"Hold still, damn it! I need to see if they're in your bloodstream." I placed a drop of her blood on a slide and put it aside as I cleaned and bandaged the wound. I used a 'My Little Pony' bandage I had in my bag. "There, you big baby."

"You will pay for this assault, I assure you." She hissed.

"Yeah, yeah." I waved her away as I slid the slide under the microscope. "You got the full dose as opposed to Mr. Alfenheim. His system purged almost immediately upon consumption. There you are, you nasty little asshats." I stepped aside so Ms. Corvis could look for herself—the nanites were attacking all of her cells versus just certain ones. Most likely because she wasn't human at all.

She rolled her eyes and looked into the microscope. "What am I seeing here?"

"Those little spider things are attacking your cells. Your immune system doesn't quite know how to identify them as they are mechanical rather than biological."

"I—those are inside me?" The venom that had been in her voice quickly turned to fear.

"And everyone else who ate at that table. If left untreated, they can, and will, do untold damage to your body."

"Then why aren't I feeling sick?"

"It's only been a couple of weeks. They haven't had the time to do the kind of damage they are capable of. Mr. Alfenheim purged immediately because of his allergy, but those who haven't purged will likely start showing symptoms soon. I'd estimate symptoms begin a month or so after consumption. The victim may feel a little off but unsure as to why. The nanites don't appear to be fast-moving, but they are extremely destructive." I moved the microscope to show the little buggers in action. "Without further study, it's unclear if they are programmed to attack certain organs or just cause wanton destruction like we're seeing here. I don't want to take the risk of waiting."

I wasn't the kind of doctor who would postpone treatment on something like these nanites just to see what ultimate destruction they could cause. To just sit back and watch as someone slowly died was . . . monstrous. This was like treating an unknown poison. I'd rather try as many things as I could to stop further damage to my patients.

"I have a couple of different methods in mind to be rid of them, but I'll need a few things to get it done properly and, most likely, without pain." I studied Ms. Corvis's face. It was as flawless as ever. I had no idea if that was an illusion or not. If she were human, I would expect clammy skin at the very least. Possibly a fever if the immune system got its act together and recognized the nanites as a threat. Then I noticed a twitch as her jaw clenched—the woman's only sign of stress.

"Name them and they are yours." She strode away, calling over her shoulder. "I must inform High Raven of these developments immediately. Tell Horace and Larson what is needed and the extreme speed at which it is needed."

I nodded and took my time over the threshold this time to get the ball rolling. I already had a plan as to how to knock these things out of commission. I needed to set up an electromagnetic pulse emitter.

I've got to give those two guards credit. Between the two of them, they had put together all the bits I needed to make a small portable EMP emitter. By "small," I mean it ended up about the size of one of those tall white kitchen trash cans. It fit very nicely on a rolling handcart Horace found. Google was our friend that day. We put it together in the Time Lab. I also had to test the device before using it on patients. Fortunately for us, we had a nice, dead, infected sandwich to test on.

Larson was handy to have around in this room. Because he was a lesser Fae, he knew what time was doing outside. I felt like a mad scientist as I donned a set of black rubber gloves to insulate myself from the electric power needed to produce an electromagnetic pulse. I had the guys unplug everything we didn't absolutely need for the test fire. We had put the sandwich in the middle of a stainless-steel table behind a blast shield.

"Do you truly feel the food will explode?" asked Horace fearfully. He sounded like a knight with grave concerns.

"Naw, blast shields are just cool." I smiled at him. "Theoretically, unplugging the machines may save them from the pulse, so we shouldn't have too much damage. That's why we shut down and unplugged everything." It was also why I had three backup programs on two different flash drives in case the laptop fried.

"Theoretically?" said Larson. He pronounced each syllable slowly; it sounded like 'Thee-or-ret-ick-cally.' Horace was right; Larson did sound like a cartoon. "I don't know how I'm feeling about theoretically."

"It just means it hasn't been tested very well yet." The emitter was humming, storing up the energy needed for the pulse. I had needed to make sure I was going to be using the best type of pulse for what I needed to get done. I didn't have the expertise to set up one using nuclear fission—that would have taken too long anyway, time dilation or no—so I was limited to either an electronic or magnetic. I thought a combination of the two might do the trick. While Larson had worked on the small threading of insulated wires, I helped Horace set up the larger parts, though nothing could be too large because I wanted a smaller area of effect. I didn't want to knock out a whole building. I wanted to keep it confined to a room. Tesla coils were involved. I had to stop myself several times from cackling when something worked.

"I don't like it in here, Doc," Larson complained. "There's too much metal. It's gonna make me sick." His tiny stature made him very sensitive to the materials we were working with. I already had him in a makeshift hazmat suit we'd made out of a pair of medical gloves.

"Just a little longer, Mr. Larson. We need to test this before I can administer it. Come around to this side of the blast shield if you would, please. This should be the final one. Everything else looks right where we need it to be. Ready boys?" I couldn't suppress a grin as I typed in the final command to fire the EMP for the final test. My pinky hit the enter button and the world went dark.

"Doctor! Doctor Hall!" I heard panic in Horace's voice. He sounded a lot closer than he had been. "Awaken, my lady, please!"

I found myself cradled in Horace's arms. His equine body was kneeling on the floor, his hooves tucked under his belly. I blinked up at him.

"Oh, thank Zeus," he said in relief. "Larson has gone for your Zauberer, but I have no idea when he'd be back with the time distortion. You would not respond, my lady."

"How long have I been out?" My head ached like a rotten tooth. Horace propped me up to a semi-seated position slowly. I blew slowly out as my distance vision became clearer and in focus.

"You have been comatose for but a few minutes. Enough time to put a few gray hairs in this old tail." He flicked the tail in question against the floor. It sounded like someone had smacked a broom or a mop against the ceramic tile sheets.

"I apologize, Horace." I sat up further and my head spun a little, but not as badly as before. I should be able to stand *if* I was careful. "I don't know what came over me. Walk me through what happened from your perspective."

"You turned on that bedeviled device and were suddenly overcome at our feet. Your face lost all color as if someone walked over your very soul. Larson screamed . . . do not tell him I told you that. He would get self-conscious and impossible to work with for the rest of the day. He lit into the air out of the room as if Hades himself was chasing behind. I imagine he will not tarry long in the procurement of your Zauberer." I managed to get myself into a chair using Horace as a brace. He then went about the laborious task of getting himself back on all four feet.

There wasn't much traction for his hooves, but he managed to get to his feet much faster than I thought he would. "How did you do that? I've seen my cousin's horses stand up pretty quick when they have earth under their hooves, but you've got them beat."

"I'm shod with rubber-lined shoes, my lady. They do not leave as many scuff marks on the floor." He smiled. "A benefit is that they make it easier to stand again if needed. The distortion was rather severe the last we checked. We should probably go out into the hall to meet them."

"I'm—" I stopped and looked up at him. I was about to say I was grateful. I fisted my hands in my lap in frustration. I'd been warned about that when it came to Larson. Horace must've read the concern on my face. He gently patted my clenched hands. He was being very kind, and I really appreciated that.

"Have no fear, my lady. We Centaurs do not have the same laws as the Fae." He smiled kindly at me.

I took his hand and smiled back. "Thank you, Horace. I don't know what could have come over me."

"That is the second time you have said as such, my lady. Mayhap that machine harmed you more than you thought."

Great, I was repeating myself. I shook my head again to try and gain some clarity. "The body doesn't work that way. If that were the case, why didn't it hurt you or Larson? I have a suspicion that I'd like to check out before we go out to the hall." I could only think of one reason I would have passed out when an EMP went off.

Methodically, I drew my own blood, put it on a slide, and slid it under the microscope.

My suspicion solidified into fact as the picture came into focus. I sucked in a breath through my teeth. Nanites were floating inert in my blood. They were similar; very similar to the ones that were on the sandwich. I swapped the slides. These nanites were inert too. Well, good to know my device worked. I swapped the slides back to get a closer look at the ones in my blood. Mine were slightly bigger. Why would that be? I didn't have to wait long for the answer. Mine were already starting to move again. I switched back the slides and watched. No movement. I swapped the slides back and forth for twenty minutes with Horace silently watching. The sandwich bugs were dead. Mine took those twenty minutes to become fully operational once again. My headache disappeared as soon as the nanites were fully functioning again.

Why would they put a bug that would die and stay dead in the sandwich while mine were rebooting? Mine must have a different purpose. The nanites in the sandwich were there to do a specified task: hunt and destroy anything not sporting one hundred percent human cellular structure.

"Doctor? Are you feeling faint again? You have lost color." Horace clipped up behind me, politely ready to catch me again.

"Just found something unexpected." I took one final look at the sandwich nanites before turning to Horace. "I have to have the delegates lying down when we administer the treatment."

"Most will not wish to be prone in front of the others. It would cloud their viewed strength." He shifted from foot to foot as only a horse can do. "I know the Grand Dam will not like the idea of being so vulnerable. Dam Punch is my wife's dam as well."

"I have to say I love the fact that you call your leader the 'Grand Dam.' Is she a fan of Broadway, by any chance? Never mind." I stopped myself. "Not important. Do you know any others who were at the meeting?"

"No, only Dam Judith Punch, whom I know personally. She makes the decisions for the herds in this area. My lady, I do not want you to be on her bad side. I will offer my protection to her during the process so she will not be vulnerable." I was surprised Horace was so well connected.

I frowned. "Damned politics is all that is. If the rest of them want to be babies about this, then we're going to just have to convince them. Privacy screens should help."

Horace visibly paled. "I would not wish such an arduous task upon you, my lady. Mayhap request your Zauberer do it."

"The oath I took when I earned my doctorate demands I help whoever needs it. They won't be my first cantankerous patients, and odds are they won't be my last." We carefully wheeled the emitter out into the hall. Larson, Jove, and Ms. Corvis were rounding the corner at top speed. Jove got to us at the exact same time as Larson. I secretly think he used his magic to teleport.

He gently held my face in his hands. "Kleine, are you all right? The *Elfin* said you had fallen?" His eyes searched mine. "Are you hurt or injured? You are not ill, I hope."

I took his hands off my face and held them. "It's all right. I'm okay now. I passed out there for a couple of minutes. An unfortunate side effect of the treatment." I grinned hugely at him. "But, by God, it worked!"

"Well then, let's not waste any more time." Ms. Corvis motioned to the machine Horace was rolling out from the lab. "Just what is this and how does it help us?"

"Nanites are essentially very tiny machines. Usually, they are beneficial, used to kill off cancer cells, or to place very small sutures in delicate surgeries. The ones I found in your blood, and Mr. Alfenheim's sandwich, are not so benign. These were programmed to seek and destroy. Anything that doesn't match the human genome is fair game." I patted the emitter. "This will generate a pulse of power that will permanently disable the devices, allowing your body's defenses the time to isolate and expel them naturally."

"You mentioned a side effect?"

I nodded. "You may pass out for a couple of minutes."

"Is that all?" She looked incredulously at the emitter.

"It also may potentially wipe any hard drive and cell phone in the immediate vicinity. It also could turn off any heart monitors or insulin pumps. We'll need to start medical history charts." I handed her a flash drive. "I have a standard one on this under 'Chart templates.' Have your people print out as many as we'll need and put them onto clipboards. We may want to do this in one of those chamber-like rooms you guys have that looks like it's supposed to be in a castle. Stone and candles. No electronics other than the emitter, a screen to show what these little nasties look like, and the laptop used to command them."

I crossed my arms, thinking about what we'd need. "Beds or gurneys are a must, or at the very least chairs, unless they want to fall on their asses. Partitions for privacy, pillows, liquids for afterward—then they should be right as rain. I'll need another laptop to run the program on. They have a tendency to get fried if I'm in the same room with the emitter. What would be better is if we could set up a separate room to use the laptop in, away from the emitter. Sort of like the setup you see in an X-ray room."

"Unfortunately, Doctor, we do not have such a room . . . yet." Ms. Corvis crossed her arms to mirror my own and gave me a small smile.

A good technique, that. "Were you able to discover how this mess was carried out?"

"Whoever did this put it in your food as a condiment that wouldn't be easily tasted. I suspect olive oil, as it doesn't have a hefty taste and can easily hide something this small. As to when the perpetrator did it? I have no scientific way of knowing. I'd look into every step they took in the process, down to delivery, if I were you. There had to have been a compromise somewhere along the line." I was a doctor, not a detective, damn it. Not that I wasn't inquisitive as all hell, but it still wasn't part of my contract. I now had an inkling as to how it got into my patients' systems, but that was all I really cared about. That and how I was to get them OUT of their systems.

"We have that angle covered." The look she sent me told me she knew damned well where the compromise happened and probably also had a suspect. But there was no way she was going to pass on that information to the likes of me.

"The sooner we get the delegates here, the better," I said plastering a smile on my face. Ms. Corvis stalked away, already barking orders into her cell phone.

Jove reached an arm around me for a sidelong hug. His voice was full of pride. "'Not magic,' she says. I would very much like to differ. Just look at what magic you have wrought."

I flushed and shrugged. "Just some science. I wouldn't have been nearly as quick with the results, or the build for that matter, if it weren't for that glorious room and the help Horace and Larson gave me. It saved some precious time to have Larson get into the little nooks to fix a wire or two. We had to modify a couple of surgical gloves to keep him safe." I certainly couldn't doubt the Pixie's bravery. That had been a lot of metal, wires, and diodes that had surrounded him while we were building. I felt like I owed him a cupcake.

"So, what now? How many shots do you have with this . . . What do you call this monstrosity?" Jove waved a hand at the machine.

"Electromagnetic pulse emitter or EMP emitter," I said proudly. "We should only need the one 'shot' to fix the problem. I'm trying to think of it as a treatment for the disease they are afflicted with."

"I worry that I will not be able to stand by your side if you want your . . . emitter"—he chewed on the strange word; it was adorable—"to work. Especially if I need to use magic."

"I was pondering that while we were tinkering. You told me you gave up the radio, right?" I'd been thinking about this while I was up to my elbows in computer parts. There isn't a ton of a relationship between computers and radios.

He arched an eyebrow at me. "*Ja*, and . . ."

"The computer was never based on the radio. It owes its origins to adding machines born of the Industrial Age. You and computers should be hunky-dory."

Jove blinked at me. I guess the thought had never dawned on him that not all modern technology was based on the radio. He frowned. "An *abschwören* is a very personal thing, Kleine. I know you are trying to help, but in this case, please do not. It is for me to have faith as to what it should be or not. Not for you to tell me how to get around it. Every time I have brought a computer into the shop, if I try working with it, then it breaks. This is what my faith tells me, so this is what it is. I ask that you respect it."

It was my turn to blink.

I didn't realize how much of his magic had more to do with his faith. I had my own faith—I went to church almost every Sunday—and I shouldn't have thought that my own way of thinking was the only one. "I apologize, Jove. I didn't know that's how it worked for you. If it were just proximity, then Katie and I couldn't have our smartphones at work," I said, trying for logic. "We should still be okay with you in the room if you're far enough away from the equipment. Just like how it was at my apartment."

I really didn't want to be in that room without Jove. The Unkindness had already shown me what they would do if I were unprotected. I noticed then that Jove was carrying something. "What's that you have there?"

His face bloomed into one of his rare smiles. "In the excitement, I had forgotten. While you were working, I conjured this up for you."

He held it out in both hands and gave his wrists a quick flick. White cloth fluttered, unfurling into a gorgeous, long lab coat. Jove let go and the garment swirled around me, placing itself on my arms and shoulders. It felt like a dream, light and soft. I gave the pockets an experimental tug. It felt durable, strong even, and perfectly tailored. It looked like the twin of the one given to me at my ceremony.

"We cannot have you treating patients without the proper attire, true?" Amazed, I looked inside the coat I was wearing, proving to myself that I really was only wearing Jove's gift. "No trying to return this either."

"You have to stop giving me gifts I can't give back." I snuggled into the coat. "Aren't you just the sexiest lab coat ever?" I cooed.

It purred.

My eyes went wide. "Jove?"

"She is a guardian for you, Kleine. For when I cannot be there." He rubbed his hands up and down my arms. "I was unsure if she would choose to bond with you; they are usually shy of humans. Especially ones not of Japanese descent. However, it seems my fears were unfounded."

I looked down at the coat. There were a few Japanese beasties I could think of, most of them not very nice. There was an emblem sewn into the vest pocket. I tilted it gently up so I could get a better look at it. It was a multicolored fox made of fire, with four tails. I swallowed. "I thought Kitsunes were guardians to gods."

"How did you—" He pouted. I think he wanted to impress me with knowledge and I beat him to the punch again.

"Nerd, remember? Kitsunes are portrayed a couple of different ways. Tricksters in their own right, but they usually play more chaotic good than true neutral." I looked skeptically at the coat. "And never worn as a garment."

Jove nodded thoughtfully. "Again, some things are true, some things are not. We really must sit down and compare notes."

I shrugged, still marveling at the Kitsune coat. "Sure, I'll bring my D and D books over to the shop for you to go through." I glanced at Jove. "What does she eat?"

A fluffy white head poked out from under the pleated front collar. If you'd been looking at me from the front, it would've looked like I had a Pomeranian under my coat. My heart melted looking into her little eyes. Her face wasn't all white; it had these gorgeous, intricate black markings. "Oh! Hello, Pretty. Or maybe you like Suteki better?"

The fox face closed its eyes; it almost looked like it was smiling.

"I think she likes it," said Jove with a laugh. "You should be able to feed her what you usually would a fox."

"I am not hunting squirrels," I said in disgust.

"Somehow I do not think that will be a problem." He chuckled as the little fox face snuggled under my chin for a moment before disappearing back into the coat.

The quick staccato clack of Ms. Corvis's heels announced her return. "Everything should be in order. I want you to do a final once-over in case there is anything else you may need." She gave me a pointed nod. "Good. That coat makes you look more professional. That is exactly what we want to portray here. These people are . . . strenuous allies in the Community. Each are very wary of each other. We do not need any infighting here. At least, no more than usual." We started walking at a brisk pace down the hall. I was pushing the emitter.

"Do they know they've been infected?" I increased my pace to match hers.

"No, and you will not tell them. All it would do is cause them to blame one another, or worse, blame us for trying to make a power grab." Ms. Corvis gave a dismissive wave of her hand.

"I don't think that's the best course of action here." I paused in the hall, stopping our quick march. "When I turn on this machine, all of you guys are going to be taking a quick nap. The delegates are going to think you have a weapon capable of putting them out cold that you are all too willing to use on them." I crossed my arms over my chest. "I'm not going to let you show my medical equipment as a weapon."

"Might I make a suggestion?" We both looked over at Jove. "We keep them in the loop about the investigation. Let them know it is another party that is to blame for this obvious attack."

"How do we keep them from retaliating against every human they meet?" asked Ms. Corvis. "They will not be happy that humanity has started to target us again."

"Well, how do you do it now? With today's technology, I'm honestly shocked that the wrong people don't already know about the Community's existence." I looked over at my emitter. "Unless this is the first sign that they already do. Someone had to create and program those little bugs, program them specifically to do harm to something *not* human. The only other practical use for this type of tech would be to destroy any other species on the planet." I shivered at the thought. "Dangerous, very dangerous. So far it looks like the creator of these has only figured out how to put a vial or two in food. God help us if they figure out how to make them into a virus. They replicate! That would be very bad for us if they get to that point."

Ms. Corvis nodded, conceding the point. "I don't like showing that we let the delegates get harmed on our watch. This makes us look weak."

"They need to know there is a danger that is coming from outside the Community. They would then have a common enemy to stand against," said Jove. We started walking faster.

24

THE HALL ENDED abruptly in a set of familiar-looking, carved wooden doors. The sharp contrast from modern architecture to medieval jarred me. I felt like I was in Doctor Frankenstein's lab, or Dracula's castle. Either way, it had a very gothic feel. The doors opened by themselves into a room that reminded me uncomfortably of the grand chamber in the dungeon where I'd met High Raven for the first time. The same stonework and architecture surrounded us. There were Bird-boy guards here. I did my very best not to look at them.

Eight partitions were lined up next to one another in the large room. Each had exactly what you would expect to see in an ER: a gurney, fresh sheets, and white pillows. There were also tables and chairs, one of each per "room." The rooms were set up in such a way to not be able to see inside anyone else's, but it left a spot right in the middle for me to set up and still be seen by my patients. There were large candelabras everywhere to give us plenty of light to see by. A huge chandelier hung over our heads; two ravens finished lighting the candles on it with lit tapers held by their claws. The only pieces of technology in the room were a big-screen television, the laptop, a big-ass power cable, and the emitter.

Ms. Corvis walked up beside me. "Well, is everything in order?"

I nodded.

"Good, I'll make the call." A red phone rose up out of the stonework on the floor. It was a rotary phone. The fact that it not only worked but didn't seem to have any sort of cable going anywhere was fascinating. She only dialed one number and put the receiver to her ear. "This is Second Raven. I am calling an emergency meeting of the Council of Eight for the Community of Philadelphia. All members please converge at this location immediately. This is a matter of life and death."

Second Raven? That meant Ms. Corvis was much higher on the food chain than I'd given her credit for. It made me wonder about the Unkindness. Did Ms. Corvis take her rank from her spouse? Did she inherit it when he died, or did she earn it? She sure acted like she'd earned it. If she hadn't been so cruel under all that gloss, I might want to be her when I grew up.

As soon as she hung up the phone there were various flashes of light. Some were accompanied by acrid smoke that made my eyes water. It didn't take long for all members to teleport into the room. They were equally made up of both men and women, four of each. Most of them were in business suits with very stern looks on their faces. Mr. Alfenheim was among them. He gave me a warm smile and a courteous nod. They had to have had their various glamour on, because every single one of them looked as human as anyone I'd pass on the street.

Ms. Corvis made a disapproving sound in the back of her throat. I glanced over. "Something the matter?"

"We're one low-born idiot shy."

My eyes widened, and I counted the people in front of me again. "I count eight, including yourself."

"The councilman for the Dwarves decided that he isn't required to answer an emergency summons from 'an animal' like me."

"We have to try again! He doesn't know the damage these things can do!"

She rolled her eyes and leveled a cold look at me. "I tried five times, Doctor Hall. On his own head be it." She cleared her throat. "Council members," started Ms. Corvis, "thank you for coming so promptly."

"Just what sort of threat are we facing, Second Raven?" asked an older woman. Her hair was steel gray, but she didn't look terribly old. I saw Horace out of the corner of my eye straighten his uniform. This must be the Grand Dam Judith Punch. I would wait for proper introductions before saying anything.

"As I said on the phone: life and death. Namely our own." She stopped the outraged murmur from becoming shouts with a slowly raised hand. "Allow me to introduce Doctor Mira Hall."

Showtime. I took a step forward and nodded to the council members. But before I could speak, an older-looking councilman spoke up. He had an obvious limp in his left leg, causing him to adjust his stride. His voice drawled like someone born and raised in the Southwest as he spoke. "We are aware of a Gewalt who just moved into the Community Charter with that name. Is that you, my dear?"

I smiled my professional smile and nodded. "Yes, Councilman . . ."

"Rhoades. I am the councilman for the Zauberers. I also train Zauberers when they are new, as I did Zauberer Brandt there." If he had been in a robe with a pointy hat, I would have thought he was dressed up as a Wizard. Instead, he looked like a university professor with a white shirt and brown tweed vest and matching dust-brown pants. I tried not to grin when I took in his shoes. The man was wearing the gaudiest pair of cowboy boots I've ever seen. Tall, teal, embroidered leather shafts flowed down the councilman's calves to the black lower part of the boot. The intricate embroidery and beadwork seemed to sprout from the instep like loving, living tendrils that traveled up and branched out. Boxy toes and at least an inch of heel connected somehow with the rest of the boot, but I couldn't see how as there were no obvious connection stitches. They were the most epic footwear I've ever seen before.

Zauberer Rhoades didn't give me the creepy feeling like Zimmer had. He looked more like a kindly old man. I glanced back at Jove. He was pale. He didn't have that reaction to Zimmer . . . I decided to make an effort to be more respectful. I clasped my hands behind my back and gave a little bow to all the councilmen and councilwomen with my confident doctor smile on. "Yes, I am the Gewalt who registered. I have been employed by the Unkindness to look into what happened to Councilman Alfenheim during your last meeting."

"You saved my life, Doctor Hall. Plain and simple. Welcome to the Philadelphia Community," said Mr. Alfenheim. Today he was dressed like a typical European businessman who is trying to be trendy. He wore brown ankle-height boots, tight, skinny slacks, and a blazer with the shirt underneath slightly unbuttoned at the top. As he had a swimmer's body, the look worked for him. It also made me wonder just what kind of half-Fae he was.

Alfenheim took a few steps to separate himself from the rest of the council, making sure everyone knew he was the center of attention. He bowed deeply, eyes to the floor. "I owe you, Doctor Hall. I am in your debt for the return of my life. I say it a third time: you are owed a debt by me, to be called in at any time, and I will gladly answer to your need."

Breaths were drawn around the room and various eyes widened. I gulped, knowing this was a bigger deal than just words. He looked up from his bow; our eyes met, and he gave me a flirty grin. I flushed. I was starting to think all the Community had been hiding all the handsome men for a while.

"I'm Councilman Amos," growled a large man to Mr. Alfenheim's left. He was almost as big as Jerimiah. His eyes were a piercing green in an angular face. Strength was radiating off his body, but it wasn't a bodybuilder power I saw roped in his arms; it was a fighter's. This was David's alpha! His arms were thick with muscle, so he looked more like a bodyguard than a council member, but he carried himself as someone who did not put up with being disobeyed by anyone. Councilman Amos was dressed in a high-powered business suit. The kind that says you were not even worthy to be on the same block as them, never mind in the same room. I noticed no one would meet his eyes. It seemed the best thing to do the same. Amos made a circle motion with his hand. "You did say this was life and death. Didn't you? Shouldn't we get on with it?"

I cleared my throat and looked away from the powerful Werewolf. "Indeed. I was charged with the task of finding out just what had made Councilman Alfenheim sick. What I found was disturbing, and it is threatening your lives as we speak."

I motioned to the big screen and brought up a picture of the nanites. "I found these in the remains of Councilman Alfenheim's meal. And these"—I clicked a button and brought up Ms. Corvis' blood—"I found in Second Raven's blood. These are microscopic machines that are attacking any cell in your body that doesn't match up with the human genome. They are slowly tearing you apart and, if left unchecked, they will cause your internal organs to shut down." I let the implications hang in the air.

Concerned murmurs flooded the room. Then one of them started to laugh. She was one of the female council members. Where Councilman Rhoades didn't hit on my creep-o-meter at all, this woman hit so hard it maxed out. I felt fear make my heart pound a little faster. Her eyes landed on me and her smile widened.

"Is that what that was?" Her laughter grated, sounding like her body was trying its damnedest not to do what the entity inside wanted it to do. The lady in question wasn't as tall as Amos, but she was fit and looked like she could handle herself in a fight.

She wore a fire-engine-red power suit with a blazer that looked a size too small, as parts of her seemed to want to fall out of her top. Instead of slacks, the councilwoman wore a pencil skirt cut three inches too far above the knee and stiletto heels that had flames that licked from the toe up the sides. Too brazen for my taste. She reminded me of a gender-bent Lex Luthor. Beautiful, commanding, and not bald at all. She just exuded evil as she ran a hand through short black hair. "I'd wondered why this body was starting to rebel more often."

She smirked as she sauntered up close to me, leaning over a little to get closer to eye level. Or to give me a look down her shirt. I couldn't tell which. I think her goal was making me uneasy. Her eyes had a red glow to them that had nothing to do with the candles in the room. Fear had me wanting to look away, but this person was to be a patient, and you don't show you're scared to a patient. It undermines your credibility. I kept my face stony and professional. Her glowing eyes landed on the Celtic cross on the charm bracelet and traveled up to the traditional cross I had under my shirt. It felt like she could see through the cloth as her eyes traveled up and down my body lasciviously. I crossed my arms and felt an embarrassed flush hit my cheeks. Her smile grew, showing way more teeth than she needed to.

"Little girl, do you know what I am?" She took another intimidating step forward. I had to fight to stand my ground and not retreat. You don't run from predators—not if you want to live long afterward.

"Oh, I'm getting a strong inkling," I said. The woman wasn't trying overtly to catch my gaze, but I was finding it hard to look away from her. Like you do when there's someone in uniform in the room.

Her skin wasn't overtly pale . . . but I wasn't sure if vampires worked the same way as they did in books and movies. Even then, there were so many varieties that it boggled the mind to pin down precisely how to identify one type from another. She could be a vampire or something more sinister. Then I caught a whiff of sulfur on her breath and knew.

I was going to have to deal with that moral quandary after the emitter had done its work. My plan was to get to church and pray for the poor soul that body belonged to as soon as we were done. This wasn't the place to try to perform an exorcism . . . not that I knew how to exorcise a Demon anyway. Well, I did, but only in the context of Dungeons and Dragons, and I was no cleric. "I was taught to love my enemies as well as my friends, so I'm still going to save your life."

"And what about the soul of this body I'm inhabiting?" She ran her hands over the curves of her body from the boobs down.

"That has nothing to do with the treatment of the nanites, and frankly, way out of my league as a doctor. Since you are an invader of the mind and spirit rather than that of the body, I'm supposing the nanites have been more concentrated on your cerebral cortex. Especially since you are losing control so quickly." I shot a significant glance at her hands, which trembled involuntarily as if she had palsy. I stood my ground, though my body was screaming to retreat. I took a steadying breath and remembered that my God is more powerful than anything this bitch could cook up. "Depending on how you infect your host, the nanites must be doing their dirty work well. So, sit your ass down and let me do my job, Councilwoman . . ."

"Edwards." Her voice was a sultry, whispering hiss as she told me her name. She thrust out a perfectly manicured hand.

I didn't take it. "Take a chair or a bed, Councilwoman Edwards. This will be over soon."

I purposefully turned away, relieved to have that woman out of my line of sight. "Councilmembers, I have a machine here designed to permanently disable these nanites. It is called an electromagnetic pulse emitter. It will cause weakness and possibly make you pass out for a couple of minutes. That is why we have the beds and chairs behind you set up. There will be a questionnaire on a clipboard on your tables. Please fill them out so we don't have any unforeseen complications."

"You're positive this will permanently disable them?" the older councilwoman asked. She had a more matronly look to her, but with a competent air. She reminded me of a stateswoman who had the best intentions for her people. She wore a much more subdued business suit in navy blue and comfortable-looking slacks. No nonsense would come from this woman's mouth. "Have you tested this procedure?"

"We have, Councilwoman Punch." Ms. Corvis snapped her fingers and nurses clad in black scrubs with the gold Unkindness logo on their breast pockets came into the room. They started to lead the council members to the different privacy areas. "Please take your seats or your beds. The sooner we get this done, the sooner we can get on with what we plan to do about this attack."

As I flicked a switch on the side of the emitter to let it gather power, I was surprised to see how efficient the nurses were. The general grumbles were met with smiles and pats. I was starting to feel right at home. Though, if the Unkindness had nurses, then logically they should have their own doctors. Why the hell did they need me to treat the fledglings?

I had to leave that thought for further analysis. I grabbed the clipboard with my notes on it. I'd scribbled a lot of notes in the margins that I was going to transfer onto my computer as soon as I got a chance. I started making my way to the different 'rooms' the Council of Eight occupied. The one closest to me was the Zauberer councilman who had introduced himself earlier. Jove was chatting with Councilman Rhoades.

"Can we trust this girl, Zauberer Brandt? She is very young." His German was clean and unaccented. Rhoades sat in the chair we provided, though I doubted it was because he didn't want to be caught prone. Even from here, I could tell he was having an ongoing problem with his left hip. I paused just before walking into his line of sight. To his credit, he let the question stand without any backtracking to apologize for me having heard. Maybe he didn't think I spoke the language.

"Impeccably, master." Jove took my hand as I stood next to him. I felt heat rise to my cheeks. Why did this feel like I was being introduced to Jove's father? Was it because Rhoades was his Obi-Wan? Jove saying 'master' felt more like him meaning teacher. *"She has managed to see our world and not go mad. Doesn't this mean that maybe there is a chance for others?"*

"There are many kinds of madness, my boy. We will have to wait and see how hers may make itself known." He looked me up and down without being overtly offensive about it, unlike Edwards, though it did make me squirm a bit.

I gently took back my hand from Jove and made a show of writing more notes down before giving the councilman my best doctor smile. *"Are you finished with your paperwork, Councilman?"*

He blinked at me, then he smiled. *"You speak my language, then?"*

Ha! Called it. "*Taught on my grandmother's knee. Make sure you drink that water next to you after the procedure. I want to make sure your body purges the little bugs after I've deactivated them.*"

"*Yes, Frau Doktor.*" Rhoades leaned forward, handing me the completed form. "*I hope I have not insulted you with this talk of madness.*"

I shook my head and smiled. "*No, sir. You haven't offended me. It's something I, myself, worry about. We'll get started as soon as everyone is settled. Sit back and relax. We'll be done with this business soon. Oh, and nice shoes.*" I left him laughing like a loon.

I paused by Mr. Alfenheim's area where he was already lying on the bed. His nurse was giggling at him and smiling. I put on my friendly doctor face again and knocked gently on the partition. "All done with your paperwork?"

He pouted at me. "Do I really have to do this again, beautiful?" He eased himself out of the bed like a large cat and came up to me. "Are you so worried for me, Doctor Hall?"

"You may not have purged all of the invaders, Councilman Alfenheim. While you didn't get a full dose, I'd still like you to go through the procedure to be on the safe side," I said, writing on the chart and handing it off to one of the nurses.

"You *are* worried for me." He grinned again. "I like it. I would be so much more willing if you joined me in this bed, dear Doctor. And seeing as we already know each other so well, call me Aiden."

I'd forgotten how he sounded like Ireland. His red hair and green eyes brought images of spring and summer places just after a rainstorm. Alfenheim obviously wasn't his given name, but a name he'd chosen for himself. I gave myself a little shake; I had other patients. "Fill out the papers. I'll be back around after I get the others. Nurse, don't let this charmer keep you from doing what needs to be done. I don't want to have to hold the procedure for too long."

"Is that Summer Court dandy causing you trouble, Doctor?" asked a light voice from the next room. "I could always neuter him for you."

"Ah." Aiden sighed. "D'ya see what I have to put up with from that frigid bitch?" He rolled his eyes and sent his attending a mournful look. "Nurse, I tell you it's a hardship with her being my sister."

Well, that must make for interesting holidays, I thought. "Are you finished, Councilwoman?" I said as I walked around the corner. The woman was sitting up in the bed. She'd had the nurse prop it up. She was one of the few people not in a business suit. Instead, she had on brown leather pants and boots I'd kill for. They rode mid-calf, had zippers and buckles in all the right places, and a nifty little pocket that I don't know what I'd use for but I would have found an excuse to have.

She had paired them with a lacy black halter top which perfectly complemented her hair and skin. Her eyes danced with mischief as she thumped her boots together. "Nice, aren't they?"

"No kidding. Nothing like Councilman Rhoades', but still impressive. I'm curious as to where I can lose a fortune on them, Councilwoman—"

"Call me Meriah, sweetie. I don't like titles. I got these from a place run by cobbler Elves in New Hope. Lovely family, they are. Local is always better. And, unlike my procrastinating little brother, I'm all finished with my paperwork." She smiled and handed me the chart, and I got a good look at her face. Where Aiden reminded me of bright green fields, his sister reminded me of rich autumn forests that were just on the cusp of changing to winter. Her skin was ivory, like piano keys. Her tightly curled hair and long eyelashes were a pale red that reminded me of frosted leaves that I would find on walks in the woods. In sharp contrast, Meriah's eyes were a deep twilight. It was the kind of color you could get lost in. This was the kind of beauty that would make one question their sexuality.

"Wonderful—" I cleared my throat and looked away. I hoped I hadn't been too forward by staring. Her features were fascinating, but what could you expect from a daughter of the Fae.

"Though, I really don't know if I need this either." She shrugged. "I brought my own food to the table. Can't trust anybody, you know, and

I wasn't about to trust that my food wasn't poisoned. Huh, who's the paranoid one *now, Aiden*?" she shouted over the partition.

"Aw, shut it, ya flaming git!" came his less-than-clever retort.

"You shut it! You're a sorry excuse for a half-blood! Spring court is filled with good-for-nothing pansies and pop stars!" she yelled in the general direction of her brother. She then turned back to me and said in the most reasonable of tones, "But my point, Doctor, is that if this procedure is something as new as I'm betting it is, especially as I haven't heard anything about it coming out of the NHS, is it safe for us to get fried by this contraption you've made?"

"To my knowledge, nothing bad will happen if you get this done and don't need it. Nanites may not need to be inside a host to function. That means they could still be on your skin. We'll zap them and be done with it."

In the next 'room' one of the nurses was helping Councilwoman Punch to step onto the bed, which had been lowered all the way to the floor. I thought this a bit odd, but shrugged it off. Horace stood sentinel to the side, out of the way of the busy nurses. There were bound to be stranger things I was going to see today. The Councilwoman regarded me with a steady glance once she got herself settled onto the lowered bed.

"Are the twins giving you trouble, Doctor Hall? They fight like cats, but it is one of the few ways we've found to keep the peace between the courts is to have family be bridging the gap. I wouldn't be surprised if fighting was their way of showing affection." Her body appeared to be kneeling on the end of the bed, but there was a large indentation that took up the rest of the mattress.

I gave her a smile and knelt down myself to keep us both at eye level. "I have family of my own that does the same thing. I've heard worse during rotations. Are you comfortable, Councilwoman?"

"As well as I can. May I ask what exactly you intend to do with this information we've given you on these questionnaires?" She held up her unfinished clipboard. "Some of this information, if it made its way into the wrong hands, could be very dangerous for us."

"I have to have accurate information before performing any sort of medical procedure. Say I turn on this machine and one of you hasn't told me you have a pacemaker. I would effectively be turning off your heart, thus killing you. In medicine, information is everything. Symptoms are clues to lead a doctor to what the problem is, tests to identify the disease, and form a plan to treat, then you have the execution of the plan to cure the problem."

"You make it sound like a war." She frowned as she filled out the forms.

"In a way, I suppose it is." I smiled at her. "I like the rush I get when I win a battle against a disease."

"I like knowing you're fighting for us. There are far too few doctors not beholden to one group or another." Councilwoman Punch paused and arched an eyebrow at me. "You will be working for more than just the Unkindness, I hope?"

"Oh, yes, Councilwoman. My practice is going to be open to everyone in the Community. I did promise to put their symbol on the building, mostly for being my biggest investors."

"Hmm, is that so?" She casually handed me the clipboard. "I would like to be another one of your investors then. I will match whatever the Unkindness has given, and I may even have land you may want to build your practice upon."

I was floored. I almost dropped the clipboard. Words stumbled out of my mouth. "T–that's very generous, Councilwoman Punch."

"Not at all, I just want my herd to have the same opportunities and options as our . . . allies. Horace speaks highly of you and your quick action with Councilman Alfenheim. I will have someone contact you to speak about the particulars."

She spoke like a queen more than an elected official. That made sense. With horses, it was the head mare who made all the important decisions, like where to get good water, where to graze, where the herd was going to move next. The Stallions were just there for breeding, and protection, but always deferred to the lead mare when it came to anything else. The

Councilwoman had to have something very strong to make me see her as human. I didn't even see an anomaly.

She was proposing to match what the Unkindness had already given me. That was more money than I'd ever imagined having access to as a business loan. I'd always dreamt of building my own practice, but creating the building it was to be housed in? That was . . . staggering. I clutched the clipboards in my arms a little tighter. This offer obviously came with just as many strings as it did with the Unkindness. I had to be careful not to get strangled by them.

"Provided this procedure is a success, of course, dear," she said, folding her hands in her lap.

"Of course." I swallowed and walked on to the next partition.

I could have kissed the nurse at the next station. It was Councilwoman Edwards' 'room' and the nurse simply handed me the completed chart and chatted a little with me as we passed. I didn't have to look at Edwards. But damned if I couldn't feel the heaviness of her eyes on me. Yup, church, right after this. I looked down at my hands, as it seemed I held something heavier than just her paperwork.

I came to the last 'room' that was set close to the emitter but on the opposite side. Councilman Amos was right where I expected him to be when I got to his area: sitting in the chair because no alpha worth his salt would be caught lying on his back. "I hear you know my new packmate," he grumbled as he handed me his paperwork. The nurses left him mostly alone in his room, making sure not to crowd the Alpha.

"Yes." I put his paperwork with the others. "My friend David. Did he tell you about me?"

"Jerimiah informed me." Amos almost looked peaceful with his arms crossed over his wide chest, but something told me it was an illusion. "The boy will have to be punished for lying to me. He told us you were his woman, not his friend. I am his alpha, not his father. I will not stand for deception."

"Please . . ." I made sure my eyes were anywhere but on his; if urban fantasies had taught me anything, it was that. Wild wolves don't really have alphas, so much of what I knew could be horseshit, but I didn't want to chance it. "Don't be too hard on him. He didn't even admit his feelings to me until just recently. He's a good and strong person. An asset to any pack. He's also a doctor in his own right. He can take care of your pack as wolves while I can take care of them as men."

"I'm not offering you money like Punching Judy and the Unkindness are," he said with a sneer, as if he suspected that was what I wanted in exchange. Amos didn't have the same attitude as Jerimiah, though he was every bit as much of a badass. He felt almost more like a military commander, if anything.

I felt my spine straighten and tried to tamp down on the impulse to remind him of who was in charge in this situation. That would have been stupid.

"I know that," I said softly, though now I wanted to know the story behind the nickname for the Centaur leader. "I'm not asking for another donor. All I want is to be able to help people, your pack included. Copays and deductibles may apply with your insurance once I get things up and running. What we are doing today has already been paid for by the Unkindness." I held the clipboard close to my chest before I left his room. "Please take care of my David for me."

The nurses were proving to be very efficient. They not only got the paperwork Aiden procrastinated on, but also the one from the remaining councilman: Myles Sakis of Olympus. I sorted them alphabetically before loading up the program for the emitter.

While it booted up, I read through the paperwork, scanning for keywords or problems that could come into play with having a pulse of magnetism flying through the air. I marked each folder with a number I assigned to the different councilmembers. There were some questions I'd have to ask if they ever decided to see me as their primary care doctor. I saved a copy of the program on the same encrypted flash drive that held my research and slipped it into my pocket as Jove joined me.

I smiled, putting on my gloves. "I'll keep the charts with me for now. How do people of the Community keep paperwork safe? I have a heavy-duty safe at my apartment, but I worry about how long it could take for me to get home."

Jove made a motion with his hand, and the charts disappeared. That was just so cool. "Will you be able to keep them safe with the recent break-in at your home, Kleine?" He spoke as quietly as possible.

"I will, especially once I ask you to enchant a safe for me. I have one at the apartment that should serve until I get something better." I looked at the screen and smiled at the power reading from the emitter. "It's showtime. Everyone! May I have your attention, please? I'm going to need you to close your eyes and concentrate on breathing in and out. This machine will emit the pulse in three, two, and—"

ZWORM

I grinned triumphantly as my emitter did exactly as advertised. Most of the Council members passed out on their beds or in their chairs. Nurses swarmed to get them in positions to be monitored. My head gave a thump of pain, but this time, I didn't pass out like my patients had. As expected, the only person not to pass out was Meriah, who was busy screaming at the top of her lungs as tiny zaps of electricity danced over her skin. I rushed over to assess the situation. It wasn't anything worse than the kind of static shock you get when you wear wool socks on a shag floor, but to have them all over your body had to be disconcerting. I just bet she got her skin from the human side of her lineage, as she didn't have as big a reaction to the metal as her brother did. She'd written in her chart in big, bold letters: Aiden is a pansy; I have piercings. Those piercings were acting as electrical conduits, causing pain every time one of the little buggers popped.

"Let's get her grounded, boys and girls. I need rubber for the electricity to dissipate into and get her a thermal blanket to take care of anything that tries to catch fire," I shouted over the councilwoman's screams. Jove handed me what looked like a square of thick black rubber. I nodded my thanks and put it into Meriah's hands, looking into her eyes. They were stormy: fear riding lightning.

I talked low and slow, willing the woman to calm. "Take a breath in and out. Slowly now. That's the way. I know this feels weird; just hold onto this. It'll give all the electricity from those little nasties somewhere to go. There we are. See? Dissipating already."

"Doctor!" shouted the nurse from Edwards' bed. "We need you over here!"

I rushed over in time for a pitcher of water to be thrown at my head. I *caught* it with my ability just before it had a chance to crash on the floor. Edwards had come out of her momentary forced slumber in a wild panic and was fighting the nurses with the fury of a trapped animal. "Don't keep me here! I don't wanna be here! I gotta get outta here before it comes *back*!"

"Calm down, Councilwoman. Take some deep breaths," one of the nurses tried to soothe.

"I ain't no stinking 'councilwoman.' Just let me up!" The woman's wild eyes landed on me and my white coat in the sea of black-clad nurses. "Doc, you've got to help me, please!"

I went to the side of the bed and took her hand. She clamped on like I was a life preserver that someone was trying to snatch away. "Miss, I need your name, your real name, quickly before it settles back in."

"Eva, Eva Strom." She sobbed out.

"I'm going to do my best to help you Ms. Strom, be strong for a little bit longer. Can you do that for me?" I held her shaking hand. "Just a little longer."

She nodded and then started to seize. The nurses and I held her down until it passed. It was as if Eva turned into a completely different woman. I suppose, in a sense, she did. Edwards looked down at our joined hands. "Oh, Doctor, what have you been up to?" The council-woman purred. "Tut, tut, giving this body false hope." I made to let go. She reached out and grabbed my forearm, giving it a quick, vicious twist. It felt as if her thumb alone was grinding the bones together. "She is *mine*."

I yelped in pain as the nurses scrambled to get her off me. The pain seared where her thumb pressed into my arm. Suteki's little fox face appeared under the sleeve cuff above my elbow and bit, fast and hard, down on Edwards' well-manicured hand. The councilwoman raged at being forced to let go of fresh prey.

"You little bitch!" she screeched. "I'll see you fry!"

"You'll do no such thing here, Councilwoman," came the frigid voice of Ms. Corvis. She strode toward us, power in every step. This was Second Raven, Councilwoman of the Council of Eight. She stood in her impeccable suit, the logo of the Unkindness glowing on her lapel pin. The fact that she had already recovered to the point where a person couldn't tell she'd just been unconscious was a show of strength. I could just feel the authority she put behind her words. It was impressive, it was intimidating, and I could've hugged her. "Doctor Hall has healed your body of invaders, as promised. Feel free to leave once the nurses are done with you. Doctor, please follow me."

I had to put a little effort into catching up. "That was amazing! Good for you, putting her in her place! I'm really—"

"Don't speak," she hissed through her teeth. "I should have known someone like you would stir up Edwards. You're just so . . . good, you seem so . . . nice. It's like you secrete it from your skin!" She stopped suddenly, jabbing a finger into my shoulder. "You listen to me. We have a very delicate balance here. A tip in any direction could mean war in our corner of the country. A Community at war isn't a pretty thing. A healthy Community brings balance to where we live." She straightened her suit. "Not all of it is Community doings. We have a tendency to keep things more peaceful and harmonious with our human neighbors. Part of that is due to the work of the Demons to keep evil in line, so to speak. No one likes working with the Demons, but they are a necessary, if rarely palatable, evil. Is there anything else that needs to be done?"

"Just a quick blood screening to make sure the bugs are dead. I then suggest immediate incineration of all samples. We won't need them for future tests. I'd like to oversee it myself." I knew all of my patients had more than valid worries about their privacy. I also knew, in this brand-new world I'd gotten myself into, much could be done with a single drop of blood.

"Do as she says," she snapped to a passing nurse.

"Yes, Second Raven." The nurse nodded smartly.

"You have some very well-trained nurses here. I have to say I'm a bit surprised," I said with admiration.

"Feeling superfluous, Doctor Hall?" she said with a smirk. "High Raven took you up on your offer because you were more expensive than your agreed-to price. We would be able to solve our own problems in due time."

She left me standing by the desk near the emitter while I felt smaller than the nanites. She'd just made it clear that she didn't think the Unkindness needed me at all. That the only reason I was standing here instead of being shipped off to whomever had purchased me was because I had caused too much trouble and offset the costs. I shook; if the buyer had gotten there before Jove, I might not be standing here at all.

All tests came back negative. I got all the samples done rather quickly thanks to the time room. I had the time to make sure all the bugs, except for the ones floating in my blood, were dead. I was escorted back to the chamber by Jove, where the Council of Eight waited for the final verdict. I cleared my throat to get their attention. "Ladies and gentlemen, I'm pleased to announce the treatment was a complete success. You are free to return to the rest of your evening."

"Evening?" Zauberer Rhoades laughed. "It's barely half past noon, young woman."

I flushed as the rest of the Council laughed at me. I must've lost more time than I thought in the time lab. "I've been working hard on this project, so I may be a little muddled. If you have any questions or concerns, please contact me through Zauberer Brandt." I gave a small bow. "It's been a pleasure working with all of you, but I must take my leave." I held the samples of blood close. "Second Raven, will you please escort me to your incinerator?"

"Doctor, I think I'd prefer to have mine back, if it's all the same to you." Councilman Amos rumbled. "Not that I don't trust the Unkindness, but I don't trust you."

I nodded, unoffended; after all, the man had just met me. All of them had, really. I had all the samples clearly marked. If what I'd read throughout the years was true, then blood could be used for some very nefarious purposes with this sort of crowd. "That's fine with me. Does everyone feel this way?"

There were general murmurs of assent. Councilman Amos muscled his way to the front and glowered down at me expectantly. I gave him my doctor smile and gently laid the sample in his palm. He snorted and stepped to the side, pulling a small, crumpled piece of paper from his pocket. Amos growled something in a language I didn't understand and disappeared in a puff of white smoke. I shrugged and turned to my next patient. Councilwoman Punch gave me a nod. She remained in human form the entire time and pocketed her sample in her smart blazer before leaving the room, followed closely by Horace, who had been waiting to escort her out. I wondered what her horse portion looked like, but it somehow felt rude to ask.

Meriah and Aiden were still bickering when it was their turn. "I didn't pass out. I should have mine back first. Or at the very least, before you!" Meriah sneered.

"Well, as I've known the good doctor longer, I think she'll want to give me mine first." Aiden waggled his eyebrows at me. "Unless you want to keep it with you, my lady." I smiled and *floated* both specimens into their waiting palms at the exact same time. Aiden laughed musically. "You are something special, Doctor Hall."

Meriah just rolled her eyes and dragged her brother along into a portal that had opened beside me. It smelled like flowers, and there was a warm breeze that wafted out from it. I managed an "Oh, so cool!" under my breath before turning back to the line. My blood froze as I was once again faced with Councilwoman Edwards. Her eyes reminded me of a cougar who'd just spotted a fawn alone in the woods.

She was going to do something. As if I were watching her in slow motion, the councilwoman shoved one of the nurses out of the way, her hands curling into black-and-red-veined claws as she made a desperate grab for the slide tray holding the remaining samples. I used my ability to *grab* them out of the tray and zipped them high into the air.

Edwards screamed in some unholy tongue that felt like oily scum from the bottom of a polluted lake. Several of the nurses started retching. I struggled to keep my eyes on the samples in the air and not on the Demon-possessed woman currently being wrestled to the ground by the Ravens and Horace. If I looked down at her, I knew my concentration would take a nosedive and Edwards would get what she wanted. My body was tense, and I was starting to shake when someone stepped in between the Demon and me. Two someones, in fact.

"Enough, you soul-riding monster!"

Jove! Damn, I'd never been so glad to hear his German ringing out. I risked a look over at them, still holding the samples well out of reach. He and Councilman Rhoades stood sentinel, blocking Edwards' path to me. I almost bobbled the samples. Holy hand grenades, the Zauberers were wearing robes and held honest-to-Potter wands. The designs on Rhoades' boots pulsed and glowed with an otherworldly light. I would have loved to study that when I had the time. Unfortunately, the councilwoman didn't give me the time. Edwards charged, looking as if she were going to barrel right through the two men to gleefully rip my head off. She snarled and started throwing off the Unkindness nurses as if they were toys. Her target was clear. Me.

25

The Zauberers waved their wands in precise unison. "*Schild!*" they shouted, almost in the exact same voice. The Demon-driven woman bounced off the air in front of us as if it had been made out of rubber. She flew back into a stone wall. Faster than any human could move, Edwards was back on her feet and rushing the magical shields.

I had enough. This was nothing more than an erratic patient trying to steal someone else's medical information. I remembered David being flattened by the gravity spell in my apartment. I gathered my concentration and, while *holding* the samples in the air with one hand, I focused on my Demonic adversary and envisioned a giant hand. It descended from above and smushed Edwards against the stone floor, pinning her. She made a perfunctory attempt at moving, but was unable to regain her feet. She let out a frustrated growl. Black, mottled, red eyes glowed up at me.

Unfortunately, all the magic being tossed around was too much for my lovely little machine to handle. There was a vibrating clunking sound coming from deep inside its casing as it shuddered and started to smoke. The smell of burning electrical wires was strong in the air as it gave an anemic warning beep before it died. I would mourn it later. After the Demon bitch from hell was gone from my immediate vicinity.

I *stacked* three of the remaining samples in my hand and curled my fingers protectively around them. The fourth belonged to Edwards. That

I *flew* right to her as fast as my ability would allow. Then, I slowly let her up. Rhoades's steady eyes regarded the still-raging councilwoman, who was quickly getting back to her feet. Though her eyes glowed, I was certain she wasn't going to make another attempt. The stone beneath her feet scorched under her still-perfect pumps.

"Councilwoman, you are no longer welcome here. Take what's yours and be gone until this council is called again," intoned Rhoades.

"Stay behind us, Kleine." Jove quickly glanced over his shoulder.

"Like I'm dumb enough to move," I hissed at his back.

Edwards, sample in hand, straightened her suit. "I saw an opportunity and I took it. You smell human to me, little girl. Humans are toys. Maybe you'll be *my* toy. We'll have so much fun." She smirked, and a chill raced up my spine. "Dream of me, little girl."

With that, she disappeared in a cloud of thick, acrid smoke that easily overpowered the scent of the EMP machine's untimely demise. I was going to have nightmares about that woman. A small hand tapped me on the shoulder, accompanied by a polite little cough. I turned around to see the final member of the Council of Eight. Councilman Sakis' glamour had been unremarkable. He had looked like a man who'd been stuck behind a cubicle for too long and didn't mind it one bit. The slim shoulders and barely-there upper body were the same, but the councilman hadn't yet replaced his glamour. His lower body was covered in coarse fur, with his spindly legs terminating in cloven hooves.

"Um, may I have my blood back now? Please?" He was shaking. I put the sample in his slim hand. He gave me a nod and walked through a door that hadn't been there before. Well then, huh, Fauns were real too. This new world just kept getting better and better. I suppressed the huge smile on my face before the Zauberers turned around. They would have thought I'd finally reached crazy town.

"Well, that was definitely one of the most cantankerous patients I've ever had. Thanks, guys." I gave them a not-crazy-at-all smile and handed Councilman Rhoades back his blood. My hands were still shaking, and my smile must've come off a little insane after all, because Jove took me by the shoulders and had the most intense look on his face. He was quiet for a long moment, milk-chocolate eyes searching mine.

I sighed, and let myself shudder once. "I'm scared, really scared. I'll need to get to my church after this."

I started to feel like squirming when Ms. Corvis, bless her little black heart, cleared her throat and shoved an expectant hand between us. I gave her a sheepish grin and placed her sample in her palm. "Am I needed for anything else, Second Raven?"

"No. Other than almost causing our members to kill one another—"

"Oh, come now, Second Raven." Rhoades smiled. "If there isn't a little tussle once per meeting, we'd feel cheated."

She clenched her teeth. "If you would allow me to finish, Councilman Rhoades . . ."

"By all means." He gave a gracious sweep of his hand.

"*Other* than almost causing our members to kill one another, you've done an adequate job. I will report what happened here to High Raven. Your payment for today will be wired directly into your account. Expect to hear from us again soon." Ms. Corvis gestured to the door. "Larson can see you to the car. Tell the driver where you wish to go and he will take you there."

"Thank you, Ms. Corvis."

"No 'thanks' are necessary," she said with a sarcastic sneer. "Any sane person would seek spiritual comfort after dealing with a Demon."

Whoo! A sign of sanity! I'd take it. "I also wanted to mention something. My neighbors are starting to ask questions as to why I'm getting picked up in a limo all the time."

She huffed out a disgusted breath, like I was the stupidest person on the planet. "Simply tell them you are working as a concierge doctor with an eccentric client."

She didn't call me an idiot out loud, but it was heavily implied. Ms. Corvis then turned and walked briskly away.

I supposed a little gratitude was too much to ask for. Still, it was slightly better than how she'd treated me before. I turned to Jove, but he and Rhoades had disappeared.

I followed Larson out of the medieval room and was again surprised by the instant contrast between the chamber and the hallway. I blinked as we came under the harsh light of fluorescents.

"Gotta say, Doc. That was real impressive." The little Pixie gave me a tiny bow. "You even fixed the Heralds of the Courts. My girlfriend is going to be sooo impressed with me today."

"She should be anyway. You did very well with the tasks I had you do. Expertly done, Mr. Larson." It was as close as I could get without thanking him. "However, it may be best if no one outside that room hears anything from anyone."

The hallway was empty except for myself and Larson, so it was easy to hear the sound of Jove's shoes hitting the floor. He was in his tailored dress shirt and slacks again, shrugging into his overcoat.

"That was a quick change."

"Magic." He smiled. "May I accompany you, Kleine?"

I quirked an eyebrow at him. "You want to come with me to church?"

He gave a quick nod. "Herr Rhoades and I do not trust the Demon wench. We've agreed that you should have an escort. He has a few things here that he needs to finish up. Namely, making sure that all are sworn to secrecy. That includes you, *Elfin*."

"Damn it! That was going to get me laid!"

"You can still tell her you helped build a groovy machine that saves lives."

"Not the same as saving the life of the Herald," he grumped as he flew away. "But it'll have to do."

Truth is, I really didn't mind the company. I'd never been so frightened of another woman in my life. I smiled. "Well, okay, but no snark. This place is special to me."

"Kleine! I would never 'snark' in a holy place." His voice was teasing as he put his nose up in the air. "I snark elsewhere because it is funny and I like the way you snort when you are trying not to laugh."

I gave the driver the address, and we rode in a tired quiet, neither of us wanting to bring that woman up again so soon. Eventually, we pulled up to the white, double-front doors when Jove stopped short. "I want to walk around the perimeter." He opened the door and held it for me. "I will join you shortly."

I gave God Eva Strom's name, letting them know that this particular lamb needed a bit more than what I had at my disposal. I felt more tension ease away from my neck and down my spine. I could only hope they heard me, and gave Eva the help she desperately needed. Jove walked up and waited while I prayed for a damned soul, silent in everything. He stood next to the pew I was sitting at. It was just what I needed. The sun was finally starting to set on one of the longest days of my life. It made the window glow as the sun's rays hit it in just the right spot.

"This place has its own kind of power, Kleine."

"Yeah. It really does." I stood up from the comfortable pew, rubbing my arms. It was chilly in the sanctuary that evening. It's not like we were alone in the church. Someone was almost always bustling around St. John's. I could hear the bell choir practicing down the hall, and could smell the cookies that were no doubt baking in the kitchen next to Fellowship Hall. We were going to be selling them at the chicken barbecue on Wednesday. I signed up for fire pit duty.

It gave me a wonderful feeling. I opened the door into the narthex. Jove and I had almost made it out without seeing anyone. Poor Sandy Funk almost dropped a tray of cupcakes for the bake sale when she saw Jove and I exit the sanctuary.

It was going to be all over the congregation that I brought a 'friend' to pray with me after hours. I just *knew* it.

Jove and I got back to the apartment at eight, and I was so ready for bed. We got to my door and, damn me, I hesitated. I kept feeling Matthew's hand touching my hair.

"Kleine?"

"You said before that you had an idea about what to do about someone who could teleport into my apartment?" I said in a rush.

"Yes. I have been playing with a few theories that may take care of your instant intruder problems." Jove stepped to the door and drew a complicated design with his finger. It flashed for a second. The light pulsed, and for a quick instant, there was a pattern that showed on my door in blue. It faded almost as quickly as the light had.

"Whoa."

Jove smirked. "Mira, you have no idea how much I enjoy the wonder on your face when you see my magic. The fascination and joy I see in your eyes is a heady thing."

I blushed while ushering him inside. Time to get back to the subject. "So, what will happen now if Sable pops in?" Jove gave me a curious look—one that clearly asked who the hell I was talking about. "The woman from the tape. Matthew said her name on the video. You can put your bag on the couch while I'm feeding the cat." I heard Jove shut the door behind us as I walked into the kitchen to feed Toria.

"You know his name too?"

"He's been the creeper in my nightmares lately. He told me his name in the dream," I said over Toria's indignant meows. "I'm putting the food in the dish now, you impatient cat." Her fuzzy little head bumped my hand lovingly as I set down the food dish. I loved that cat, no matter how much of a brat she was.

"You only heard her name once, and that a few days ago. His you only heard in a dream. That is very impressive, Kleine."

I tapped the side of my head as I put the empty can into the recycling bin. "My recall has been almost eidetic since the accident. That's not always a good thing."

Suteki decided that now was the perfect time to introduce herself to Toria. She flowed down my arm and came to a swirling stop as a fox next to the dish of food. Toria arched, hissed, took a quick swipe, then ran.

Suteki, being a fox, gave chase. I put a quick stop to that by *lifting* them up into the air with my ability. It kind of looked like a cartoon. Toria wheeled mid-air, suddenly losing traction and essentially losing gravity.

If you've never seen a cat in zero gravity, look it up. You feel horrible for the sheer terror the little darlings are going through, but damned if it isn't hilarious. I strode up with a very serious expression on and tapped Suteki smartly on the snoot.

"None of that jazz! Toria was here first, and I will be very upset if you try to make her into a meal." I narrowed my eyes. "'Upset' as in I will tell all of Japan how a Kitsune killed my other protector. This cat also saved me from the Unkindness by killing one of their flock."

The little fox's eyes went wide, and she looked at the still-struggling cat with new interest. Then she looked at me questioningly. Just how was I supposed to tell all of Japan? "The internet is a wide and indestructible thing," I said direly.

Suteki seemed to shrink back into herself, properly chastised. I put both animals back on the floor. Toria bolted for the bedroom.

"She will most likely keep a far distance from the Kitsune for a long while," said Jove.

Suteki jumped up to the dish and started eating Toria's food happily, which was probably the whole point.

"Well, that answers the question as to what to feed her for right now. It's not like I have filet of vole just lying around." I was going to have to hit the internet to figure this one out, but for now, this was fine. I got another little bowl out and put it under the bed, near Toria's favorite hiding place. I blew the stray hair out of my face. "She's gonna hate me for a while. So, what is the spell you put on the ward supposed to do?"

"Instead of pressing the intruder as it did with your friend, the ward will now put them to sleep. A slumber that can only be rescinded by my presence. Then we will have the answers we seek. It will also affect anyone who is not expressly invited into your home, so be careful with those silent gestures of welcome."

My brows shot up; that sounded impressive. "Well, that'll do it."

He smiled. Why hadn't I realized how charming his smile had always been? It was sneaky, slow, and so rare that it was always special to see. It did nice things to his face that made my stomach jump.

"I thought it would. Now, you should get some sleep, Kleine. I bet Councilwoman Punch will have her people contact you soon. Centaurs usually wake with the sun."

"Thanks, Jove. I mean it. I don't know where I'd be if you weren't around." Probably still in a dungeon or, worse, in the mysterious ACS's clutches being brainwashed.

Jove took my hand and brought it to his lips. My heart did another impressive kick in my chest. "I would be lost among the books in my store, barking at the customers. You have brought joy into my life. I would not replace you for anything else in the world. I would like to see you Saturday for a date. We can go over your books then."

I swallowed, nodded, and blinked at him as he gathered his satchel, adjusted his floppy brown hat, and left. I heard him grumble as the door was closing. "She says she can't do magic, then she squishes a tier three Demon into the stone floor like it was being held by the hand of God. *Einfach unglaublich!*"

I blinked a couple of seconds more as my brain processed the information. Then I leaned heavily on the counter, blinking at Suteki. "Holy shit! He said date! It's a *date*!"

26

THAT NIGHT I had been too exhausted for dreams, thank God. Between Edwards asking me to dream of her and Matthew's random visits, I had no stomach for such things. True to Jove's prediction, I got a call that morning, but not from Councilwoman Punch. I woke to the melodious tones of "Close to you." Ms. Corvis was calling. Looked like Ravens woke up earlier than Centaurs did.

"Hello?" I answered with a yawn.

"Doctor Hall. You and your escort are required to present yourselves to High Raven this morning at precisely eight. We will send a car for you."

"Good morning to you too, Ms. Corvis." I blinked at the red clock next to my bed. "Jeez, it's only five!"

"Which should give you plenty of time to put yourself together and call your Zauberer." She hung up without so much as a goodbye. I took it as an improvement to our relationship.

I groaned and heaved myself out of bed. Toria jumped up to fill the spot I'd just vacated and meowed indignantly. "I'm not getting rid of Suteki. You and she have to come to an agreement. One that doesn't involve murder." I felt a little pressure on my right calf. I looked down and saw Suteki's marbled face. She crooned up at me, the picture of innocence. "You're adorable, but I do want there to be some sort of peace, okay? No bloodshed. God, I need a shower."

I stripped off my oversized Captain America tee and tossed it in the hamper next to the bathroom door. I'd decorated my bathroom in earthy tones and a wildflower shower curtain. I mostly kept my nerdom in my bedroom, but there were a few other things around the apartment that gave me away, mostly in my wardrobe.

I hummed while I turned on the water, letting it heat up to the temperature I wanted. I left the door open so the bathroom wouldn't steam up. I had to be quick; I still had to call Jove to let him know we were going to see High Raven. Lather body, rinse, lather hair, rinse, conditioner, rinse. One of the fastest showers I've ever had. I dried off and wrapped my hair in a turban-like wrap with another towel.

I didn't scream until I saw the mirror. Written in scrawling, blood-red letters, just where my face would be in the mirror, read:

Now I know you exist, little girl.

The glass split from corner to corner as I screamed. It crunched as the cracking spread along like it was under constant pressure. There was something oozing out between the broken shards. It was black as pitch tar. I gasped in a couple of breaths as Suteki ran in to see what the problem was. She jumped up onto the counter, hissed at the mirror, and flicked her tail at it.

The mirror rippled as if it were a pond of water and someone had dropped in a pebble. The ooze reversed its flow, the cracks retreated, and the words erased, until it looked like the episode never happened.

I looked down at the little fox. "Can I hug you? Is that a thing I'm allowed to do?"

Suteki bounced at me as I opened my arms to catch her. We sank down to the floor because my legs couldn't hold me up anymore. "Thank you, Kitsune. Thank you, Suteki." I cuddled with her, giving her the petting of a lifetime. "Aren't you fantastic? Aren't you pretty? Best Kitsune ever." I cooed. "Let's get you and Toria fed. I need some breakfast tea with possibly a shot of vodka. We're going to go see High Raven. But first, breakfast." I looked down at my still-dripping body. "After I get dressed."

I called Jove while making bacon and eggs with an extra side of bacon for Suteki. Toria got treats with her meal, too, so she wouldn't feel left out. I told him about the message in the mirror and about High Raven's summons. "So, you're going to have to make your way over here sooner rather than later. Ms. Corvis made it sound . . . dire, but then again, I bet she sounds that way when she's describing the weather."

"I am already here, Kleine." I looked suspiciously at my door and went over to open it. Jove hung up the old rotary phone he held in his hands and put it into one of the pockets on the inside of his coat. The pocket stretched to accommodate the much larger phone, then went flat against Jove's hip as if nothing bigger than his palm had been put in there.

"How did you—"

"Magic of course." He chuckled.

"Oh, well, of course." I stepped out of the way and offered to hang his coat on my antique coat rack. I wasn't about to tell him I found the thing at a yard sale for five bucks.

"I would like to see your mirror before we go," he said, removing the coat and hanging it himself. It felt homey having his coat there. That made me blush. He'd only just asked me for a date, and here I was thinking about how his coat looked like it belonged there? Phew, keep it together, Mira!

"I'll make some more eggs then. How do you take them?"

"Over easy? Mit some toast?" His accent was at the forefront again. Jove was more upset by this than he was letting on. "You said you did not have any dreams with the soul rider in them?"

The phrase caught my attention. "You called Edwards that before. Did you mean it literally? As in she is riding on Eva's soul?"

"Yes, Mira. The same way you or I would ride a horse. The Demon takes control of the soul that inhabits a body and controls it with extreme prejudice. They also take great joy in causing all sorts of pain onto that soul while it is being ridden, like spurs being raked over the spirit. Demons cause physical and emotional pain. They break apart families and friendships, isolating the victim until all that is left is the soul and the Demon.

Then it slowly breaks down the body, so that too brings pain to the soul, until the body finally gives out and dies. By then, it is time for a new host." He looked to the bathroom door. He knew which one was my bedroom, so it was only a process of elimination. I shivered and walked back to the stove to take in some heat while I was cooking. He called from the bathroom, "What did the message say again, Mira? I need to know what it said exactly."

I swallowed once as I plated my breakfast first and started on his. "It said, 'Now I know you exist, little girl.' I screamed and the glass cracked. Suteki fixed it. She really is some guardian." I saw her preen at the praise out of the corner of my eye. The cat jumped off the counter where she was eating with an annoyed flick of her tail and sulked out of the room. I'd probably find a hairball in my bed later.

"That does sound like a threat. However, with Demons one must be very careful. Cruelty is as common with them as a handshake."

Two slices of bread *floated* their way into the silver slots as I *pushed down* the lever on the toaster and I *flipped* the eggs gently with my ability before gently sliding them onto the plate. There were times when I loved my ability.

Jove came out of the bathroom with a frown on his face. "I could feel the remnants of Demon magic. My ward should have been able to prevent this." I handed him his plate. Jove placed it down at the table. "*Danka. Kleine*, did Edwards touch you at all yesterday during the healing?"

"The healing? Oh! You mean the EMP treatment," I said around the fried egg sandwich I was eating. I swallowed and rubbed my arm where the woman had grabbed me before my coat bit her. "Yeah. She grabbed me right here." I motioned to the place on my arm just below my elbow. "There's a pressure point there. She knew right where it was to cause the most pain with just a little twist." Gently, Jove took my arm. His hands were warm as he murmured the healing spell again. The warmth spread as it had on my knees, but this time it didn't give the same relief it had before. I chalked it up to being freaked out about the mirror. "If you guys can do that with just a few words, why does the Community need a doctor?"

"We can only do a certain number of spells a day. A foolish Zauberer is one who wastes his spells, leaving himself defenseless at the end of the day."

I blinked at what Jove had just said. "Wait, really?"

His eyes narrowed. His gaze intense on my arm. I'd have to ask about spells later. "She did something here to your arm. My healing spell should have done more to ease your pain than it has."

Panic sliced through me. "What? What did she do to me?" I heard a loud clatter as the spatula that had been floating in the air crashed to the floor.

"It is much like a brand. Here on the muscle of your arm." His thumb gently rubbed over the spot Edwards had grabbed. "I worry that it may be even deeper than that, possibly on the bone itself."

"Is there any way to get it off?" I pulled away, feeling shaky.

"We need a priest who specializes in such things to cleanse the site. No, your pastor will not do; she is not a member of the Community. I will take you to one who is as soon as possible. A Demon brand is a nasty thing; they bring bad luck as well as pain." He sat and ate. I was a little surprised at the . . . voracity with which he ate. Like he'd never had eggs and toast before.

"I do have more eggs if you want . . ." I floated my dishes to the sink.

"What? Oh, *nein*, Kleine. We must go, yes? The limo should be here soon." He smiled as he drank down the orange juice I'd set in front of him. I wondered if casting spells caused the caster to get really hungry afterward. He chugged down the glass of orange juice. I couldn't help but smirk and let out a snort of laughter. "*Vas?*"

"I often see you as this worldly, sophisticated guy." I chuckled again. "And here you are, sitting at my kitchen table, yolk on your chin, well on its way into your beard, chugging orange juice like it's the only liquid on the planet."

He cursed in German and grabbed some napkins from the holder.

My chuckle turned into a belly laugh. This was the first time I saw Jove being 'cute.' I got up and got him a wet towel.

"You're right, though. We've got to get a move on. Time to work, Suteki." I reached down, unsure of what to do next. Light swirled around me, and I felt the weight of a jacket around my shoulders. I looked down to see a light leather spring jacket, white with black accents. I supposed that a lab coat isn't appropriate for all occasions. I grabbed my now fully stocked Gladstone bag. It seemed pertinent, figuring how much I'd already had to use my skills when dealing with the Unkindness. I paused, wondering if maybe I should be more disturbed by that.

We headed to the front door while I pondered why High Raven would want to see me. Another test, maybe? Or maybe I'd finally proven myself to the point where he'd let me look at whatever was harming the fledglings. The black Unkindness limo pulled up once again to the curb in front of my building. Jove opened the door to usher me inside. He'd done this for me before, but this time felt different. It was the first time he'd opened the door for me when we had a date coming up. My cheeks flushed and my heart started pounding.

He stopped me before I got into the limo. "Now, I know what your wolf friend was talking about, Kleine. I too, have waited for you to look at me with a blush to your cheeks. You did so once before when you helped me with my gremlin. I wanted to see it again."

The flush went up to my ears as I swallowed the lump in my throat.

"If you would *please* hurry up," said the frosty voice of Ms. Corvis from inside the limo. "High Raven is waiting. I will be *plucked* before I let some Zauberer make me late for a meeting because he feels like flirting with his charge."

"Sorry." I mumbled and quickly ducked inside. I didn't look where I was going properly and hit my head on the top of the door frame. Feeling like an idiot, I scooted over and buckled in. I hissed as I gingerly touched where my head hit. Damn it all to hell, I was going to have a bruise when I met High Raven again.

Jove sat down next to me, his eyes dancing with humor. He knew exactly why I hit my head, the smug bastard. Gently, he ran a hand over the wound, his fingers brushing aside my short, growing bangs. I felt the heat of his touch ease the pain. The healing spell he'd used earlier had to still be in effect.

"Hugin and Munin save me from flirting Wizards." Ms. Corvis rolled her eyes skyward. "You will both be presented to High Raven when we get there in an hour. You will be presentable. Did you bring your lab coat?"

"In a sense," I replied, running a hand over the sleeve of the jacket. "Where are we going?"

"Home," she said and turned her face to the window. She sounded so wistful. It made me want to look out the window as well. Already, we were along a stretch of highway I didn't recognize. I'd lived in PA my whole life and it never ceased to amaze me how one moment you could be in the heart of the city with all its lights and sounds and then, seemingly in two turns of the car, you were on a lonely country road surrounded by farms and woods. Then, just as suddenly, you'd be back to a place you recognize again, back to civilization. Momma calls it 'Portal Magic.' We figured it was because she was really bad at directions. She would have been ecstatic to learn portals were real. Not that I could tell her.

"What gives you such a sad smile, Kleine?"

"Just thinking," I hedged. "This is going to be different than the last stronghold, isn't it?"

"Pfft," grumbled Ms. Corvis. "That is where we hold the livestock. More equivalent to a barn instead of a stronghold."

Livestock. She called those people *livestock*! I felt my temper spike but felt Jove holding me back. "She is baiting you. Bored, Second Raven?"

"We have been forbidden from taking her mind and turning it into Swiss cheese. For a human, you have something to you that High Raven . . . almost admires." She crossed her arms, almost sulking. "Why didn't you become as lobotomized as the chattel in our pens, Doctor?"

I shrugged. "I'm a special little snowflake?" That got a snort that may have been laughter from the usually sullen woman. I'd been thinking a lot recently on that very subject. Things were only going to *get* stranger from here on out. I had no doubt that unless I was careful, something would tear my mind to shreds. What frightened me more was what would happen in the aftermath.

I saw visions as my head swam with the terrible possibilities. Me, in my insanity, hurting everyone who would get within my range. Killing anyone who scared me, or worse, succumbing to the corruption and killing as a way to achieve power. After all, who would know better than me what was wrong with my country? Those evil people play with the laws like they are simply things to move to suit their needs. So many people suffer, stunted, because the ones in power have no frame of reference to relate to the people they are supposed to serve. Who wouldn't want the power to fix that?

I felt the rage at the injustices I saw during my rotations. People! And children who could have easily been taken care of if their benefits hadn't been cut. We shouldn't live in a country where a woman with a grievous wound begs for no one to call an ambulance due to the financial cost. The rage felt black and consuming.

"Kleine." Jove's voice cut through the rushing sound in my ears that I hadn't realized was there. I blinked to find both of my companions staring at me. My heart started pounding; what the hell had just been going through my head? I looked up at him, panicked.

"I believe the need to get you to the Community priest is becoming more urgent." Jove turned to face Second Raven. "You see Ms. Corvis, Councilwoman Edwards left a mark on the dear Doktor. It seems to be having some adverse influence on her."

"I see." Ms. Corvis nodded, business-like. "Seeing as it is still in its early stages, she will still be able to do what High Raven wants today. However, take her to a Community priest. I'll have a list ready by the time we are done. The Councilwoman pulls something like this often. We have priests from various faiths on retainer as a result. If we didn't need to have a representative from their part of the community, things would be a lot cheaper when we host the council meetings."

That reminded me . . . "Did you ever find out who tampered with the food from the last meeting?"

Her scowl deepened. "The employee who had made our order disappeared after it was sent out for delivery. I'm using the word literally. Another employee had been having a conversation with her when the woman winked out of existence in front of his eyes. He searched the establishment for her and then went to call his sponsor. There were no signs of any residual magic in the area."

Jove and I exchanged a look. We knew of a person who could do that, but should we tell Second Raven? These are the same people who set me up to have the kind of vehicular accident that most people don't get to walk away from. Fortunately, Ms. Corvis was back to gazing out the window instead of paying attention to us. Her focus lay on a particular location on the mountainside that looked like a dense forest to my eyes. Birch, maple, pine, and poplar grew the best there.

'Home' must be *there*.

There was little doubt in my mind that the reason for the Unkindness to be paid to hurt me so badly was to get me into the room for the secret procedure. Best to hold back for now. See what was wrong with the kids. If the nanites were at fault, I would tell Ms. Corvis about Sable. If those damned bugs were already virulent, then the group of self-proclaimed monster hunters was already too dangerous.

We soon turned off the highway and went down several back roads that got increasingly more rugged. The road had been gravel for twenty minutes before the limousine finally came to a stop.

Stepping out into the tree-mottled sunlight, I took in a deep breath of fresh air. The car had started getting stuffy. We were at a campground of sorts. A circle of gravel for cars to drive in on, with a teardrop-shaped camper sitting squat on the perimeter with its back to the forest. Large trees stood sentinel to either side of the camper, and several large boulders were positioned inside the semicircular parking area. They looked a little too perfectly placed to just be decorative.

Standing in front of the trailer was High Raven, flanked by two burly-looking Bird-boys and a thin-looking man in a black, feathered cape.

"Showtime, Suteki," I murmured to my coat, stroking one of the sleeves. As we walked toward the Ravens, Suteki flowed over me, becoming the long white doctor's lab coat.

Ms. Corvis strode forward, bowing deeply with her arms outstretched before her leader. "High Raven, Lord of the Pennsylvania skies. I have done as you bid and brought Doctor Mira Hall and her escort to you."

"Impressive, Second Raven. You never disappoint me." High Raven smiled benevolently down at her before turning his piercing gaze on me. "So, Doctor Hall. It seems you've done well for yourself with this first foray into our Community. How are you finding it?"

I gave a respectful bow, but not as deep as Ms. Corvis'. "It has certainly been interesting, High Raven. I learn more every day."

"And you haven't yet gone mad." His words made my heart kick in fear, remembering the people in the dungeon. "Impressive. Have you found our accommodations to your liking?" His eyes were dark and bore down on me. Creepy and potent.

I struggled not to squirm as I told him the absolute truth. "The workspace was good. However, you spent too much money on things you didn't need. For example, you didn't need to buy a mass spectrometer from each manufacturer. If not for the nature of the laboratory, I wouldn't have had the space to move, let alone work. I do commend my lab assistants on a job well done. Larson and Horace were invaluable in helping create the EMP emitter that we used to treat the Council of Eight of Philadelphia."

I stood at what was commonly called parade rest, but my hands kept clenching and releasing behind my back. Nerves. I took a breath before continuing, "I also commend Second Raven for her quick and decisive action once she was made aware of the problem. None of the Council felt anything attacking their bodies, with the possible exception of Councilwoman Edwards and Councilman Alfenheim. This malady is pure science and has nothing to do with magic, so their own wards and warnings of danger had no frame of reference."

"It is similar to the problem plaguing my flock, Doctor. The magics we've employed have done nothing to cure what has struck down our young, weak, and elderly."

"Only because their faith was weak." The thin man croaked.

My eyes snapped to the thin man. He was much older than High Raven and dressed in what looked like Indigenous ceremonial garb. His eyes were narrowed into disgusted slits as he glared at me. This was going to be a bigger project than I'd anticipated.

"You have shown not only quick and decisive action yourself," High Raven continued, ignoring the thin man, "but also for people not of your own race."

High Raven matched his stance to mine but somehow looked more regal in the enterprise. Like he was showing me how it was supposed to be done. I didn't really care about the posturing, but it was apparently something important to him, so I did my best to look like the country cousin and not try to make myself look better. "Therefore, we have summoned you to fulfill your function as agreed to in the contract to secure your freedom. Will you perform this function?"

"I will." I nodded.

"Step forward." As I complied, the thin man reluctantly stepped forward. The long, black, feathered cape moved with him in an odd way, and I realized those feathers were his own. They moved, ruffling and unruffling. This was not a happy Bird-boy.

The feathers across the man's thin chest were smaller, matching what is found on his wild cousins. On his legs, he wore light-colored leather with a patterned leather sash. His feet were talons, each spindly toe tipped with silver. On his hip was what I thought was a black sword. It was longer than my leg but didn't swing with gravity like a sword should. This long, black thing was the biggest feather I'd ever seen. It was fastened with an ornate silver ball chain to the thin man's waist. I'd seen metalwork like that at some jewelry shops that catered to big, burly people who like shiny things but still want to be seen as badass.

We stood there staring at one another until High Raven growled, "Shaman Corax, do your duty."

"This gift should only be bestowed on friends of the flock. This human is no friend, as no human can be a friend. She even wears a predator that could cause harm to our flock." The voice was old, croaking. His disdain tainted every word. "Turn away from this low being. We should be depending only on Raven's power to heal our own. As I have told you before."

"I didn't ask for your opinion. I told you to do your job."

The branches above us exploded in raven calls and croaks. They sounded indignant . . . angry. Invisible birds shouting at us. High Raven shot a warning look over his shoulder and the invisible voices stilled.

The shaman held a painted earthenware bowl up to High Raven in one hand and the impossibly long black feather in the other. Comparing it to the feathers that hung down from his limbs, it didn't look like one of the feathers from his own arm. It had a rainbow iridescence that seemed to shimmer across the black. It moved as if there were a breeze ruffling the barbs of the vane, though there was no wind. He waved the feather over the bowl a final time and offered it again.

High Raven dipped two fingers into the bowl held out for him. "I grant entry to you alone, healer. I give you vision to see through illusion this day to help you find a cure for those who need you."

The substance on his fingers was dark and chilled my skin. It smelled as much of the earth as the bowl it came out of. Loamy, with floral, natural oils. "Your entourage must stay here, healer." High Raven put his hand, now covered in feathers, lightly on my shoulder. "That includes you, little spirit, for foxes are well known to eat the eggs they find." Suteki slid off my shoulders, gave High Raven a little bow of her muzzle, and bounded off to sit prettily next to Jove.

"I ask for assurance of her safety if I may not accompany her," rumbled Jove in German.

"You may have no such assurance as I do not know what the malady is or if it will infect her as well. However, she will not experience any violence from us," High Raven spoke back. The shaman flinched like he would have very much liked to have me experience violence.

Usually talking around me like that put my back up, but now I could see the true faces of the Unkindness, including the ones hidden in the trees. What I'd seen before, when I'd seen through their illusions, had been an odd mashing together of features between human and corvid. Now, they looked like something one should find on the internet while looking up character art. They were beautiful, their bodies finally proportionate and something my brain could wrap around. The females differed from the males as human bodies did in shape. The females tended to have slimmer waists but no breasts to speak of. That made sense biologically. A species that lays eggs rarely needs to produce milk for their young. I couldn't tell if the feathers went all the way down because all of them were clothed. High Raven and Ms. Corvis were still in their business suits, and Shaman Corax was still in his ceremonial garb, but the rest of the parking lot had suddenly filled with a lot more people. And no one wore shoes. There were many toes that were adorned with shiny things like rings, many talons that were painted and polished.

The perimeter of the parking area was filled with bird men and women dressed . . . normally. T-shirts, jeans, dresses, and slacks. I'd see the same walking down South Street. Some were sitting in the boughs above us, some on the rocks, some were hidden among the trees. I noticed something off about the faces we passed as High Raven led us deeper into the vegetation. Some of the eyes that stared at me were full of malice and disgust, just like I'd read in Shaman Corax's eye—as if I had no right to be here and High Raven had no right to invite me. The intense gazes made me swallow, but then I straightened my shoulders. I remembered what these people were capable of. Just how easy it was to treat other sapiens as chattel in their dungeons.

"Are you well, Kleine?" Jove's voice had worry lacing through it. I looked back at him from where we were standing, just before leaving the parking lot. His eyes were intent on mine as I looked back at him, roving over my features searching.

"I—I'm all right, Jove. See you in a bit." I tried for sincerity as the Unkindness flanked me.

"You never could lie to me, Kleine." He started to take a step forward when two other members of the flock flew down to bar his way. "She is frightened. If you would simply allow me to accompany her, then—"

"It's okay, Jove. This is what I've trained for." I gave him a smile. "I've also taken an oath. I can do this."

Corax's head whipped around. "To whom? Who else do you owe your allegiance to?"

"Calm yourself, Shaman. She's speaking of the Hippocratic Oath." High Raven's eyes were hard to read as they studied me. "Does that extend to us, Doctor Hall? As you can now see, we are not human."

"I'll do my best. People are people. If they need help, then I offer my services. I will need to consult with your own physicians. I don't want to waste time going over what they've already tried." I looked over my shoulder to Jove. "Watch Suteki for me."

High Raven held out a surprisingly elegant hand to me. "Are you ready, Doctor Hall?"

27

I squared my shoulders and strode forward, my Gladstone in hand, with the flock closing in around me. The weight of their eyes was heavy as we walked. I followed the three most powerful beings of the flock into what had once looked like a large boulder. Now, with the magic swept away, I could see that it was an enormous bowery. The walls of the entrance bowed outward, forming an inviting entrance as the light flitted through the branches and fronds that could only have been woven by so many feathered hands. This place was made with such obvious love. This was the safest place for the flock to be, or rather it was supposed to be. It was so beautiful.

I was here to do a job. I filed the grandeur away to admire later. "Show me to your sick."

High Raven and Ms. Corvis walked in front of me, two tall, burly guards flanked us on either side, and the shaman stalked behind me. I really didn't like him behind me. I felt like he'd love to introduce a blade to my spine if he had the chance. We walked in tight formation, so most of what I could see was the 'ceiling.' Everything I could see looked very organic, as though it had been grown rather than built.

The air wasn't as musty as I had been expecting from the last time I had been at their mercy. Should I have insisted on Jove coming, too? What if this whole thing was a sham and I was walking into the arms of the person who 'specially ordered' me? I took another breath to center myself. I was no longer just a human driving home from a party. I'd been working on the use of my ability daily since the accident, only recording new tests as they occurred to me. I was no longer defenseless.

We soon came to a new clearing. Sunlight filtered through the leaves of the largest tree I'd ever seen in my life. "Whoa," I breathed.

"'Whoa' indeed, human," croaked the shaman. "You stand in the presence of one of the trees Raven asked the Great Spirit for to protect his children. Raven knew humans were quickly becoming the greatest threat to us. He gave us his cunning, his trickery, his intellect, and these trees so that we may survive. You humans," he said with a sneer in his voice. "Always take, sometimes not even for the good of your own people. How many innocents have died, tortured in your prisons? How many children ripped from their parents' arms for trying to seek safety? How many of your 'war heroes' languish in the streets?"

This was obviously something this raven had been ranting about for years. I saw eye rolls from some of the Ravens around us. Others were nodding in agreement. The shaman spun me around, his long beak clacking in my face as his words rose in volume. "Empty houses gather dust while people are forced to live on the streets. You disgust me, and the fact that High Raven has brought you into our most sacred place offends me."

I winced as his talon-tipped fingers dug into my arms.

"According to the Charter, Shaman, she is not human. She is a Gewalt." The procession had stopped with all parties turning inward. It was Ms. Corvis who had spoken, her wing-like arms crossed her chest.

"The magic of the Charter isn't infallible. Somehow, the Zauberers have spelled the book!" The shaman cracked. "She smells human, she looks human, and I say she *is* human. Take her back to the pit with the other humans and when her mind breaks make what use of her you want."

I felt the flock's eyes on me. I straightened my back and stood silently waiting. This was a political stunt on the part of the shaman to make High Raven look weak in the eyes of the flock.

"How dare you question the will of High Raven?" Ms. Corvis hissed.

She stepped between me and the shaman. Her beak opened in a threat and clacked as she spoke. "You, above all, know he is the closest to Raven Lightbringer. That you do this in front of the Gewalt shows just how little respect you have for Raven himself, who chooses the leaders of our flocks."

The air felt uncertain, on the brink of either disaster or salvation. I felt my pulse quicken as I watched the exchange between Ms. Corvis and Shaman Corax. His feathers were ruffled like a rooster in a cockfight; hers were smooth, but the look in her eyes promised death, not a fight. I was trying to gray rock it—be as uninteresting as possible.

"Enough." High Raven's voice echoed in the silence, though I swear his volume was lower than that of the shaman. Corax's fingers relaxed. I'd have bruises, but thankfully, he didn't break the skin. "Blindfold Doctor Hall for the remainder until we get to the hall of illness. However, I don't see the point of Shaman Corax insisting on giving her the sight if he did not agree on her being a necessity."

Quietly, I took a roll of bandages out of my bag and handed it to one of the four guards who had started moving menacingly toward me. He blinked, clearly expecting me to cower and fight. Why would I? High Raven and Ms. Corvis just saved my bacon. "Please, not too tight. I don't need a headache when I consult."

The air grew colder as I was led forward. There was a subtle incline, but we didn't climb any stairs. At one point, we were bustled into something that worked with pulleys to move us upward. I heard creaking ropes and felt wood under my feet. I heard the wind rustle through leaves that seemed to surround us overhead. My hands weren't tied, mostly because when the Shaman suggested I may be able to cast a spell, High Raven grunted and said, "You can't have it both ways, Corax. She is either human or she is a Gewalt. Neither of which cast spells."

So, I kept my hands holding my medical bag and waited for the next part of our journey. Have you ever noticed that when you cover your eyes, there's always a spot near your nose where you can still see? I didn't want to advertise it. No sense in causing more friction in the Unkindness flock. I started counting the steps and turns, having grown bored with the lack of visual stimuli. I also wondered if all of the building equipment had been locally sourced or if the pulleys on the elevator had been made out of the wood from the tree we were ascending. From time to time, I would hear titters and whispers around us. Never from too far away, but also never so close that I could make out what they were saying. My guards acted as the inflatable tubes in bumper bowling, with me bouncing lightly against them to keep me on the correct path.

"You know this would be a lot easier if one of you would just lead me instead of us playing hu—Gewalt pinball." I felt my face flush as I stumbled over the word for what I was. I held out a hand, waiting. We stood there for what felt like ages until I heard a female snort.

"Cowards and idiots, the lot of you." I felt feathers under my hand as Ms. Corvis placed my hand on her forearm, or whatever the equivalent of that was on a wing. "I will lead you to your patients, Doctor Hall."

"Thank you, Second Raven." We were able to proceed much faster after that. The smell of sickness hit me first. It made the hairs on the back of my neck stand up. 'Death is a close colleague of the doctor,' one of my professors had told me. 'You fight him with all you are, but breathe with relief when he ends the suffering you could not.' I stopped walking abruptly enough for the entire party to stop short.

"Is there a problem, Doctor?" asked Ms. Corvis.

"I just need to put a mask on. If their immune systems are vulnerable, I don't want to make it worse. It would be useful if I could use my eyes. Are we almost there?"

"Ah, Doctor Hall! I've heard so much about you," chirped a happy-sounding voice from somewhere in front of me. "I am Doctor Thaddeus Blackbird, and I couldn't be happier to see you. This malady is beyond our understanding, and we desperately needed outside input. I'm so glad you decided against using that other human, High Raven; there was something about him that—URK—"

The happy voice sounded as if it had been literally choked off. I imagined High Raven's hand around the doctor's feathered throat. "We do not speak of other deals with those not involved with them," he rumbled.

"If it's any consolation, I've figured most of this out already, sir. You made a deal with a physician for him to treat your people in exchange for me, as I was 'specially ordered.' I am grateful that you, in your great wisdom, chose a counter-deal with myself. While I would love the name of the—*ahem*—customer I realize it isn't for me to ask at this time. I would like to see my patients now, if you'll allow it. The sooner we can get to the bottom of this disease, the faster we can eradicate it." My heart was hammering in my chest as I spoke, making sure my voice didn't betray the absolute terror coursing through my veins.

After a pause so pregnant I thought I'd have to prep for delivery, High Raven started to laugh. The sound was a terrifying amalgamation of the rasping call of the Unkindness' wild cousins and laughter that would erupt from the throat of a hyena who just spotted an easy meal. It caused me to involuntarily shudder. "You do have some spine to you. I'd wondered if that had just been an act when you cowered in my receiving room before."

A gentle hand loosened the wrap over my eyes. I blinked at the sudden light. It was brighter here than it had been down at the base of the tree. We were now in the canopy, on a bough much farther away from the rest of the flock. Sensible. They kept the infected separate from the others without denying them sun and air. It was thicker than any bough I've seen on any tree native to this state. It was more like standing on a wooden road.

Doctor Blackbird had the tanned skin of a Native American and short black hair that somehow had the same style as it did when I could see through his illusion. It was like an overlay that moved as the man moved. Currently, he was hunched subserviently between High Raven and Ms. Corvis. He had brown puppy-dog eyes that made you want to tell him everything that was wrong so he could fix it. I would have thought he was cute if it weren't for the whole 'I'm actually a seven-foot bird' thing.

Ms. Corvis stepped back, allowing me to view the patient floor. The floor itself was firm underfoot. It was dark, the same color as the branches above our heads but with a dark mossy green coating it like a carpet. On closer inspection, it was indeed a kind of moss. The beds the patients lay on were more reminiscent of the metal beds found in hospitals in Europe. My heart ached as I counted how many patients I now had. This was a large group. No wonder Doctor Blackbird was so happy to see me.

He walked up to stand grimly beside me, smoothing down his ruffled feathers. "As you see, Doctor Hall, we have been trying to keep contamination to a minimum."

"Is it affecting any of your healthy adults yet?"

He shook his head slowly. "Not that we've seen. Primarily it has been the children and the elders."

"What are your standard practices for vaccinations?" Temper threatened to spike. Were these people just ignorant as to what you have to do if you have kids? I just bet they had anti-vaxxers here too. I counted twenty-four beds with someone in them. I had to take a breath to avoid clenching my teeth. "Do the readily available vaccines work on your young, or do you have to create your own?"

It's harder to tell if someone is sad or pensive if they have a hard beak and feathers, but the Unkindness doctor's shoulders slumped and his eyes lost the spark of excitement. "This has come on much faster than we could have anticipated. We do have vaccines for most things that our researchers have created, but from infection to gestation, it's less than twenty-four hours with the infected showing no signs of illness until days three to five at the earliest."

I felt my stomach drop. There was no way this could have been parental negligence if it was that fast for the onset . . . "How many have succumbed?" I asked quietly.

"Too many," rumbled High Raven. "Far too many of my flock have been taken by this disease. Find out what it is and eliminate it."

I nodded and locked eyes with Doctor Blackbird. "Let's get started."

That first day, we took samples from every patient in the ward. The youngest among them looked more bird than biped, the oldest more biped than bird. The symptoms ranged from sore throats and coughs to pink eye and diarrhea. One of the elders had fluid going into an IV due to advanced dehydration. I could see he didn't have much longer to live and felt a familiar ache in my heart. This was why I chose not to go into geriatrics. They all remind me of my grandparents and just how heart-breaking it is to lose one.

Quietly, I turned to Doctor Blackbird. He was the only one of the Unkindness to follow me into the ward. He wore one of those long-beaked masks that used to be popular when medical science was still in its infancy. "Do we know who patient zero was?"

"Is. She is one of the fledglings and a fighter. Her symptoms showed first and have lasted the longest. We aren't sure how she has survived this long." He gestured to the bed farthest from where we left our entourage. "This is Jackie."

The little feathered body shivered under the heavy blanket on the bed. She snuggled with a stuffed toy bird that looked like a superhero. Someone in the flock had some craft skills. She wore pajamas with rainbows speckled over them and had a breathing tube attached to her little beak. From her size, I judged her to be five or six. A fighter indeed. I was going to help because of the bargain I had with High Raven. But now, after laying eyes on this kid, I was ready to tear into whatever this was to give her the best chances at survival.

"I want to talk with her and her parents. Are we able to do that?" The more knowledge we had, the better I could help her.

"Her father was recently killed in service to the flock." Blackbird sighed sadly. "Her mother is Second Raven."

The world seemed to stop a moment, my heart along with it. I'd had a hand in the death of the father of this tiny fighter. Yes, I'd been defending myself. Yes, it was my cat who did the killing, but it was my hands that opened the cage. If I'd just gone with the Unkindness when Deep Raven answered the door at Bindings, then this baby would still have both parents. I risked a glance over at the entourage. Ms. Corvis stared in our direction, but I felt like her eyes were only on her daughter. The rest of the room could have been empty as she regarded the small bed. And she had to work with me every time the Unkindness needed me. I blinked away tears that I prayed Doctor Blackbird didn't see. Thankfully, most of my face was behind the medical mask.

I swallowed twice before I spoke again, trying desperately to keep my voice clinical. "I'm going to need access to the samples. Blood, saliva, urine, fecal, whatever you have. We have so much we have to examine under a microscope. I'll send over a copy of the pictures I took of the nanites I found before to make sure they aren't here making a second appearance. High Raven purchased every kind of testing device on the market. I'm going to use the best ones for the job. God willing, we'll get our answers and help these people win their battles."

"I'll have them sent to the lab." His eyes seemed to smile over his mask. "Brilliant move with that EMP. We'll be doing most of our clinical work there. I'll have their charts emailed to you. The samples should be ready for you tomorrow morning."

"You're a handy guy to have around, Doctor Blackbird." I smiled behind my mask.

"Please, call me Blake," he said with a little bow.

I looked at him incredulously. "Your name is Blake Blackbird? You introduced yourself as Thaddeus."

He shrugged. "Thaddeus is the name on my diploma. Blake is my middle name, and I like the alliteration. And sometimes—" he whispered with one wing-like hand on the side of his mask like we were sharing a secret. "Sometimes, I pretend I'm a superhero fighting all the bad guys."

I grinned. Geek minds think alike. The humor slid from my face as we turned back the way we'd come. This felt more like a war rather than a one-time battle.

"Why can't you fix them now?" rumbled the Shaman dangerously as we rejoined the group. "This is the whole reason you have been brought here!"

"With great respect, Shaman Corax, medicine doesn't work like that. I need time to truly identify this enemy to decipher the best way to heal your people. I should be able to work the fastest in that lab in the office building you have. The time distortion makes it so I get more done in less time. I should go in at the same time as the samples and the reports." I looked over at Ms. Corvis. "Hopefully it has some amenities as I will be staying in there until I have an answer."

"There is a full kitchen and a bathroom. We can put in something for you to sleep on."

"That would be fine. I would also like some time to consult properly with Doctor Blackbird. I have a few suspicions as to what the disease is. Speaking with him in depth about it may get us the answers we need faster." There were flu-like symptoms, but there are a myriad of different diseases that have flu-like symptoms. I was praying we weren't dealing with a new COVID variation.

Our group started to walk toward the exit, High Raven leading the way. He somehow managed to never set eyes on me without making it seem like he wasn't paying rapt attention. I continued as we walked, "I also would like if the parents and family members could be interviewed. We are looking for common threads, like if they all went to the same restaurant or if we can trace the disease back to a batch of people or just one."

"Ms. Corvis," he rumbled as a quiet command.

"It will be done, High Raven." She nodded. I resolved to talk to her more about the type of precautions High Raven should be taking to ensure his own well-being later. It didn't seem to be the right time now. Tensions seemed to be rising higher the longer I stayed in the sanctuary. I could feel the eyes of the flock on me as if I were a fox who'd just entered the henhouse. Thankfully, High Raven led our party briskly back to the entrance after I was blindfolded again.

Jove sat in the middle of the gravel lot, legs crossed in a meditative position, when the gauze wrap was removed. "Hello, Sweetie." I smiled in my best imitation of River Song from *Doctor Who*. "Did you miss me?"

His eyes were intense as he slowly stood. They made it hard to breathe. So much for joking around. Why was it so hard to resolve what I felt for him, given the revelations I'd just had in the home of the Unkindness? How long had I been putting my feelings for Jove to the side? Had he felt this strongly about me this whole time?

I had to find time to think and re-evaluate. I don't know how long we stood there, but it was long enough for Ms. Corvis to discreetly cough to break the spell. I flushed and walked down to where Jove was waiting for me. Suteki jumped into my arms and once again became my coat.

"Hey, girl," I murmured, stroking the sleeve. "I guess you missed me." I had the mental impression of her sniffing all over me to make sure everything was as it should be. She growled slightly at my right forearm. I turned back to the Ravens. "I need to pack a bag with some essentials, then I can go right to the laboratory."

"Agreed," said High Raven. "Take the rest of the day to prepare. The car will return for you at six tonight. Second Raven, you may remain here. I don't think the doctor will be needing you for the rest of the night."

Ms. Corvis bowed low, her arms spread to the sides. "Thank you, High Raven." She walked to us and gave Jove the list of names and phone numbers of the priests the Unkindness had on retainer and a wet nap package to me. "You may take off the sight now. Please, Doctor, work fast."

"This is a mistake," croaked Corax. "A human is lower than the lowest member of our flock. We should pray to Raven Lightbringer to send us a miracle. He's done such things before for his beloved." He rattled his staff at me. "Instead of trusting the highest of us all, you trust a dust crawler. You shame us and doom us to die of this plague."

"Raven once brought us light; why would he not bring us a doctor at our time of need?" asked High Raven. "Taking no action will doom us faster than using the assets we have. I will not let our flock fall. Didn't Raven himself use others to bring light to the world? Then so shall I. If I have to use a slug to save our people, then I will." With that, High Raven snapped his fingers and the clearing was suddenly empty.

I felt Jove take my arm. "We must go, Kleine. We will leave the Unkindness to their own."

He escorted me back to the limo, where there was water waiting for us in a refrigerated minibar. It made me long for something frozen and alcoholic. I found myself staring out at the forest as we drove away. Jackie's little face kept flashing whenever I closed my eyes. Only she was awake, and her eyes were accusing. *'It's your fault my daddy is dead. It's your fault my mommy is gone all the time.'*

There were other things that were my fault. My fault for dragging Jove into being my warden. My fault the Moms had to rescue me. I hadn't checked back with them since I'd gotten the new car! What kind of a daughter was I? Such a selfish bitch, more concerned with what was going on in my own life to check on theirs. I hadn't even called Sandy at the church to let her know if I'd be at the barbecue tomorrow. Was I even going to go to that now? It wasn't like they really needed me. No one really needed me anyway. The Unkindness had way more resources than I did; they'd be able to figure things out on their own.

"Kleine?"

Jackie's eyes were black and staring at me, her jaw elongated, getting ready to take a bite out of me. I deserved it. I did this to her and her family. I ruined a family. It didn't matter that they weren't human. They had loved each other, and I'd destroyed that. How could I call myself a healer? I needed to atone for this. I held my breath and waited for the first sharp slice of her beak, which had become razor-edged. There was a hissing, growling sound that I had been assuming was Jackie. 'Let me in, you stupid bitch, give in to me. You don't have the power to stop me.'

"Mira Hall! Snap out of it!"

I took a huge breath of air and coughed. "What was that?"

"I had to use your *titel*, Kleine. You were not *breathing*." Jove held my hand tightly. "I suspect you were almost possessed."

My breath shuddered. "Jove, w–why didn't the charms you put on the bracelet work to keep me from being possessed?"

"Councilwoman Edwards is a much stronger Demon than what your bracelet can ward off. I will get another charm to help more against Demons. However, it is a short-term solution. I will consult with other Zauberers to see if we can come up with something more long-lasting."

"In the meanwhile"—I started ticking off things on my fingers—"I have to start work on the project for the Unkindness. I still have to get in touch with Councilwoman Punch to see about which land she has to offer for building the practice. I have to find some way to fend off a Demon stronger than a Wizard, and I really need to call my moms." It was going to be one long-assed week and it was only frakking Tuesday.

28

I GRINNED INTO the camera. I'd needed a distraction from everything. I hadn't eaten dinner, and comfort food was the way to go. I splayed my hands out flat on my little table to prove I wasn't touching anything. "I am Dr. Mira Hall, and this is Experiment Six. I need to make this ability work better for me. I want to get to the point where I won't need someone to hand me a tool while I have something in my hands. The way I'm doing this is by making dinner. Tonight, it's a sloppy joe. Hopefully, this will end better than Experiment Three."

The camera turned to point at the white refrigerator door that opened by itself. One by one, the ingredients came out to settle on the counter, out of my reach. The camera moved itself behind me to frame both me and the ingredients.

"Now, Momma would kill me if the canned stuff was to ever get made in my kitchen, so we're doing this the long way."

I spent hours talking with her when I called asking about the recipe. She could tell I was freaked out; she always could. I'd told her I had a really vivid nightmare. I laughed. It felt good to laugh. No, I'm not manic at all! Not me!

"This experiment could double as a cooking show this time around if everything goes right. Okay, so what we have is a pound of ground beef we thawed last night."

The beef unwrapped itself, and the plastic flew over to the trash can, which opened its own lid like a Muppet ready to eat a cookie. It was nice not to get the blood from the meat all over my hands.

"Diced onion." A red-lidded food container opened itself and settled next to the meat.

"Ketchup, mustard"—the two condiments stood sentinel on either side—"and the weirdest of all, maple syrup. I do not know where my mother came up with this recipe, nor why it works so well, but it tastes amazing when it's done. We're also going to throw some fries in my little air fryer as a side dish."

The freezer door opened, and a bag of frozen fries came out to line up next to the other ingredients.

"The trick is going to be doing this without my hands. I'm also going to stay seated as a way to push myself. I'm not always going to see everything, and I'll have to figure out what to do in that scenario. First, let's turn on the burner. I'm going for medium heat on mine, but every range is different, or so Momma tells me."

There were a couple of clicks and a soft *fwoosh* sound that came from the stove as the burner turned on.

"Olive oil . . ." A slim glass bottle with a pointed nozzle tipped gently into the pan for a few seconds before gracefully tipping back and floating back to its place on the counter. The spatula next to the pan spread the oil around before settling back onto the counter. The container of diced onions lifted and dumped itself into the pan of the now-hot oil. It hissed like an ill-tempered cat as the juice from the onion reacted to the heated oil.

"Ohh, this is a nice side benefit!" I smiled. "No burns from splattered oil. I want the onions to be caramelized, so I'm turning down the heat." The dial moved again with no actual motion from the only person in the room. The video continued with the meat sliding into the pan, the spatula breaking it up as it browned, and then the condiments added themselves to the browned meat.

"Fries into the fryer while we give that a sec to cook." Fifteen of the frozen, golden rods danced out from the open bag and slid into the fryer that opened for them on approach. The drawer closed behind them and the dial turned to start.

I bit my lip. I had already added the condiments. "Momma said to drain out the oil before putting in the ketchup, mustard, and syrup, but I couldn't think of how to do that without it getting dumped on the floor for the monsters. So, extra sloppy on the joe then."

For a few minutes, my eyes were on the pan with the sloppy joe. I stirred it occasionally to make sure it didn't stick to the bottom. The fryer dinged. I stopped the spatula, turned off the heat, and used my ability to open the cupboard. A plate eased out and slid itself gently in front of me. I had yet to make a physical move. The now-crisp fries flew out of the fryer, did a little loop, and landed artfully on the plate.

"I feel the slight weight of these, but, again, I don't feel the heat."

Two slices of honey wheat bread settled themselves next to the fries as the pan with the saucy meat lumbered over. It wobbled in the air a moment. I focused a little bit more on its flight. It stopped its drunken motion and eased forward. One of the slices lifted off and floated to the side as the spatula doled out a portion onto the remaining slice on the plate. The top slice set itself on the sloppy joe before I sent the pan on the return trek to the range. The spatula knocked itself twice on the side of the pan before putting itself in the sink. A glass lid slid over the top of the remaining meat.

"Can't leave this out for the monsters. Onions are no good for them."

The door of the refrigerator opened again, and a small bottle of cola joined the party. The cap twisted off with a little hiss. A fork floated its way over from the cutlery drawer and settled itself next to my motion-less hands. The whole affair looked as if there had been some invisible person making the food, apart from the whimsical flight of the fries.

I took up the fork and smiled again at the camera as I cut into the meal. "And that's Momma's sloppy joe and the end of Experiment Six. This is a much better outcome than Experiment Three." I swallowed a perfect bite of sloppy joe. "I'm very pleased with the results of this, and hopefully, as time goes on, I will get more and more adept with my abilities."

The rest of Tuesday, after a very well-made lunch, was spent packing a bag. I needed at least a week's worth of clothing, toiletries, and some other essentials.

Wednesday started early. I didn't want the fam to worry about me, so I made sure to take care of that while I was making breakfast that morning. My family uses group texts as a way for all of us to share information without having to call. It never felt as impersonal as it sounds. Momma and her siblings have had a messenger group chat called 'Sup Sibs' for years.

When I had asked her what they talk about in there, she said, "Almost everything, really. Years of worries, hopes, and joys are in that chat. You should have seen it when your cousin was born. Plastered with baby pics for a year. I hope it never goes away."

I sent my family a message saying I'd be out of town. I made sure to be vague on where I'd be. I'd taken Second Raven's advice and told them I'd been hired as a concierge doctor by Jemma Corvis of Raven Enterprises for a project that required immediate attention and discretion. After some begging and pleading, Annie agreed to take my slot for the church barbecue pending a favor later. Mom reminded me about 'The Checklist.'

'The Checklist' is something my moms put together when they were younger to prep for vacations. It included things that made sense to take, like a towel and medications, and things that seemed silly, like board games if you were going to be with a bunch of people or had three daughters to entertain. One of my favorites was a gunny sack. You can fit just about anything in one, and it makes a great laundry bag for when you are ready to return home.

Mine had a cross-stitched stethoscope on it, courtesy of Grandma Smith, Momma's mom. It was adorable how she would sit in her chair with an adjustable lamp over her shoulder, readers on the tip of her nose, and would work on anything from gunny sacks to tablecloths to give people as gifts.

The car came at six, as promised, one Zauberer already in the back. The driver just sat in his seat and glared at us. I guessed it was beneath him to help any more than what was minimally required. I heard and ignored his comment of "Fucking low animals."

Jove and I packed the car and were at the lab before I could digest the whole 'the last time I was in this car, I was possessed' thing. While Horace was placing my bags in the part of the laboratory that was to be my home for a little while, Jove took my hand and clicked a new charm onto the bracelet. I didn't recognize this one. It was a pendant-type of charm with intricate lines and symbols.

"I met with one of the Community priests on the list we were given. This is one of the strongest charms he and I could come up with. It is the Seal of the Seven Archangels. Rooted in your Christian faith, this should act like a strong lock on the door that Edwards created to your spirit. It will help keep the Demonic at bay until we can have the mark removed. Zauberer Rhoades is in negotiations to have her remove the brand herself as we speak."

He brought my hand up to his lips and kissed the inside of my wrist, making my heart pound. I heard the driver retch.

"You could have left us at the door, yanno."

"I had to make sure you could find your way to the right place." He sneered. "Shaman Corax is right. Humans are always getting into and taking over places they shouldn't."

"Doktor Hall is a Gewalt, *Rabe*. You best remember that." Jove turned his back on the disagreeable being. "I may not be permitted to be in that room with you, Kleine. However, my protections are. Are we still on for Saturday?"

I gulped and blushed. He meant to catch me off guard like that, probably to take my mind off of our driver's rude comments. "As long as I can get this hammered out. Especially if the time differential works like it did the last time. W-what should I be expecting? I mean, originally, I thought we would just be going over my D and D books."

He smiled wickedly. "Concentrate on your work first. I think I can make our date worth your while."

"Just what have you planned, Mr. Brandt?" I felt playful but suspicious. He just smiled, pecked me on the cheek, and walked away, leaving me feeling off balance.

Apparently, I was a bit rusty on my flirting game. I'd spent the last few years focused only on studying and working to earn my doctorate. But I had been so immersed I failed to notice that two important males in my life were looking at me differently than they had before. I felt like an idiot for not noticing earlier.

I shook out my hands. Time to put personal matters aside. I had to get back into the work headspace to solve the Unkindness problem. I had a suspicion, based on the symptoms, but I wanted to consult further with Doctor Blackbird to see if he had tried that route. I picked up my gunny sack and went into the laboratory.

29

THE INSIDE HAD changed substantially. Many of the superfluous machines had been removed, giving the area much more space to move around in. The sprawling room had new partition walls to block off an infectious area, as well as a room with two bunk beds and a couch.

"The Unkindness never seems to do things small, do they?" I murmured to myself. High Raven must have taken my suggestions to heart. He'd kept the equipment I'd used and the ones that had the highest online ratings. I smiled. These would make things easier. I also saw three hazmat suits hanging on the wall next to the infectious room.

I wandered over to the helpfully labeled room and flicked on the lights. Overhead fluorescents flickered on, illuminating beautiful wooden tables topped with white marble, beakers, and test tubes through the glass of the double doors. The entryway was broken up to keep the area hermetically sealed. I chewed my bottom lip as I inspected the wooden tables. Usually, only stainless steel tables were used for lab work, but with the unique nature of the patients involved, I could understand why more natural materials were used instead.

"Everything to your liking, Doctor Hall?" A male voice cracked like thunder through the silence behind me.

I jumped and lost my footing, stumbling backward into a now very human-looking Doctor Thaddeus Blake Blackbird. He had stronger arms than what one would expect when the person in question secretly had wings. That was one strong illusion. I couldn't tell the difference; his arms felt like arms. His hands felt like hands. There was no way to discern the reality beneath the deception.

"What happens with your wings in human form? Are they illusionary, or are your arms really this strong? Is it a physical shift, like the werewolves, or are your illusions strong enough to fool other senses like touch? Touch would be a hard one to get past." I squeezed the forearm holding me. "This feels real. I don't feel feathers or the texture of feathers under the cloth."

"I'm not sure what any of that has to do with our problem." He helped me to my feet. "I'm also not sure how much I'm allowed to say."

"The more I know, the more I can help. If it is a literal biological shift in form, it could change the direction of this investigation." I straightened my shirt and hefted my sack from where I'd placed it on the floor onto my shoulder. "Want to pick bunks while I pick your brain?"

"You certainly have a different personality today from when I first met you, Doctor Hall. A lot more outgoing and curious." Blackbird smiled. "I think I like it."

"I was blindfolded, paraded through the sanctuary like a dangerous animal, and heard some of the contention between High Raven and Shaman Corax—one of whom doesn't care if I live or die and the other actively wanting to break my brain and strip-mine the knowledge *before* killing me. I knew I wasn't welcome to your home. Forgive me for being a little on the subdued side." I shrugged, walking to the sleeping area.

I turned on the lights. They had a softer glow than the harsh fluorescents in the lab area, which I appreciated. The bunks were very stylish, as was the rest of the room. It felt like a designer had been hired to make a dorm room fabulous. It was almost more like being in a chic hotel rather than just a bunk to crash in when we'd pushed ourselves too hard. The image of Jackie clutching her little superhero made me determined to push myself as hard as I could. Time was on our side with the time lab, but that was no reason to slack.

"Your people are in danger from a microscopic, invisible threat. I am an unknown factor. People fear the unknown." I chose a bottom bunk and placed my sack on the floor before testing the mattress. "I experienced the hospitality of the Unkindness before. It's not exactly an experience I want to repeat."

Blackbird watched me with very steady eyes. "I'm sorry. That place is not one of my favorites to visit, either."

I looked up sharply at him. "You've seen that bastardized Bedlam and haven't done anything about it?"

"I would if I could!" He sat hard on the lower bunk across from me and looked into the middle distance. "I was disgusted by what I saw the first time I was brought to treat someone over there. I told the enforcers not to feed the prisoners rotten food. Our systems can handle it. Humans can't. They laughed at me. Sadly, I'm not high enough for them to listen to. I'm not old enough, not powerful enough. I had to change that first. We are supposed to be better than those who are below us. We have to watch over the world that Raven left for us, and that includes the Veil-Struck that we are responsible for."

"Veil-Struck?" I'd heard that term before, but maybe Blackbird had more insight into the problem than Jove did.

"It's what we call those humans who go mad when they are exposed to members of the Community. It happens most often when a veil fails for one reason or another. Like if someone put theirs on but the enchantment was due for renewal and failed while they were on their way to work, for example. It's, sadly, becoming a common occurrence."

"Have they been failing more often lately?" I probed gently.

"Yes, and the Fae haven't told us why. They blame users for not using them properly. They say that Community members need to come in for renewals more often to make sure they have the most up-to-date enchantment. But the renewals are expensive, and for some of the less affluent, the cost of maintenance is becoming prohibitive. The end result is more humans who have to be taken care of by the people who struck them down. Not as many as the Zauberers would have us believe, but enough for those of us in the medical field to give the condition a name."

"But why treat them like that? You should know as well as I that when someone has a mental condition, an environment like that isn't going to make anything better for anyone."

Blackbird wrung his hands. "Only some of those humans in the dungeon did anything malicious; most of them were just a case of wrong place, wrong time. But the focus of the flock is always on those who have harmed us in some way."

"Like Issa and her Escalade."

Blackbird nodded. "The 'ethical' treatment of the people stored in the dungeon is under the dubious supervision of Shaman Corax. He preaches that the Unkindness have the right to treat such low beings by the fullest extent of our laws. Ignorance of the law is not an excuse of that law. He has said humans are so stupid and easily broken that they wouldn't *understand* what was happening and wouldn't *remember* what they had done against the flock. He took it upon himself to remind them. He *campaigned* that the dungeons fell under the aegis of those able to hear Raven's will."

The more I was finding out about this Bird-boy, the less I liked him. It was one thing to be racist. It was another to torture the people you're racist against and beg for the ability to do so.

He looked away and snorted. "Like he would *know* Raven's will. I fought to raise my rank in the flock to fight against that hypocrite. I am now the youngest to be appointed to head of our medical division. Our people were rarely sick because of the care and services that my division cultivated . . . Until this damned disease. I fought hard to get my staff into the prison. I went to High Raven myself to beg to let the prisoners get treatment rather than being left in their cells to die in pain. I can talk and talk until I become a blue bird, but with my current position, I can't change anything about how the prisoners are treated."

Blackbird's voice was bitter, and my estimation of his character went up. He didn't agree at all with what Corax had done. "But, you're not higher than Corax, not yet."

He lay back on the lower bunk and sighed. "He and I are not on the best terms. He's fought me for every wingbeat of power. Last month, I got High Raven on my side to stop the active torture of the prisoners. My next goal was to stop the rotten meals. My people take care of the medical treatments for the humans. They let me know there was a woman in one of the cells who actually knew what she was talking about. We have to send people out every other month to take care of problems like what happened to your neighbor. That was because of Corax. I would much prefer everyday sweeps, if only to make sure that whatever infects the humans won't spread to the flock."

"How is Issa? When I saw her last, your people were taking her out of the cell to be 'healed.'" I started pulling things out of my sack to put away in one of the drawers under the bed.

"I'll have her chart copied to you. With the plague, I haven't had the time to look over the prisoner health checks like I usually do. I'm worried that things have gotten worse while I've been distracted." Blake didn't sound callous about the situation, which was the only thing that kept my temper in check. "My people told me about you. How you called us by the scientific name for our lesser cousins, how your silver tongue convinced High Raven to hire you rather than sell you. Ever since then, I was extremely interested in meeting you. You are very intuitive for a human."

I smiled wryly. "Didn't they tell you? I am a Gewalt." I *lifted* the empty gunny sack into the air between us with my ability, *folded* it, and *placed* it at the end of the bunk.

"Well, that certainly explains why they placed you in the same cell as the Fae. Putting a power in with a non-power is just asking for someone to be Struck. Sometimes that can end violently."

Blackbird's shoulders seemed to relax a bit now that he thought I wasn't human. That rankled a bit, as I *was* human, but I understood better now why Zauberer Zimmer was so insistent on not admitting it outright. "Do Veil-Struck humans always go crazy in your experience?"

"All of the ones who have come through the prison are unable to take proper care of themselves anymore. Whether that is because of the conditions or being Struck is uncertain. Usually, if they come in twitching, we know they've been Struck." He started putting his things away in the other drawer set in the bunk across from me. When he got down to his suitcase, he put it on the top bunk.

"The Unkindness seems to have an almost religious obsession with heights," I said, and watched him climb the ladder to test his bed.

"Oh, we most certainly do." My colleague nodded as he rolled onto his mattress. "It has to do with the legend of Raven the Lightbringer. Are you familiar with it?"

"I did some research on ravens and stories related to them after I'd reached an *understanding* with High Raven." I nodded. "There are a few different stories that deal with Raven being a lightbringer. I don't know which is the truth."

I couldn't see Doctor Blackbird's face, but his one hand gesticulated in the air as he talked. "Ah, but you still read the stories. That is the point." A feathered finger pointed at me. "To be remembered."

"Coyote also likes to be remembered," I said, testing my mattress. It felt supple and very comfortable, a vast difference from the threadbare blanket and dirty pillows on a stone floor. This would be fine for when one or both of us got too tired to stand. "There are just as many stories about him."

"True, but you should thank your lucky stars you didn't run into one of his kin. Nothing but trouble magnets. Raven's power runs through our veins and gives us a chance to see the world as no other people on the planet can." His voice took on a beatific, reverent sound. "We can fly as high as we wish and with more style than any other bird on the wing."

And not vain at all, I thought, rolling my eyes. "So, then, which story do you follow? The hero who returned warmth to a winter-weary world, or the thief who used some twisted subterfuge to steal the light for himself only to drop it into the ocean?"

His bunk creaked, which I took to be a shrug. "Some follow one, others the other. I like the first story better, but I could see him doing the other just as easily. I find it comforting to have a deity that isn't perfect."

"Whatever floats your feathers, Doctor."

30

THE NEXT MORNING, we got down to business. I was poring over comprehensive reports that had been delivered via a pneumatic tube that connected us to the outside world. I tried to wrap my head around just how the time difference worked with such a delivery system, but I had to chalk it up to magic before my brain exploded. Damn it, I'm a doctor, not a theoretical temporal physicist!

"I approve of your approach with treatment," I said when I heard movement behind me. "Fluids are going to be vital if we don't want any more casualties."

"It fit the symptoms the best. Do you agree that it is highly likely to be some version of influenza?"

"I would have boxed your ears and sent you back to med school if you didn't recognize the flu in your own house. Even with the fast incubation period and the low white cell count, I suspect it's H5N1. The symptoms are too textbook to be anything else, but we'll confirm it using that spiffy centrifuge to isolate. We need to find out if and how Jackie managed to come into contact with it before bringing it back to your flock to germinate." I nodded and turned around to face him.

He sighed deeply. "I was afraid you'd say that."

"Oh, come on, you had to have known. The signs are too classic to not be, and given your avian nature . . ."

"I agree, but I'm not happy about it. Shaman Corax and his followers have been putting the pressure on to rely on more . . . ahem . . . *traditional healings*." He sneered.

"The kind that doesn't require a degree and leans more toward laying on hands? And because he's a spiritual leader . . ."

"Those are *his* hands he wants to heal with." He drilled his fingers into his black hair.

I woke up to him in human form. I assured him that it was okay for him to let his feathers out, but he insisted that it was easier to move around the laboratory 'in the skin,' as it were. It was easier to read his face in this form, though.

Disgust was plastered on his features as we talked. "That bastard has half of the flock arguing with me to allow him to perform a ritual to 'make the evil of the human world fly from my patients.' It's enough to make me pull out my pinfeathers!"

I used my ability to *float* a sample over to the machine in question. "Have you talked to Second Raven about it? This disease is a real danger to your entire flock."

Blackbird grinned. "That is amazing, Doctor Hall. You can be your own nurse."

"It's like having two extra hands at this point. Anti-vaxxers piss me off, too. While spiritual healing has its place, our deities gave us tools to take care of things medically so we don't have to tap their power all the time. And, hell, what happens if you roll a one on the prayer? Your deity ignores you, the person you love suffers, and or dies, and the religion loses followers."

"D—did you just explain why not to use spirit healing in terms of tabletop gaming? I don't know if this helps your credibility or hinders it."

Either way, he knew I was right. If God sends you a manned boat when you're drowning, you take the damn rope and thank God for sending it to you. You don't turn the boat aside to wait for God to pluck you out of the ocean with giant, etheric hands.

I turned to the table and started to prepare microscope slides. "Well, assholes aside, we still need to come up with a way to prevent your flock from collapsing. I would strongly suggest getting the rest of your people vaccinated pronto."

"If they agree to it," Blackbird said morosely.

"I don't think they should have a choice, given how many of your flock are already infected. I'm not kidding about the flock collapse here. I don't know how much faith to put in the miraculous healing of your Shaman." I aggressively wiped a glass slide with alcohol. "If High Raven wants to go that route, why not have Shaman Corax heal the lot?"

"Corax tried," said the Unkindness doctor softly. "You were right. I knew it was the flu from the onset, but I am lower in the flock than our Shaman. He demanded that I leave the girl in his care for healing, that Raven Lightbringer would answer his pleas, and she would heal. It seemed to work at first; she went back to school and played with the other fledglings for a week before she succumbed to the fever."

And vaccinating the flock was then suddenly a show that Shaman Corax was weak and didn't have the power he claimed. Every step after that was for the Shaman to save face and keep ahold of the clout he already had by discrediting everything that wasn't religious in nature.

"Goddamn politics are going to kill your flock, Blackbird." I clicked the clean slide into the tray and picked up the next one, quietly raging.

That stupid Shaman can't see that his god had already given the flock a healing option in Doctor Blackbird. Why should a god work at the command of a mortal when the solution to the problem already existed? Corax isn't happy with the proffered solution and wanted to show off his own damned power and rolled a god-damned one on his religion check. People are suffering because of that Bird-boy!

I hissed as I felt a sharp pain in my palm. I stared owlishly at the broken glass slide in my hand. Blood was welling up where the shards had dug into my flesh. I watched in fascinated horror as the glass pushed itself out from beneath my skin. The wounds closed as I looked up at Blackbird, who was watching me with suspicious eyes.

"Still new to the whole 'Gewalt' thing, huh?" His head tilted in a way more avian than anything I'd seen him do. "That wasn't the reaction of someone who grew up knowing what their body can do. So, what, did you start human and then get turned? Is that what Gewalts do?"

I schooled my expression, disposed of the glass, and said evenly, "At least you have the victims quarantined. That's something, at least. It seemed really open to the air. Aren't you worried about the patients getting cold?"

"So, we're just going to ignore all that, huh? Okay, we can play that way." Blackbird's voice chilled. "We keep convection heaters around to keep our people warm. A member of the flock is never denied the ability to see the sky, even if they cannot fly at that precise moment. It's something *humans* wish they could have."

His voice felt accusatory. I cleared my throat. "Look, we should work together to get this all ready before the rest of the cultures and samples arrive."

"They arrived while your body was doing weird things with glass." Blackbird motioned to the boxes in the area I was starting to think of as the living room. It was just inside the door that led to the rest of the world and had a coffee table, a white couch, and a set of matching chairs. There were four bankers' boxes stacked to the side of the couch. They looked full and heavy. "All of my research, notes with theories, blood tests, charts, the works."

I gaped. How the hell had those fit in a pneumatic tube? Magic was really starting to mess with my mind.

"We should get a whiteboard in here, too, to start a timeline. We need to know when the first patient was exposed to the virus and how."

He and I got through a box each, moving silently around one another. It was like walking on the glass that had gotten pushed out of my palm. While we were working, another two boxes, a cold box with samples, and a whiteboard were delivered to the laboratory, which was a pretty creepy trick, seeing as neither I nor Blackbird asked for it. It made me wonder if the lab was bugged, but then I shrugged that off. Time dilation would render keeping tabs on the room impossible. Ms. Corvis had to be just that good at planning. The boxes contained samples from the patients, complete with day and time stamps. We put those into the hermetically sealed portion of our lab in a cold storage unit.

"I think I'm about at my limit for tonight." Blackbird yawned. He arched backward, stretching more like a cat than a bird.

I rubbed at the grit in my eyes and nodded. "We'll pick this up in the morning, then." I stood and stretched, too. I heard the bones in my back pop. I really hoped a night of sleep would reset our attitudes. We had people to save, and they deserved our full attention.

31

"So, how do you like being a traitor to your kind?" Matthew asked as soon as I dropped into REM sleep.

"You again? I thought I kicked you out of my head."

"No, you hurled me through your curio cabinet. That's entirely different from getting me out of your head. Especially since we've had physical contact. Besides, you saved my life." He brushed phantom fingers through my hair in my dream, and I shuddered. "I'm going to do my best to keep you from facing too many repercussions for your actions. I'm sure I can figure out a way we can use this to our advantage. It's the least I can do to thank you."

I jerked away from his fingers; they felt like spiders. "I'm a doctor. Saving people is what I do."

"Just where are you, anyway?" He looked around as if he could see where I was. "It's too early for you to be this deep asleep."

"None of your business. Get out of my head, creep, or we're going to find out what a party cannon can do to your pretty face."

"You're talking far too fast for me to understand, darling." Matthew grabbed my wrist and pulled me close to him. I could feel his hand bruise my skin.

How the hell was I feeling that in a dream?

He was way too close; his blue eyes bore into me, radiating mad obsession. I looked down. I was suddenly in a tulle ball gown; small, embroidered purple flowers decorated the low-cut bodice. My hair was impossibly long again. It tumbled over my shoulders in loose ringlets.

Matthew was now dressed in a dark Regency uniform and slacks with shining boots. Medals glinted from a spotlight that was suddenly overhead. A possessive arm wrapped around me and swung me into a head-spinning twirl. "You never called, Mira. You were supposed to call. I'm going to start thinking you don't care about me."

"Seeing as I don't, then you're on the right track." I tried to pull away, but his grip was too tight.

"You'll change your mind once you're here. It'll be perfect! Me, out with the team kicking ass; you, back at base waiting to heal me up. None of these outside distractions. We'll be together every day. We could be heroes! Saving humanity from the monsters! Well now, that's rude."

I'd been flipping him the bird for a while now to see how long I had to hold it before he noticed. The time distortion must still be in effect. Good. I gave my hands a quick jerk and shoved Matthew away. I added a bit of my ability, forcing the man back ten feet. I snarled. "Don't you dare make decisions for me."

I ran like a speedster, shucking the dress and diving into a labyrinth of thorned hedges. I could do this. I'd get a full night of sleep and hopefully confuse the hell out of Matthew. I treated him to continuous scenes from my favorite movies and TV shows. It was hilarious to watch David Bowie dance the super-soldier around the ballroom in the obnoxiously floofy dress.

"Apparently, Mira, you are feeling childish today. I'm okay with that. Can't have my woman being super serious all the time. Until next time, babe." With that, he disappeared.

The next few days were grueling. We had some of the family members come in for interviews. They would only talk to Doctor Blackbird and wouldn't open their mouths when I was in the room. So, we made sure I could hear but didn't let them know I was within earshot. There was a handy intercom in the sealed lab. All we had to do was turn it on before the people came in. There was, understandably, a lot of anxiety about the prognosis of the victims from their families. I would float notes onto his clipboard if I needed any clarification.

I felt like a poisonous pet in a terrarium.

Thankfully, only a few of the interviewees had the anti-vax mentality. All of them said that Shaman Corax assured them that their families would already be healed if they followed the 'true word of Raven Lightbringer.' When the victims just got worse, all of the families were doubting their god—not the shaman, but their god. How twisted was that?

We started the timeline on the whiteboard. Jackie Corvis and the rest of her class had gone on a field trip to a local Community-owned farm to learn about animal husbandry. When we checked with the farmer, it was confirmed that his flock of chickens had been infected with H5N1, but they had been treated. By the time the fledglings had come for their tour, the chickens were symptom-free. Symptom-free didn't always mean infection-free, however. The entire class had been exposed. Little Jackie was just the first to succumb two days later.

"We need to start them on antivirals ASAP," Blackbird said. We'd been at this for what felt like weeks now. The mood had only marginally improved since the day I'd cut myself. We were at professional courtesy rather than friendly.

"I'd agree. We can have the onsite nurses add that into their IVs," I said over my shoulder.

Blackbird looked once again into the microscope. "Wait. Wait wait wait wait. Son of a bitch!"

I put the samples I was working with on the countertop. I turned to see what the excitement was about. "What is it? Did you find something?"

"What the hell are those nanites doing in this sample?" His brow furrowed in confusion. He double-checked the label on the slide. "This is Jackie's sample. How the hell did nanites get into her bloodstream?"

Did I somehow infect the samples? The ones floating around in my blood hadn't been destroyed when we'd done the treatment. They were different. What if that meant they could reproduce? I'd been masked when I'd visited the quarantine area, but I hadn't been here, in the time lab. Why hadn't I thought of that possibility earlier? My heart pounded as I strode toward the microscope.

"Shit. Let me see." They were the same variety that had infected the council. They weren't shaped the same as mine—no spare battery—but they were still diligent in the insidious work they'd been programmed to do. Destroy anything not human. If I hadn't contaminated the sample, then why were they in that little girl's blood?

"Let me isolate this, and then you let me know if you've seen these in anyone else's sample." Blackbird got to work, taking the sample over to one of the machines.

"I haven't seen this in any of the samples I've run so far. I should have." How could I have missed something this important? I scratched at my arms, practically feeling my own nanites crawling around under my skin.

"We've been going for two weeks now, our time. We start as soon as we wake up and go until our eyes get blurry. This is a lot of work for only two people. Even when we have all the time in the world." He gave me the first small smile I'd seen in days. "Do you think the kid was exposed via her mom?"

My head was spinning. "If she was, I don't think we should tell Ms. Corvis. Can you imagine the guilt she'd feel? How did you spot them?"

"I saw something hide behind one of the infected cells. When I turned the sample, there it was, happily munching on a neutrophil. We need to see if these are in all of the samples." He gestured to the stacks of trays.

"Ahh." I sighed. "You're right. Damn it. Let me get my stack, and we'll see if we find them there, too."

We found them in almost all the samples from the children. The samples from the elderly didn't show as many signs of nanite infection, but there were still a few. These little bastards were vicious. They would hide, destroy the closest immune cell like a spoiled child in the middle of a temper tantrum, and then go back into hiding. The nanites were acting like intelligent hunters. It was chilling to watch. The creator still hadn't nailed down self-replication, thankfully, but now I felt like it was only a matter of time.

"You know, this explains the low white blood cell count we've been seeing. Why aren't they going after the rest of the cells?" I murmured, "That's what they did before."

"It's like they are just targeting the ones that would stop or hinder the proliferation of the influenza virus. If you can get another entity to do the work for you, then all the better. Work smarter, not harder."

That was far too much intelligence for a single-celled machine to have. Could it be that these nanites were still receiving instructions from somewhere? The microscopes were better in this lab than any others I'd used before. We were able to zoom in far enough to find a maker's mark. The letters *PZ* were on the 'leg' of one of the microscopic robots, written in atoms.

Whoever this was, they had a lot of blood and suffering on their hands. But how much of this was just them, and how much was the ACS?

My eyes were glued to the eyepiece as I tried to separate them with my ability. I felt sweat roll down the back of my neck, but I must have focused too hard. The one I'd isolated fell apart like a bug on a windshield. It was like trying to use a hammer to separate an ant from the rest of the colony. "*Godamned son of a bitch* don't BREAK! Argh!"

"I take it from your expletives you're having some trouble, Doctor Hall?" Blackbird said calmly.

We had been at this for three weeks, our time, by this point.

I pushed away from the microscope before I threw it across the room in frustration. "I'm trying to use my ability to corral the nanites. I want to see if they are receiving outside instructions or if they are just running off of a pre-written program. I can get them bunched up no problem, but when I try to isolate one, then it just . . . squishes."

"How can something so small be receiving outside instruction?"

I moved back to give him access to the scope. "I don't know, but they look way more complex than they should. It's like someone built this a lot larger, then shrunk it to the scale they needed. It doesn't look like a single-celled organism." I raked my fingers through my hair. "And, because I'm not the size of a cell, my ability squished it. I barely thought *at it* at all, and it still squished it."

"So, what you really want is to be able to see it and manipulate it." Blackbird leaned back and gave me a look. "This feels like a waste of time. Be practical, Hall. How is finding out how they are being controlled going to help our patients?"

"Well, if they are receiving an outside signal, then we may be able to track it and stop them from doing this again." I huffed.

Blackbird put a hand on my shoulder and gave it a comforting squeeze. "Leave that to us, Doctor Hall. The Unkindness is far better equipped. Our job is to use these microscopes to get the most accurate images of these nasty little bugs to give our warriors the best chance to track them down."

"It just makes me so angry." I gestured at the microscope. "Someone did this on purpose. It's a microscopic mechanical monstrosity built simply to destroy. Thankfully, nanites can't replicate, so we can easily find those who were first infected. But *who* were first infected makes my blood boil. Targeting children is just . . . wrong on so many levels." My hands fisted and shook with rage in my lap. I clenched my teeth. "Those kids didn't deserve this. No one deserves this. Left untreated, these nanites lead to a slow, agonizing death . . . Their families should get the EMP treatment as well to be on the safe side. A kiss goodnight could have transferred enough to start damaging their immune systems. I'll send the specs to Ms. Corvis."

"You're not like other humans, are you?" Blackbird's eyes softened a bit. "You see us as people. I'll send word to Second Raven as well, just to give it some extra *oomph* on the necessity and to keep Corax from squawking too loud. In the meanwhile, you should hit the bunk and get some rest. You've been going nonstop for a few days now."

"Any idea what time is doing out there? I have a date Saturday." I smiled tiredly. My head gave a pleasant little spin before the world righted itself.

"No idea. Go to bed. Your eyes are doing that thing they do before you pass out."

"Okay." I went into the bunk room. I hadn't realized how sleepy I was until Blackbird said something. My temples were pounding as my head hit the pillow.

My dreams had been more like typical dreams since entering the time lab. Matthew had given up invading them because of the time dilation. His slowed speed made it far too easy to mess with the jerk. One time I trussed him up like a turkey, hung him over a pool of rainbow dolphins, and they would jump and hit him with their noses. It didn't actually hurt, as it was all in my mindscape, but it'd still been fun.

32

I JOLTED AWAKE the next morning as we heard a thunk from the pneumatic tube that had been our only communication with the outside world. It was always surreal reading the notes, as they were on a slower time stream. Thankfully, Ms. Corvis had the decency to put timestamps on all communication to help us keep track, though I severely doubted it was for my benefit.

Aug 1st 7:00am EST

Doctor Blackbird,

You and the Gewalt have been in isolation for three days. Twenty new cases have been discovered, some with no link to the previous victims. Their blood samples are included in this communication. We have followed your instructions to treat the patients with the device the Gewalt invented and started them on the medications you've indicated. We were able to get the device recreated thanks to the Gewalt's instructions. Shaman Corax sends his prayers that you fail so he can fly higher, as usual, and spouts that Raven would save us all from this disease with a quick wave of his wing if only our people come to him first.

Second Raven Jemma Corvis

So many new cases with no connections to previous patients made me frown. We shouldn't have seen that many new cases when a quarantine was in place. What could have gone wrong? "We need more information. How do that many people get exposed to a contagion we supposedly have isolated? How is your quarantine situation with the current patients?"

"We took all necessary precautions." Blackbird scowled. "The infirmary is farther from the main flock than you think. We also have restricted visitation to limit the exposure."

"Ms. Corvis said they were unrelated to the current victims. Let's get these samples under a microscope. I want to see if they have invaders or if they only have the disease." We took the samples to the lab, the doors hissing behind us. I prepped the slides and *slid* them into the slot of the microscope with my ability.

"Thank you, Doctor Hall." Blackbird leaned into the eyepiece and cursed soundly.

"Aww, you've been learning from me." The levity left my voice. "I take it the bugs are there?"

He nodded, then tilted his head as he read the label. "Let me see the names on the other samples." His head moved from side to side as he read the names, like a bird who's spotted an interesting shiny bit.

"You have something, Blackbird?" I handed him the vials.

"Maybe. The list of the newly infected is a who's who of piety," he said, looking through the paperwork.

"Pearl clutchers?" I remembered some of the more extreme churchgoers. A person was always doing something against God in their eyes. The wrong color hair, the wrong spouse, the wrong clothes . . . None of which had anything to do with God at all.

"If you asked me who the most devoted to Raven were in our flock, the most pious, these would be the people I'd choose. They attend every one of Corax's sermons. Practice everything in our teachings almost obsessively. They ask for Raven's blessing for just about everything that happens in their lives. As if they cannot turn a corner without Raven guiding their every step."

"I know people like that in my church as well."

"But can you imagine how EXHAUSTING it is for Raven to try to follow a single person's every step?" For a second, I could see the exhaustion etched clearly on my fellow doctor's face. Almost like he wasn't talking about his god, but himself. "Ours is the largest flock on the Eastern Seaboard. This time of year, we all start coming together for the winter to roost; we can number as many as five hundred. Miracles take a lot of juice, and gods who can't count their followers in the millions don't have the same kind of oomph."

"Sounds like you're pretty devout yourself, bud." But the prospective commonality of coming together for the holidays made me think. "At church, we have the sacrament where we share wine and bread from the same metaphorical plate for communion. According to the Moms, it was a literal plate before the pandemic. For kids who aren't old enough, they can still come up to the altar for the pastor to bless them. Does your religion have something like that?"

"There is a feather the shaman uses to call on the power of Raven. Raven's Pinion. It is *supposed* to be handed down from Raven himself and passed from one shaman to the next. It is *SUPPOSED* to be used only in important blessings. It is usually kept as a treasure to the flock." If he'd been in raven form, I'm sure his feathers would have been ruffled. "Instead, Corax uses it to bless . . . everything . . . constantly."

And an item like that could easily spread a contagion if it weren't properly cleaned. "Where does Corax keep it?"

"On his hip, connected with a ball chain like a rabbit's foot!" Blackbird sneered in distaste.

I'd seen it before then. Raven's Pinion had to be the sword-length feather I'd seen when I'd first met the shaman.

"As if he were the master of Raven and not the other way around."

I pulled out my cross and arched an eyebrow.

"That's different." He snorted. "That's a mass-produced symbol. This is more like having a piece of the original cross on your keychain, then demanding the Son of God come down and unlock your car every day."

The mental picture of Jesus looking annoyed before unlocking a car with a heavenly-sounding chirp made my lips twitch. I sat on a stool and faced my colleague. "So, Corax uses his fairly often, then. Is the artifact cleaned regularly?"

"Ritualistically." Blackbird nodded. "The process is passed from shaman to shaman through the years. Medicinal herbs, oils, and plants are used."

It could have been something in the cleaning process. The original nanites were found in the oil used on sandwiches. "Is there any way we could get a sample? Maybe the ingredients have been compromised?"

"Something like that. Hmm, my feathers are itching. It feels like we're on the right track with this. If only someone could pry The Pinion from his old, gnarled talons." Blackbird scrubbed his fingers into his scalp in frustration. "High Raven *might* be able to do it, but then he'd have a religious coup on his wings. Corax has been undermining him for years now. The shaman says we've strayed too far from the flyway Raven set before us. I say if a damned tree has grown in the flyway, then you have to change course to avoid hitting the damned tree."

"Words to live by." I was impressed by the imagery.

We were distracted by a second thunk in our friendly pneumatic tube. What was written this time had my blood boiling. The quarantined were worse, especially the children. They'd been showing signs of improvement after the EMP treatment, but then Corax had forced his way into the ward and "blessed" them with Raven's Pinion. Immediately after, one of the children who'd shown signs of recovery collapsed. Another blood sample had been included. It was our little warrior, Jackie.

We sent back a note with just five words.

BRING CORAX FOR INTERVIEW NOW.

33

BLACKBIRD AND I talked, and I agreed to stay in the lab while Corax was here. It was the best place for me to keep out of sight of the racist shaman.

Doctor Blackbird went to the doors that hissed as he walked into the decontamination section. "So, stay put. Corax is dangerous, but only if you're the squishiest thing in the room. So, stay out of the main room, Squishy."

Doctor Blackbird stood with his back to the entrance but not blocking my view of the room. He had his super-serious doctor look on his face—the one we usually reserve for cancer patients.

High Raven entered first. The entire process was fascinating, as the transition from normal time to our fast time caused the shaman and Ms. Corvis to stumble as their bodies acclimated. High Raven didn't have any trouble at all. It was like he walked through time dilations every day and couldn't see what all the fuss was about. He was more imposing than I remembered. Granted, this time I didn't have the benefit of the 'see true' goo.

I slid further back into the lab, quietly seating myself on one of the stools. It somehow felt safer and more familiar being sequestered there rather than being closer to the leader of the Unkindness with nothing protecting me. His face was practically serene, maybe even a little smug, in comparison to the thunderous expression twisting the features on the face of Shaman Corax.

The bastard chose to come in the Bird-boy guise, somehow making a scowl with his long beak. He stalked into the room on the heels of High Raven, followed by a stalwart Ms. Corvis. I had just enough time to shut the door to the lab, turn on the intercom to hear, and zip over to a work area to look studiously into one of the microscopes.

Even through the intercom, the sound of Shaman Corax's outraged voice was clear and distinct. I wish I'd had popcorn. If Shaman Corax was about to get reamed out by his boss, I wanted to be able to hear every blessed word. I sat back at the microscope, changing the slide to look busy.

"What is the meaning of this, High Raven?" he hissed as soon as the door to normal time had closed. "Is this because I was called to do my work to heal our sick? I'll have you know Raven himself called to me in a dream and instructed me to heal those you let that low human touch."

"Doctor Hall isn't human. She is a Gewalt," Ms. Corvis said evenly.

"And I'm a cat. You may be able to pull the clouds in front of everyone else's eyes, but *not* mine!"

Bringing up cats was a dick move, seeing how her husband died. Granted, this sacrosanct shaman seemed to be made of dick moves. I sneaked a look over my shoulder at the tableau and had to bite my cheek to stop from laughing at how hard Ms. Corvis rolled her eyes. Good for you, lady!

High Raven's voice was a low rumble in comparison to Corax's hiss. "We need to see the Pinion of the Lightbringer."

"You dare! The only person allowed to handle this is the head Shaman of the Flock, and to the best of my knowledge, that is *not you*!" The shaman grabbed at the feather like a child who's been told his favorite toy needed to be washed. He clacked his beak angrily at High Raven.

High Raven struck me as feeling calmer and more collected—still angry to be sure, but his rage didn't have the flash and scald. He stared dispassionately as Ms. Corvis shoved the shaman away, forcing the older bird to land comically on his tail feathers.

"The young ones got *worse* after your visit," Ms. Corvis hissed. "You bottom-feeding charlatan! Jacqueline was getting better. She read a story with me yesterday. *You* forced your *blessing* on her, and she got *worse*!" Her voice broke, and she covered her face with one hand.

My heart went out to her. I wanted to kick that asshole for her.

Ms. Corvis sobbed only once before rage lit in her eyes. "I'll kill you for this, you sacrilegious fraud."

"Hold, Second Raven." High Raven held her back gently.

"I demand satisfaction, High Raven," she said, her voice as strained as her muscles. He was the only thing stopping Jemma Corvis from pinning that Bird-boy and laying into him. "He's harmed my fledgling."

"We do not yet have proof that it was his fault. That is why we are here." He looked down at the creature at his feet with disgust. "Give us the Pinion, or we will relieve you of it."

Ms. Corvis snarled and pulled back a leg to kick at the shaman. He made a small sound of fear and held out the feather to High Raven. The leader of the Unkindness handed the artifact to the waiting Doctor Blackbird, and I was reminded of how large it was. It looked more like a saber than a feather, black as pitch, and as long as my leg. The door hissed open as my compatriot entered the lab. I was gently nudged aside from the workstation. He took a pair of shears out of the drawer to his right and snipped the end off.

Shaman Corax squawked at the top of his lungs. It was high-pitched and made me flinch. "*Defiler!* You've destroyed a treasure of the *Flock*! When the People hear about this—"

"Silence," said High Raven. Corax settled into rage-filled mutterings.

A smell permeated the lab—the scent of burning wires and electricity. "You smell that, Doctor Hall?"

I nodded. "I take it your sacred artifact doesn't typically smell like you cut a live wire in half?"

"No, it does not. Nor does it spark like this." Blackbird held it up for me to see, then held it higher for our observers with a scowl on his face. "This is not his gift to our people. *This* is *not* Raven's Pinion."

I leaned over his shoulder and looked through the microscope. Their 'Pinion' was a nanite factory. From every simulated barbule, more of the little beasties emerged, festooning the faux feather like lice on a child's head.

Every blessing performed with this thing would have been covering the person in more nanites, which would try to enter the body by any means necessary. Wiping the eyes, eating without washing the hands, a small paper cut—any of those things would be like a wide-open garage door to these things.

"Y–you lie! I've never let the Pinion out of my sight!" Corax shouted, climbing to his talons from where he'd fallen.

"Not even when you got it mounted so you could wear it on your hip like a sword?" I said under my breath.

"*You* have *no* voice here, Gewalt." High Raven's voice was quiet and firm. "However, you bring up a valid point. I have known you for a very long time, Corax. You have no skill at a forge to make a mount like the one on that feather, the Dwarves don't like you enough for a commission, and you are too vain to have it done by a novice. Where did you take the Pinion to mount it? Did you take it to a human? Did you reveal our flock's most precious thing to *outsiders*?"

"What right have you to question me?" The shaman snorted. He crossed his feathered arms over his chest and looked away from the Unkindness leader as would a petulant child who didn't like that the rules applied to him. "I no longer recognize you as the highest, and neither will the rest of the flock as soon as they hear about this blasphemy!"

High Raven made a motion with his hand faster than my eyes could follow. With a thunderous crack, Shaman Corax was again on the ground at his feet, blood spotting from the older bird's nostrils. "I no longer recognize *you* as a member of this flock. You will be driven from our roost and far away from our lands. But not before you tell us where you took the Pinion."

There was a heavy moment in time following his proclamation, as though the words held far more meaning than the shaman's had. I felt it ripple through the air like a stone being dropped into a lake.

"Y–you can't do this to me!" shrieked Corax. "I am the High Shaman of this flock! I, above all others, was chosen by Raven to lead our people! It was my right to improve the Pinion. To make it more than what it was. The People will follow where I fly! You—you fear me and my power! That is why you and your second bitch have brought me to this place! Well, don't you forget my followers are many, and will have your head buried beneath the ground feeding our trees."

"Strange." Ms. Corvis's voice was calmer when she spoke. "I wasn't aware 'High Shaman' was a position in our faith."

Neither was I.

I froze. I heard that voice with what felt like every cell of my body. I stood so fast I knocked over the stool I had been sitting on. I turned toward Dr. Blackbird to see if he'd heard what I had. His stool was empty. The good doctor was no longer in the lab with me. Nor was he out with the other ravens.

Stay where you are, Mira. This is a matter between this flock and myself.

I peered through the large window separating the lab from the rest of the space where we'd spent the past few weeks. I saw Blackbird's long white coat flutter to the floor in front of the representatives of the Unkindness. It suddenly came to mind that I'd never told Blackbird about the nanites. They had never come up as a topic of conversation, and I didn't say anything about the treatment of the Council of Eight.

'What are the nanites doing in this sample?'

The nanites, not *'Are these nanites?'* not *'What the hell are these sci-fi looking things?'*

He didn't ask any questions when Ms. Corvis mentioned the EMP machine. He'd just agreed to the procedure, calm as you please. At the time, I'd just been happy he wasn't hostile to me anymore. But Blackbird must've already known about the nanites that infected the council and how I'd treated them.

Everyone was sworn to secrecy that day.

With *magic.*

So how did he know? Easy, because he was a little 'g' god.

Huge, spindly talons clicked and clicked on the tiled floor. They looked sharp and wicked. I swallowed, suddenly very happy to be on my side of the glass. Its feathers, while primarily black, shone with iridescent colors that seemed to move on their own. Its beak looked sharp but not cruel. In fact, it felt more like a wise person looking down at foolish children. I could actually feel the disappointment and sadness in those intelligent eyes. It croaked once, loud enough to shake the window I was looking through.

High Raven and Ms. Corvis had both taken a knee in front of this impossibly majestic creature that could be none other than the living embodiment of Raven. Corax lay prostrate before his god, caterwauling like a bully who'd just been caught by the teacher.

"OH! My lord Raven, highest of the high! We are but lowly ants in your presence! Our bellies scratch the earth like snakes—no—like worms—yes—we—"

Yes, yes. Protestations, blah blah.

"I'm just so happy to see you, my lord! We have prayed so hard, begged for so long for you to come down and help your people! I am the first shaman, obviously the highest among your shamans, to view your visage with my own eyes! The fact that you have come to my prayers must mean I am more powerful than I thought."

Don't flatter yourself. Raven snapped.

It was interesting hearing this voice in my head as well as seeing this gigantic bird's body language. His feathers puffed in what I could only assume was anger. I blinked, and suddenly Corax was under Raven's talon like the worm he'd said they all were. *In your arrogance, you have single-handedly caused more harm to this flock than any human who has walked this earth in the last decade. I had my doubts, of course. Who would believe one of my shamans would have done what you have? You have allowed the Pinion I gave to my children to be taken . . . By humans no less! In your idiocy, you failed to notice the Pinion they returned to you was a fake. My true Pinion would never be able to be modified like that. You have killed members of the flock to show off your so-called power. Did you think that I would not hear the cries of my children? Did you think that I would not seek your corruption out as I sought light itself for this world? I strip you of your power . . . Worm.*

Ms. Corvis made a protesting sound.

Raven turned his impressive head to her. *What is it, little daughter? You do not agree with my judgment?*

"Please, my baby. He hurt my baby." Her voice was strangled and tight. My heart went out to her. I'd want revenge, too, if any of my family had been hurt like that.

Your chick will recover. I and the good Doctor Hall here have made it so all those in our ward will be saved from this disease.

"I demand satisfaction."

Demand?

Ms. Corvis ducked her head. She must've remembered she was talking to her god. "Humbly request," she amended.

My mind was in a strange place as I watched this unfold. I'd been working with a god for a long while now. We were in the third week in our time lab.

Blackbird was funny, smart, and sneaky with his humor. This being felt the same . . . but different . . . *More.* Like Raven was just borrowing Blackbird's existence for a while. The nerd part of my brain was geeking out. THIS WAS SO FREAKING COOL. I was looking at the raven that all other ravens were modeled after. Not many people can name-drop a little 'g,' but hey, I could now.

Raven gently brushed a wing over her head in a very light rebuke. *You are forgiven, little daughter. The love you have for your Jackie is like a warm wind lifting us up. But no arguing, hmm? I don't want to set a precedent. How would you have your satisfaction?*

"If it pleases you, highest of high, I would have my satisfaction by way of combat." Her teeth clenched together with her next words. "I will have his throat 'neath my talons for the wrongs against mine."

Raven nodded, and as his head came back up, I realized we weren't in the lab any longer. We stood on an open, oval, wood-covered floor. The light from above us was mottled. I looked up to see the sun peeking through branches of the most massive tree I've ever had the pleasure of seeing.

34

THERE WERE WEAPON racks built into the stone wall that separated the spectators from the combatants. It reminded me of a gladiatorial arena. The spectator seats were made of stone, with an ornate viewer's box facing the rest of the spectators' stands. The box was decorated with brightly colored fabrics and jewels.

Raven stood in the guise of Doctor Blackbird once again—the Bird-boy version—though now his beak was longer and sharper than the others. High Raven and Ms. Corvis stood on his left. I stood on his right. Shaman Corax stood across from us. I saw them all in Bird-boy feathers, but I didn't have the goo. I think Raven was being nice to me.

I was the only human there and felt as if I were meant to be aware of that. This was not my home, not my place to have any say here.

Raven's eyes were cold and indifferent as Ms. Corvis stepped forward, away from our little group. He snapped his fingers, and the perspective changed.

Suddenly, High Raven, Raven, and I were in the viewer's box, looking out upon the arena and the two combatants. There were three chairs, the largest of which was in the middle. It could have actually been classified more as a throne than a chair. Raven sat himself there and motioned for High Raven and me to sit on either side of him again, with High Raven on his left and me on his right.

The deity then clapped his hands and the stands were filled with the entire flock of the Unkindness. There were surprised squawks and screams from the panicked flock all around us.

High Raven stood and raised his arms for silence. The Unkindness quieted, though uneasy murmurs still carried throughout the crowd like the wind through reeds. High Raven then bowed low and held one arm out to the side. Raven stood and walked forward into the light to be seen by all. As he walked, his doctor's coat flowed into some ornate, colorful robe. The cloth was fashioned to look like feathers.

Ivory lines drew the form of the 'feathers.' The lines of the blindingly white fabric pulled the eye to the colors at the 'tip' of each 'feather.' Blue, green, purple, and red were all in attendance. This display had to have looked really impressive from the front, but from behind made me feel as if I were an actor who knows all the secrets behind the curtain.

My Children, said Raven, using the voice that rang in the head as well as through the air. *I, Raven, have heard the cries of your fledglings and croaks of your elders. Have heard the lamentations of your dead. I have come to rectify that which is wrong.*

"Pfft. There's no way that's Raven. It's gotta be just some new shaman showing off power as *usual*."

My eyes went wide. That had sounded like some teenage, angst-ridden, asshole. And they had to say this in the utter *silence* that followed Raven's proclamation. Raven's beak clacked together once and a huge, shadowy hand launched from our seats into the crowd. A squawk sounded loud as a body clothed in black was lifted from the seated throng and floated up to the viewer's box.

What did you say, boy? You don't believe that I am Raven of song and story? You believe that any old shaman can sing in your head and your heart like this?

The boy was skinny and in the tightest pair of black jeans I'd ever seen. He reminded me of the pictures of the kids who loved punk music in high school. He had a militant look on his feathered face. Gotta give the kid credit; he had balls for facing down his ultimate authority figure.

"If you are Raven, why did you wait so long? My mom prayed for months for you to save her so she and m—my sister would get better." The boy's beak clacked as his emotions took over his senses. "They b—both died because you couldn't get off your *f—freaking tail* to heal them!" Tears were rolling down each side of his flattened beak.

I felt my throat tighten in sympathy. I couldn't imagine losing my sisters or the Moms. This poor kid.

So then, you do *acknowledge me. What should I do with you now? I could crush you for your insolence. I could drop you from here, and you would join them with the One.*

The boy visibly shook in the clutches of that hand. He was obviously terrified. "I—I d—don't c—care what you do to me."

The shadowy hand loosened from around the boy and cupped under him gently so he wouldn't fall. His body sat in the middle of the palm, still shaking, as Raven stepped into empty air and walked out onto the flattened hand. He then knelt next to the boy and pulled him in for a fierce embrace.

I am so sorry it took me so long to hear your pain. My connection with this flock was strained because of the duplicity of another. I couldn't feel your wingbeats or hear any prayers. So, I had to fly silently among you to know for certain who was at fault.

Raven's features slid around, and his outfit flickered back into what he wore as Dr. Blackbird. Gasps of recognition flitted through the stadium. After a few moments, he was Raven once again.

It took me too long. I'm so sorry, Kendall.

The boy jolted at Raven's voice. "Y—you know my name?" His voice cracked with emotion.

Of course, I know your name. You are one of my blood. You all are. I knew you from the moment you cracked the shell of your egg. The moment you first breathed and shouted your presence to the world. I know all of you!

Cries of joy and tears of sadness rang throughout the arena. Those who didn't believe just got their faith shoved in their faces. It was impressive, to say the least. I sniffed and wiped my eyes at the beauty of that moment. Raven pulled Kendall to his feet, and the hand brought them to the box. Raven made a motion for me to get up. I could easily understand why. I was an honored guest, but I was *not* one of the Unkindness. I stood, and gave the teen my chair.

Raven twitched a feathered hand and another chair appeared further to the left for me to sit. Kind of him, really. Kendall sat, but only had eyes for Raven, who would pat the kid's head from time to time, like a proud parent.

High Raven took the position of announcer. "My people! Today we have been blessed by the presence of Raven, from whom we all came. The duplicitous one Raven spoke of is he who you see before you. Shaman Corax. His desecration of our most sacred artifact, Raven's Pinion, made it so our voices were muted!" He held the broken faux feather above his head for the entire flock to see. "He took what belonged to all and let hands not of this flock touch it. His foolish actions not only let our treasure be stolen from us, but this disgusting perversion *caused* our plague."

Kendall jerked in his chair at this. "He what?"

Be at ease, Kendall. This is to be his punishment.

"Second Raven has begged for her talons to be the ones that mete out justice for our flock, and Raven has granted this to her!" High Raven shouted. Cheers erupted at this news.

Shaman Corax looked quickly around for any faces still loyal to him, or at least I assume that's what he was looking for—any friendly face in that sea of disappointment, betrayal, and rage. He turned his desperate eyes to Raven.

"My lord, why have you done this to me?" he shouted over the crowd as best he could. "I have sung your praises to the clouds. I've blessed all the Unkindness in your name! Why do you side with High Raven? He works with those lower than us! He has worked with *humans*! Why do you side with someone who touches those so much lower than us?"

All are part of the One's creation. While we fly so high above our brothers and sisters, they are still part of our family. You seem to have forgotten this in your desire to place yourself as superior *to all others. You've forgotten the trees we live in grow out of the ground, nurtured by the depths of the earth. You've forgotten that you cannot survive without those beneath you lifting you up. Your blind desire to be superior to all is what makes you the lowest of all.*

"Your arrogance is making my fledgling suffer." Ms. Corvis's voice was quiet. The shape of the stadium—or hell, maybe magic, seeing as how big this place was—made her voice heard. She walked to one of the weapon racks and ran her fingers along some sharp-looking implements. She chose a set of metal bracers and started to tie them on.

"I had to listen to your rhetoric for *years*. All this 'We are higher than *all* others. They deserve to be as servants under our feet.' We are *done* with you and your *poison*." She kicked against the bottom of the wall. Form-fitting metal clamped around her exposed talons. Ms. Corvis then took a stance that reminded me of something out of a Kung-fu movie.

"This flock would be *nothing* without me." Shaman Corax croaked. "I sacrificed what I needed to in order to make us the most powerful flock this side of the Mississippi. You turn your backs on me now? So be it." He clacked his beak once. A tall black staff appeared in his hands. He slammed the end onto the ground.

Power ripped across the arena, causing the people in the seats to be thrown back into the rows behind. Ms. Corvis was the only bird left standing. I noted the set of her legs had braced her body against the invisible wind that had thrown back the others.

Raven looked sheepish and suddenly sounded a lot more like the man I'd been working with for a month. *Oops, sorry about that; I forgot he still had access to pull from me. I hereby rescind my power from you, Corax. There. That should make this a much more fair fight.*

"What?" Corax shrieked, "You can't *do* that!"

Just did, asshole.

The crowd laughed with derisive, croaking voices.

"You know what? Fine. Just FINE. I'm still in good standing with other powers as things are."

You were cheating *on me with other gods? Just for that, I'm going to do* this. He flicked a finger toward Ms. Corvis. Her body stiffened, and she rose a foot off the ground. Her chosen armaments became inscribed with beautiful, bright silver lines and swirls. The armor also sleeked into something that looked like it was specifically forged for her. *I name you, Jemma Corvis, my champion in this battle.* He leaned back and lounged in the chair. *Go get him.*

Ms. Corvis darted forward. At first, I thought she'd simply ram the older bird onto his tail feathers, but at the last moment, she leapt into the air. The silver on her talons flashed as she flexed them toward her prey. Corax arched his back and swung the staff upward to catch the attack before it had a chance to strike.

Ms. Corvis flapped her wings to keep the sweep of the wood from connecting with her cranium. Corax adjusted his grip on the weapon and swung like a batter aiming for the cheap seats. Ms. Corvis landed hard on the staff, bringing it to the ground beneath her silver-clad talons. "Is that all you've got, charlatan?"

"Oh, you thought that was all I had, Second Raven? I have only just *begun*!" Corax's body started to shift into a different form from the Bird-boy guise he'd sported up until now. His torso stretched to an impossible height as his features sucked in to make him look terrifying.

You absolute bastard, growled Raven. *You struck a deal with OWL! His kind kill ours on sight!*

"Your power wasn't enough. Owl gave me what I needed." The shaman sneered at the viewer's box.

Corax must have lost access to a lot of the power he had when the Pinion was stolen from him. So, he went to another in the pantheon to supplement what he'd been missing. From how Raven was talking, it sounded like the shaman had made a deal with the devil.

Corax's body continued to shift until he was skeletally thin and the feathers on his arms and shoulders had flattened until they resembled a cape. I blinked in my seat. No wonder Raven knew it was Owl Corax had cavorted with. This was a threat display of the Northern White-faced Owl. Momma had shown me a video of this thing in action, and it had been fascinating to watch.

"No amount of power is enough for the likes of you, charlatan." Ms. Corvis scooped Corax's staff from under her feet with a flick of one foot. "And no amount of so-called power you've weaseled out of our enemy will keep you safe from me."

With this threat, Second Raven of the Unkindness winked out of sight.

My eyes searched the arena for her. There was no way she'd just cut and run. Not the Ms. Corvis I knew. That's when I noticed the upturned smiles on the faces of High Raven and Raven. Ms. Corvis was using her power from her flock—a power now denied to the disgraced shaman. Her illusion was absolute. I had no idea where she was until Corax suddenly dodged to the right.

The staff appeared and danced in the air. It was the only visual cue and another ploy. Corax flew back from where he'd been standing as an invisible fist launched him into the air. He then stretched out a long, misshapen arm to the sky from where he lay on the ground. Lightning streaked across the sky, followed instantly by a clap of thunder.

Raven clacked his beak a second before the torrent of rain fell from the sky in a deluge. That clack put shelters over the seated Unkindness, protecting them from getting wet.

My eyes went wide as I realized Corax's plan. In some cultures, owls were thought to be able to redirect lightning and, like Daredevil and Elektra, the rain made it so he could see where Ms. Corvis was.

"LOOK OUT! HE CAN SEE YOU!" I shouted—or rather, I tried to shout. No sound came out of my mouth. I felt the pit of my stomach go out from under me. I touched my throat and tested for any pain. Nothing wrong there. I had plenty of air, so I should have been able to shout my warning.

You were told you had no voice here, little doctor. Second Raven is aware of the many powers of our ancient enemy. But I will remember how you were willing to warn one of mine.

Corax was on his feet again with his arm still in the air. His other hand came up and pointed precisely where Ms. Corvis stood. The hair on the back of my neck stood as the lightning came down. Corax acted like a living lightning rod, his right hand focusing the electric bolt into a deadly weapon.

Jackie's face flashed in front of my eyes. I couldn't just *sit* here and do *nothing*! I narrowed my eyes and focused on the muscle that controlled Corax's bicep on his right arm. It was just a pinch. It would have felt like a muscle cramp. Corax's arm jerked up, causing the lightning to misfire and strike harmlessly on the wall behind his quarry.

Ms. Corvis took instant advantage of the opening this left. Her form darted in close, and she used her hands to quickly break the neck of Shaman Corax.

The rain stopped, the clouds dispersing as quickly as they had formed. Second Raven stood victorious over the dead body of her foe. Raven clacked his beak, and we were suddenly standing in front of the combatants.

You are needed to declare the dead, Little Doctor.

I looked up at Raven. 'Little Doctor' felt like a title now. I pointed to my throat and arched an eyebrow.

He chuckled. *Yes, you can speak now.*

"Thank you," I said as I knelt by the body. Corax's form was shifting back. What surprised me was that the shift didn't stop with Bird-boy form. Corax shifted into what I would call human. I looked back up at Raven questioningly.

Ms. Corvis was the one to answer. "Raven stripped him of everything to do with us. He had nothing left that connected him with our flock. If he would have lived, he would have gone to be with Owl's people and taken the secrets of our flock with him."

I did the final checks I was taught to do in medical school. When

I'd graduated, I'd hoped I wouldn't have to do this again. Obviously, I was wrong. "Time of death: six fifty-three p.m., today. Cause of death: Spinal cervical fracture. Do you need me to fill out something official?"

Ms. Corvis ran a hand over the top of her head, getting back into corporate mode. "I will send the paperwork to your email to fill out and sign. We have people in place to make this official. I'm planning on saying he fell into a zoo enclosure and was mauled by a chimpanzee. It's ridiculous enough to make my daughter laugh."

"He'll need wounds that reflect that."

"I'll send you the pictures when it's done." She put a gentle hand on my arm and helped me to my feet. "Let's get you home. Your Zauberer has been camped out in front of our doorstep for days."

35

As Ms. Corvis led me to the entrance, I noticed how much brighter everything seemed. It could have been, in part, because this time I was not blindfolded. I suppose being seen with the creator of the people tends to change some opinions. We were treated with reverence as we passed. People ducked their heads in an avian-like bow as we made our way through the labyrinthine corridors.

"I want to thank you for everything you've done," Ms. Corvis said suddenly. I jumped a little, as she'd been stoically silent since we'd left the arena.

"Your daughter should have no problems with recovery now that we've identified the agent of infection."

"If Corax hadn't made that mistake with his final move, I would have been the one you had to write a death certificate for." She sounded a little shell-shocked. It made me look at her face and try to read what was in those avian eyes.

"I wouldn't count you out so quickly. I've never seen Crane-style kung-fu used that way before. Very impressive."

"We call it 'Raven Style.' It has more attack options rather than purely defensive. I'm surprised you recognized it."

"My mom loves kung-fu movies." I shrugged. "When my siblings and I showed an interest in learning, my parents showed us the different styles online to choose a school to learn in."

"Did you get very far?"

I laughed. "No, I didn't have the concentration the instructor was looking for. I have some of the stances down and the defensive moves from time to time, but they aren't my strongest suit. I became fascinated by the different pressure points I learned about while in the class." I looked around at the intricately woven fibers that made up the walls. "What did you use to make your home so beautiful? I don't recognize the material."

"We use anything we can find on our flights or through our businesses. Usually, things discarded by others. Our builders then strip the material down to its base components, then weave them together into something that can last for generations."

That was incredible! These people were the ultimate reusers! The wall we were looking at was as solid as any I'd ever seen at the construction sites I'd visited as a kid when we'd pick Mom up from work. "Does the Unkindness have interests in waste removal or recycling? You'd get your pick of the materials that way."

She smiled a little at the corners of her beak. "We do, yes. Humans bring us treasures and we get to select the best for ourselves. It is one of our most lucrative business ventures."

We turned the last corner and the entrance of the Bowery was in front of us like the opening to another dimension. Hell, with all I've seen since coming into my abilities, I wouldn't have been surprised if it was a portal like the ones I'd seen the Council of Eight go through. I smiled as I noticed a large, colorful tent set up on the gravel. It was situated exactly where I had left Jove and Suteki what felt to me like weeks ago. I was about to step out into the sun when Ms. Corvis grabbed my arm.

"Not quite yet, Doctor Hall. There is something I must prepare you for. You spent three weeks, ten hours, and forty-five minutes in the laboratory. While you did sleep and eat, it will take a toll on your body. This is the cost of such magic. Sadly, there is nothing that can be done to mitigate the effects. Mr. Brandt has been made aware that your—*ahem*—date will most likely be canceled." She looked wistful, like she was lost in a memory . . . maybe a happy one from when she was with her husband. "I'm sorry."

I gave her a resigned smile. "Not the first time I've had to reschedule a date. Doctors' hours can change at the drop of a hat. Call me when you need me again, Second Raven."

I sighed and took a step through the arch of the Bowery and exited on the steps of the broken-down RV. I looked behind me, and the majesty of the home of the Unkindness had disappeared. The promised toll came as soon as I stepped through that doorway. A wave of dizziness struck with the force of a tsunami. My knees became jelly, my stomach dropped to my feet, and my world spun. My training took over, and I eased myself down to a sitting position and put my head between my knees. I *needed* to get horizontal soonest.

I heard Jove call my name, but my brain couldn't process what he was telling me. I heard Ms. Corvis hiss something at him and felt the softest, fluffiest blanket wrap around my shoulders. It felt glorious. I heard a soft purring sound in my ear and felt myself being lifted from the stairs. I am not a small woman, so the ease with which Jove lifted me into his arms was impressive, to say the least. I found myself snuggling into his chest and enjoying the rumble of his voice as he talked to Ms. Corvis. It didn't take long for the exhaustion to claim me and for the dream to begin.

I know what you did, Mira.

Raven's voice sounded the same in my subconscious as it did in the arena. Neat trick.

Flattery will not distract me, Little Doctor. You should not have interfered in Second Raven's battle.

We were back in the arena, but somehow, I knew I was sleeping. That this was a Dream with a capital 'D.' The kind the dungeon master role-plays so you can speak with gods.

Keep on topic, Little Doctor.

Raven's beak clacked and the final scene of the battle was suddenly before us. Bright lightning connected to the tip of the staff, Corax's face a macabre mask of joy and rage. That was the face of someone certain of their victory. Ms. Corvis' hidden form, beautiful and deadly, was silhouetted in the falling rain, poised to strike.

Blackbird worked with you for weeks, Mira. I've never been able to feel when you use your magic.

"I don't have magic. It's a scientific thing. It's what makes me a Gewalt." I crossed my arms over my chest. "I couldn't let her die. Not after so much that happened to her was my fault. I couldn't just stand there and do nothing."

You were not responsible for Second Raven's choices.

I shook my head, hard. "I'm not talking about her. I'm talking about HER." I pointed to the stands, where a hospital bed was now standing. The fledgling's form lay under a thin, threadbare blanket. The one she had in reality had been much more robust, so I knew this had to be a construct of my mind making her situation more woebegone than it was. Her chest rose and fell, proving she was alive.

"This child has just been through so much. First, my cat kills her father, then she comes down with this disease. She's fought so hard, and if her mother had just THOUGHT about anyone other than herself and her anger FOR TWO GODDAMNED MINUTES, she would have realized she was going to leave this little fighter as an orphan."

I gently touched her little head. I knew she was just a product of my subconscious, but I needed Raven to understand why I'd interfered— why I had helped Ms. Corvis.

I see. Raven mused, *You feel responsible for the child. Very well, but there will be repercussions for this. I cannot let someone defy a direct order from me. It would tarnish my reputation as a god.*

"Pfft. You're no god. You are one of the first people. Powerful yes, but not a god. Not MY God, either."

Then you should show me respect, Little Doctor. You're a lover of tabletop games. So, your punishment will be a quest. Find and return my Pinion to the people. I can feel it deep under the ground, where feathers are never meant to be, surrounded by those little nasties.

Raven clacked his beak again. My special medicine bottle floated in front of us. NAN-06. The letters glowed.

The 'medicine' you were taking . . . it feels like them . . . the nanites. If you crack one of those open and put it under a scope, I bet you'll find more of them. Every time you take a capsule, you put more of them into your body. I can practically see the threads that bind you to their creators.

"I kind of suspected that." I knew there were nanites inside me already. I'd suspected that the medicine Alden had given me had something to do with them. But I was still taking them every time the little bottle beeped at me.

Why do you still take them?

I crossed my arms over my chest, started to shrug, but this was a dream . . . I couldn't even lie to myself here. "I'm scared, Raven. I'm scared that if I stop taking the medicine, I'll lose my powers. That I'll stop being a Gewalt."

Raven turned to me and held out his arms. I walked into them and accepted the comforting hug. His voice rumbled in my head, *Once a person has signed the Charter, it is almost impossible for them to be scrubbed from it. You will always be a member of the Community now, Little Doctor. Find where the creators of the nanites are hiding, retrieve my Pinion. Do this and your debt is paid.*

"Will Blackbird not be around anymore? He was kinda fun. He got most of my jokes."

Perhaps. He laughed and pulled away. *You are a good doctor. It was a pleasure working with you as Blackbird. You will see him again. It is hard to make a vessel only to unmake it after so short a time.*

That could have meant anything, but seeing as I was on thin ice with Raven, I decided not to push.

A wise decision, Little Doctor. I will allow you to rest now. Mortal bodies are not meant to function well in compressed time.

We were suddenly in my bedroom at my apartment. Raven tucked me into bed as a parent would a child.

You have had some hard nights with your sleep. Even as I watched over you as Blackbird.

I felt my face flush in my dream. "Did I talk in my sleep while we were in the time bubble?"

No, I AM RAVEN. His voice reverberated in my mind for a moment. It made me wince with the power of it. *One of my realms is that of Dreams. I liked what you did to the funny man who thinks he has power. So, for saving the people . . . And making me laugh, I will give you a gift. A boon for your help weeding out the corruption of my flock.*

He waved a hand over the wall above my bed, and a dreamcatcher unlike any I'd ever seen before appeared. It wasn't like the ones you see online or at a retail store. This was made from natural materials like branches, leather, and (of course) raven feathers. It wasn't precisely round, but it looked perfect to me.

I will send you into a deep, healing sleep, he promised. *And this will help guard you from nightmares from here on. Sleep now; you will be well-rested when you awaken.*

Raven touched my forehead with one finger, and I felt my eyelids grow heavy. My pillow felt sooo good. I was warm and safe, and I smiled as I felt two little bodies jump onto the bed and snuggle with me—Suteki and Toria, one on each side of my body. It was the most restful night of sleep I'd had since my accident.